I0669453

TITLES BY KOSOKO JACKSON

I'M SO (NOT) OVER YOU

A DASH OF SALT AND PEPPER

A
DASH
OF
SALT
AND
PEPPER

KOSOKO JACKSON

BERKLEY ROMANCE
NEW YORK

BERKLEY ROMANCE
Published by Berkley
An imprint of Penguin Random House LLC
penguinrandomhouse.com

Copyright © 2022 by Kosoko Jackson
Excerpt from *I'm So (Not) Over You* copyright © 2022 by Kosoko Jackson
Penguin Random House supports copyright. Copyright fuels creativity, encourages diverse
voices, promotes free speech, and creates a vibrant culture. Thank you for buying an authorized
edition of this book and for complying with copyright laws by not reproducing, scanning, or
distributing any part of it in any form without permission. You are supporting writers and
allowing Penguin Random House to continue to publish books for every reader.

BERKLEY is a registered trademark and Berkley Romance with B colophon is a trademark of
Penguin Random House LLC.

Library of Congress Cataloging-in-Publication Data

Names: Jackson, Kosoko, author.
Title: A dash of salt and pepper / Kosoko Jackson.
Description: First edition. | New York: Berkley Romance, 2022.
Identifiers: LCCN 2022028504 | ISBN 9780593334461 (trade paperback) |
ISBN 9780593334478 (ebook)
Subjects: LCGFT: Romance fiction. | Novels.
Classification: LCC PS3610.A356439 D37 2022 |
DDC 813/.6—dc23/eng/20220616
LC record available at https://lccn.loc.gov/2022028504

First Edition: December 2022

Printed in the United States of America
1st Printing

Book design by Daniel Brount

This is a work of fiction. Names, characters, places, and incidents either are the product of the
author's imagination or are used fictitiously, and any resemblance to actual persons, living or
dead, business establishments, events, or locales is entirely coincidental.

PRAISE FOR

I'M SO (NOT) OVER YOU

"With beautifully drawn themes of family ties, foundational friendships, and the importance of choosing a love that makes us better, stronger, and happier, here is the queer rom-com the genre has been waiting years for! As tender and unflinching as it is uproarious and joyful, Kosoko Jackson's *I'm So (Not) Over You* is, quite simply—a spectacularly satisfying read."

—Christina Lauren, *New York Times* bestselling author of
The Soulmate Equation

"A snappy, sizzling, downright delightful book from Jackson, a welcome and fresh new voice in rom-coms."

—Julia Whelan, author of *My Oxford Year*

"A witty and fast-paced romance full of rapid-fire dialogue, laugh-out-loud one-liners, and spot-on pop culture references. *I'm So (Not) Over You* is full of swoon-worthy and sizzling romantic moments, but it's also about following your heart and figuring out what you want to do with your life."

—Kerry Winfrey, author of *Very Sincerely Yours*

"A delightfully hilarious romp. Kosoko Jackson's writing zips along with an electric, playful energy, making Kian and Hudson impossible not to root for. It's been a while since a book made me laugh this much!"

—Rachel Lynn Solomon, national bestselling author of *The Ex Talk*

"Such a fun read! *I'm So (Not) Over You* gives us witty, complex characters that you want to have a (Rivers & Valleys) beer with, just to keep them talking. Kosoko Jackson is a sassy, fresh new voice in romance, and I can't wait to read more from him!"

—Jen DeLuca, *USA Today* bestselling author of *Well Matched*

"Swoony, witty, and utterly fun. Jackson will have you falling in love while laughing out loud."

—Denise Williams, author of *The Fastest Way to Fall*

"Full of humor and heart, this romance about second chances and taking risks will have you laughing one minute and swooning the next. A delightfully fun and sexy read."

—Ashley Herring Blake, author of *Delilah Green Doesn't Care*

"This is a rom-com that isn't lacking in either the romance or the comedy, and the end result makes for an excellent, ultimately satisfying book."   —*Paste* magazine

"Putting a fun twist on the beloved fake-dating trope, Jackson's rom-com debut *I'm So (Not) Over You* offers snappy writing, complex characters, and an ode to pop culture!"   —The Nerd Daily

"Jackson has a knack for building nuanced and multilayered characters. . . . Ultimately, that character development is what makes this queer, Black romantic comedy such a delight. It is, from start to finish, full of laughs and heart." —Shelf Awareness

"This nuanced romance marks Jackson as a writer to watch in the adult sphere."   —*Publishers Weekly*

"[A] delightfully outrageous romantic comedy full of pop-culture references, strong families, and a ride-or-die BFF."

—Library Journal (starred)

For Talya (and, of course, Arthur).
You'll never know how much our walks saved me.

A
DASH
OF
SALT
AND
PEPPER

CHAPTER
ONE

You up?

In most circles, that text would read like a very ineloquently crafted booty call, one that absolutely should not warrant a response. Or, as Miranda Priestly—a fictional god among men—would call it, *Boring, dull, and derivative.*

If a boy texts you at 4:00 a.m., don't answer it, I would always tell my girlfriends in college. *If he can't text you in the daytime, why should you answer him when the lights go out?*

I have firsthand accounts that my guidance has helped many girls in my resident hall—Clark Street pride, baby—avoid some embarrassing situations. I would even give the same advice to the (few) straight male friends I had.

Don't you dare go texting a girl at 4:00 a.m. and ask her to come over. If you care about her, you'll message her when the sun is high. Ask her out. Wine her. Dine her. And THEN, and only if she consents, you can finger blast her in the back of a movie theater. #Romance.

Because remember: When we let boys succeed by performing

the bare minimum, we'll never see them blossom into the men we know they can become. No, it's not our responsibility to help boys achieve their full potential, but if we don't do it, who will? It's a hard job, but someone has to do it.

Someone, obviously, in this situation, being me, a gay, and my fellow female partners in crime.

But, going back to the topic at hand, this isn't a booty call text I'm sending, for three key and very important reasons.

ONE: The message was sent to my friend Mya, and I do not hook up with friends. Point-blank. I don't have many rules I've set for myself that I've followed—which is probably a mark of my flightiness or inability to stay focused on any goal that doesn't have strict consequences if I fail, which is a topic for my therapist, when I get a therapist again—but that is a hard-and-fast one.

FBI—friends, bosses, idols—the trifecta of people you should never EVER have sex with. Someone always gets hurt and the night ends with some sad ballad written by an airy breathy white girl who sings in cursive on repeat, causing the neighbors to bang on your door or issue a noise complaint and lead you to being homeless on the street, begging for change, realizing a boy completely and utterly destroyed your life.

Dramatic? Maybe. Factual? Absolutely.

TWO: This can't be a booty call because, even if Mya is up, there's no potential for her to be free to actually, you know, do the big nasty. She's a teacher and they—especially those who teach second grade—never sleep because they're always working. So, the whole suave acting-like-she-might-not-be-up thing is a moot point. Mya is as close to a vampire as one could personify, which we all thought our teachers were when we were in second grade. Vampires who lived at school and went into their coffins during summer vacation.

TWO POINT FIVE: It's only 4:00 a.m. That's not *that* early. Many people in the United States get up at six to start their day. In fact, roughly 23 percent of Americans get up between six and six thirty, and if you include those up between five and six, that adds another 32 percent, for a total of 55 percent of Americans—more than half are up to make the world their bitch.

And THREE: Probably the most important bullet of all these: I am a raging homosexual. Like, a big ol' "knew the lyrics to 'Rain on Me' twenty minutes after it came out, makes a point to analyze each queen on *RuPaul's Drag Race* each season to pick the top contender" homosexual.

Ergo, in conclusion, as you can see, Your Honor (etc., etc.), there's no possible way, given the facts presented, this could be a booty call. In truth, though? I just can't sleep. A logical person would just give up and start their day, like a normal member of the 55 percent of America, but being awake—truly, fully awake—means I have to deal with my life. And I'm not at all ready for that.

If I lie in bed, maybe just for a little bit longer, the real world lurking outside my window will stay at bay. I won't have to deal with the fact I'm a twenty-six-year-old who just lost his job. I won't have to address the heartache and embarrassment of three days *after* losing my job, my boyfriend of five years saying to me, *I feel like my life is on the express train and yours is on the local,* before kicking me out of the house. All of that is a distant concern, like a poorly formed dream. I won't have to deal with the growing cloud of self-doubt, or the ballooning feeling of failure that threatens to shroud every accomplishment I've achieved. And I most certainly won't have to deal with the fact that I'm in fucking Harper's motherfucking Cove motherfucking MAINE when I should be in Chicago, Paris, London, England, Edinburgh, or New York. LITERALLY anywhere but goddamn Maine.

I was supposed to be better than this. To succeed. To make it out of this town and create a life for myself more than "the Black boy Rory Gilmore of Harper's Cove," where the three biggest industries are fishing, miscellaneous mom-and-pop shops, and the school where Mya teaches. Me, the one who got a full ride to NYU, and then a fellowship to the University of Chicago's Booth School of Business. My life was S-E-T. I was going to be the Cristina Yang of business school, with a touch of Meredith Grey to balance out the sassy.

Everything was perfect. But you know what happens when things start to look a little *too* perfect in someone's life? Whoever controls the universe laughs in your face and throws everything out of whack.

And now I'm back here. End credits. Twenty percent on Rotten Tomatoes.

Let me be perfectly clear: There is nothing wrong with living your whole life in Harper's Cove, population nine thousand. Stars Hollow, I mean Harper's Cove—seriously, we're nearly the same population size, the same single high school and middle school combined, everything—is a great place to settle down and raise a family, if the quiet life is what you want. It's why my parents moved here from Washington, DC, when I was barely six months old.

It's just not the life for me.

Which is why, as soon as I graduated from high school, I got the fuck out of here and intended to never look back.

I thought my future and, by extension, my happiness, was in

New York. Every homosexual does. New York, LA, London, Atlanta, the four homosexual metropolises for us. That, of course, as luck would have it, is why I ended up in Chicago, thanks to a professor who invited me to a speech by another professor from UChicago who spoke at NYU when I was an undergrad. Going to Booth School of Business and living in the Windy City made sense when the bones were thrown on the table. And getting a job (while still at Booth) at TixFlixs, a start-up that helped pick movies based on your interests and sold you discounted tickets, was supposed to be my stepping-stone into the big professional world. Helping start-ups better themselves in the first two years of their inception, the most critical point of a start-up, is where I thrived. By helping companies, I help the owners, and by helping the owners, I help people. And the fact that it was owned and created by a nonbinary Asian American? Even better. This fit my professional goals and my personal goals.

I might have an MBA, but I'm not a monster who is only money driven, like so many people think. My parents taught me better than that.

To make my time in Chicago even better, my boss at TixFlixs then nominated me for the Carey Foundation, a twelve-month-long study fellowship in Berlin that would allow me to take a mentorship under a professional in one of twelve specializations, one of them being start-up support. That would rocket me down the fast lane of success. And I deserved it. I'd earned it.

I know that sounds cocky, but I did. Life isn't a meritocracy, but I worked hard to get there. And finally, *finally*, I had everything I wanted out of life. A great first job. Great education. Great boyfriend. I had all the right checks. I did all the right things. My life résumé was padded to the max. I was a Black person who was going to be a success story by all metrics.

And then, like a poorly constructed gingerbread house made while drunk on eggnog, it came crumbling down around me. Now I'm right back to where I was seven years ago—in my bed, in a room that seems frozen in time.

The company I worked for went under. I got the infamous *thank you for applying* email from the Carey Foundation two weeks after my seven two-hour-long final-round interviews spanning three months. Then my *boyfriend* fucking broke up with me and blocked me on all social media platforms. All of this happened one after another in a span of two months; blow after blow, gut punch after gut punch.

"What a great and anticlimactic fucking ending," I say to no one in particular in the empty room.

I roll over and check my phone again: 5:05 a.m. No message. Just me and my shame. Love that for me.

When I was younger, I loved waking up with the sun. It's why my parents switched bedrooms with me, so my room—though it is slightly larger by about sixty square feet—faces the east. The sun illuminates the alt-rock posters of Paramore, Relient K, Fall Out Boy, and Panic! at the Disco that plaster two of the three walls. On the third, birth charts of me, Mya, and a kid from school I barely remember thanks to losing touch that pepper the remaining three walls. Cities and countries I wanted to visit. Companies I wanted to work for. What would teenage Xavier say to me now? How would he feel, knowing we failed at every single thing we aimed to accomplish?

"He'd say we're a loser," I mutter. I know how vicious I was as a teen. How driven and only focused on succeeding and getting out of this town I was. People made excuses for it. Forgave me for it because I was going places. I was getting out of here. I was an *inspiration*. I fucking hate that word.

And now look at me, back home in a bed that's too small for me.

A ball of fluff and weight at the bottom of my bed shifts and presses against my right leg. That fuzz ball is Naga, my family's Samoyed. She's more my parents' dog considering my parents got her only two years before I moved out as a not-so-subtle way to get me to stay in Harper's Cove. It didn't work, obviously—but maybe it did. I mean, after all, I'm still here, aren't I? And they got a cute dog out of it. Win-win for everyone.

Naga rolls over and sighs, her bright eyes blink at me, like there isn't a thought behind them.

"Can't sleep either, huh?"

She says nothing in response because, well, she's a dog, and dogs can't talk.

I reach down and give her head a quick pat and a rub. Naga may be almost ten years old, but she's as spry as she was when we first got her. A bundle of white live-wire energy that can go from one side of town to the other in a matter of seconds, it seems.

Spry. Jesus, how old am I? They say living fast and hard ages you quickly, and that's why you shouldn't take high-stress jobs like, I dunno, being the CEO of a Fortune 500 company, but I think the complete opposite is true. Moving at a glacial pace makes me want to throw myself off the top of a building.

Moving at a glacial pace is everything that makes Harper's Cove appealing to some people. Some of those people aren't me.

"I need to get out of here, girl," I say to Naga, swinging my legs over the side of the bed. Pressing my feet against the cold wooden floor, I close my eyes and let my shoulders fall into place. My body slips into gear, relaxing my muscles and bones cramped from sleeping on a twin-sized bed my parents had no reason to replace. "Maybe I'll take you with me next time."

The only thing I miss about this place—besides seeing my parents and my best friend Mya—is the house. The stillness in the air isn't oppressive like the rest of the town. Harper's Cove's silence makes me feel like everyone can hear every mistake I make. But the house? It's like I'm safe here. The stillness in the air absorbs every bit of fear, of panic, of self-doubt and—

What the fuck was that sound?

Like some comical duo, Naga and I both look up and toward the half-cracked-open door at the same time. Our heads turn to one another in sync, too.

You heard that? her cocked head says.

You did, too? I ask silently, nodding.

Now, again, I know she can't really talk. I'm not that stupid. But there was 100 percent a sound downstairs. I reach for my phone, tapping the screen once. A text from Mom forty-five minutes ago.

MOM: Went into Portland to meet with Robbie. Biscuits on the counter. Siri input Love you emoji.

Robbie is one of my mom's closest friends and a fisherman, meaning she's getting some fresh lobster from him, which also means I know what's for dinner tonight. Assuming we make it to tonight. Harper's Cove isn't the place where you see grisly murderers, but you know what they say. Cabot Cove in *Murder, She Wrote* is technically the murder capital of the world, if you judge by population-to-murder ratio. Who's to say Harper's Cove isn't following in its footsteps with me being the first victim? A morbid thought, but at least I'd be known for something.

Mom never misses the meeting with Robbie; it's every other Wednesday. Not only does my mother pride herself in being on time and not prescribing to CP time, but Robbie's fishing skills are unparalleled, his fish won't stay for long, and there's always a wealthier buyer willing to pay for whatever he has for the day.

Between me and Mya, I always told her that Robbie just wants to get in Mom's pants, but she refuses to accept that. Good to know that if Dad kicks the bucket early, Mom has a decent backup plan, though.

But, more important than Mom's impending *How Stella Got Her Groove Back* moment is that Mom isn't downstairs. So who made the noise?

Maybe Dad? No, he's off with his *brothers*—yes, my sixty-one-year-old father still says *brothers*—on an annual camping trip he's done since before I was born. The location might change, and what they do on the secret Illuminati-like trip might shift and adjust based on age, but it's always a weeklong event. He won't be back till tomorrow.

Which means only one thing; the thing I didn't want to admit.

Someone is trying to break into my house, and all I can think about is *I'm going to fucking die in Maine. Oh joy.*

No high school, college, or CW prime-time drama prepares you for what to do when someone breaks into your house. I mean, sure, you should probably hide under your bed, *Taken*-style, or hide in the closet or close the door and press your back against it, but in the moment? None of those thoughts come to fruition. This is one of those kill-or-be-killed, "happy Hunger Games, may the odds be ever in your favor" situations. The killer is already here, so it's too late to call 911, right?

Luckily for me, Naga's already standing at attention on the bed, which lets me know something bad is about to happen. She's the sweetest dog, who, yes, is energetic, but unless it concerns her or something or someone she cares about, she's a lazy bunch of nothing. She only goes to the door when it's either her favorite postman or someone she gets a bad vibe from. So her standing up now? That means I should be paying attention, too.

I stand slowly, using my memory of which floorboards in my room creak and which don't. Initially, I pick up the first thing I can grab to use as a weapon. For most people it would be a bat, maybe a book, or maybe even a dumbbell. All valuable and smart choices.

Me? It's a fucking bottle of lemon-lime Gatorade. The absolute best flavor.

"Great. Fucking great."

Thankfully, I'm not alone. Naga is right next to me, her soft paws making no sound on the overly polished floor, my mom's second-favorite obsession. Gatorade is all I need when I have a beast like her next to me. Hopefully.

I push the door open all the way, stepping onto the carpeted hallway. Whoever is in the house made a beeline straight for the kitchen. Which makes sense; they used the back door, which goes right into the mudroom, and then into the largest room in the recently remodeled house. But it's also the room with the most expensive gadgets. I'd know because while some people obsess over TVs, cars, homes, shoes, or dolls, my mother obsesses over cooking equipment.

America could be building a colony on Neptune, and my mom wouldn't be able to discuss it. But ask the difference between the Chopper 451A and the Chopper 451B, and she'll be able to explain every single change down to the gears.

I walk down the steps as quietly as possible, one foot over the other. Naga follows suit, one paw in front of the other. My muscle memory kicks in. Skipping the last step and treading on the center of the carpet, balanced on my toes, I walk carefully down the hallway.

"Where are they . . . ?" the deep voice mutters in the kitchen.

Where are *what*? It only takes me a moment to put two and two together.

My mother's china.

When my grandmother passed ten years ago, she gave my mom her most precious gift—her expensive china. The will said she was getting them because of the treasured memories they shared in the kitchen. My mom's three sisters were pissed, of course. The china is worth more than $10K in total. In this town—in most towns—that's a lot of money, and people would be *happy* to have it. I told Mom that. I warned her about that.

See, baby, the thing you never understood about Harper's Cove is that people are nice here. This is a big, happy family.

A family that wants to steal from you.

That's the real American Dream.

Is it, Mom? Is getting robbed by your neighbors the American Dream? If we *do* get robbed, can I then tell her *I told you so* without getting a backhanded slap against the back of my head?

I slowly open the cap on the Gatorade as I step over the alcove and into the kitchen with the island in the middle. The plan is simple: throw Gatorade on him, sic Naga on him, maybe grab a cast-iron pan, hit him, and call the police. Easy. A four-step process.

Alright, Xavier. You got this.

One step closer.

That's it.

Another step.

Just get a little closer. Throw it on him. And then Naga will do the rest.

Just one more step . . .

Suddenly, the man closes the fridge and turns. I was *hoping* I'd be able to get a foot closer before having to confront him, but . . . well . . . that didn't happen.

Before he can open the mouth on his handsome face with his sharp jaw, slightly salt-and-pepper scruff and hair, my body reacts. I throw the Gatorade bottle at him, the bright yellow liquid staining his face and his white T-shirt, blinding him.

"SHIT!" he yells, covering his eyes. He stumbles back, his surprisingly long (and fit, based on how snug those jeans are) legs tripping over the mat by the sink. He falls on his ass.

Perfect.

"Naga! Attack!" I order. I think that's an easy command. She's a dog, I'm under assault. *Attack* pretty much covers what I want her to do.

Except, for whatever reason, my message gets lost in translation. Maybe in Dog, *attack* means something different, but it sure as hell shouldn't mean *jump on him and start licking the man's face.*

Some protector she is.

CHAPTER
TWO

THE ONE THING THAT makes me, well, me, is that I'm a lover, not a fighter.

Even when navigating the cutthroat world of business school, or navigating the roads of, you know, trying to make a name for myself in a school where being a—and I quote—*small-town hick*, makes me lesser than, I never resorted to violence or name-calling or sabotage. If I was going to succeed, I was going to do it on my own merits, not by beating other people down.

Might be the Cancer sun in me. Or is it the rising that tells your personality? I'll have to ask Mya. Assuming I make it out of this straight-out-of-a-Blumhouse-production invasion.

But seriously, *passive* is one of the five words people would use to describe me. I'm not kidding, one of my reviews at an internship said, *Xavier doesn't take enough initiative, despite his strong intellect and business mind. If he doesn't, I'm worried his intellect will be wasted.*

A nice way of saying I'm a wallflower who needs to "level my pussy up" if I want to succeed.

Even when a lot of my girlfriends (rightfully so) went through their we-need-to-learn-how-to-protect-ourselves montage of two months of training, thanks to a Groupon for sixteen kick-boxing classes for the price of eight, I never signed up. What situation would I be in where I need my fists—or, rather, my legs? I'm smart. My brains will get me out of any situation. When I *do* buck up, it's usually with my words, like sharpened, folded steel dipped in the most venomous of poisons. After all, anything can be solved when two sane minds put their heads together or when one person's words cut deep enough. Whichever one comes first.

But there lies the flaw in my logic. Someone who breaks into my home to steal my mother's china isn't of sane mind, nor are they going to give me time to try to logically reason with them or buy enough time for the police to come.

Which means I have to use my fists.

I don't hesitate, gently pushing Naga out of the way—we'll have a talk later about her usefulness as a guard dog—and tackle him hard. Putting the full weight of my chest on him, I pin him down as successfully as I can. He has a strong body, sharp from well-defined muscles. The type of body that tells me he spends a good amount of time in the gym. It feels, you know, good. The type of muscles on someone that Jennifer Coolidge would idolize in some rom-com where she plays the lovestruck woman who gets the muscular man to notice her.

Focus, Xavier, I scold. *You can think about how Jennifer is a queer icon later. Right now? You need to make sure this guy doesn't move, since Naga is no fucking help.*

Easier said than fucking done. The guy under me keeps squirming, doing his best to use any leverage he can to throw my balance off.

Not going to be that easy, bud.

To ensure, you know, that I'm not just talking shit, I put my full weight on his body, effectively sitting on his chest. I pin both of his arms above his head, bearing as much weight as I can down on his chest. At least, not enough to hurt him, but enough that he can't use his strength against me.

And he has a lot of it. I can feel the definition of his pecs, the curves of his muscles, the slight indentation toward the center of his chest. He is nowhere near himbo status, much more defined and toned than that, but he definitely does not miss chest day.

It's a nice feeling; no one can deny that.

"You work out," I blurt out.

Shit.

The thing is, I didn't intend to say that out loud. It was supposed to stay in my brain. Maybe filed away somewhere in the spank bank—there's absolutely a subsection of porn that focuses on home invasions, and they are all very hot scenes, thank you very much. But that's not the type of thing you say to someone out loud. Especially not someone *actually breaking into your home.*

He stops squirming, just for a moment; long enough for me to know he most definitely heard what I just said.

"I'm sorry, what?"

Cue the record scratch.

When I thought about coming home and all the things that would happen, this wasn't part of it. Getting blackout drunk with Mya? Sure. Maybe helping my mother with some recipes, since we always said we would finish making *The Reynolds Family Official Recipe Book*—and my dad can't cook worth shit? Probably. Do a lot of brooding about a future that's crumbling in front of my eyes? Absolutely.

Sitting on the chest of some hot man? Not at all.

But then again, I've never really thought about the type of person who breaks into someone else's home.

"Did you just say I'm hot?"

"I said you work out," I correct. "Big difference."

I know it sounds dumb, because there isn't really a connection between physical looks and crime, but this guy is too handsome to be a criminal. His face is . . . honestly perfect, with a tapered chin, high cheekbones, and just the perfect amount of scruff, beard, and mustache, and just the right level of salt and pepper. Messy, shaggy black hair and a firm body that shows he goes to the gym but doesn't overdo it. He's . . . well, he's fucking hot. Why turn to crime when you could smile?

I bet his smile is beautiful.

I didn't fall asleep and wake up in some Brazzers porno, did I? Wait, wouldn't it be like a men.com porno? Unless Brazzers broke off into doing gay porn, which, to be honest, would be a—

"Get the fuck off of me!" he growls, and then bucks, breaking me out of my thoughts.

I tighten my grip on his arms and squeeze my thighs.

"Not until the police get here. I called them; they'll be here in a few minutes."

He doesn't need to know I haven't called them yet.

"You're a fucking liar," he snarls, blinking away the Gatorade. His eyes are red from the sugar and electrolyte mixture thrown in his face. I don't feel sorry. Okay, maybe I do a little.

"I guess we'll find out in a few minutes then, won't we?"

How I'm going to actually get the police here . . . that's another question. Am I going to have to sit on his chest all day until Mom comes home?

All those thoughts go out the window when suddenly, in the span of a blink, I find myself on my back with the attacker on top of me. One hand has my wrists cuffed together. His other hand is under my right leg, slightly raising it, ankle on his shoulder, hips pushed forward, giving me absolutely no leverage . . .

And also putting me in a position that I'm 10,000 percent sure would be on the cover of some newfangled sex-position book an influencer is hawking. Me being in only boxer briefs doesn't help either.

Or does it?

He leans forward, dark strands of hair skimming my face. His lips are barely an inch away from me, close enough that his soaked T-shirt collides with my bare chest.

"What were you saying about not getting off of me?" he whispers in a raspy voice.

I narrow my eyes and buck my hips, but the man's weight is too much. He pushes his hips forward.

"Nuh-uh," he whispers, tightening his grip and clenching his jaw. It's the first time I notice his arms are covered with tattoos, mostly animals, from wrist all the way to under the shirt. I can tell from the translucent shade—you know, thanks to me throwing Gatorade on him—the right sleeve is completely done while the left ends at his bicep.

And honestly? The way his muscles flex is one of the hottest things I've ever seen, made even hotter by the tattoos.

"Say you'll stop, and I'll let you go."

"Fuck you. You're breaking into my house and you want me to apologize?"

"You're not my type. But, hey, I might know—"

The man blinks, the sharpness in his face replaced with

something warmer. His eyes go wide, and he pulls back suddenly, completely giving up his advantage.

"Wait, hold on for a moment. You think I'm breaking in?" he asks, gesturing between us with his hand.

I scamper to my feet as quickly as I can. Idiot, giving up his advantage like that.

"Well, considering this is *my* house and *not* yours? What would you call it? Coming for Sunday tea with a fucking queen?"

"It's Wednesday."

"Exactly! You should know Maine is a stand-your-ground state."

"I'm pretty sure it isn't," he mutters, reaching into the pocket of his jeans.

I tense up, fumbling blindly behind me. My back is against the sink, and I can feel the handle of a frying pan against my hand. A perfect weapon. Operation Defend Our House is still absolutely underway.

But he doesn't pull out a knife, a gun, or even a Taser. Instead, he pulls out his cell phone: a cracked iPhone at least three generations old.

"Interesting weapon choice . . ."

"You're insane," he mutters, tapping almost gorilla-like at the screen before showing it to me. "No, that's ableist. My daughter would kill me. You're—"

"Ridiculous? I get that a lot." He shoves the phone in my face. It takes a moment for my vision to focus on the words. My eyes skim the text exchange. Two people, one telling the other to stop by and pick up . . .

"Cupcakes."

"Did you see the number?"

I know those digits instantly. They're my mother's, one of the few numbers I actually have memorized.

"Okay, hold up one moment! Let's assume I believe you."

"Are you really going to try and save face by saying I somehow planned this text in case, as an intruder, someone tried to stop me?"

"I don't know who the hell you are, I don't know what you're . . ."

The flimsy ground I'm standing on completely breaks apart under me as Naga trots over to the man and sits in front of him. She smiles, sticking out her tongue, jumping up and putting her front paws on his thighs.

The man grins, kneeling to her level. One hand combs through the longer strands of his dark black hair, pushing it out of his face as his other hand scratches Naga's Bitch Spot, about an inch behind her right ear toward her skull.

No one would know that except someone who came over often.

"Believe me yet?" he asks, standing up.

I cross my arms over my chest. "Not fully. Why wouldn't my mom just have me get these so-called cupcakes? And if you *were* asked, why don't you know—"

The man holds one finger up, pressing it against my lips, making my eyes cross in order to focus on the tip. Did he . . . seriously just . . . ?

"From your mom—and forgive me, because I'm not going to try and replicate her voice—"

"Thank God for small miracles," I mutter against his fingers.

"But she said, *Let yourself in. My son is asleep so try and be quiet. Cupcakes should be on the counter or in the fridge, depending on if*

Xavier got a hold of them. Considering they are in neither place, did you get a hold of them, Xavier?"

There's a lot to unpack in this moment. For one, a random man has his hands on me. Secondly, I'm standing in front of him, mostly naked. Thirdly, he's dripping wet, and the T-shirt does little to hide how fucking lean he is. Like four-pack-very-evident lean.

But most importantly of all, it seems I'm wrong and he's right, which is the biggest fucking offense out of all of this.

I slap his hand away. "I'll be right back."

Before he can say anything, and ignoring his question, I make a beeline upstairs to my room, taking the steps two at a time. I yank my phone out of my pocket and dial my mom. And I mean actually dial. Not telling Siri whom to call or pressing the call button from our sparse texts. No, fully type out her number.

That should tell you how serious this is.

Two rings later, she picks up, and judging by the windy sound in the background, she's driving.

"You know how much I hate talking while driving, Xavier. Are you trying to kill me?"

"There is a man in our house. Who is he?"

"Is this a man you slept with and forgot his name and now you're asking me, or . . . ?"

"No!" I hiss, trying to keep quiet. "A man, black hair, salt-and-pepper beard?"

"Oh! That's Logan."

"Logan Paul or Logan Howlett?"

"What?"

"Never mind. So, he's not coming to kill me?"

"No! Xavier, why would you—"

"Or to steal your china? You know that sixty-six percent of two point five million burglaries that happen annually are classified as home invasions? That's one point sixty-five million a year. If you break that down to an equal amount per state, that's thirty-three thousand three hundred per state, roughly ninety per day per state. The odds are in our favor that . . ."

"Xavier," she says in that firm, motherly tone that's the equivalent to a boot against my throat. "None of that. Stop being dramatic. He's picking up cupcakes for the bake sale today. Did he find them?"

The cupcakes. All of it is clicking now, like a video of a watercolor painting dipped in water playing in reverse. I came home late last night. I wasn't out drinking like Mom thought I was, I just didn't want to be home. Even being here for one week was starting to make me itchy. I went to Mya's house and spent the evening there with her husband.

Mom didn't judge me; home was always a safe haven for her, but she respects that it isn't for me. Even if she doesn't tell me how upset she is, even if she doesn't vocalize how she wishes I would embrace the fact we're home together and get to spend some quality time, she understands it's the last place I want to be.

We're Reynoldses, after all. We walk through fire. We don't run when things get tough. We find ways to make the shitty things rosy. At least, that's the mantra Mom repeats.

And I didn't want to deal with her subtle disappointment or have to explain to her I never intended to come back home unless she or Dad were on their deathbeds.

"*Please* tell me you didn't eat them in a drunken pity stupor . . . I spent all night baking those."

"I gotta go." I hang up before Mom can ask me any questions.

Shit. Shit. SHIT. So, Logan was actually right. Which, on one side of the coin, is good. At least he's not trying to break into my house and kill me. But it also means I have to go downstairs and see that smug face of his. It means I have to apologize.

Part of me wishes he were a robber. At least I could put on my grave *Here lies Xavier Reynolds, he died being right.*

Naga pads her way into the room, pushing the door open with her rump. She jumps onto the bed and walks around twice before settling down, resting her pretty face on her paws.

"What, you have nothing to say for yourself? You're supposed to be my protector."

All I get in return? A yawn.

"Asshole. You're lucky you're cute."

Sighing, I grab a nearby pair of sweats and slip them on, along with a blue T-shirt. I'm going to have to apologize to this guy, explain to him that I screwed up, and hope to God he doesn't press charges or anything.

He won't, I think. That's not like the people of Harper's Cove. This is a town where you can hit someone with your car and all you have to do is fix their fence for them and they'll call it even. But this guy didn't seem like a native. I don't remember ever seeing him growing up. And believe me, I would have noticed a man with a strong jaw and a deep, rumbling voice like that.

I shake my head to clear my thoughts, smooth the wrinkles out of the shirt I pulled out of my bag, and swallow my pride. *Just get it over with, help him get the cupcakes, and this will all be over. Just a bad interaction you can chuckle over when you see him at the corner store.*

"Hey, so it turns out you might, might have been correct," I say, beginning my spiel before I round the corner. "So, considering that there is a slight chance I'm in the wrong, I just wanted to—"

Except no one's there. Not a single person is in the kitchen, just emptiness and the memory of Logan, his wet T-shirt and . . .

A single fucking cupcake on the counter.

THREE

DESPITE BEING SOMEONE WHO went through seven years of school, I'm not much of a drinker.

Seriously, you don't understand how much of an accomplishment that is. Did you know that roughly 20 percent of college students check enough of the boxes to meet the criteria to have a toxic relationship with alcohol? Twenty percent; one in five. Some studies say as much as 30 percent.

Generally, I like to be considered exceptional, but this time, I'm glad to be part of the common group. And, trust me, it's not because I haven't tried. It's common for gay guys, and academics, to be in situations where alcohol is often served. Try to go to any club, bar, or school mixer; the one thing they all have in common is alcohol.

It's just never done anything for me. Alcohol tastes just . . . *meh*. I add it into my cooking when the recipe calls for it, but I'm not the type of person who needs a beer with them while they relax for the night or tries to drink someone under the table. I don't need alcohol to have fun. That doesn't make me better than anyone, it just makes me, well, me.

Which is why the only reason I'm at the bar right now is because, as a second-grade teacher at a school that teaches year-round, Mya drinks alcohol like she drinks water. Her words, not mine.

She's already on her third margarita for the night, and we've only been at the second-best drinking place in Harper's Cove for about one hour. Second best out of five. Six if you consider the arcade, which serves alcohol and allows you to play board games until 2:00 a.m. But, like I told Mya, the Brook isn't bad, and we have fond memories of this place. We should have our ceremonial Xavier-is-back-in-town drink here for old times' sake.

Mya has other ideas. Then again, Mya *always* has other ideas, and they are usually better than mine.

"You know, I'm still upset you're making me drink this swill instead of—"

"I told you already," I interrupt. "You should be happy I came out."

"Because being in your presence is such a grace?"

"Exactly, and you love me."

"Debatable. I love alcohol and you provided that."

"Correction, I agreed to come out with you so you can get alcohol," I remind her. "You're paying because—"

"—because you're broke, I know."

"That's true, but also because I'm gracing you with my presence, so it's the least you can do. You know, quid-pro-quo and all that jazz."

Sure, the reason we're here is because I want to see Mya. She's like a safe harbor in a sea of discomfort. But it's also because there is no universe where I would want to talk about why I'm back home, when I said I'd never come back home after high school with Suzy Sue or Betty Gin or Amber Rae or Sally Q. None of those are real Harper's Cove residents, I don't *think*, but I'm happy sacrificing "top-shelf" alcohol for my anonymity.

"I know, I know. You're all *I cannot be seen, doth best not set eyes on me, or thou will suffer*," she teases, putting the back of her right hand over her forehead and lounging dramatically in the wooden chair.

"What are you even quoting?"

Mya shrugs. "Just riffing."

"Move over, Barden Bellas. Mya Kennedy is in the house."

"Fuck you! I could have been a poet!"

"Sure you could have," I smirk. "Keep telling yourself that."

Mya gives me the middle finger. "I would make you pay for this but OH WAIT."

"That joke is getting stale."

"Never."

Part of me wants to remind Mya that I, Xavier Reynolds, can *technically* afford the drinks. If I'm willing to inch even closer to the red on my credit card. Suddenly packing up and moving cross-country isn't cheap, despite what rom-coms make you think. My stomach tosses and turns just thinking about my fracturing bank account, the exhausted savings, and the thin credit limit I'm pushing. How my parents are going to eventually want to know what my future plans are; am I staying or am I going? I already know which one they'd prefer.

It's nice to just exist with her. To be out of the house and pretend, even for a moment, the shitstorm waiting for me at home doesn't exist. So if the price I have to pay is a few cheap jokes, then so be it. Plus, I know they aren't serious. If I really needed it, Mya would help me any way she could. Without question.

That's what friends are for. That's what a Harper's Cove resident does.

Mya leans back in her chair, downing the rest of the drink. The Brook's patio faces the Harper Sound. The sun bounces off the water and refracts off her deep-brown-colored skin. Tendrils of locs lay over her exposed shoulders, and the yellow sundress she rocks—because Black people own the color yellow—plays beautifully off her skin and eyes and everything.

Screw poet, she could have been a world-class model and given Naomi Campbell a run for her money.

Mya and I have been friends since we were both assigned to Miss Lawson's first-grade class—she still teaches at the school, by the way, and helped Mya get her job. We bonded over being the only two kids in a class of twelve who liked the color purple. Since then, we've been nearly inseparable. I talked to her more often than my parents when I was gone. In fact, they got most of the updates *from* her.

"But let's get down to business, and if you quote *Mulan* I'm going to punch you. I know you've been gone for . . ." Mya counts on her fingers. "Eight years, but really? You seriously thought someone was going to break into your house?"

"It's because I've been gone for eight years, I know people *do* break into homes," I object. "You all are just too trusting."

Mya shrugs, tipping her glass to me. "That's why I like it here. Perfect place to raise a family."

I don't reply to the statement about staying here. I don't want to start that age-old argument up again. I never saw Mya anywhere else. She met Derek, her boyfriend and now husband, here. She went to college—University of Southern Maine—but she commuted the forty-five minutes each way. Same for her master's in education. There was no other future for her, and I don't mean that in a negative way. There was no other future for her because she *wanted* no other future, because she made sure that was the case. Harper's Cove was her home, and she wanted to give back to it as much as possible.

Sometimes, I wonder if she looks down on me for wanting to leave so badly.

Who am I kidding? I know the answer to that. Everybody does.

"But more importantly, please elaborate on how you and Logan almost fucked on your kitchen floor two days ago."

A spray of Coke leaves my mouth and almost coats Mya's face, but I have enough sense to turn to the side, instead giving the potted plants in the outdoor part of the bar a shower. Mya smirks, resting her chin in her hand, her well-crafted locs draping in front of her dark-skinned face like shutters of a window. Her brown eyes are like liquid fire, burning into me, begging for more details, with that cocky *I knew it* grin.

"Don't give me that look," I warn, wiping my mouth.

"Whatever do you mean?"

"That look like what you just saw meant something. You just caught me off guard with how crude you are. I forgot that about you."

"You love it," she winks.

"Debatable." A beat. "You're not going to drop this, are you?"

"Absolutely not. Do you know who you're talking to?"

"Unfortunately," I mutter. "I didn't almost fuck him in the kitchen, by the way."

"But you wanted to."

"I didn't say that."

"You didn't have to," she replies. "Your—"

"If you're about to say, 'aura says it all,' I'm going to throw myself into traffic."

"Demeanor says everything."

I try to find comfort in the silence between us. Sometimes I forget how goddamn annoying Mya can be. That perceptiveness makes her such a good teacher. It's frustrating to be on the receiving end of it.

"He was there. I was there. He didn't make himself known as a normal person would," I try to justify.

"Mhm."

"Things got out of hand."

"No, sure. I get it."

"It was a miscommunication."

"Totally was."

I narrow my eyes at her. "I feel like you're not taking me seriously."

"Really?" she asks, hollowing out her cheeks as she slurps down her drink. "What would give you that idea? Gosh, that NYU education was really worth it, huh?"

"Okay, okay, beat-up-on-Xavier time is over."

Mya blows me a kiss and flags down the bartender, mouthing, *Another*. He gives her a thumbs-up before she turns back to me.

"Look, I'm just saying, most of the parents in my class—hell, the school—would love to have a romp with Logan. Even if it's a fake one, like you said."

"People can't be that thirsty."

"You haven't met mothers then," she mutters. "He's a single father who's good with his hands and has an adorable fourteen-year-old."

"How do you know he's good with his hands if you haven't experienced it?"

"Don't ask me things like that. I'm a married and taken woman, Xavier," she scoffs.

"But, if the chance happened to come along?"

Mya waggles her brow.

"You're disgusting."

"So now you're saying a woman's sexuality is disgusting?"

"AND you're putting words in my mouth!"

Mya smirks again, a lopsided grin that fits perfectly on her beautiful features. "Plus, he's a chef. AND available. There isn't anything wrong with this guy."

"Sounds like a cliché from a bad rom-com," I say, arms resting on the table, blowing carbon dioxide bubbles into the last third of my Coke. The ice has mostly melted now, cutting through the sugar.

The chef bit makes sense. Mom owned a restaurant in DC before my parents moved out here to Harper's Cove. She gave that up for Dad and me when we moved here. She didn't have to; she wanted to. Trading spatulas and broilers for flyers and microphones running the Harper's Cove community center. Mom wanted to make sure she had time at home with me. To help mold me into the man I am today. Her father and mother weren't role models in her life. She wasn't going to repeat that cycle.

Plus, it meant all of her cooking knowledge was passed on to me, instead of some sous chef just trying to use her restaurant as a stepping-stone.

It's one of the things that makes me such a goddamn catch of a boyfriend, I'm a fucking awesome cook, if I do say so myself.

"I mean, if all clichés looked like that, I'd do more reading," Mya mutters.

I arch my brow. "Don't you teach second-grade English? And, *AGAIN*, aren't you married?"

"Doesn't mean I can't look. And besides, I'm discussing things like *Stuart Little*, *James and the Giant Peach*, Paddington Bear, and *Charlotte's Web* with my students, not the difference between tropes and clichés. How old do you think second graders are, anyway?"

"Twelve?"

Mya's face looks like someone tried to imitate Picasso with clay but realized they were not the reincarnation of the famous artist and settled on just an emotionless face made of Play-Doh.

"You're not serious. You're serious. Oh my God, my best friend is stupid as shit."

"Oh, for fuck's sakes," I groan. "Siri, how old is the average second grader?"

"The average second grader is seven to eight years old."

Okay, that wasn't the answer I was expecting. Mya looks at me, one brow perfectly arched.

"I know Logan has a kid," I say, diverting the conversation from my ignorance. "He just doesn't seem like the type of person who I would peg for being a parent."

"Oh, this is going to be good. What, pray tell, does a parent look like?"

I shrug. "Not like he does. When I picture a parent, I don't picture them buff with tattoos."

"I know what you mean. But, funny you mention that because he does have nice tattoos," Mya says, her eyes glazing over like she's no longer part of this world anymore. "And he used to be a musician . . ." I wait patiently for her to exit whatever dreamland she's in, a dreamland where her sole focus is Logan. Eventually, when her elbow slips and her chin almost hits the table, she snaps out of it.

"What were we talking about?"

"Logan's daughter. And how much of a cliché he is."

"Oh, yeah. Anne. She's a doll. Sometimes works with him on weekends at the Wharf doing deliveries for those who can't leave their homes but still want seafood. See? He even delivers food to those who can't leave their homes. That has to be worth at least ten-kay points toward the Good Place."

More (unearned) praise for Logan. But I'm not focused on that. I'm more curious about this employment of his daughter. The curiosity manifests itself as an arched brow. Mya arches both of hers in response.

"I know small towns have their own . . . *we handle our own here, and how we get by is for no one to judge but ourselves and God* mentality, but letting a kid work in a wharf? That sounds . . ."

Illegal. That's the word I'm looking for. Has the town changed that much since I left?

"I sometimes forget how long you've been gone," Mya says, shaking her head. "The Wharf is a restaurant. Cute little place thataway." She points west. "Anne helps out as the dishwasher on evenings ever since Logan's previous one quit and does deliveries on her bike during the weekend. Well, not quit, Logan fired him, but that's a story he should tell, not me."

Having a summer job is a rite of passage in Harper's Cove. It may be a place where almost anything can be done by favors, but manning a lemonade stand, mowing lawns, helping clean Mr. Robinson's corner store, running the *Summer in the Park* movie series every weekend—those are just a small sample of jobs kids did when I was younger. Every person in Harper's Cove has a role to play in order to keep this community thriving. And the kids' job is to find a way to carve a space for themselves in Harper Cove's ecosystem, anyway they can. That's just how it is.

My God I sound like I'm about to apply for an AARP card.

"We should go there sometime," Mya suggests. "You know I love you and Janice's cooking, but Logan's food is . . ." She makes a chef's-kiss-like motion with her hands.

"Simping for a white man over a Black queen like my mother? In this economy? Th—OW! Shit, Mya! That *hurt*!"

"You deserved it. You're going to say stupid shit like that, I'm going to hit you. Like our parents did when we were younger."

"That is *not* how this friendship works!" I squirm, trying to get out of her reach. "And my mom never BEAT me!"

"Maybe she should have! And also, I'm your best friend, which means I can say or do anything, and you can't argue with me."

"That is not what that means!"

"But most importantly . . ." Mya takes a long sip of her drink, a pregnant pause that's intentional in the anticipation it causes. "Logan is exactly your type. Trust me. I'm right. I'm always right."

I've already spit once, and that's more than enough times reverting to my past life as a camel for one lifetime. So Mya just gets a well-placed scowl instead.

"He is *not* my type."

"Oh, sorry, sorry, yes, your type is what? Trust fund babies without an emotional bone in their bodies, who kick you out when you need them the most?"

Mya's face shows she knows how deep her words cut without me having to say anything.

"That was a low blow."

"You think?"

Mya sighs. She leans back, crossing her arms under her breasts, making them rise up slightly.

"Are we having a fight right now?" she asks.

The silence between us is uncomfortable, and I don't think Mya and I have had a moment like this in years. Since knowing her, I think we've had what we can really call a fight maybe three times. I like to think there's something positive about that. Only three fights in nearly thirty years. That's a good record.

But Mya, in typical Aries fashion, can't keep her mouth shut.

"All I'm saying is, you both would be cute together," she blurts out. "He's single. You're single. He's hot. You're hot. He's good with his hands. You're good with . . . what are you good with?"

"Alright, that's enough." Fishing out a twenty, I throw it on the table, even though I know what Mya and I agreed. "I'm going home. Before we both say something we're going to regret and can't take back."

I know Mya means well. As my friend—my best friend—it's her job to push me. To want the best for me and to see opportunities that I can't, be it because I'm too nervous, pigheaded, drunk, or whatever. But there is no opportunity with Logan, for many reasons. For one, he lives in Harper's Cove, and I don't intend to be here for much longer. He is absolutely—no matter how much Mya thinks otherwise—not my type. He has a kid. Which means he's probably straight. Or he could be bi. Sexuality is a construct and fluid.

But most importantly, I don't trust Mya's ability to tell if someone is gay or not. I still remember when we went to Portland and went to a gay bar after graduating, she picked the one guy there who was straight and swore up and down he was *my prince charming*. I made a fool of myself so badly my whole body almost became a singularity and imploded on itself. I would like to not go through that again.

Mya frowns but doesn't try to push the issue any further. She may be the fire sign in the relationship, but I'm a Taurus rising, the resident earth sign and stubborn as a bull. She knows when not to push me, and this is one of those times.

"One more thing," she says, standing to hug and kiss me goodbye. "You free this weekend?"

"Depends on what for and depends how I feel about you this weekend."

"It's the annual Harper's Cove Junior Olympics at the school. I could use some support."

I groan. "You all still do that?"

While most schools have some sort of state-mandated test you have to pass to prove you're physically fit, our school has a day where middle school, elementary school, and high school kids all participate in an Olympic-style array of games to prove their physical talents. It's a low-stress day and no one ever really fails. Everyone gets a participation trophy and pizza, and parents get to cheer on their kids as they let off some energy. It's, like, the third-most-popular day in Harper's Cove. Everyone turns out.

How could I have forgotten this was happening?

"Trust me, if I could call out sick and not have to go, I would. But you have to admit, it's a little cute watching a whole gaggle of four-foot-tall kids trying to run a mile. They don't stay in their lanes, no one makes an appropriate time, and we all just have fun. But I need someone to man one of the ticket booths."

"Your husband can't do it?"

"Derek's out," she says in that matter-of-fact tone that tells me this isn't something she's happy about or wants to discuss. "Last-minute trip."

"And now you need me to cover for him. I told you, you can't trust men."

"Oh, I know." She smirks at me. "I'm only asking you because I have no other options."

"We can do this song and dance, but you know I'll be there."

Mya grins, a type of smile that shows off her white straight teeth and makes her brown skin seem brighter.

"Just say the word, and I'll break up with him and marry you in a heartbeat," she says, kissing my cheek while hugging me before picking up her drink and doing what Mya does best: going to the bar and starting up a conversation.

I stand for a moment, just watching Mya chat with the bartender and two other men sitting at the bar. She seems in her element, casually holding court with these gentlemen. Does she know them? Are they friends?

"Stupid question, Xavier," I mutter. Everyone here knows everyone. It's what makes Harper's Cove feel like such a tight-knit community and home. Unlocked doors. Neighbors doing favors. Everyone knowing everyone by name. It's quintessential happy, small-town America.

And I'm counting down the days until I can leave. How do you tell the people closest in your life that you want to get as far away from them as possible, because everything they believe in is exactly what you want to run away from?

Answer: You don't tell a soul.

CHAPTER
FOUR

THE DISTANCE FROM THE Brook to my parents' house is less than a five-minute drive. Yet still, sixty minutes after I left the bar, I arrive home.

Part of it is because I feel bad letting Mya drive home alone. Harper's Cove may be one of those small towns that border on lawless, but I'm not letting my best friend drive drunk. So driving her car home, walking back to get mine, and then driving myself home takes a total of nearly an hour. At least the hour gives me time with my own thoughts. I forgot how much I missed those since being attached at the hip to Bradley.

The only problem with spending so much time with your own thoughts is that sometimes they betray you. Validating turns into confusion. Confusion turns into second-guessing. And eventually, second-guessing metastasizes into catastrophizing. Such as maybe I should just give up and open up a soap-making business. I like soap. Soap smells good, and I like smelling good.

"Honestly, that doesn't sound like a horrible idea . . ."

Harper's Sound is where the fishing community troop has their home base. Most of the boats are small ones—Harper's Cove is known for its fishing, but it's not like an A-plus fishing community—but the group who call themselves fishers are loyal. They've been doing this since the dawn of time it seems, and a lot of these families pass down their knowledge from one to the next. I've never found enjoyment at the sound, not like my fellow *Covers*—I hate that word, but it's better than the alternative, Covians.

I know better than to say that to my parents. It took me a long time to learn this little trick; but when you know your attitude is going to be shit, it's always best to remove yourself from any triggering situations. It's no one else's job but your own to handle your emotions. I love my parents, but they are absolutely triggers.

I should feel ashamed, and maybe a part of me does, for being so open with the fact that I don't want to deal with my mom. I don't want to have to navigate the seas of her invasive questions, trying to figure out what happened between Bradley and me. I don't want to have to deal with her repeating, *But he seemed like such a sweet boy*, unable to understand that *I* wasn't the one who broke up with *him*. And I certainly don't want to deal with Dad trying to fumble through discussing a gay relationship with me that he doesn't fully understand.

More importantly, I don't want to have to deal with her trying to probe into what I'm going to do with my life next. I know she means well; I know she just wants me to maybe consider making Harper's Cove my permanent home, but I'd rather die than do that.

"My parents are good people, I'm lucky to have people who love me, I'm blessed," I repeat over and over again, whenever I feel myself going down this spiral. Yes, my parents are nice people, great people, even. I don't know how to tell them, though: they aren't perfect parents.

When I finally arrive home, the sun is almost set on the horizon, a burst of purples and oranges like paint swatches in the sky. I let my Prius quiet for a moment, just sitting in the car. These are the moments I love most about Harper's Cove. Not the people. Not the small-town vibe, or the nature. It's the stillness. The fact that I can think and hear myself think.

Maybe I'm more of a hermit than I like to admit.

"You can do this, Xavier," I mutter. "You just need to go inside, chat with your parents, and then go upstairs. Your computer is waiting for you. Monster.com and LinkedIn are waiting for you. You'll be out of here in a week, maybe two. Just hold on a little longer."

Am I being overly optimistic, thinking I can get a job in two weeks? Absolutely. Am I going to keep that same optimism and try my very best to keep my anxiety locked in the closet like the Babadook? Absolutely.

The living room and kitchen lights are on. I can make out Mom's and Dad's shapes at the large table they've had for as long as I can remember. Mom's eyes lit up when Dad brought it home; a solid oak, expandable table whose flaps came out and allowed us to turn the six-person table into a twelve-seater whenever Mom hosted any holiday or random occasion to cook for people. We had every meal at that table, unlike other families in my high school who ate in front of the TV in their living rooms. Mom was insistent on family time, that it was important for us all to catch up with one another.

But who is that other shadow at the table? Those other *two* shadows? One is obviously Mom; the other is Dad . . . but the last two? Maybe one of Dad's friends? Maybe . . .

"No fucking way."

For a moment, I think that my mom would have somehow convinced Bradley to come all the way up for dinner. It's not the most unreasonable thing. My mom is a force of nature; if she wants something, really wants something, she'll make it happen.

But why should I be ashamed? This is my home. He's on my turf. The tables have turned, bucko.

Buddy? Bucko? Which sounds better?

"Neither, Xavier, neither of them sounds good."

I frown, jumping out of the car and slamming the door. I don't care if my parents have company over—as long as it isn't Bradley. They had a life before I appeared on their doorstep a week ago. That's a good thing. I want them to get over empty-nest syndrome.

But there's an opposite side to this point. If we have company, that means I have to perform. I have to put on a smile, pretend like I have my whole life figured out, like coming home is all part of my plan, or doesn't make me feel like a complete and total loser who failed at the simplest thing in life: surviving on your own. Whoever is sitting at the table is going to want to hear my life updates, and I don't have the energy to lie or beat around the bush for them. I'm not in the mood to force fake smiles, make sure my laugh sounds pitch perfect, or pretend I know what I'm doing.

For once in my life, I don't know what I'm doing, and that's scary enough.

Which means the only option is to be rude and go up to my bedroom, which also means Mom is going to give me an earful about how I'm being a horrible son, a bad host, etc., etc.

"Great."

But before I can think of a plan for how to handle any of those competing end results, I'm already pushing my way through the front door. An assault on my senses almost throws me off my feet. The sounds of soft jazz mixing with laughter and constant chatter. The smell of caramelized onions, roasted chicken, brussels sprouts, and more dance around my nostrils. The cold air tingles against my skin, and the bright light of every single bulb turned to the max almost blinds me.

"Xavier?" my mom asks before I can even toe my shoes off. "Come into the living room!"

There's no arguing with her; I can hear it in her voice. Sighing and staring at myself in the mirror by the door, I flex my smile and force it to look natural. The scowl that is constantly on my face slowly disappears and is replaced with something a little more natural. It isn't a full-on grin, but it will do. At least whomever my mom wants me to meet won't think I'm a bitch. That's a small win.

"Just a few minutes," I tell myself in the mirror once more, quickly fixing my coils of curls so they look decent. See, if I had been drinking, this would have been even more of a problem. Sighing, I give myself one more smile before walking into the living room. I'm quickly going through the list of faces I expect to see. One of Mom's friends from the library where she volunteers. The Clancys, Dad's best friend who moved here right when I left for college, and his son who works at the scrapyard. A few other names and faces come to mind, many of whom I haven't kept up with for the past seven years—and that makes a pang of embarrassment flood my body.

But no one I expected, absolutely none of them, included Logan and his daughter, sitting at the table, in the exact same spots where Mya and I would usually be sitting.

"What are you doing here?" I say before I can attempt to make the words sound nicer.

Mom glares at me in that way that every kid knows is just the tip of the emotional iceberg, but I do my absolute best to ignore it. Instead, I focus on Logan, who barely seems fazed. He glances over at me with a sideways, almost bored look, and then back at my mom.

"This chicken is amazing, Janice. Seriously. Some of the best I've ever had."

"It's the vanilla." She grins. "Just a little of it mixed with the sauce and cooked for a bit longer. Helps to bring out the sweetness of the meat. I repurposed it from a honey garlic chicken wings recipe my mother taught me."

"I've made something similar. Madagascar vanilla curry chicken. I'll send you the recipe sometime."

"The chicken's good, but the vegetables . . ." Anne mutters under her breath. She makes a *blegh* face that's nothing short of dramatic.

"Anne," Logan says sternly.

That's all he needs to say to shut her down. "Sorry."

"Sorry what?"

"Sorry, Mrs. Reynolds."

Mom waves it off, as if the disrespect is nothing but water flowing down her back. "My son used to hate his vegetables, too. Trust me, it's nothing I haven't heard before."

"So now, not only are we just giving away family secrets, but we're also just throwing me under the bus in front of strangers?" I ask. "Are we in the twilight zone or something?"

"Xavier," Mom says, as if my name is a full sentence, while standing. "Kitchen. Now."

She almost sounds like Logan. Funny how the parental tone is something all parents have mastered without even trying.

There's no question of whether I'll follow her; it's more, will I follow her fast enough that she won't yell at me. I turn quickly on my heels, trotting behind her like a lost dog.

"Someone's in trouble," Anne says, dragging out the word trouble so it has a singsong tone to it.

"Eat your brussels sprouts, Anne," Logan gently orders. "It's not nice to gawk at people."

Fuck you.

Mom uses the dividing shutter-like doors to dampen the sound just a bit.

"What is wrong with you?" she hisses.

"I—"

"That wasn't a question for you to answer, Xavier Malachi Reynolds."

Oh, so we're pulling out full names now.

"We have company. Have you been gone for so long you don't remember how to act? I know I taught you better. Seems you haven't forgotten all your home training."

I open my mouth to throw out some quippy reply, but the way my mom arches her right brow makes me shut it. It's not worth it, especially when my mom gives me *that* look. Everyone in town knows what that look means. This conversation is over.

Let's try another question then.

"Why is he here?" I ask, quieter this time, correcting my tone to be more curious and less accusatory.

Mom doesn't answer at first, instead gesturing for me to follow her to the fridge. She opens it up, and without saying anything, I know what she wants and what I need to do.

There's a cake, in cling wrap, with homemade frosting in there. Frosting cakes was always my favorite part of cooking with my mom. Maybe she thinks doing this will trigger some dead spark plug inside of me. Maybe she just wants me back in the kitchen with her, reliving old times. Maybe it's a mix of both.

I take both the cake and the frosting out, one in each hand, and place them on the island. She gets out the wooden spoon, taking the cling wrap off the upside-down strawberry cake that's glistening with its layer of simple syrup.

"Logan is a family friend, Xavier," she says, handing me the wooden spoon. Spreading the frosting seems to still be my honor. "Your father and I have friends, you know. We didn't just stop living when you left. And . . ."

Nope, not going to have that conversation.

"And you're apologizing for the whole cupcake scenario?" I ask. I know that famous chicken recipe Mom was talking about. We fine-tuned it before I left for college. It's only rolled out for major occasions—including apologies or celebrations. Something tells me, since I got into grad school, besides birthdays and anniversaries, there isn't much here to celebrate anymore.

Mom doesn't say anything, maybe because she doesn't want me to feel ashamed. Which would be dumb, because I'm not ashamed. Perhaps I should be, but I'm not upset for defending my home. I was wrong for throwing Gatorade on Logan, but he still came into our house. It was self-defense. I had no reason to think otherwise.

Mom dips her right finger into the frosting, flicks up a bit, and holds it to my mouth. Without any more words, I lick it off her finger.

"Anything missing?"

"You know there's nothing missing from your recipes, Mom."

"Anything we can do to make it better? And don't say there

isn't; cooking is an art form, it can always be improved. You know this."

"I'd argue that if it's art, then my thoughts on it are as subjective and valid as yours, and thus it can't be."

The correction is important. Mom's Black, and passing on recipes is a big part of our culture and tradition. Now, she's nowhere near the age to be worried about that—she's barely sixty-two—but I know mortality is something she's been thinking about, ever since her cancer scare a few years back. For us, and our people, it's not about forgetting the past, or completely changing it; it's about building on it and using the previous foundations as blocks for our future offspring. This cake recipe and dozens of others were different when my grandmother made them. They were different when her offspring made them. But that's what makes them so special. When I inherit them, I won't make them better, I'll just add my own spin on them. And if I ever have kids, they'll do the same.

Maybe this is my mom's way of asking me to start thinking about how I'm going to build on her legacy.

"I think . . ." I smack my lips. Walking over to the spice cabinet, I pull out some nutmeg and cinnamon, dashing a little of each inside. Using the hand mixer, I blend it until it's smooth and add a little salt during the mixing process.

"This will cut through the sweetness of the cake." Once the mixing is done, I return the favor, putting the spoon to my mom's lips. She licks it, eyes glancing up at the ceiling in thought, as she decides if I made her recipe better or worse.

Finally, the verdict comes in: a nod and a smile. "I knew I taught you well," she praises, cupping my cheek. "Which also means I taught you manners. Can you please be decent tonight? For me?"

"For you," I say a moment later, kissing her hand. She pats my cheek, gently working with me to quickly cover the cake in frosting.

I promised my mom I would be decent. I didn't tell her I'd be social, and those are two very different things.

I bring the cake in.

"Only half for me," Dad says, raising one hand.

"But you love Mom's cake."

"Diabetes," Mom says. "Doctor says he needs to watch his sugar."

"Should I be concerned?" I ask, frowning. Dad has always been a stubborn man. He doesn't show his emotions well or ask for help. Maybe it's a by-product of his generation, maybe it's just who he is, but the idea of Mom being here alone is almost enough for me to consider the option of staying in Harper's Cove. Especially if what Dad is saying is worse than he's letting on.

But, then again, Mom has Robbie.

Dad waves his hand dismissively. Even if it was worth being concerned over, he wouldn't tell me. "I think it's a load of BS, if you ask me," he grumbles.

I give Mom a silent sideways glance, asking her again, without words, if I should be concerned. Her eyes calm my anxiousness. Until Logan opens his very nicely proportioned mouth.

"Now, Mr. Reynolds, your health is important," Logan scolds gently. "We want you around for a long while."

My hand almost drops the plate as I put it in front of Logan's red-haired daughter, which would have led to a mess Mom would have made me clean up. Maybe that would have helped me focus my frustration. What does *he*, Logan, know about my father? What right does he have to suggest anything? He isn't a doctor. He's just a restaurant owner with very nice stubble, very nice biceps, and . . .

Mom must feel the rage wafting off me. She puts her hand on mine, guiding the knife back to the plate. It's not like I was going to stab him or anything.

Maybe.

Probably.

"Listen, if I have to pick between eating greens for the rest of my life and eating a piece of cake every now and then, kill me now because I love cake too much," Dad says proudly. "But for your mom, today, I'm going to be good."

"And that's why I love you," Mom says, kissing his cheek.

I sit next to my mom, across from Logan and Anne. I try my best not to focus on his face, on how his hair is pulled into a small ponytail. I try not to stare at the falcon and osprey tattoos on his left arm and the wolf and lion tattoos on his right. Mya is right, despite how much I don't want to admit it. Logan's looks check every single box of a guy I wanted when I was younger and playing MASH: my dream guy.

But dream guys are just that—dreams—and they often turn into nightmares because you overlook all the red flags. Being an adult is about learning to compromise and making choices that help you accomplish your goals. That doesn't always align with happiness and the happy ending people want.

Though, if you asked my parents, they would disagree.

You see, my mom and dad's romance is one that rom-com directors would dream of creating. They met in high school. He was there illegally—wrong zip code—and her parents grew close to his parents. When he needed a place to stay during the week so he could claim residency, her parents suggested he live with them. Mom and Dad hated each other at first, but over the next year and a half, they grew closer and closer. Mom went to college, and Dad ended up following her; driving her to Spelman and professing his feelings for her when he dropped her off.

He stayed in Atlanta the whole time for her. They moved to DC to be closer to my dad's family, Mom's family moving out west like they always dreamed. They never dated anyone else. Never broke up, rarely fought, and now have been married for almost forty years. It's ridiculous.

"Xavier, baby, do you mind serving everyone?"

Of course I do, I think, but I'm not going to say that. I can tell, by the way Mom speaks, she's asked me this before and I wasn't paying attention.

"Of course I don't."

I keep my answer short and sweet. Black kids don't talk back to their parents like that. I remember when I went to an ex-friend's house during Thanksgiving one year at NYU, when I couldn't afford to go back home, and I watched her parents have a knockout, dragged-out verbal fight with her in the living room. And then just pretend like nothing happened? It was fucking weird.

I swiftly cut the cake, dividing it into halves and separating it. The left half, I split into five pieces with three even cuts. One for me, Mom, Dad, Anne, and sadly one for Logan. Part of me wants to find a way, but you know, that would defeat the whole being-a-good-son thing I'm trying to do.

"Thank you, Mrs. Reynolds," Anne says without even being prompted.

"You're welcome, sweetie," Mom replies with a warm tone.

"Here you go, Mom," I say, placing the best slice of the remaining three in front of her.

Mom smiles one of her soft, gentle grins at me, a silent thank-you for doing what I'm told and putting whatever feelings about Logan I have behind me. I smile back, staring at the last two pieces. One is a little small and was the first slice I made. Cutting cake is like having sex for the first time; it's never great, and this slice reflects that. It's lumpy, almost broken in half, and the icing is falling off one side like a snowman snowboarding down a mountain in some YouTube skit.

Then there's the last piece. It's perfect. Not as perfect as the one I gave to Mom, but damn good. I should give it to Logan. I should take the ugly piece. It's all aesthetics, sure, but it's the right thing to do. He is the guest after all.

I can feel my mom's eyes on me. She knows what I'm thinking. She knows me better than I like to think or let on.

Be the good son, Xavier. Do the right thing, Xavier. It's just a piece of cake, Xavier. Both are going to taste the same.

Screw that.

I push the ugly, malformed piece toward Logan. Xavier, one; Logan, zero. Even though Mom lets out an audible sigh, and, from the corner of my eyes, I can see she shake her head, it's still all worth it. A small act of silly rebellion that really doesn't mean anything.

Until fucking tattoo indie-painter-looking Logan flashes a perfect smile, completely unfazed. Doesn't he know what the ugly piece of cake means? It means I won and he lost. It's a passive-aggressive act of rebellion. He just can't SMILE at me like nothing just happened. But that's exactly what he fucking does.

"Thank you," he says. "It looks delicious."

I take it back. Logan, one; Xavier, zero.

"Course," I reply through gritted teeth. "Eat up."

"Xavier," Mom warns.

"I mean you're welcome."

"You'll have to excuse my son, he hasn't eaten all day. He ran out of the house this morning without breakfast."

"It's 8:00 p.m. What does breakfast have to do with it," I mutter under my breath.

"Xavier," my dad says. "Don't talk back to your mother. Did you lose your manners when you went to the big city?"

You make it sound like I traveled across the ocean on a one-man boat in the 1700s, I think to myself.

"Don't worry, Janice and Shelton, I understand, Anne gets the same way when she hasn't eaten," Logan says, flicking his eyes toward me for one brief second. "I know what it's like to have children."

Is he really comparing me to his teen daughter? In my own fucking home? My pride deflates in a matter of seconds, and shame balloons inside of me, pushing my organs out of the way.

I feel like I'm a high school kid all over again, and that's the worst feeling anyone can feel. Some people think when you turn eighteen, your parents can't tell you what to do anymore. And sure, maybe in some families that's true, but not mine. I'll always be my parents' kid. Even in Harper's Cove, I'm known by the residents as Shelton and Janice's boy. I hate that. I want to be my own person. I don't want to be attached to them because, if I settle for that—if I decide that's enough—I'll never leave. I'll never try to discover who I am on my own.

And I can't—I won't—let that happen.

Logan, two; Xavier, zero.

We eat the cake in silence for just long enough for that comfortable flatline to fill the air. The decibel level flickers upward every now and then with the occasional clink of a fork against the plate, or a sound of pleasure from someone's mouth. Eventually, of course, Logan breaks the silence.

"I have to say . . . this is some of the best cake I've ever tasted."

Kiss up.

"Stop it, Logan," my mom "modestly" says. "You're flattering me."

She fucking loves it.

"Can I have another?" Anne asks.

"Sure," I say, in a half stance. At least it gives my hands something to do.

"You already had enough," Logan interjects. "One is more than enough."

"But—"

"What did you get on your algebra test again? Tell you what, if you can tell me what the answer is to $3x + 5 = 26$, then you can have another piece of cake."

X *equals seven.*

Anne scowls. "That's not fair. I don't *need* algebra to go pro."

"Everyone needs math, and you sure as heck don't need another piece of cake."

Anne huffs and sits back, muttering what sounds like *ass* under her breath.

"Come again?" Logan asks.

"Nothing."

"That's what I thought." Without missing a beat, he morphs as if he's taking off his parental mask and replacing it with his kiss-up mask. "The icing, especially, Janice, is perfect."

Logan makes the kissing motion with his three fingers, thumb, pointer, and middle, to show his appreciation.

My eyes snap up to my mom, trying to secretly warn her not to say anything. But I can see the mischievousness dancing off her lips. I can see the gears turning.

"Mom."

"Well, if you like that icing, did you know that it's Xavier's recipe?"

From the corner of my eye, I see Logan's eyebrows rise. "Really?"

"Mom, seriously."

"Sure is," she says, no signs of stopping and ignoring my little outburst—again. "Made it when he was fifteen years old. My son is a very good chef, you know."

"I didn't," Logan says, turning directly to me. "Is that true?"

"I'm more than just a pretty face," I say, mostly a joke.

"Color me surprised."

Wait, did he mean that he's surprised that I have talent or was he admitting that I am pretty? Before I can ask, my mom interjects, singing my praises.

"Xavier made his first meal when he was six years old."

"Learning how to make cream-chipped turkey isn't an accomplishment."

"But learning how to make both sides of the toast crispy while only using a hot plate? That is. Most people can't do that or know that about you. My son is a man of many talents."

Because I don't go around telling them. I want to be known for being a badass business mogul. Not some chef. Not that there's anything wrong with that; it's just not me. That's not my dream. That was always Mom's dream for me, but not mine. I wonder if she sometimes resents me for not molding her dream with my own blood, sweat, and tears, and turning it into a reality.

"And, if I'm correct, you're still looking for a sous chef? I think my son would—"

"Excuse me," I say quickly, dropping my fork and knife, letting the loud clamoring of metal against ceramic break my mom's train of thought. Standing up quickly, I push the chair from behind me and walk to my room.

Suddenly, I'm not hungry for cake anymore.

CHAPTER
FIVE

WHEN MY PHONE RINGS at 4:00 a.m., I think someone is dying.

At first, I think it's my parents, despite how illogical that really is. I wouldn't wish that fate on anyone, not even my worst enemy—not even Bradley. Or Logan. I'm not sure whom I hate more at the moment. Why do I have to pick?

As logic begins to push through the fog of sleepiness, I think, *Maybe something horrible happened to Mya that would cause her husband to call me at 4:00 a.m.?* Again, not a fate I'd wish on anyone. That shit can fuck you up for life.

It's surprisingly common, too. Considering that the odds of dying in America are 1 in 107, that basically means every 107 times you drive, 1 of those could lead to your death, and most people average two trips a day . . . well, the numbers add up, and that "less than 1 percent" isn't so small.

There's also the third option, the less likely one yet the least morbid one: You won the lottery. Funny how the horrible things are always more likely than the positive thing in my head. I wonder if other people's brains are as broken as mine is.

It takes me a moment to process, one by one, in the matter of seconds, how none of those choices are probably likely. My parents are in the room on the first floor. If one of them were dead, God forbid, I would have heard the other wailing through the house. I don't have a loved one, and I wouldn't be the first person Bradley's family would call if he were somehow unconscious. The one time I met them, it was a very *Get Out*–like situation, and I was not feeling it.

And, if I had somehow won the lottery? Well, there's no reason that couldn't happen. I've seen *In the Heights*. I know how lucky some people can be. But I've never been one of those people. Not in ninety-six thousand years.

But there is a phone ringing, that's for sure.

At first, I think the sound is in my dream, which wouldn't make sense considering said dream was Katy Perry as a Popsicle dancing on top of a banana while it rained Skittles. But when it stops—and then a minute later starts up again—I know it's for real. And I know it's serious.

"For fuck's sakes," I mutter, opening one eye. I'm met with Naga glaring at me.

"Oh, I'm so sorry, Your Highness, sorry my phone is disturbing your sleep."

She simply huffs in response.

Groaning, I pat around on my bed, feeling tangled sheets, the coolness of my laptop, Naga's fluff, and then my phone, somewhere under the other pillow on my left-hand side.

"Hello?" I hoarsely call out, rolling onto my back. Naga rolls away from me, yawning loudly before burying herself in the blankets.

You and me both, girl.

"Good morning, is this Xavier Reynolds?"

The voice is British and far too happy for 4:00 a.m. I pull the phone back from my face. The string of numbers means nothing to me, besides confirming it's not an American number. Maybe I'm still asleep?

I pinch my left arm to check. "Shit."

"Pardon?"

"Nothing, sorry, yes, this is he." A beat. I can't ignore saying it. "Do you know what time it is?"

"1 . . ." The sound of shuffling on the other end is almost soothing enough to put me back to sleep. The shrill squeak that follows most certainly wakes me up. "Oh, my goodness! I am so sorry! It's ten a.m. here in Berlin."

Berlin. Berlin? BERLIN!

If I was asleep before, I'm up now—like, physically and mentally. I'm standing before I tell my brain to issue the string of commands to make my body stand. Naga yelps, the surprise throwing her off the bed. She glares up at me, quickly righting herself almost like a cat.

"You'll forgive me later," I say, quickly stepping into the bathroom and closing the door. I don't know why, but the bathroom connecting to my room has always been a safe haven for me. During my first breakup when I was crying my eyes out, or when Mya and I had a fight that I swore was going to be the end of us, or when I was trying to come up with how I was going to tell my parents I intended to go to NYU instead of the University of Maine . . . this bathroom has seen me at my best and my worst.

"You're with the Carey Foundation, aren't you?"

"That I would be. How are you this morning? Besides being woken up at . . . what time is it for you?"

"Four a.m., and don't worry about that. It's fine." The memory of that rejection letter still stings. It was the start of my personal Mercury retrograde, like someone had pulled a pin from a latch and caused a cascade of shit, of astrological proportions, to fall on top of me. But, nevertheless, I persisted. Barely, but I did.

Maybe this was all worth it?

"May I ask why you're calling me, Ms. . . . ?"

"Cunningham."

"Cunningham. If I remember correctly, and I may be wrong, you all told me I didn't make the cut."

I'm not fucking wrong. If you told me right now you would give me one million dollars to recite four Nicki Minaj songs word for word, I'd fail. But if you told me to recite my Carey Foundation Fellowship rejection letter forward, backward, and every other -ward? I wouldn't miss a beat. I pored over that fucking letter hoping to find some sliver of hope.

There was none. But I'm trying to keep my cool. Trying to act like this doesn't faze me and that my mind isn't going to the most illogical yet hopeful choice. What good does hope have in a place like this? Sleepy small towns are where hope goes to die.

God, please don't let this be where I end up.

"Yes, yes, about that." More shuffling. More awkward pregnant pauses that make me want to scream, *Tell me what you fucking want to tell me, or I'll jump through this phone and beat your ass like we did during the American Revolution.*

"There's been a change of plans."

"A change of plans?" I meant to say that in my head. "What does that mean?"

"One of our applicants . . . unfortunate, really, but he got married."

"Congratulations to him."

"If you're into that sort of thing," Ms. Cunningham says. There's a sugariness to her tone of voice that is deceptive. She just dragged a guy for being married, and I feel like I can see clearly the smile on her face. "His priorities have shifted, and he passed—"

I don't hear the rest of her words because I don't need to hear them. My heart is pounding so hard it sounds like Niagara Falls in my ears. He's passing on the fellowship, which means a slot has opened up and they are giving it to me. *Me.* A Black kid with no job is going to Berlin for a year on a fellowship to learn from some of the greatest minds about business. Coupled with my MBA, and the experience plus the recommendation and connections I'll get from this place? I'll be running a Fortune 500 company before I'm forty. This is it. This is my time. This is my moment. This . . .

"Mr. Reynolds, did you hear me?"

"I accept," I blurt out. "I accept the fellowship."

"Oh, I'm so happy to hear that! We think you'll be a great addition to the cohort. But that's not what I was asking about."

And then it drops. The other shoe. What's that expression? Humans make plans and God laughs?

I bet he's fucking laughing up a storm right now.

· · · · · · · ·

"FIVE THOUSAND DOLLARS?!"

As with everything in my life, the first person I told wasn't my parents, or Naga, or Bradley anymore, but Mya.

I was good this time, though. I didn't call her while she was on her Peloton, or having breakfast with her husband, or during class. I waited until her first free period, a twenty-five-minute recess, and made a beeline for the school.

The wait was excruciating.

I didn't play nice guy with Ms. Abby, the front desk attendant whom I've known for years. I didn't stop in Principal Meadow's classroom, or reconnect with her son, who's my age and the first guy I had sex with (it wasn't great). I headed to my best friend to complain about what was supposed to be a happy moment.

"Right?" I ask, taking a carrot from her lunch pail.

"I thought you said this was an all-expenses-paid fellowship? Right? I'm remembering correctly?"

"It is, once you get there," I explain. "The five thousand dollars covers everything I need for the program, including induction into the Carey Foundation Registry of graduates, and the payment we have to make to the program."

"And there's no payment plan?"

I shake my head, taking a sip of the Diet Coke we're sharing. "The payment plan date passed. I was lucky enough they took fifteen hundred to hold my spot; I emptied out my bank account for that."

"Okay, but *hold your spot* can mean a lot of different things," she corrects, glancing past me through the window. I see Mya's eyes narrow, and I know she's locked eyes with a student who thinks they're slick because whoever is on recess duty can't see them. That's why Mya sits in this exact empty classroom. You can see the whole playground from here. She's like . . . a female Mufasa. "Because, like, can you get them the money in a week? A month? In three months when you start? It starts in November, right?"

"They need it in two months."

Mya lets out a whistle that is akin to someone saying the words *fucking shit*, but she's trying to cut down on her cursing, supposedly. Not sure how well it's going, but the sound tells a full-bodied picture of how screwed I am.

"So you need basically thirty-five hundred dollars."

I nod, munching on a carrot while doing so.

"In eight weeks."

"Bingo."

"No one says *bingo*. You know I'd give you the money if I had it."

"I know, Mya."

"But with Derek and I wanting to try for a baby, and IVF is expensive . . ."

"I know, you don't have to explain it to me."

"And we're still paying back the loans we took out for the wedding."

"Mya," I say more firmly. "It's fine. Really."

Mya always had a specific wedding in mind and nothing stopped her from getting it. Once Mya has set her mind on something, or decided someone is worth her time, you'd have to probably paint the world in blood for her to even consider changing her opinion. She, more than anyone, deserves to be happy.

So, after her two failed pregnancies, when she called me, telling me she was doing IVF, I didn't hesitate to support her. And I'm not going to do anything to jeopardize her getting the fairy-tale ending in life she wants. The husband, dog, kid, white picket fence; all of it.

"I'm guessing your parents are out of the question?" she asks.

"They don't have that much money. They barely have four hundred dollars of extra money lying around."

My parents worked middle-American jobs. There was no pension, no 401(k). My dad didn't even go to college. They've saved well, own their house and their car, and I helped right the ship as much as I could. But having enough money to give me $3.5K? That's not a reality I live in.

"You could always sell your body," she says, shrugging. "I mean, you're hot. Sex work is a legit form of income. OnlyFans is booming right now."

"You've been reading too many rom-coms."

"More like smut-coms."

"Oh my God."

"I'm just saying," Mya says in a singsong voice, crunching on a carrot. "It's an option."

It's not an option. The Carey Foundation wouldn't take me if they ever found out I did that to make money. Make no mistake, I'm very pro-sex work and pro-legalization of it. What people do with their bodies is their choice. How people make money is their choice, and the stigma surrounding sex work greatly affects women and trans women, especially those of color. But I don't live in a world or function in circles where that nuance is discussed and accepted. The Carey Foundation is not that progressive.

So, an OnlyFans is out the window.

Mya and I spend the remainder of her lunch break trying to decide a reasonable way to make money.

"Selling plasma?"

"The body doesn't make enough blood."

"Uber Eats? Postmates?"

"Not enough restaurants in the area signed up for it," she informs me. "People in Harper's Cove are too trusting and at the same time, not trusting enough. Robbing a bank?"

"Are you going to drive the getaway car?"

"You missed a perfect chance to quote Tracy Chapman."

"I was going with Taylor Swift."

She pauses and shrugs. "Fair enough."

"If I can't make an OnlyFans, I don't think robbing a bank is going to work."

The bell rings, cutting our brainstorming session to a close. Dozens of humans under the height of four feet come rushing into the classroom from outside. Mya's already up, her body on autopilot, conducting a humanoid symphony to navigate the classroom.

"Well," Mya says while children dance around her feet, doing her best to not step on them, "I do have one last option."

"As long as it's not, you know, as bad as the other options you suggested, I'll say yes." Seriously. I need the money. The Carey Foundation Fellowship is all I've dreamed of since getting into grad school. To be so close? I can't let this slip away. This could change my life. This could set me on the path I've always meant to be on. This could be—

"Logan's place is still hiring. A sous chef, I think."

"No."

"And he's hot."

"You say that like that changes things?"

"And he has a man bun," she argues.

"Is this 2012?"

"And tattoos. Those are timeless. Did I mention he was hot?"

Suddenly, donating blood—maybe on OnlyFans—doesn't seem like such a bad idea.

CHAPTER
SIX

PART OF LIVING AT home with my parents, rent-free, means I have to make myself useful. And wallowing in my room, like a sullen teenager, bemoaning my dwindling prospects is not making myself useful.

This edict isn't coming from my parents; they love having me, but I know I can't just sit around like a bump on a log and not do anything. What type of son would that make me? So, while my mom is out with her girls around town, and my dad is doing—well, I don't know exactly what he's doing—I work to complete the list I had to pry from my mom's hands, so I feel like I'm earning my keep.

Take out the trash? Done.

Water her plants in the backyard? Done.

Fix the fence in the driveway that Dad said he would fix for years? Okay, not *really* done, since I'm not a fix-it gay, but done enough. And by *done enough* I mean I researched a cheap and reliable handyperson in the area and scheduled a visit via an app.

Which only leaves one thing on the list: taking Naga to the

groomer. Which I find H-I-L-A-R-I-O-U-S, because when I was younger and we got Naga, Mom told me being a responsible dog owner meant doing shit like this yourself. Now we just pay someone to do it.

"You know you're spoiled, right?" I tell her as I open the door of my Prius for her so she can get out of the car. "You're living the life of luxury out here, and you don't even appreciate it. Some of us, like me, are suffering. Drowning in a pit of failure. Do you even know what failure is?"

She just looks at me with those big eyes and obvious doggy smile. Not a single thought in that brain.

"And now I'm asking a dog if she knows what an English word means. I've completely lost it."

Naga is so well trained, I don't need to have her on the leash as we walk down Main Street to the groomer. Supposedly, Maria Beth Clements—yes, all three names—and Naga have some sort of relationship that Mom trusts.

Sure enough, Naga knows exactly where to go. She trots ahead of me and makes a right, walking straight into the groomer. I hear Maria Beth Clements's squeal before I even enter.

"How is my favorite ball of white fur!" she coos on her knees, smooshing Naga's face. Naga has her paws on her shoulder. "You're the best girl ever, yes you are!"

"Careful, give her too much attention and it'll go to her head."

Maria Beth Clements grins at me through Naga's licks, strands of her neon-colored purple-and-pink hair clashing with Naga's fur. "It's worth it for her. You're Xavier."

Not a question, just a statement, but I nod all the same. "The one and only."

Not the only. Xavier is a common name. In the year I was

born, it was the forty-third most common name and has been in the top eighty names for over a decade. I bet my parents thought they were being original by giving me a name that started with an *X*. Point zero two percent of men taken from the 2000 census have the letter *X* as their first initial, after all.

But neither Maria Beth Clements, nor Naga, cares about that. She stands, and Naga moves by her side obediently. A twinge of jealousy floods me. That's *my* dog! Not hers!

I mouth, *Traitor*, to Naga, but she doesn't even see me. Insult added to injury. I should be used to that by now, because, you know, dogs don't understand English.

"You can pick this beauty up in about two hours, if that works for you?"

I nod. "Do you all accept credit cards?" It sounds like a dumb question, but there are still places in Harper's Cove that don't.

Maria Beth Clements waves her hand. "Don't worry about all that, your mom and I are already squared away."

Squared away. In Harper's Cove, that's code for *exchange of goods and services not done by money.* As an MBA graduate who is always thinking of every which way a business can collapse into a heap of dust, just the idea of trading services for favors like it's 1300 or something makes my skin crawl. That's not how anyone should be compensated. If you do a job, you get paid. It's cleaner and prevents resentment. It also erodes the idea that people should do things, like internships, just for experience or exposure. We're leaving that in the last decade.

Yet here, people still just . . . do things out of the goodness of their hearts? No need for compensation?

My mind rebels against me, going over the estimated costs I assume are required in running a dog-grooming shop, and, based on the disposition I know of people in Harper's Cove, wondering how often Maria Beth Clements offers this "squared away" payment option. How much cash is she missing out on? Does it generate return customers? Do people pay it forward for her in town? Is she, actually, coming out ahead?

I push the thought out of my head as much as I can. Which isn't saying much. Once I get hooked on something, it's near impossible for me to let it go. It'll nag and claw at the back of my mind until it pushes its way through my skull like some B horror movie.

I really did try, though. I turned, walked to the door, even had the handle in my hand and was in the motion of pushing it open when the thought got the best of me.

"You know," I say to Maria Beth Clements, turning around. Any willpower to shut the hell up? Gone. "You could make a killing in Hartford grooming dogs."

"I make good money here," she says, happily and gently.

"Yeah, but you could be making great money just a few hours' drive away. Take, for example, Chicago. When I was looking into getting a dog, one place charged three hundred and fifty dollars for a dog Naga's size."

"Three hundred and fifty dollars?!" Maria Beth Clements says, whistling. "That's criminal."

Maria Beth Clements doesn't say *criminal* in the way someone might say, *Holy gee, Annabeth Lee, that's highway robbery!* but she says it like she's actually disdainful, like she actually thinks it's a crime to charge that much and someone should prosecute those offenders.

A bubble of regret, covered in a sheen of shame, grows inside of me. Maybe I overstepped. I might not be a Cover anymore, but I know that people here actually do care about their neighbors. People in Harper's Cove rise and fall together, be it right or wrong. I should have known better than to assume, even if I am right, that Maria Beth Clements would want to change that about herself. It goes against everything this town stands for.

Instead of digging myself a bigger hole and causing the bubble to expand in my chest until it cuts off blood flow to my brain, leading to a stroke, I give her a half wave. I need to get out of here as quickly as possible. Before my mouth betrays me again.

"I'll come by in a few hours."

Two hours to kill. It's not like I'm short on opportunities. Main Street is filled with cute little shops like the one Maria Beth Clements owns. That was the good thing about growing up here. Small-town chic that makes you feel safe and at home. You want ice cream? Amy's Armory is open. Want to get your clothes tailored for a night downtown? Marsha's Menagerie is open on Sundays now. Need to get some new sports equipment? Daryl's Dugout is your place.

There are hardly any chains in Harper's Cove. You could view that as a positive or a negative depending on how you look at life. My parents, and the booming amount of fortysomethings moving here to grow their families, view it as a positive. People like me, who moved away, view it as a negative.

I stop in at Oliver's Olive Shop, a—you guessed it—deli, to get some lunch (turkey on rye with mustard and garlic mayo) before heading to St. Amos Park. When I was younger, before I went to work my shift at the movie theater, or when I needed to . . . well, to be anywhere else but here, I'd imagine a life for myself. The bench I used to always sit at is still there, with its worn and paint-chipped wooden slats and its dedication to Harper Amos, the founder of Harper's Cove, almost nonexistent and buffed away from how many people have sat in this exact same space.

I used to wonder—still do—how many people who sat here

thought about their future and how many of those people imagined a life for themselves outside of Harper's Cove. And of all
those dreamers, how many of them made it out of town and how
many people resigned themselves to staying here? Are they
happy? Do they regret it? Do they wonder what their lives could
have been if they took a leap of faith and just . . . left?

"It's not all that it's cracked up to be," I mutter to myself, de-
vouring the sub. It tastes just like I remember, a memory so rich
and so pure, it's nearly impossible for me *not* to let my bones and
muscles relax as I sink into the splintered wood. This place is a
place stuck in time. Everything is the same and that—

Wait.

Everything is *not* the same.

Directly across the street from me should be an art gallery. I
know because I used to watch the patrons go in and out, and
wonder what drew people to specific pieces of art. Why, for example, does someone pick a piece about birds when another person picks a knockoff pointillist landscape? By the way, the only
reason I know that word is because of an art history class I took
as an elective.

But that art gallery isn't there anymore. Instead . . . instead
it's the fucking Wharf. Right fucking there. Right in the open.
Like Logan is flaunting his success at me.

The emotions I feel flowing through me don't have any
words. It's not anger, though the white-hot pulse feels like that.
Truthfully, I have no reason to be angry. Gerri's Gallery could
have closed for a dozen reasons. It's not sadness. Gerri always
talked about how she wanted to go abroad, to be swept off her
feet by Mr. Right and see if the world she saw in the paintings
and photographs she sold actually existed in the real world.
Maybe she finally did.

You go, girl, I think. Except it doesn't come off like pride. It's more like resignation. At least someone made it out and is living their dream with the man of their dreams.

Instead, I'm here, looking at the home I don't even want to claim slowly morphing into something else, while some guy everyone seems to love, and thinks would be great for me in one way or another, is living his perfect small-town life.

I'm not a fix-it gay and I'm definitely not an OTP type of gay, so the whole you're-designed-to-be-aligned-with-someone bullshit? That doesn't fly. I do believe people can be in *lust* with one another. And I also believe it's possible to click with one person more than another. To be more compatible for a plethora of reasons. It's even possible to match with someone perfectly. There are billions of people on the planet; that's statistically probable.

But believing in destiny, and the universe having a plan for you and all that? Miss me with that bullshit. It's exactly as I said. A game of statistics.

Although . . . after hearing my mom talk about Logan, hearing Mya talk about Logan, and just having his restaurant here right in front of me? I can't help but think it's a sign. Not the sign everyone else thinks it is. This isn't the last shot of a rom-com before the credits start rolling and some pop star sings over the wall of text. No, this might just be a sign that all of my problems can be solved if I just swallow my pride and put my skills to use for six weeks.

There's only one thing more dangerous than a woman scorned and that's Xavier Reynolds on a fucking mission. And if the only thing standing between me and Berlin is a guy, who, yes, is fairly handsome if you are into that sort of thing, with a voice that is objectively smooth and rough in just the right ways? Then I'll do it.

Shoveling the rest of the sandwich into my mouth, I quickly wipe my face, using the reflective surface of my phone as a mirror. I cross the park and the street before my mind can convince me how stupid and bad an idea this is. If Logan is as smart as Mom and Mya say he is, he'll see my talent and realize we can both help each other succeed here.

On second thought, though, I'm not sure Mya said he was smart. Talented, and hot, sure. She hit that second note multiple times. But smart?

Doesn't matter. This is pure business and nothing more. He's a business owner. He has to see when a good deal is in front of him. I have a lot to offer. I just need to think of what exactly those things are that would be useful to him.

Once I'm in front of the restaurant, with the driftwood sign that has the blocky title of the Wharf burned into the surface, I take a deep breath.

"This is good practice, Xavier," I mutter. "You'll have to deal with plenty of pompous, stuck-up, cocky business owners if you want to work your way up the corporate ladder. Consider this practice. Like . . . a write-off on your Personal Life Lessons section on your taxes."

Rolling my shoulders and counting to five three times, I push the door open and step inside. I'm hit by a burst of chilled artificial air that makes me shudder. The restaurant is more spacious than I remember the Gallery being. It has a metallic minimalist design to it, each table with some metalwork sculpture of a specific utensil in the center. Silvers, woods, and blacks play off each other perfectly, with black-and-white photos of cities across the world. The space feels high-end, but at the same time welcoming, like Logan is striking a perfect balance between sophisticated and down-to-earth all at the same time. The restaurant is bigger than I remember, as if some giant made of polished wood holding his breath had just inhaled. It reminds me of . . .

"A wharf," I say, actually slapping the side of my head. The blue-sky ceiling. The wooden theme. It all makes sense now. And it only took me twenty seconds to get what vibe he's going for, which I'm sure translates to his menu, a fish-based menu that leans into what Harper's Cove is known for. He's captured a feeling in a matter of moments and set expectations without having to actually tell you directly.

That's something many places, especially start-ups, fail to do. So, one point for him.

But he loses that point when I notice there's not a single person inside the restaurant. I check my watch: 2:45 p.m. on a Thursday. Shouldn't I hear the sounds of chefs in the kitchen getting ready for the evening rush? There's no reason this place should be empty. Right? I've watched enough *Kitchen Nightmares* to know this is a red flag.

Maybe they're closed? No, the door is unlocked. It's not a holiday, because if it were, Mya would have been bugging me to hang out with her, and I wouldn't be about to compromise my morals for some cash.

Is it too late to make an OnlyFans account?

"This is a bad idea," I say. But that doesn't stop me from going in.

Walking deeper into the restaurant, I hear the faint sounds of music in the back, where I'm guessing the kitchen is. At least Logan has good taste; Dua Lipa's "Levitate" is playing on the radio. The off-key singing I hear, though, as I venture deeper in? That's another minus point.

If I'm keeping score, I think he's about negative two, which makes up for the positive two he got during dinner. Now we're even.

I take a deep breath and round the corner, doing my best to put a smile on my face, but I lose my words when I see him. Dressed in a black T-shirt that shows his inked zoo covers more than just his forearms, Logan is standing in the middle of the kitchen, reenacting a poor man's version of *Risky Business*. He has a wooden spoon in hand—a spoon I'm assuming is supposed to be stirring whatever is bubbling in the large cast-iron pot on the stove—belting into it while gyrating his hips and dancing on the one and the three, instead of the two and the four.

And the key? Where is that? Surely not here.

To be fair, I sound bad singing in the shower or when I'm cleaning, too. Singing when alone in a room isn't meant to be on key—or seen by anyone besides maybe your dog or your plants. So, I don't blame him. And, to be fair, I don't think he expected anyone to just barge into his kitchen. I also don't look as suave or as good, moving my hips and sliding across the floor, as he does. He has the whole "rock star in progress" thing down pat.

At least, that's the vibe I get when he turns around, doing a Michael Jackson–like spin on his shoes and coming face-to-face with me.

"What in the hell . . . ?"

"The door was unlocked, and yes I see how this looks considering how we first met," I say quickly.

Logan throws the spoon down and taps his phone quickly, cutting off the music. "You've got ten seconds to tell me what you're doing here."

"You know that's rich considering you broke into my—"

"Eight seconds."

"Again, the door was open."

"That doesn't mean you can just barge into places."

"If it helps, your singing and dancing weren't . . . bad?" I say. "Very 'single father at his daughter's first school dance.'"

"That does *not* make me feel any better or help your case! Five seconds."

"I just gave you a compliment and you're threatening to kick me out?"

"Your 'compliment' basically said I danced and sang like an out-of-touch old person. I'm thirty-nine."

"The new twenty-nine!"

"You're really not helping yourself here, you know that? Four seconds."

"Okay, but I feel like we—"

"Three."

"Got off on—"

"*One!*"

"Are you still looking for a sous chef, because if you are, I think you should hire me!"

I yell the words so loudly, I'm sure everyone outside of the restaurant can hear. But that is the least of my concerns when a pot of—I'm guessing tomato soup?—explodes. Like, literally explodes on the stove right after I confess my intentions, covering us both in tomato puree.

CHAPTER
SEVEN

LIFE COMES AT YOU in two different speeds: fast and slow motion.

When you're having the best sex of your life? Or seeing the best movie of all time—*Sucker Punch*, in case you were wondering—with live director and lead actor commentary? Those moments go by in the blink of an eye.

But when a seemingly bottomless tub of tomato sauce bubbles and splashes like Sauron with IBS? That shit happens in slow motion.

Pun absolutely intended.

Being further away from the epicenter saves me, mostly. Besides some splatters of red on my black shirt and dark blue jeans, I mostly just look like a guy who has no idea how to eat and not make a mess—aka a straight. But Logan? And the stove? Oh, they look like a nuclear wasteland.

"Shit, shit, shit," Logan curses, not even caring that there are

chunks of tomatoes in his black-and-white hair. He's more focused on saving the dish than his clothes. Which, I mean, I get.
He probably spent a good amount of time on the soup. "Fuck!"

I hate most things in the world: loud noises, amusement
parks, Halloween. But yelling men? That's top of the list. There's
just something so . . . obnoxious about it, no matter the reason.
So, when Logan goes through the five cycles of grief over his
tomato soup in the span of a few moments, I take a step back.

"If it helps at all," I say slowly, "it looks like it tastes good?
Tasted? Not sure the tense here."

Logan doesn't even perceive me. He hisses, grabbing the han-
dles of the ten-gallon container, shifting it from the flames to
the counter. He waves his hand, floundering them in the air
wildly. I see glimpses of his palms covered in hot tomatoes.
That's going to hurt like a bitch later. What's that expression?
You have to sacrifice for your art? And cooking is an art. The best
chefs would agree with me.

Like some actual, real-life witch auditioning for one of the
roles in *Hocus Pocus*, Logan grabs spices, sauces, and containers
from the expansive cabinets above the stove. A dash of this here.
A splash of this there. He mutters under his breath like an incar-
nation needed to summon some tomato demon.

"Eleka nahmen nahmen. Ah tum ah tum eleka nahmen . . ."
I chant.

"What?"

I wave it off, a silent gesture for him to ignore me and my
Broadway musical obsession.

Logan easily does it, trying to salvage the mixture he created.
For all the weaknesses Logan has, and he has many, he looks like
a person who cares about his food. His daughter, his restaurant,
and, apparently, this pot of tomato sauce.

He licks at his fingers and looks at the steel ceiling for guidance, like Simba looked at the stars for his father.

"I think it's okay," he finally says, sighing. I watch his shoulders relax, like the bones are locking into place.

"Praise be the tomato gods."

Logan rolls his eyes. "Seriously?"

He's right. I'm here wanting something from him. Being quippy doesn't help anyone.

I hold my arms up in defense. "Sorry. Can we try again?"

"I haven't decided if we're going to try for the first time yet."

"But who could resist this wonderful face?" I ask, flashing him the brightest, best smile I can muster up, resting my chin on the back of my fingers, like I'm trying to beat some beauty queen in a pageant contest.

The stoicism of his face tells me Logan is *not* convinced. He crosses his arms over his chest. "You want to try again? And be honest this time?"

"Honestly, I'd rather be anywhere else but here, but it seems fate has another idea."

"You know what. You can—"

"Sorry, sorry." I hold my hands up in defense. I'm not going to be able to wittily talk my way out of this one. I let out a large exhale. I can't avoid what I came here to do any longer. One of my professors at the University of Chicago told me (after a mock meeting for a telecom company merger) that coming off as begging means you'll never get your worth.

"It's always best to be the person who makes the other person in the debate talk first. Be it salary negotiations, or trying to catch someone in a lie, or an interview, or anything. Talking second is a position of power." My professor told me.

Except, this time, Logan has all the power. He has the job I need. He can turn me down with a simple no and destroy my dreams, crumpling them right in front of me. He doesn't know it yet, but my life is literally in his hands, and that's not being overly dramatic. That's the truth.

But I'm not in a position to try to talk my way out of this. Nearly four thousand dollars. That's how much I need. And working as his sous chef is the fastest way to get it. I just need to push my hubris aside and make it happen.

"I was wondering if that offer still stands," I repeat.

Logan arches his brow but says nothing.

"From before? When you came over for dinner?"

His eyes look like those of a golden retriever, not a single thought behind them. Not a single piston of recognition firing.

Either he's doing this on purpose, or he really doesn't remember. Neither of them are pieces of good news.

"When my mom suggested I work for you? That offer?"

He's really going to make me work for it, isn't he? If the situation were reversed, I'd make me do the same thing, so I can't really blame him. It's human nature to try to get one over on another person.

I see the light behind his eyes twinkle as the engines fire.

"Oh," he says. Plain and simple.

"That isn't the reaction I was hoping for."

"What type of reaction were you hoping for then?" Logan asks. "I never made an offer at dinner," he corrects. "Your mother mentioned that I needed to hire someone. I agreed with that fact. She mentioned that you were a good chef. That's all. And, furthermore—"

"There's a *furthermore*?"

"If I remember correctly, you were very against working for me."

"I stormed out."

"How else was I supposed to take that?"

"Fair. But, if I'm being honest, you were against it, too."

"For good reason."

"Such as?"

Logan laughs, a deep bellowing one from his diaphragm that echoes off the walls. "Are you forgetting that you threw Gatorade on me?"

"You broke into my house!"

"You *assumed* I broke into your house," he corrects.

"Same thing! I was defending myself. You'd do the same thing, too, if the situation was reversed, don't tell me any differently."

Logan opens his mouth to say something I'm sure is going to be incredibly witty and sound, and a conversation ender, but he pauses. That's my opening.

"Look. You need a chef and I need a job. You need me as much as I need you."

"Okay, I've had enough of—"

"And before you try and argue that you don't"—I gesture wildly with my hands—"your restaurant opens in, what? Three hours? And no one is here yet?"

"We aren't open for lunch today," he replies, not missing a beat in this tit-for-tat verbal argument we're having.

I open my mouth for a moment, then close it.

"You didn't consider that, did you?"

"I did not. BUT!"

"But?"

"You need someone to be your second-in-command, and obviously no one has stepped up to the plate. If they had, you would have said that first."

"Maybe I like watching you sweat?" He shrugs. "You seem like a guy who always knows what to say, what to do, and watching you flail a bit right now? It's fun."

"It's evil."

"One man's evil is another man's pleasure. But I'll humor you. You think you're the one? To work in my restaurant? You think you're that person?"

"I know I'm that person."

The way Logan's lips go into a thin line tells me he isn't convinced. "Are you trained? Have you ever worked in a kitchen?"

"I haven't, but you heard my mom, I'm a great cook."

"Every person's mother says that." Logan turns his back away from me, grabbing a towel to start dabbing at the red splotches that cover his shirt. In business, you never want to lose the attention of your mark. Once you've lost that, nothing else matters.

I quickly walk around the side of the island with the burners, cutting him off before he can reach the sink.

"Face it, Logan," I say. "You need me as much as I need you. So, let's both help each other."

Logan's nostrils flare, and I can't tell if he's going to yell at me to get out, shove me against a wall, or throw the remainder of his hard-salvaged tomato puree at me. Which, I mean, you could argue I deserve any of those three options.

But instead, he says something I couldn't have predicted.

"I have one question. Answer it right and the job is yours—on a trial basis."

"Shoot."

"Who says I'm even looking for a sous chef?"

I open my mouth, but no words come out.

"What if your mom was wrong, hm?" he adds. "Did you think about that?"

I want to say, *My mom is never wrong*, but Logan doesn't give me a chance.

"Would you still want a job if it's not sous chef?"

It's a good question. I didn't even consider the fact that maybe my mom misheard. But I need a job. That looming $4K bill is hanging over my head. Four thousand dollars keeping me from me and my dreams.

Even some of the greatest people in the world have to eat crow every once in a while. Consider it my hero origin story.

"Let me modify that question. What's in it for you? What do *you* get out of helping me?"

Every person in life reaches a crossroads at one point or another. A time where you have to decide if you're going to go left, or right. I could be honest here, tell Logan what my goals are. I could explain to him I need this job for a few weeks, in order to get the job I want and rocket myself into my future career. Maybe he'd understand. Maybe he wouldn't.

Which is the other option. A lot of people in Harper's Cove will say how they always believed in me. How they knew I was going to make it out of here and be someone. How proud they were to have known me. That's all correct. But I remember the students in high school who teased me for missing out on parties. The snide comments of *nerd* and *dork* and other harsher words kids would say behind my back just because I wanted to be someone, and that was a dream worth fighting for.

Those moments, those small cuts that never really heal? They change you. They affect how you navigate the world, like it or not. Lies hurt people. Each one is a choice. Even now, looking at Logan, knowing that once I lie to him, that'll be a piece of our relationship forever going forward. I won't be able to take that back.

"I need a job," I say directly instead.

That's not a lie. He doesn't need to know exactly *why* I need a job. I don't need him judging me, thinking that I'm just using him to get out of this town. Everyone, despite what they think or say, always has an opinion about other people's lives and how they go about handling it.

It doesn't change, no matter where you go. Closed-mindedness isn't just a small-town phenom. It's all over the world. When I went to New York and Chicago, a small group of people figured I wasn't good enough because I *came* from a small town. It was almost as if, stay or go, there was no way for me to win. No way for me to impress people and to show I was no worse or better than them because of where I came from.

I don't want to invite all that, Logan's opinions, his thoughts, his assumptions, back into my mind. I don't need those whispers pushing me under the surface and fighting alongside my own army of insecurities I carry with me daily. It's true that I *am* doing this to leave town and I'm not trying to hide that from myself. I'm not ashamed of wanting something bigger than this. I'm only trying to leave town because the version of myself I know that I can become is just a few thousand dollars away from being realized. And I'll do anything to make that happen.

But Logan shakes his head, refusing to let me off so easily.

"I don't buy it. There are plenty of places in town you can

work if you just need a job. And you're some hotshot graduate of a big-name Chicago school. Can't you do remote freelance or something?"

I also don't wanna spend the rest of my time arguing with him about what I can and cannot do. I clench my fist, digging my nails into my palm to steel myself.

"I could," I say slowly. "But that will take too long. I don't have the time to go through all the hoops I need for one of those gigs."

"So, there *is* something." He smirks like he just discovered the secret to making a man come, gay or straight, is playing with his prostate, and has a plan to market it to all the middle-class Dudebros in America. He takes a step forward, then another. I step back, trying to keep the space between us, but bump into a perpendicular counter.

Logan ignores the space between us, shrinking it. He stands close, so close I can feel the heat wafting off his body and smell the mix of sweat and some generic evergreen cologne. It works for him. Objectively speaking.

"You know, if we're gonna work together, starting our working relationship off with a lie doesn't really make me want to hire you. Especially if I can't trust you."

"I never lied," I correct. "I just said I needed a job."

"I asked you *why* you wanted the job. You omitted a crucial piece of information. A lie of omission is still a lie. I have a daughter, Xavier. I know when people are hiding something."

"You don't need to know. All you need to know is that I'm a good, reliable worker. *Why* I need a job shouldn't affect if you're going to give me the position or not."

"Don't you think I should be the decider of that, not you? This is my restaurant, after all."

I clench my jaw so hard I think my teeth might crack—which is an expense I can't afford, considering dental in this country is literally a criminal offense. If Logan doesn't take me as a sous chef, there's not gonna be many options left for me. I might have to give up my dream of getting the fellowship, which means staying here in Harper's Cove for even longer, which means any hopes I have of being something and making something of myself are pretty much going to disappear like the wishes, hopes, and dreams of a starry-eyed high school senior who doesn't know how the world works but is quickly going to learn.

I won't let that happen. I can't let that happen.

"What do I need to do to prove to you I'm good for the job?"

"Besides telling me—"

"Besides that."

Logan shrugs. He returns to moving around the room like a puppy that can't stand still, fiddling with pots, organizing pans, and opening the large four-door freezer-fridge combo on the right side of the room. He begins to heave plastic containers with piss-poor chicken-scratch labeling out, setting them on the table.

Trying to be helpful, I shuffle over and hold the door for him.

Puppy. That's a good analogy for Logan. He has that kind of DILF-y look about him that makes me understand what Mya was saying when she tried to sell him to me like a slab of meat in a corner store on a Sunday after church. But he also has a boyishness about him, one that makes him look charming and warm and safe.

"That's not an answer."

"Who says there is anything you can do?"

I roll my eyes. "This is a business transaction, so—"

As Logan squats down to get something off the lower shelf

that requires both hands, I see his shirt rise up, revealing, for a second, the black boxer briefs with neon-green trim he's wearing. His pants also stretch a bit around his ass in that position, accenting how fucking nice is it.

Focus, Xavier.

"There's always something that can be done to reach an agreement.

"Did you learn that at your fancy business school?"

"No, I learned that from YouTube."

A smile appears on Logan's face. He's got one of those smiles that when he's actually smiling, you can see it fill up his whole face. His eyes light up, dimples show on his cheeks, and there's a burst of light that comes from him that I have to admit is a little infectious.

"Alright," he says. "I'm interested."

"Interested in hiring me?"

"Interested in giving you a shot," he corrects. "I want to be clear, though, I'm not looking for a sous chef. And even if I was, I wasn't going to give it to someone who has no professional cooking experience. I'm sorry, that's a nonstarter. You're a hotshot MBA holder, would you let someone run your . . . I dunno, crypto farm?"

"Not how it works," I mutter.

"You know what I mean. Would you?"

"Of course not, but—"

"But what? My job is different because it's not some billion-dollar company? This is my life, Xavier. This is how I provide for my daughter. You want to be part of it? Sure, but you're going to play on my terms. You decide. In or out."

Part of business is learning when you've pushed your client too far. Logan is unmovable. We've reached an impasse where if

I try to shove him any further, this relationship is going to crumble right in front of me.

And I really, really need this job. "How much does it pay? This 'not a sous chef, actually a prep chef' job?"

"I can give you twenty dollars an hour. You'll work about thirty-five hours a week."

I do a quick calculation, looking up at the ceiling. Math isn't my strongest suit, but . . . It's tight; but it'll work. My eyes finally turn down, looking back at Logan. He's arching his brow at me, arms crossed (im)patiently.

"Find what you need on my ceiling?"

"What time do you want me?"

"Come by at four."

"That's in an hour."

"And? Do you want a job or not?"

I don't even hesitate to reply. "Of course."

"Good answer. I want to be clear, Xavier—this is a trial run. I wanna see what skills you actually have in the kitchen. See how you get along with the rest of the staff."

"I understand."

"This isn't a guarantee that this'll work," he adds, repeating himself. "I'll pay you for your night working here, no matter what. And I can give you some leads in town if it doesn't."

"Oh, you're so generous. Thank you, Gordon Ramsay," I tease, rolling my eyes. But the joke doesn't seem to land.

"That was a joke," I say, adding, "I appreciate it. Really. But, to be clear, that was a joke. Most people would snort or roll their eyes at that."

"Most people have shitty humor, then," Logan mutters, turning back to the fridge. "Four p.m. Don't be late. And, Xavier?"

"Hm?"

"I'm fucking ten times better a chef than Gordon Ramsay."

"What about Julia Child?"

Logan grabs salt and quickly throws it over his shoulder. "Don't use the Lord's name in vain like that. I'm not trying to have her ghost haunt this place."

CHAPTER
EIGHT

I'M GOING TO BE fucking late.

It's not my fault. No, seriously, it's not my fault. It's not like when people say that it's not their fault, when it actually *is* their fault, but they don't wanna take responsibility. This is really, actually, 100 percent not my fault.

I had no way of knowing that today would be the day that the power would go out in our house. Yes, climate change is absolutely a thing, and the East and West Coasts have been hit with fires, colder weather, and more violent thunderstorms. You won't find me disagreeing that capitalism is the cause of most—if not all—of our problems . . . which I know is hilarious considering I'm literally going into a field that thrives off capitalism.

But I didn't expect the storm would be bad enough, and strike our house so perfectly, that the power would go out.

Because Harper's Cove is, well, Harper's Cove, it has direct access to water. It's how the town gets most of its money. Half of it comes from tourism, since it is a cute little Maine town, and the other half comes from the fishing community. Because we're so close to the water, storms can be more violent here than in other parts of the country. Our house, for example, is right on the watershed. That's why we don't have a basement, and why flooding on our road is common.

Like today. Something I completely forgot.

I had to double back and go the long way into town, just to get to work. And by *long way*, I mean literally going out of town and doubling back from the north side. Driving in the water was a bitch. Parking on Main Street was a bitch. Just everything about the whole situation was a bitch.

But worst of all was knowing the smug look on Logan's face I was going to have to deal with when I parked in the employee parking lot behind the Wharf, seventeen minutes late. Or knowing he might turn me away at the door because I am, in fact, late; the one thing he told me not to be.

"Alright, you got this. You're going to do great," I mutter to myself as I quickly look in the rearview mirror. I adjust the color of my gray shirt, a generic nondescript T-shirt I had in my suitcase that I hadn't yet unpacked. I smooth my palms over my dark pants (at least, I think that's what chefs are supposed to wear) and grab my umbrella from the back of the car.

I have this interview; I have a job. If I have a job, I can pay for the fellowship. I can pay for the fellowship and get myself to Berlin so the life I've always wanted can begin. The only thing separating me from that is this one test session with Logan.

"How hard can that be?"

I expect the Wharf to be like it was when I visited before—quiet, maybe half-full if we're lucky, with Logan and a few staff members doing their best to keep the business afloat. This is Harper's Cove; it's not Boston or Chicago or New York. My hometown made me who I am, which is a positive and a negative depending on how you look at it, but it's not someplace you would ever think about when naming East Coast cities. The sad truth is, if you polled one hundred people, none of them would know Harper's Cove existed. So, I'm not expecting a very populous crowd on a Wednesday afternoon.

This will teach me to assume things about small towns.

"Move it!" a Latine woman about my age roars as she barrels past me at speeds that no human should be able to fast-walk. She's carrying that same large damn pot that plagued Logan before.

Standing in the doorway with the pot in her hand and a red-checkered bandanna wrapped around her neck, she glares at me and looks me up and down. "Customers usually enter through the front."

"I'm looking for Logan." A beat. "I'm Xavier."

"Who?" I can tell that she does not care about this conversation, nor who I am. It's probably only manners instilled from when she was a child that require her to keep talking with me. Or maybe it's just curiosity. Could be a mix of both.

Suddenly, recognition flashes on her face.

"Oh." Another beat. "The new guy."

"Is that what he's calling me now? And to think, I thought I meant more to him than those other boys."

A smile appears on her face. "You got a sense of humor. You might just survive here. Help me?"

"What type of gentleman would I be if I didn't?"

"Like most guys in this town."

I take the left handle of the pot as she takes the right. It's fuller than it was before; I can hear the sloshing of liquid and suspended pieces of something inside of it. With two hands, we carry it through the back of the restaurant and into the kitchen, the woman using her back to push open the double doors.

The Wharf is like night and day compared to before. The kitchen looks and feels smaller now that it's filled with workers. There's only me, the woman from before, another guy on the far side of the room, and Anne, sitting on a stool, texting on her phone. She glances up when the woman and I bring the pot in, a flash of recognition passing over her face. I give her a soft half wave and a gentle smile. She returns it, but a notification sound on her phone pulls her attention back to it.

"Put it here," she says. "Move, Kyle." The woman hip checks a redhead who is easily six foot six, about a foot and a half taller than her, knocking him an exaggerated distance.

"Jesus, watch how you wield that WMD," he teases with a baritone voice that makes the room shake.

"You better be talking about this pot of bisque."

"I'm talking about your ass, you know that."

"Oh, shut up." She grins. In unison, we hoist the pot up and put it on the stove, right next to two sizzling pans—one with three slabs of beef and another filled with roasted vegetables. "How about next time you be helpful?"

"I was tending to the meats. Like you told me to do!"

"Oh, so this time you decide to listen to what I ask of you?"

"Aw, don't be like that." Kyle grins. "You know you love me."

"I tolerate you," she says. Her eyes turn back to me and then back to Kyle. "New kid."

Kyle gives me a once-over that doesn't seem to take enough time to actually analyze me or make a decision. But before I know it, he flashes a bright, rakish grin and brings one of his large hands to my right shoulder. The force is enough to almost make my whole body fall apart, as if my bones were a poorly constructed Jenga tower and his hand was just the catalyst needed to destroy the structure.

"Well, hello, new kid," he teased. "Kyle. This is Angelique."

"And my name is Xavier, not new kid."

"And no one calls me Angelique."

"It's her government name," he stage-whispers.

"Angelique" rolls her eyes. "Call me Angelica."

I arch my brow. "There's a story there, isn't there?"

"Last more than one night, and I'll tell you."

The ominous weight of that statement makes my whole body feel heavy. It also reminds me why I am here; not to get to know Angelique—sorry, Angelica—and Kyle, but to prove to Logan that I can do the job. I scan the restaurant, quickly noticing the other four or five people going about their duties. I feel them glance up at me and expressions pass over their face that tell me each one has a different thought about me, but none of them bothers to say anything.

"Can you point me to where . . . ?"

Kyle puts a finger to his mouth, the universal sign of silence.

"Seriously. Both of you seem like great people, the best type of people. A true Janis and Damian for the modern era, but I need—"

Angelica repeats the action Kyle did. "Just wait."

"Is this some type of culinary cult I'm not aware of?" I ask, looking around. "Are we waiting for our overlord or something to come and give us instructions?"

"Three . . ." Angelica says.

"Two . . ." Kyle continues.

"One," Anne finishes.

With enough force to cause the two panels to smack against

the wall, Logan pushes through the double doors that separate the kitchen from the dining room. I'm the only one who jumps, while the other two return to their work, as if they're afraid to catch Logan's gaze. Like when you're in class and a teacher asks for someone to answer a question no one knows the answer to and you're just hoping they don't call on you.

Logan scans the room slowly, dressed in a white chef's coat with the sleeves rolled up, dark pants, Crocs, and a bandanna.

The bandanna, with colors that looked like water stains, I imagine, is very much like McDreamy's scrub cap in *Grey's Anatomy*. A quick check of the room shows me that every person has a different-colored bandanna, and you can tell a lot based on the patterns or graphic designs that people chose. I'm guessing choosing one is like choosing which lunch table to sit at on your first day of high school.

I hated the first day of high school.

His eyes settle on the back of Angelica's and Kyle's heads, and then moves to Anne's, where they soften for a moment before landing on mine. We hold our gaze for a second longer than I think is necessary, before he walks briskly through the kitchen, quietly checking some of the pots and pans on the stove.

He dips his spoon into the red, berrylike reduction sauce for the meats and gives an approving sound. Moving to the salad, taking a new fork, he stabs it into the bowl, pulling out a fistful of shimmering greens covered in what I'm guessing is some homemade dressing, plates it, and takes a bite. He chews slowly before gesturing with one hand for me to come over to him.

"Taste this," he says. "Tell me what you think."

"Is this part of the test?"

"It's part of being in a kitchen," he says. "A kitchen is a family, Xavier. We help each other, and we also critique each other. We rise and fall together; we succeed together. So, oftentimes, we check each other's food to make sure it's up to par. I want to see what your palate is like. I want to see what you add to the family."

Someone calling a restaurant, a job, a family raises my hackles, but I can see in the way Logan looks at me, he truly believes this. It's not just some talking point for him.

"And what if I don't like it?" I ask. "Sorry, I'm just not used to most places valuing outside opinions."

"Not saying I'll change the whole menu just because you say I should, but your opinion matters here, I can promise you that."

"If I get the job," I remind him.

A flicker of a smile graces his lips. "If you get the job."

He holds the fork up to my face, with his right hand under the lettuce to catch it from falling on the floor. Leaning forward, I take a bite, chewing slowly.

"Well?" Logan asks.

The flavors absolutely explode in my mouth. The tanginess of the balsamic sauce floods my senses, melding with the sweetness of some fruit that's mixed with the dressing to balance it out. I think it's blueberry? It's also not lettuce that's used for the salad, but Swiss chard. I know that roughness anyway; it's an acquired taste. Walnuts and warm goat cheese make the salad come together in perfect harmony.

But there's something unusual here. Something . . . different that I can't quite put my mouth on.

"You taste it, don't you?" he asks.

"What is it?"

"You tell me, Mr. Hotshot Chef."

I roll my eyes at that fake compliment but focus on the flavors in my mouth. I let them roll over my tongue like waves before pausing.

"Did you put watermelon in there?"

"Watermelon puree," Angelica corrects.

"It helps balance out the tartness of the other flavors and gives it a refreshing taste," he says proudly, tossing the fork into the sink. "You think it's good to go out?"

"You're asking me?"

"Again, think, Xavier. Don't just answer my questions. You want to work here, right? Cooking is an art and a science; to be successful in my kitchen, you need to know how to follow orders but also how to think outside the box and trust your senses. If you want to be responsible for something, then I need to be able to trust your palate."

It reminds me of business school, when I took a crisis management elective and I had to decide whether a company should disclose its CEO's embezzlement. The class was divided. Don't tell or tell. I voted on telling. In the end we were outvoted and failed the assignment.

"Despite what shows like *Billions* or *Succession* like to show us, it's always, *always* better to be honest, and to trust your gut. Sometimes, those two things are in conflict with one another," our teacher said during our debrief.

"It's good," I say, but hesitation lingers in my voice.

"But?"

"Nothing."

"There's absolutely a but. What is it?"

"Who is going to want watermelon salad? I mean, this is Harper's Cove. You're not trying to win a Michelin star or anything."

For a moment, the kitchen stays silent, my outburst lingering in the air before Anne lets out a snort.

"He's not wrong, Dad."

But "Dad" doesn't turn to her. He just stares at me, jaw tight, eyes steely.

"Office. Now."

With his long legs, Logan makes his way across the kitchen into a room connected on the left-hand side. Everyone in the kitchen puts their head down quickly and goes back to doing whatever they were doing, as if they weren't just on the edge of their seats watching an episode of the soap opera *Days of Our Kitchens.*

"Are you talking about me or Anne because I—"

"You, Xavier," he says deepening his voice in a way that makes the room rumble.

"Okay, okay, coming!"

There is no good situation that involves a man yelling at me like I'm some Black male version of Scarlett O'Hara, who is just going to sit by and take the yelling. But in some ways, that is exactly what I do. I scamper into the back office, filled to the brim with papers, boxes, and sketches that are obviously done by a child.

"Your daughter's?" I ask.

At first Logan doesn't answer, his body hunched over some papers. Finally, he looks up. "What did you say?"

I gesture to the drawings. There are least twenty of them, and that's one wall alone.

"She has a talent."

"Thanks. She designed my bandanna, too." A moment passes. "You can't say things like that to me."

"Like what?"

He gestures wildly with no direction. "Undermining me like that in front of the staff."

"Did I undermine you? I think I just clarified."

"Same thing, Xavier."

"You just told me to think outside the box."

"That doesn't mean completely shooting down my meals during the dinner run. If you disagree with a meal, we talk about it . . . which is easier to do if you're on time."

Touché.

"I have no problem with constructive discussions or changing recipes around. Angelica and Kyle give me feedback all the time, and we change things based on our discussions. But they're based on just that—discussions. We work together here; we're a team. Do you want to be part of this team or a solo hotshot?"

I open my mouth to say something but close it. I can feel my blood starting to boil, and having this conversation with him doesn't help me at all. *Remember, Xavier. You need this job more than he needs you.* And, more importantly, which is the most humbling of things, Logan is right. I'm so used to having to make an impression, to make a splash, to have to stick out in the crowd. Less than 8 percent of MBA graduates are Black, which is horrible considering the Black population of our country is 14 percent. I don't have the privilege of being . . . forgotten.

But this isn't Chicago. This isn't the Carey Foundation. This is the Wharf.

"I want to work here," I say without hesitation. "Won't happen again."

"Good." He pauses. "Now, how good are you at descaling fish?"

CHAPTER
NINE

THE SIMPLE ANSWER TO Logan's question is *kind of.*

I've cooked fish before in my apartment. We had some friends over to celebrate a member of our cohort in our second year of business school getting a job at a start-up that was supposed to be the next competitor for Microsoft. Each of us brought something to the party, which I was hosting in my small apartment—which definitely shouldn't have fit fifteen people, but somehow, we made it work thanks to the fire escape. And one of the meals I cooked was fish. Luckily, no one died. Which is a pretty low bar when you're cooking. But no one said that they tasted any fish bones, so I'm pretty sure I did well.

And, I mean, I'm Black. Being able to cook fried catfish is pretty much a requirement of keeping your Black card. And I've lost enough the past few weeks. I'm definitely not about to lose that.

The *problem* is the speed at which Logan wants it done.

"You have to be faster than that," Angelica mutters loud enough for me to hear.

Since I started working on Logan's task, Kyle and Angelica

have been watching me. At first, I pretended I didn't notice. Maybe if I ignored them enough, they would stop once they realized they couldn't get a rise out of me. Very juvenile, I know. But, for the past twenty minutes, they've been doing that thing where you know people are looking at you, because you can feel their eyes on you, but when you turn to look at them, they quickly look away. At least this time they finally speak.

"You're going to fall behind if you keep working like that," she clarifies, speaking out of the corner of her mouth. She's focused on her own plate.

"Give him a break," Kyle croons. "He's trying his best."

"Sometimes best isn't enough."

"Does Logan want this done fast or does he want it done well?" I ask.

"Both," they say together. Kyle, on the right, is working on segmenting some of the pork chops into edible pieces, while Angelica shifts from chopping up the carrots and dumping them into a large pot between them. The smells tell me they're putting the finishing touches on some sort of thin stew.

"Here, move over." Angelica encroaches on my space without waiting for me to actually move. "Time me?" she asks Kyle.

"You got it, Mama." He grins, pulling out a stopwatch. "In three . . . two . . . one . . . go."

She twirls her knife before cutting the fins off the side of the fish's head, smoothly and in one even cut. She slides the knife down the back of the gills to remove them, before inserting the point of the knife into the vent hole and making a shallow cut. With one quick swoop, she slices up the belly toward the head, before opening it and removing the guts in a matter of seconds.

"Teaspoon," she says without looking at me, kind of like how a surgeon on a TV show would ask for a scalpel. I look around quickly and find one just a few inches away. After handing it to her, I watch as she uses it, not to scoop anything out, but to break what looks like a long vein inside the fish. Angelica then slaps the fish down with a heavy thump on the table, throws her arms up, and steps back.

"Time?"

"Twenty-seven . . . no, twenty-eight seconds," Kyle informs. "Three seconds longer than last time."

"Damn it," she hisses. "This is somehow your fault, you know. You're bad luck." Wisps of jest dance in her voice.

"You don't actually believe in that, do you?" I ask.

"Beware of bread bubbles," Kyle says without hesitation. "If you cut open a loaf of bread and it has a large bubble or hole, then someone you know will die in the near future."

"If you don't crush the ends of your eggs, then a witch will collect the shell, build a boat, and start a crazy storm out at sea," Angelica adds.

"If you're cooking noodles and you cut them short, you're cutting your life short," someone else behind me says.

"Never hand a knife or a hot pepper to someone," Logan says, coming out of his office. "Set it down on the table and let them pick it up."

"You have got to be kidding me." I turn to look at Logan and frown. "Don't tell me you believe in this stuff, too?"

"Believing in this *stuff*, as you call it, has helped me keep my kitchen. What and who does it hurt to believe in superstitions?"

I open my mouth to say something back, but this isn't the time. Instead, catching the cue that this conversation is over, Logan strolls over, looking at the fish. He stands over and picks it up with both hands, rolling it over his fingers until it makes a 360-degree turn.

"You didn't do this." It's not a question; more of a statement.

"What makes you say that?"

"For one, I could hear Tiny and Tim acting like this was some televised Olympic sport in here," he mutters. "And second, these cuts are too perfect."

A wave of frustration pulses over me. "Too perfect?"

"That's what I said."

Logan lets the fish flop on the table with a heavy thump. "You get bonus points for not ratting out Angelica for cutting this for you, and yes, I know it was her. But you lose points for not doing it yourself."

"Didn't know you were keeping score."

A flicker of mirth passes over his face. "You still don't have the job yet, remember? Follow me."

Based on Logan's arbitrary scoring system, I can't tell if I'm passing or failing his test. Or if I'm just breaking even. Without hesitation, I follow him, catching Angelica's eyes. She mouths, *Sorry*, to me. I shrug and give her a thumbs-up, effectively saying I'll be okay. Besides, she was the one helping me, and I wouldn't throw her under the bus for that. No matter what people think about MBA graduates, I'm not *that* cutthroat.

My phone vibrates in my pocket once. I discreetly pull it out and steal a quick look. A message from Mya illuminates the screen.

How is Logan? Is he hot? Can you sneak a picture? Did you get to see him shirtless while changing? I feel like chefs get dirty often. Oh god I sound like one of my parents. Remind me that I have a husband and I love him but—

"But how about we focus on making sure you actually have a job before the night is over and worry less about how you got the opportunity, hm?"

I shrug, not giving him the benefit of the doubt. Logan doesn't push any further and walks me around the kitchen, a crash course in how the Wharf functions.

"All I get is a shrug? You're taking a page out of Anne's book of how to talk to me, aren't you?"

"Again, you do know it's weird to compare me to your child just because I'm—"

"You already know Angelica and Kyle," he says, interrupting me. "They have been helping me out while I've been short-staffed. Angelica usually is a server in the front of house, and Kyle is the king of meats."

"In more ways than one." He smirks. Angelica slaps the back of his head so fast, I don't even see her hand move.

"Then we have Anne here. She's helping out by washing dishes after school."

"You didn't give me much of a choice," she mutters.

"I did, I said you could either take up an instrument or come work for me."

"I *hate* music."

"All music?" he asks. "There's not a single genre of music you like?"

"Exactly."

"You like your mom's music. You like pop music. You like to sing in the shower when you think . . ."

"DAD!"

Anne jumps off her stool and lets out a loud sigh of frustration.

"I'm taking a break," she yells, storming off out the back door and into the rain. Without a coat. Not like she cares.

I expect to get more of a tour of the shop than that, but Logan has made it full circle around the small room.

"This is why I tell you we're not having kids," Kyle mutters.

"We're not even married," Angelica reminds him. "Nor dating."

"So, what do you call what happened last—"

"Zip. It," she snaps. "Also, your clams are boiling."

"Shit!" he hisses.

Logan watches as Kyle hurries over to the burners. He curses under his breath, pulling the top off the clams, going into triage mode to save them.

"Kyle," Logan says slowly.

"They're fine! They're fine!" he promises.

"Do I need to come over and check?"

"Absolutely not."

"Are you sure?"

"Promise."

"So, you only have two chefs?" I ask, deflecting the attention from Kyle and the clams.

"I don't need any more. Two and a prep chef are more than enough. A competent prep chef, that's the key."

"Was that another dig at me?"

"Take it how you think it applies."

I'm not sure what the proper kitchen-staff ratio is, but all I can think about in my head is how this feels like a start-up that I would avoid like the plague. Everyone in the kitchen feels like they're doing three times as much work as they should be, and they drip stress. Angelica and Kyle are running around, bumping into each other; food is left unattended on counters. They are balancing cooking two, sometimes three different meals with completely different ingredients at once. In short, the Wharf feels like a ticking time bomb. Being down a prep chef doesn't help, I imagine, but Logan seems to think adding me will be enough to fix everything.

To say it's a mess would be an understatement. I have the smarts to keep that in my head, though.

The business manager in me is tingling. There's just so many ways I can make this kitchen more efficient, even without knowing the intricacies of what's going on in Logan's mind. It's not like the Wharf is some great restaurant that's going to win a Michelin star. Which isn't a bad thing or a dig; not every restaurant has to be in the top 1 percent. If they were, then being in the top 1 percent wouldn't mean anything. The Wharf is a decent restaurant that serves American and seafood cuisine in a decent town. Maybe he doesn't need an eighteen-person staff, but there has to be a way to streamline this.

But I can't be sure that's what Logan wants to hear. One thing I've learned about working with men in a few companies I interned with is that they rarely want someone under them to tell them how they can do their job better. It's almost as if trying to help them comes off as attacking some deep center of their mortal core, bringing dishonor to their family.

I don't think Logan is very different. He doesn't drip with toxic masculinity or privilege, which is a plus in my book. But he is a self-made man, like most restaurateurs are, at least those who haven't gotten money from Daddy or Mommy to help fund their current enterprise. The Wharf pulses with a heartbeat that is in line with him. This is as much an extension of his body as a knife is to a chef's hand, or a pencil is to an artist's dominant hand. Critiquing it is like critiquing him. And, like he said, I don't have any professional cooking experience. I'm not sure my business acumen would be welcome here; at least, not yet.

Logan walks me over to the largest refrigerator in the kitchen. It's about double the size of any of the others, and he opens it with both hands, revealing about a dozen shelves inside. Each shelf is packed full of fruits, vegetables, meats, and sauces. It's organized very cleanly, with separate quadrants for each type of food.

"Every Thursday, once a month, we make what's considered a Wharf Special. The menu only says 'the Wharf Special' on it, so it's a surprise. I want you to make the special today."

I arch my brow, scanning the fridge. I should be terrified, I'm pretty sure that's why he gave it to me. But the creative side of me is bubbling with excitement.

"No limits?

He shakes his head. "No limits. Just needs to be done by the second half of the dinner rush. We're behind on it this time because—"

"Because I'm late, I get it. When is the second half of the rush?"

He checks his watch. "In sixty-five minutes."

"Do you make every new hire do this?"

He shrugs. "Only the ones I think have promise."

"Oh, so you think I have promise?"

"I think you'd make a good addition to the kitchen, but I don't make business decisions based on my gut alone. I don't have that luxury. Prove me right, Xavier."

Okay, that I didn't expect.

For some reason, Logan's words—*I think you'd be a good addition*—bounce around in my head like pins after a strike. I thought we had an unspoken agreement. This *Taming of the*

Shrew-esque back-and-forth that we were settling into. And then he goes and compliments me like that? That wasn't in the rules.

"You good?" he asks a moment later after I've been silent for too long.

No I'm not good, I think. But acknowledging that he broke the rules gives him more power than I want him to have. And if I acknowledge that, and he notices, then he'd know I was paying attention—probably too much attention—to him. That gives him too much satisfaction, and if I were him, I'd run with that.

"Yeah, I'm good," I say. "Give me some room, I have work to do. Two hours, right?"

He grins. "Sixty-three minutes. Good luck."

"I don't need luck."

I absolutely need as much fucking luck as I can get.

CHAPTER
TEN

THE REST OF THE evening was a blur, in a good way. The type of blur that adrenaline junkies and type A freaks like me thrive on.

I remember opening the refrigerator, deciding what I was going to cook, and then what felt like ten minutes later, we were cleaning up the kitchen. Somehow, in the span of a few hours, I had made batches of the same dish four times. Each batch served six customers for a total of twenty-four orders or so. Pretty good for something I came up with on the spot.

"Okay, so walk me through it again," Kyle says as he, Angelica, and I chip in to help Anne with end-of-day dishwashing duties. Four pairs of hands are better than one when everyone wants to leave. "What gave you the idea to mix pineapple with heavy cream?"

"My mom taught me how to make a fool as one of the first desserts we ever made together. The salad-fruit mixture, the sweet and the savory, made me want to try and complement that."

"Yeah, but most people don't use a fool, especially a pineapple fool, during an entrée," Angelica notes.

"And you used it to play off the saltiness of the cod tacos," Kyle adds solemnly. "Smart move."

It came together in my head. Tacos are fun, and people love fish tacos. Then, I saw the pineapple and decided to make a fool out of it to complement the pico de gallo that was mixed with the cod. The pieces to the puzzle came together while I was cooking. It didn't feel risky, but adding the fool to drizzle over it? That was the kicker.

"Even Logan seemed impressed," Angelica says, nodding her head toward the office, where Logan's on the phone. "Which isn't easy. I'm impressed."

"You thought I was going to fail, didn't you?"

"Oh, absolutely," both Kyle and Angelica say at the same time.

"Don't take it personally, bud," Kyle soothes by clapping his large hand on my back. "You wouldn't be the first person who failed Logan's gauntlet. Hell, Angelica failed the first time."

"Keep talking and you're going to fail to come into work tomorrow."

"Oh?" Kyle asks, waggling his brows. "I love a wild woman."

Angelica rolls her eyes, though it's a playful one meant to mean no ill harm. Before she can follow it up with what I'm sure will be a well-placed perfect quip, Logan walks out and all attention turns to him, like he's a drill sergeant demanding respect.

"Good job today, all," Logan says after a moment's hesitation.

"Only a good job?" Kyle asks. "Not an excellent job?"

"I wouldn't push your luck," Logan adds. "Need I remind you how you made a dish mixing up the salt and the sugar?"

"No, you do not!"

"Oh, 1 think we should talk more about that," Angelica chimes in. "But first . . ."

Angelica moves past Logan, kneeling behind one of the steel cabinets. She is only gone for a moment before she pulls out two half-full bottles of some brown-colored liquid.

"Drinks," she says and smirks. "And before either of you idiots say you have somewhere better to be, there's no place better than drinking with me post–dinner rush. Trust me, it's science."

1 arch my brow. "Science? What type of—"

Before 1 can finish my question, Kyle throws one of his heavy arms over my shoulder, as if he's known me his whole life. With his other hand, he reaches out, grabbing a glass Angelica pours.

"It's a ritual," he says, deep baritone voice in the back of his throat. "We survive a dinner rush, we drink."

"That sounds dangerous."

"It sounds *fun*," Kyle corrects, tossing half of a small cup of alcohol back in one slurp. "And what's the point of life if not to have fun?"

"Yes, Xavier," Logan muses, leaning against the doorframe. "What's the point of life if not to have fun? Live a little. Don't you MBA boys love to work hard and play hard?"

1 narrow my eyes at him, half wanting to throw some witty comment at him out of spite, but nothing comes to the front of my brain, especially with Angelica and Kyle adding their peer-pressure gazes onto me.

"One drink," I say, taking it from Angelica as she pours three small cups.

"One drink," Angelica mocks.

"1 mean it."

"Of course," Kyle chimes in.

Why does it sound like neither of them actually think it's going to stop at one?

· · · · · · · ·

FIVE DRINKS. AT LEAST. That's how many I can remember.

I spent the rest of the evening drinking with Kyle and Angelica. I remember Logan telling us we need to make sure we lock up, I remember him telling us what time to be at work tomorrow, but that's it.

This is why I should have drunk more in college. Now it's coming back to bite me in the ass.

I wake up with a throbbing head that hurts more than a knife, or an ice pick being jabbed down the center of my brain. The feeling is a familiar one, common, though I haven't felt it since freshman year and I'm not happy that it's returned to knock on the front door of my forehead.

I lie like a starfish in my bed, counting down from thirty to zero slowly, hoping that once I reach the end of my countdown, my head will hurt a little bit less. Thinking hurts. Moving hurts. Everything hurts. On average, roughly 7,100 people die a day in the United States. Of that, 261 of them are alcohol-related deaths. That means I have about a 3 percent chance of dying from this hangover.

Unlikely but not impossible.

"Baby Jesus in a handbasket," I hiss as I roll over onto my chest. My whole body feels like lead, impossible to move. But I have to try.

If I have to call Mya to help me . . . I'd rather die. That's it for me. I'm not giving her this fodder, she'll never let me live it down.

I'm pretty sure I have some Advil in my bathroom and I'm

sure Mom has made some coffee downstairs. And by sure, I mean I'm 100 percent certain. I can smell the scent of vanilla and hazelnut drifting up the stairs into my nostrils. The question is, how am I going to get downstairs without her noticing I'm hungover as fuck so I can avoid *that* conversation?

My parents have never been drinkers, so they won't understand that I, their only son, came home drunk after my first day of work, especially after I used to call them judging others in my college who drank like skunks. They won't understand that's just part of kitchen culture, and that if I wanted to get a job at the Wharf, I had to act the part. The whole when-in-Rome conundrum.

But that's a problem for future Xavier. Current Xavier needs to get out of bed.

So, I swing my tired and weary bones over the side of the bed, channeling the same energy as Evan Hansen in "Waving Through a Window." Every fiber of my being feels like it's made from lead, not flesh. Slowly, I force myself up high, eyes still closed because I know what sunlight does to a hungover person's brain. Then I walk the path I've walked at least a thousand times before to the bathroom. I know where everything is—the toothbrush, the Advil, the toothpaste. I know it all from memory. I will open my eyes when I'm ready. Maybe I'll never open my eyes again. Time will tell.

Except where there should be a door that leads into my bathroom, there is nothing. Well, that's not true; there's something. A brick wall that collides directly with my face.

"Shit," I hiss, grabbing my nose. "Shit, fuck, shit."

My eyes swing open, and the world around me—too bright, too vibrant, too colorful—shocks me. Not because of those things alone—which are reason enough to make me hiss—but because this isn't my room.

This. Isn't. My. Fucking. Room.

I ignore the burning pain in my head from the assault of senses and look around. The room is, for one, bigger than my own and has a rustic vibe to it, like whoever lives here really loves seafoam green and old driftwood. There's a nautical theme, which isn't uncommon for this town—I'd guess about seven out of ten houses have the same theme. Quilts of mismatched T-shirts, paintings of abstract things, and clothes strewn on the floor show me whoever lives here has a specific vibe.

While looking around, trying to get a feel for the room, I notice the window faces Harper's Sound. Okay, that tells me something else. It's one of those beachfront properties, which means one of two things.

Either it's the vacation home of some yuppie visiting Harper's Cove I must have met, seduced, and slept with after the restaurant—or it's someone who is a fixture of the town and recognized I needed help.

Let me be clear: Neither of these options are good. But the first one means that somehow, I left the restaurant blasted and drunk, but not *so* blasted that I didn't have enough thought to hook up with someone and go back to their home. But I don't remember any of that. Who knows whom I could be sharing a house with?

Then again, the second option is probably significantly worse than option one. Harper's Cove is a small town, and if I were laying on the sidewalk somewhere, so drunk and blasted that someone had to take me home, it won't be long before Mom and Dad figure it out. And if Mom and Dad figure it out, that means other people will figure it out, too. Mom will go shopping, and people will give her that *look*, like they know something is going wrong in our family. They'll pretend they want to be good neighbors and ask if they can do anything to help, but really, they'll just want a piece of the drama—which means Mom is going to be the butt of every joke masked as concern.

So no, neither option here is good. Both suck, and again, as always, I just want to leave this town. Why can't I be in Berlin right now, where I could just wake up in a threesome with two other hot people? How am I supposed to live, laugh, love in these conditions?

I run my fingers through my hair and smack my lips. My mouth feels chalky and stale. At least I'm still in my clothes, I think. That leans more toward the second option than the first.

"Okay," I mutter. "You're a badass Black man who graduated from some of the top schools. You don't feel shame. Grab your shoes, go downstairs, and walk out. If you see someone, tell them *thank you* and that's it."

Since I'm close to the sound, close enough to hear the clapping of the waves against the rocks' cheeks, I'm not far from town, maybe a mile or two-mile walk. The crisp air will do me some good, though, and one of the fishermen who make their living on the water will be nice enough to give me a ride if I desperately need it. Out of everyone in the cove, they are absolutely the best people.

I look around the room, easily finding my shoes and jacket thrown over a chair in the corner. At least I didn't lose those along the way. Putting them both on, I push the door open. I feel like a kid on Christmas Day, looking left and right like I'm trying to sneak downstairs to steal presents. I'm on the second floor, and the steps are right across the hallway. Quietly, one foot in front of the other, I bridge the distance and take the steps two at a time.

Nearly there.

I just need to slip out and leave. A surge of guilt pulses through me. My mother would have me write some note, thanking . . . whoever let me sleep in their guest room for the night. But how do I know this wasn't, I don't know, a kidnapping?

Think logically, Xavier. Black men are not the most common demographic to be taken for . . . whatever purposes. But that doesn't mean it won't happen! I'm handsome! I'm smart! I'm fit! I'm a catch.

I'm sure my mother and consciousness can forgive me for forgoing manners this one time. After all, I mean, if I was kidnapped, then my parents would most likely prefer I'm, I dunno, safe and sound rather than—

"What are you doing?"

The voice makes me jump, high enough that my head almost bumps with the ceiling. I twirl around, tensing my stance and putting my arms up in a defensive boxing position. I'm not exactly sure why that's the first thing that comes to mind, or the position I think of, but it's pretty clear by the way the redheaded girl looks at me that she is not impressed.

She stares at me, a slice of wheat bread with Nutella in her mouth. She's dressed how I would imagine any teen would be dressed; her red hair pulled into two braids in a very *Anne of Green Gables* style—did that just date me?

But more importantly, I know exactly whose child this is, which means I know whose home this is.

"Were you trying to sneak out?" she asks, munching loudly.

"I was." A beat. "How was I doing? Be honest."

She shrugs. "Pretty sucky, TBH."

"Do you sneak out often?"

She shrugs again. Not an answer. Smart. Never rat yourself out to the enemy.

"Is your dad around?"

There's no other way to ask; might as well get right to the point. I'm not keen on the idea that Logan was the one who brought me home. What state was I in? Did I say anything stupid? Did I vomit? Did she see me?

While her mouth is full, she points out the window and swallows thickly. "Out back. Chopping wood."

"Of course he is," I mutter what I think is under my breath. But it's clear she heard me based on the smirk that plays off her lips. "Think I can sneak out before he gets inside?"

"Are you going to try and walk into town?"

"Is that not possible?"

She shrugs. "Just stupid."

"Ouch." I put my hand on my chest. "A wound to my heart. I bet you're that kid in school who runs circles around the other students, huh?"

Another shrug.

"I'm going to take that as a yes. How about we do this: I sneak out, and you pretend—"

"Anne," Logan's familiar and crisp baritone voice rings from the back. "Can you help me with the door?"

When I hear Logan's voice, my natural curiosity kicks in. Anne leads the way, turning swiftly on her heels and practically bouncing into the kitchen. The floor is different than the hardwood of the hallway, a plaid black-and-white tile that looks like it's been in the house for longer than Anne or her father.

Through a doorway that leads out to an expansive backyard filled with trees, what looks like an old playpen, and a shed, stands Logan. He's dressed in what I consider normal Harper's Cove clothing—simple, easy outfits: a red-and-black patterned short-sleeve shirt, and a pair of dark jeans tucked into his scuffed-up boots. It's the exact sort of thing the fishermen here in the cove wear, and the type of outfit that Mya swore her husband would wear when she finally got her hands on his wardrobe and changed him from yuppie to Harper's Cove natural.

I'm still waiting for that change.

Logan blinks at me owlishly. "Oh. You're up."

"That would be the case, or maybe I'm sleepwalking?" I pat my chest, my cheeks, and my thighs to check. "Nope, fully awake. Question: Did you know that between four and eight percent of adults sleepwalk? It's pretty common."

"And you're anything but common, right?"

"Now you're learning."

Anne snorts loudly. Logan passes half of the pile of wood he has in his hand to his daughter. She carries it expertly into the living room, connected via the right side of the kitchen.

"Still as bitchy as ever, I see. Glad you haven't lost that wonderful trait," Logan mutters. I can't tell if his voice is laced with annoyance or mirth. Probably a little bit of both.

"Can you say that in front of your daughter?"

"I've heard worse," she says from the other room.

Logan juts his thumb toward her. "She's heard worse. Her father's a chef and her mom's a musician."

I opened my mouth to make a joke, but something tells me that humor will fall a little bit too close to a personal attack, and it's too early in the morning for that. Plus, despite how much Logan annoys me, he did offer me a job and he did take me home last night. My cheeks turn hot just thinking about that, even though no one can see them under my dark skin.

"You don't need to feel ashamed," Logan says, picking up on my feels. He takes the remainder of the wood and crouches low, balancing on the tips of his steel-toed boots, and shoves the logs into a space by the woodburning stove. Because of course he would have a woodburning stove. "Everyone gets drunk all the time. And it means you're bonding with the team. That's important. Especially if you're going to be working here. Plus, no one can drink Kyle under a table."

"Oh, so we're going to talk about that, cool cool."

"Would you prefer we don't?"

I'd prefer a lot of things, if I'm being honest. I'd prefer to be in Berlin right now. I'd prefer to be in Chicago. But instead, I'm back in my hometown, in this house with a man who has a child, who is my boss but also super attractive, which is even more amplified with him squatting lower on his really nice ass—like, a really fucking nice ass—and I'm sitting here with the smell and taste of yesterday's food on my breath, feeling like a dump truck slammed into me.

So, I guess we can't all have what we want.

"Do you have a toothbrush I can borrow?"

"In the closet in the guest room. Should be on the middle shelf. Clothes are there, too, if you want to borrow some."

I'm absolutely not borrowing any of his clothes. He's done enough already, and I have a thing about feeling indebted to people . . . more than I already do feel indebted to Logan. Taking his clothes feels like we're venturing into another level of personal I'm not comfortable with. Though I'm sure many girls—and guys—in Harper's Cove *would* feel comfortable.

"Dad," Anne says as she comes out of the living room, passing me as I head to the stairs. "Can we take Xavier into town when we go?"

Logan stands up, dusting off his hands. "I don't see why not."

"Oh, no I'm good," I say. "I'm just going to—"

"You're not going to walk into town," Anne jumps in. The way she speaks like her word is law, the way that her eyes narrow into her cheeks, still slightly full from that baby fat that she has, reminds me that she's her father's daughter.

Standing from behind her, Logan grins with a look of amusement. "You heard what the lady of the house said. Go on and get ready. I'll make you a cup of coffee, then we'll drive you in. It's only a few extra minutes and we're heading that way anyway."

I sigh. "I don't have a choice in this, do I?"

"You really don't," Logan says.

"You absolutely don't," Anne follows up.

The apple in this family really doesn't fall far from the tree.

CHAPTER
ELEVEN

DEPENDING ON WHOM YOU ask, the outfits people wear in Harper's Cove are ahead of their time.

Flannels of the red and black variety with chunky boots, beanies, and ripped pants are all the fashion in this sound-side town. I think it has something to do with the fact that ever since its dawn, Harper's Cove was always a fishing town. And the outfit of choice is to look like a boho fisherman who just rolled out of bed and threw some clothes on at two o'clock in the morning before going out to the water.

In some parts of the country—some of the more fashion-forward parts of the country—that outfit is making a comeback. Rushing to my sociology finals, I would often see people who made me do a double take, thinking some residents of my hometown had come to the Big Apple just to check up and see how I was doing. The outfit works for some people.

The outfit does not work for me. Like, really doesn't work for me.

Which is why, as I sit in the back seat of Logan's rusted-out truck, I feel uncomfortable. The type of uncomfortable that reminds you of what it's like to feel itchy in your own skin.

"Are you pouting?" Logan asks, glancing over at me.

"I'm not."

"Pretty sure he's pouting," Anne adds, glancing back at me. "Yep, he is."

"I don't pout. Children pout."

"I don't pout."

"That's because you're advanced for your years," I say. That gets a flicker of a smile out of her.

Mostly, I can't admit to Logan that he might be right. Maybe *pouting* isn't the right word, but it's in the right family. I'm fiddling with my phone. I can't stop shifting in my seat, rubbing my arms against the scratchy wool like tinder that might start a fire. The clothes I slept in the night before are in a plastic bag next to me. I don't look like myself.

"You look good," Logan says, his voice a low timber. "The whole . . ."

"Harper's Cove chic?"

Logan opens his mouth and then closes it. A smile playing off his lips. "Sure."

I'm not going to admit to him that I appreciate the compliment. I don't need Mr. Big Shot Chef getting a bigger head than he already has. And besides, it doesn't make me feel any better. In these clothes, I don't feel like myself.

I might look like a carbon copy of every single other person in this town, like I belong here and I have no intention of leaving. That comment in and of itself is a reason why I hate everything about what I'm wearing.

But the other half of it? The other piece that makes it feel . . . weird is that I'm wearing Logan's clothes.

Anne sits in the front seat with her father, singing along to some pop star on the radio that I think is Olivia Rodrigo doing a slow cover of a Miley Cyrus song, but I'm not exactly sure. Logan taps along to the music with his two fingers on the steering wheel, bobbing his head like any father who doesn't want to crush his daughter's spirit. Anne is good at singing and she can hit most of the notes. It's a welcome distraction as I glance out the window, watching streets, trees, and buildings that I know like the back of my hand pass by.

"Once I drop her off to school, I'll take you home," Logan says. "Cool?"

"Cool."

That comes off more like a petulant teen than I wanted it to sound. Logan picks up on it—because of course he does—and glances back at me through their rearview mirror.

"Unless you want to go somewhere else?"

"Dad's a great chauffer," Anne says, peering between the gap on the right of her seat and the door, looking back at me. "Take advantage of it while you can."

"I'm sure your dad is good—" I cut myself off before I can finish. Logan glances at me, narrowing his steel-blue eyes.

"Good at what?" Anne asks.

"Nothing." I say. "He's good at nothing."

The innuendo in what I was about to say? Not worth it. And probably something Logan doesn't want to be said around his daughter.

Understandable.

Honestly, though, half of me, for a moment, has no idea where to go or what to do. Mya is working. I don't have to be at work, I certainly don't want to be with my parents, and I *really* don't want to just stay at home. It's not like I have friends in town whom I can hang out with. It's not like I'm a teenager all over again either. People work. People have families. People have lives. And I'm just . . . stuck frozen, like some unsuspecting debt-ridden citizen in a shitty American remake of *Squid Game*.

Which begs the question: What do people who work in restaurants do with their free time?

Sleep, I'm guessing. And my head *is* still throbbing from that alcohol. Crawling under the covers sounds—

"Shit."

"Language," both Anne and Logan say at the same time.

"Alright, profanity police," I mutter, refocusing on the revelation. I should text Mya and let her know I'm alive. If the situation were reversed, I'd be storming the streets trying to figure out where she was and what happened to her.

I pull out my phone and tap the screen twice. Nothing. Battery must be dead. Of course I didn't have the wherewithal to put my phone on the charger. Part of me wants to blame Logan; somehow this is his fault, it has to be.

The truck comes to a stop, but Anne is already unbuckling her seat belt, about to rocket herself out of the seat.

"Hey," Logan warns. "What do we promise?"

"To have a good day," she groans.

"And?"

"To give our best version of ourselves in everything we do."

"And?"

"If anyone messes with us, make sure they swing first before we swing back?"

"That's my girl." He grabs the lunch pail she left in the shared middle cubby of the car and hands it to her. "Have a great day."

"You, too." Anne glances at me in the back seat. "Make sure my dad eats?"

"I don't think I'm going to be with him that long."

Anne arches one brow, looks at me, then looks at him, then back at me. She lets out a snort, the type of snort that forms in the back of the throat and gets stuck there, before turning to leave.

What the hell did *that* mean?

Parked outside of the Harper's Cove Middle School—which is connected to Harper's Cove High School—I watch as parents I know from around town usher their children into the building. Most of them, as they should be, are focused on making sure their child gets into the building safe and sound. But a small number—a growing number—are looking over at me. And not just me—looking over at me about to get into the truck with Logan.

I kind of feel like how Bella did in *Twilight* when she and Edward take their relationship public, and he walks into school with his arm over her shoulder.

And of course, just my luck, one of those faces is Mya.

She just finished talking to one of the parents outside of the high school and just so happened to turn her face in just the right direction for our eyes to lock. A ripple of emotion like a pulsing tidal wave crosses her face. First there's confusion, then there's relief, then there's anger, and then there's some type of smart that I'm not exactly sure how to place or describe. But if I had to guess, I think it fits under the *I told you so* emotional category.

She gives me a thumbs-up and a wink. I, in return, roll my eyes at her and turn back to Logan.

"On second thought, how about I get out here?" I offer. "I know you said you'd drive me, and I appreciate it, but I want to talk to Mya before I go, and home isn't that far so—"

"Oh no." Logan shakes his head. "You didn't think I was going to let you off *that* easily, did you?"

"I mean, I was hoping."

"Nope, you're coming with me. I need some help today anyway, and you said so yourself, you're not doing anything important."

"When and how did I say that? And even if I did, what makes you think I want to spend time with you on my off day?"

"One, a chef never has an off day, and two, don't make me cash in the whole *you owe me for me making sure you didn't pass out in the street or choke on your own vomit because of how much alcohol you drank last night* card."

My body tenses up at the words, and I let out a sigh. I should have expected Logan to try to hold that over my head. The sharp cockiness of the smirk that plays on his lips, as if he knew he just served a match point in a tennis competition, softens.

"Look, I'm not asking you to do anything illegal or anything."

"Okay, when people say things like that, they are absolutely about to ask you to do something illegal, just FYI."

"But I could use your help and I could pay you. You need the money, right? For that thing you're not going to tell me about?"

"You make it sound like I'm in debt."

"Are you in debt? There's nothing wrong with that, as long as you don't owe some loan shark."

"Even if I did, eighty percent of Americans are in debt, it's pretty common and . . ."

Logan waves his hand to shut me up. "Do you want to hear an easy way to make one hundred extra bucks, or are you going to keep talking your way out of the fastest money you've ever made?"

I have half a mind to be a smart-ass about it, but the money does sound good.

"I'm listening."

He pats the passenger seat of his truck, where Anne was just sitting. "Then come on. It'll only take three hours, I promise. Maybe four depending on traffic, and then you'll have the rest of your day to yourself."

"Let the record show if it takes four hours, twenty-five dollars an hour isn't that fast. That's only $52K if you annualize it."

"Oh my God," he groans. "You never shut up, do you?"

"Never."

I get out and slide into the passenger seat, doing my best to ignore the burning looks of the growing number of single—and sometimes taken—women who are now staring at me and Logan. It's like they've never seen two guys get in a car together. But that's not how things work here in Harper's Cove. People love to latch on to petty drama. It's like their lifeblood and it keeps them feeling lively. Gives them something to talk about at their book club or church meetings or in line at the grocery story.

And I can just feel myself and Logan becoming the next topic of gossip that'll spread like wildfire. Great, that's the last thing I ever wanted: to be perceived.

"Also, four hours? There's no place we can go in Harper's Cove that should take more than forty-five minutes," I say, closing the door and buckling my seat belt.

I look up, feeling Logan's gaze on me pulling my eyes toward him. On his face is what can only be described as an almost devilishly wicked grin. No, there's a better descriptor. If the goat in one of the top five movies of all time, *The Witch*, had taken on human form and moved to Harper's Cove because he needed an R and R week after luring young, hopeless women into the art of

Satanism, the smirk Logan gives me is the one he would have when he realized he'd found his new prey.

"We're not staying in Harper's Cove, are we?"

"No, sir, we are not," he says, shifting the car into drive and heading toward the highway that connects the many small towns of Maine and leads to Portland.

I feel my cheeks once again burn hot, but this time, my heart skips a single beat. One would reasonably assume that was because, I dunno, Logan is taking me God-knows-where with no explanation at all—the plot of most good horror books and movies, FYI.

But no, it's because of how good it sounded when his deep raspy voice said *sir* when referring to me.

But he can never know that. Ever.

And so instead, to drown out the thumping of my own heart as blood rushes to my ears, I pick a random station on the stereo and turn it up as loud as humanly possible.

CHAPTER
TWELVE

"WE'RE GOING TO PORTLAND, aren't we?"

Logan and I spend at least twenty minutes not speaking once we leave Harper's Cove, which is fine by me. I like the silence. But it's given me time to think about our direction. We're going southwest, and I don't think Logan is taking me across state lines. He's driving without GPS, which means it's somewhere familiar . . . which limits my options to most likely staying in Maine. East Coast states aren't big. There are only so many places in our little state we could be going.

"Is that a statement or question?"

"Don't treat me like you're trying to teach Anne the difference between *can I* and *may I*, just tell me where we're going."

"Still didn't answer me," he says playfully.

I let out an annoyed sigh. "It's a statement."

"Well, aren't you the perceptive one?" he replies, a lopsided smirk on his face as he focuses on the road. "Want to make another obvious observation?"

"Bite me."

But he doesn't stop my brain from trying to piece together the puzzle in front of me. We're going to Portland; it's probably for something related to the restaurant. That could be one of two things: We're getting food or we're shopping for supplies. The truck has a big enough bed that we could load up with pots and pans, maybe even a new refrigerator, and take it back to Harper's Cove with us.

But if we're going with option one, why does he need me? Kyle is a bigger guy; he would be more use carrying something like that into the Wharf. And if it's the first option, Logan seems to be the type of guy who likes to have control over absolutely everything. Wouldn't having me here . . . mess with that vibe?

"You know, Harper's Cove is known for our seafood. Some of the best in Maine," I remind him.

"I know, I get a lot of my seafood from fishermen who live by the sound. A few doors down, actually. And, not sure if you noticed, but the Wharf is a seafood restaurant," he teases.

Ignoring his quip I continue. "So, it wouldn't be wise to go into Portland for seafood when we have the best in our backyard."

"Biased, but sure."

"Logical," I correct. "Am I right?"

"You're getting warmer," he says, smoothly moving into the left lane to take the exit that's a straight shot into Portland. I've done this drive maybe five dozen times. I know the route with my eyes closed.

"But you're my prep chef. So, you should be involved with these decisions." A beat passes. "I want you involved."

I put my hand over my heart, gasping dramatically. "Logan, I'm engaged! You can't say things like that. Someone might hear."

The joke falls flat. Or Logan just has no humor. Probably the latter, considering, you know, I'm hilarious.

"Has anyone told you you're not funny?"

"No, and if they did, they'd be wrong."

"Confident, aren't you?"

"It's charm. It grows on you."

"Like a fungus."

"More like how Bon Iver grows on people."

Logan frowns. "Hey, Justin Vernon is a great musician. One of the best of our generation."

"Of course you'd say that. Are you going to tell me where we're going now?"

"After you insulted my music?" he asks. "You'll see when we get there."

I roll my eyes. "You sound just like a parent, you know that?"

"Well, if I didn't, I'd be far more concerned with Anne's well-being, so at least I'm doing that right."

"You're annoying."

"I've heard that a few times before, yeah. Think people mean anything by it?"

Silence fills the car again as we merge back onto the highway. In the distance, maybe thirty-five miles or so, Portland comes into view, like some sort of small-town Emerald City of steel and glass. It's funny how when you go to other places, everything is put into perspective. When I was younger, Portland seemed like the biggest city in the world. When my family and I went back to DC a few times over the years, to visit my father's family, that felt like it was impossible to navigate. Then you go to Chicago and New York City, places that are four times as big as DC and ten times as big as Portland. You learn how to navigate those. What once seemed too big, too expansive, like it would swallow you whole, becomes natural and normal.

And then you come back home and realize this was never enough—and how did you ever think it could be?

"If we're going to be in this car and spending the morning together, I think I deserve something in return."

"Oh really? And what makes you think that?"

"Well, for starters, you did kidnap me and gave me no choice before driving me out of town."

"Gave you no choice? Debatable. Kidnapped you? Not likely, but I'll play along. Sure. What are you thinking?"

The thing everyone wants: to understand people a little better. "You answer one question for me."

He shifts into a lower gear smoothly, so smoothly I barely even feel the car jolt. "That's it? You're easy then. Sure. Hit me."

"Why are you running a restaurant in a small-town place like Harper's Cove, when you could travel out of town and be in a bigger market, with more opportunities, more people, and more of a chance for your dream to succeed?"

We go silent for a moment, and it gives me time to let everything settle in, like sediment finding its way to the bottom of a canister. Objectively, he is very handsome. The way his cheekbones and jaw protrude outwardly at a striking angle. The way his jet-black hair is peppered with white, like stars in a black canopy on a clear night; the way it's tousled lightly, giving him that sleepy-but-stylish look. The veins on his arms, which are a defining masculine characteristic everybody loves. The cuts and bruises, a few scabs here and there that have probably come from his manual labor. The tattoo sleeves, which I can tell he takes care of because the sun hasn't begun to bleed them yet.

From a purely logical standpoint, I can see why people find him attractive. Perhaps, in another universe, I would even find him attractive enough to make a move. But there are enough things in this universe barring that from happening. For one, he's close to fifteen years older than me. That in and of itself isn't an issue—I've never had a problem being with people who were older than me. But coupled with the fact that he has a child, that he's such a fixture in Harper's Cove, and I don't even know if he's gay or bi or pan—which is probably the most important thing—there's just too many factors setting up impenetrable storm barriers between us.

Plus, of course, you know, he's, my boss. *Boss* isn't the right word. Coworker? He's more than that.

Finally, Logan speaks. "I like it here."

"That's not enough of a reason to keep your business here," I say, keeping the chastising tone in my voice to a minimum. "You want the Wharf to succeed, right?"

"Of course I do."

"Then you should go where the biggest market is."

"I like what the Wharf is," he pushes further. "I like that—"

"But it could be more," I interject. "I mean, you didn't just get into this to have a hobby, right? You want it to be a business and you want it to support you and Anne? Then you need to—"

"Don't."

A momentary flash of icy venom suddenly turns the temperature in the car several degrees colder. Logan doesn't need to look at me for me to know that the venom is directed toward me, a direct shot at my heart in an attempt to stop my whole body. It's the quintessential parent move, or something I'm guessing all parents learn when they suddenly get a kid, and a stork gives them a manual on how to be an effective and terrifying parent. Every parent does it in a slightly different way, but every one is just as effective.

In that exact moment, it makes me shut the fuck up.

"Don't bring Anne into this. You want to try and argue your case, do it. But you don't need to use my kid as some bargaining chip to try and convey your point."

"I wasn't doing that," I say honestly.

A beat. Sympathy and regret burst for a moment on his face, like a flash of lightning in the sky during a thunderstorm.

"I know. Sorry, habit. When you're a single father, raising a daughter, people always look at you and assume the worst. Sometimes I wonder if Anne would be better off with Michelle."

Michelle. I haven't heard that name before, but it doesn't take me long to figure out who she is.

"Anne's mother?"

Logan nods curtly and doesn't say any more. That's the end of that conversation, I guess.

I do a quick jump down memory lane to try and see if I remember seeing any photos of her in the house.

It might sound weird, but I don't know many people with divorced parents. It was a lot more common in college and grad school, but it's not something you ever bring up when you pass twenty-two. Your parents' faults or whatever caused them are only responsible for your faults until your midtwenties. After that, who you are is based on what you make of yourself—blaming your parents' divorce for your problems is kind of childish after you turn twentysomething. So, it's not so much that I'm surprised to hear about Anne's mother, just . . . more that I find it interesting. But I have enough manners to know when a thought is an intrusive one.

Logan doesn't seem to mind.

"We divorced about eight years ago," he says without being prompted. "Just drifted apart, you know?"

I shrug. "People do that." Fall in and out of love, even when they say they love one another. I actually know that feeling pretty well. "Not the same since you two were married, but my boyfriend Bradley and I broke up before I came here. Well, he broke up with me when I lost my job in Chicago but . . ."

"His loss," Logan says without looking at me. "But your gain, sounds like a shitty guy, and you deserve someone who is definitely less shitty."

Warmth spreads to my cheeks, unable to be seen thanks to my darker skin. Before I can reclaim my mental footing from the well-placed, yet so simple, compliment, Logan continues.

"Michelle lives in Seattle; it's her home base. Musician. Travels a lot, so Anne and I see her pretty often when she's around."

"And Anne's happy? I mean, with your arrangement?"

I'm not sure I believe that a two-parent household is better than one. I think it just matters that the people are taking care of the child. It can be one person or more. The number isn't what is important; it's the matter of love in the home. But I do find it interesting Logan got custody of her. Often, it's the woman who gets to keep the child, not the man.

But then again, Logan's a stable influence. Not traveling the world because of his music. It makes more sense why he wants to stay in Harper's Cove. It's not just that he likes it because it's the best place in the world, it gives Anne that stability she needs.

"Yeah, she is. When Michelle and I divorced, we made sure Anne was okay with it. Michelle said—and I'll always love her for this—if Anne wants to live with her, she'd give up her dreams as a musician and find a way to be happy only doing local gigs on the West Coast. When Anne was okay living with me in Harper's Cove, though, it just made sense. It's a good, stable place for her to call home. And with Michelle traveling so much, Anne having that stability was important."

I nod, completely agreeing. Putting Anne's well-being over his own? That gives Logan some points in my book.

"How did you two meet? And forgive me, but I thought you'd be married to, I dunno, someone who is kinda as boring as you."

Shit. Not the word I wanted to use.

Logan pushes his lips into a thin line, but a small smile ends up forming, like he accepts he isn't the most interesting person on the planet.

"Number one, I'm anything but boring."

"Sounds like something a boring person would say," I tease.

"I'm a chef, with tattoos. That has to count for something."

"Most chefs have tattoos."

"Do you know that for a fact or are you just guessing?"

"Guessing, but am I wrong?"

He pauses. "You're not wrong, but—"

"But nothing. See? Case in point. Game, set, match."

"More importantly," he interrupts. "What's a boring profession that you see matching with me?"

"Law." The suggestion leaves my mouth before I can capture them. "Culinary law."

Logan snorts. Like a full-on snort that sounds like a pig ripe for the stuffing.

"Shit, sorry," he mutters, covering his mouth as if a glob of drool just fell down his face and into his salt-and-pepper stubble.

"No problem. I know, I'm hilarious. You don't have to try and hide it."

"You're certainly cocky enough for the both of us."

It's kinda attractive. Not the snorting, no, God no. But the fact there is something imperfect about him.

Logan's not perfect. There are many things about him—edges that aren't buffed, sharp angles that prick you like a rose—

that make him a walking hazard sign. I think, if Mya actually got to know him and looked past the handsome smile, the hipster fashion he doesn't even think about, and the deep raspy voice, she might see that he's actually a big work in progress.

Funny, because works in progress are my favorite thing.

And it's not because he's divorced. People get married when they're not the right match and for a hundred other reasons that set the groundwork for a bad marriage. In fact, getting divorced, especially when he has a child, is probably a check mark in his favor, especially if he knew that the marriage wasn't going to work.

No, what makes Logan imperfect is the other things. The things you notice every now and then out of the corner of your eye, like a shadow that changes shape based on a flicker of light to play with your senses. It's the stubbornness that's impossible to avoid. The air of confidence he has; I'm not even sure he knows it exists. Of course he does, people don't get far in life without it. To succeed you HAVE to be confident in yourself, more so than anyone else.

But—and I'm not sure if this makes any sense—just hearing him snort, experiencing him do something so . . . disgusting? His imperfections are cute. No, not cute, adorable. And though the things that make him imperfect are also the things that make my hackles rise, they make me feel . . . I dunno, safer around him? Like he isn't just a walking prickly cliché. He can laugh, he can joke, and he can snort so hard spittle leaves his mouth.

"First of all," he says, bringing me out of my thoughts. "Culinary law is not even a thing."

"How do you know?"

"I know."

"Would you bet the Wharf on it?"

That makes him pause.

"Okay, *maybe* it's a thing."

"Exactly." I smirk.

"But that's not how Michelle and I met. A mutual friend of ours is an artist. He was having a show, and we both attended."

"Wow, a real *Devil Wears Prada* Andy and Christian moment."

"What?"

He merges onto a bypass that'll take us directly into the city. A car nearly cuts him off, but Logan's reaction speed is top notch. He barely even flinches, only mutters, "Asshole."

But I'm not worried about that.

"I'm sorry, stop the car."

"I'm not stopping the car, Xavier."

"You're joking, though, right? You have to be."

"Didn't we just say you're not a funny guy? Didn't we agree and establish that?"

"We established that you're wrong. But you've *never* seen *The Devil Wears Prada*?"

"I don't even know what it is."

"It's a movie, Logan!" I boom. "Miranda? Cerulean? The boyfriend who is actually the villain? Her shitty friends? The fashion montages? The Prada boots?"

"You're saying words, but I have no idea what you're talking about."

It might seem like a silly thing, but there are few things in the world more iconic than *The Devil Wears Prada*. And it feels like a real Hague-worthy violation that Logan doesn't know about it.

"I bet Anne knows about it."

"Anne knows too much for her own good, so I'd probably lose that bet."

"So, it sounds like we're going to have to watch it then."

"Whoa, how did—"

"Shush," I order. "We're watching it. I don't know when, but I'm going to make it happen, because I cannot work with you without you knowing one of the most iconic movies of our generation."

"I thought, number one, we were part of different generations?"

"It's the most iconic film of all generations."

"That's a big statement, and number two, I thought *American Pie* was—"

"YOU ARE NOT COMPARING MERYL STREEP TO JASON MOTHERFUCKING BIGGS."

It takes me far too long to notice that infamous smirk on Logan's face.

"See," he says as we breach the city limits. "I have a sense of humor."

"If that's your idea of humor, then we really are in trouble."

CHAPTER
THIRTEEN

H OLD ON A SEC."

The moment we park in the parking garage, I'm already ready to lead the way to downtown; even though I have absolutely no idea where I'm going. I'm halfway to the elevator when Logan calls me back.

"If you tell me you forgot some spatula or something, and we have to return to the car, I'm going to carry you on my back and throw you into the Kennebec Ri—"

When I turn around, though, and round the corner to double back to the car, I expect to see Logan ruffling through the back seat for whatever he left. Frantically looking for, like I said, a spatula, or something else mundane and inconsequential. What I don't expect is to see him shirtless.

I catch him pulling his shirt off his head, strands of his dark hair falling in front of his face as he tosses it into the trunk of his car. There's a constellation of freckles on his back that map out some secret hidden location to some missing planet, I'm sure. His muscles are strong, but only pronounced enough that you can see them in the right light and at the right angle.

He reaches into his trunk and pulls out a light blue Henley, turning to me as he slips it on. I didn't REALLY notice his body before, but something's different about this time. This time, my mind makes a mental snapshot of his pecs, his happy trail, the way his waist slightly tapers . . . and stores it deep inside my mind.

"It's hot," he says as if it's a common fact. "Just needed to change my shirt. You need one? I have an extra one."

"I'm good," I choke out, clearing my throat. "I'm good."

"You sure? I think I have one that's your size."

"I promise."

He shrugs and closes the trunk before locking the car. He leads the way out of the parking garage, holding the door for me as we exit.

"Remind me when we leave, I'll get us lunch."

"You don't have to do that, I have money."

"I'm not doing it because I don't think you have money. I know you have money. I pay you," he teases. "I'm doing it because you took the time to come here with me and it's the least I could do. That's the thing people do for one another when someone goes out of their way to help them."

He says it like it's such a common thing. And maybe it should be. But thinking back to NYU, to Chicago, I'm thinking how I was usually the one inviting people out, paying for drinks, paying for dinners. Friends would always pay me back, of course, but it was the assumption that I would pay first. Even with . . .

Logan grabs my arm, gently, but firm enough to stop me and make me look at him.

"Did your boyfriend Brady—"

"Bradley."

"—Bradley never pay for things for you?"

And there he is, there Logan goes, reading into things, seeing past the wall I've learned how to expertly and quickly erect. There's no faulty foundation with my walls. There are no cracks, no spaces for water, or snakes, or mice to sneak through. They're perfect.

But somehow, Logan just barges right through them.

I swallow thickly and probably visibly. Logan lets his hand go, sparing me the moment.

"It's not my place," he says. "But for the record? He sounds like a shitty boyfriend."

"You don't have to tell me that twice."

"Funny, think this is the third time I've said it now." He smirks. "In math, according to Anne, three points are needed to verify a line or a pattern so . . . pretty sure I'm right here."

"Really only takes two, the third one is just for checking your work. And you only said it twice."

"Of course you'd call me out on that."

"But," I say. "More important than middle school geometry, are you going to finally tell me why we're here, or am I going to have to make my way to the nearest police station and let them know you kidnapped me?"

The joke sounded better in my head. But out in public, having just gotten our ticket for the parking garage, the joke doesn't land. In fact, it falls as flat as a soufflé I'd spent all day making, collapsing in on itself.

And by that, I mean a woman who looks to be about in her sixties snaps her head faster than is probably healthy to look at us, studying us with her dark eyes like she's deciding if she should pull out her phone and dial 911 for my well-being. Good on her.

"He's joking," Logan says loudly, glaring at me. "Right?"

I shrug, doubling down on the joke. "Am I?"

"Xavier."

"Who knows, I mean, maybe that's what you told me to say."

"XAVIER."

"Okay, okay, fine, Jesus."

I turn to the older woman and give her an apologetic smile. Without me saying anything, she rolls her eyes and mouths something about youngsters under her breath.

"See, she thinks—"

"If you make another goddamn old joke."

"What? You going to keep me locked in the car? That's illegal, you know. About one hundred animals die a year from being left in a car."

"Are you saying you're an animal?"

I open my mouth and close it. "That didn't . . ."

"Land like you wanted?"

"Exactly."

Logan smirks a bit, only a flicker for a moment, like a crackle of lightning across his nice features. "We're beginning to know each other so well already."

Logan holds the door open for me at the bottom of the steps. I meant to mouth a thank-you to him, but instead, I just let out an annoyed sigh. One I don't address when he quirks his brow at me.

I'm not a big fan of Portland. Like I said before, when I was younger, I thought it was a big city because it was the only thing that I knew. The quaintness kind of reminds me of Baltimore in

Maryland, or Alexandria in Virginia, two places that I visited as an undergraduate when my business elective in sophomore year took a spring break trip to DC to learn about PACs. The size of the city put it in a weird middle ground compared to other cities. It's not big enough to be a metropolis, but it's too big to be considered a small town like Harper's Cove. It leans into the idea of being a small-town city, where it feels like you could know everyone even though you can't really.

There was a time in my life when I thought this would be enough. That I could live in Portland, accomplish all my goals of being a businessman, and still live close enough to home to make Mom and Dad happy. I'd live close enough that I could see them on weekends, and if they needed me for any major things, I'd only be forty-five minutes to an hour away.

Then my dreams got bigger. And when dreams get bigger, they often explode right in front of your face. Case in point, me and the shambles I have laid at my feet.

I shake my head; this isn't a time to pity myself. We have work to do. What that work is . . .

"So now that we're here," I say as we cross one of the busiest streets that leads us down a strip of quaint shops that reminds me too much of Harper's Cove.

"Shopping," he finally answers.

"That's it? Seriously, I think I've been pretty good at—"

"Not being annoying?"

"At trusting you."

Logan lets out a bark of a laugh. "Every chance you get, you nag me about where we're going."

"Not every chance," I mutter.

"Point is," he says, turning on the heels of his boots to stand in front of me. His tall and broad form blocks the sun that's directly in front of me. "Are you going to trust me for once? You might not like me, Xavier, but you should know by now I'm not someone who is going to hurt you."

I tap my right finger rhythmically against my thigh in annoyance. He's not wrong. Logan isn't the sweetest teddy bear of a person, but he certainly isn't the intruder I thought he was. Mostly because that doesn't help him at all. There's no benefit in him kidnapping me.

I follow Logan, having to walk twice as fast to keep up with his long legs. The busy main street segments off to only let people through, not cars, and is filled to the brim with a multicolor sea of skin tones. The murmurs are equal to Union Square in New York on this warm Friday afternoon; just like Logan and me, everyone is heading down to the bottom of the hill.

It takes me a moment to realize where Logan is taking me, but when we approach the destination, I see the bottom of the hill is lined with carts, tents, and makeshift stands. The vibes are irreplaceable. Every city has one like this. And a city that doesn't? That's a place you shouldn't get your food from because you're most likely going to get a tomato that has enough pesticides you'll grow a third eye. And not the good kind.

"You know Harper's Cove has a huge farmers' market, right?" I ask. "We drove an hour for something you could get in—"

"Would you be quiet for one second?"

Logan stops at the corner as if we're waiting for a light to give us permission to go, but since no cars are allowed, we can walk whenever we want.

"I brought you here because you're my prep chef and this is my ritual. It's my thing," he explains. "Someone I can joke with is great. Someone with a sense of humor—albeit stale—is useful. But someone I can trust? That's hard to come by. We both need to be able to rely on each other. So, I thought, why not show him something that's personal to me? Did I make a mistake in that? Are you unable to be serious for just a moment?"

I could be snide here. It's so easy. He set it up so perfectly. But I can tell by the look in his eyes this isn't just some *thing* to him. It's personal. It's like if I showed him my study room in the Reg at UChicago. That was my favorite place in the world, sans next to Bradley in bed.

Instead, I nod. "You can trust me. I promise."

Logan's shoulders relax for a moment. "I come here every Friday, or at least I try to. I've been busy these last few."

Logan points, and I follow the direction of his finger. It's hard to see from where we are, but I can make out the man's bright red hat like a stop sign.

"You don't come here for fashion advice, I see."

Logan shoots me a glare. I put my hands up in defense.

"He was the only friend I made in the area when we moved, and he stuck with me through the divorce," Logan says after a beat. "So, I come here, support his little empire, get some produce, and catch up with a friend."

Something about how simple and honest Logan is strikes a chord inside of me. He doesn't try to hide the weight the subject has on him. It tells me that the breakup might not have been as good as he said it was earlier; that he lost many friends when he and his wife split up; and only one person, one man, stuck with him.

I wonder what it's like to lose your whole support system just because of a decision you made that no one outside could really understand. I wonder what it's like to feel that isolated and in a small town, trying to make ends meet, to make a young person into someone who can handle this cruel world all on their own.

"I lost my friends when me and my ex broke up," I say, before I can stop myself. "They were more his friends than mine."

A beat. Another beat. I wait for Logan to say what I would have said in response. "You're not going to tease me?"

"Why would I?"

"The setup was right there. You could have said, I dunno, *I can see how you wouldn't have any friends*, or something."

"Not everyone is looking to one-up you or belittle you, Xavier, especially when someone else shows their underbelly," he says quietly. "Being nice and genuine costs nothing. And, honestly, you don't seem like a person who always is like this or was like this. Which makes me wonder, what happened to you when you were in college?"

My parents told me something similar when I came home from college one year. They said I had changed. That I was harder, sharper, colder. They questioned what happened to the Xavier they molded into a *proper, kind gentleman who always put others first and didn't always have something sassy to say*.

Sometimes I do wonder what happened to him, too, and if he's doing okay.

"You want me on my best behavior?" I say after a moment of thinking. Logan's right, it costs me nothing and he's extending me an olive branch. The least I can do is meet him halfway.

"That would be appreciated, if it's not too much to ask."

"It's not," I say as we continue to walk. "But I'm going to want something in return."

"Of course you do," Logan mutters, weaving through the crowd. "You know you're a bit of a brat, right?"

"I've been told that before in a different context."

Logan snaps his gaze to me and looks at me with a deadpan expression. "Did you just—"

"Say what you think I said, perhaps. But that would mean I would have to know what you were you thinking in the first place. Is your mind that dirty?"

"I'm not even going to dignify that with a response."

"That means yes," I say in a singsong voice, grinning and nudging him.

Logan rolls his eyes, and I can see a small tinge of red in his cheeks. That short-sleeve shirt is doing little to hide the sudden redness of his skin.

We weave our way through the crowd to the front of the man's stall. He has maybe the third largest gathering of any individual at the farmers' market—and that totals about thirty or so vendors. And I can see why. The man is a bundle of energy, like a live wire that can't be tamed. He's dancing around in his stall, chopping fruits and vegetables, tossing them like one of those fancy hibachi restaurants where they cook the food in front of you, and keeping the crowd entertained. He reminds me of a man who might have tried to work at the fish market in Seattle but didn't make the final cut so decided to bring a little bit of that flavor to Portland, Maine.

"Alright, alright, alright," he says in what can only be a poor man's Matthew McConaughey expression. "You know the deal, folks, first come first serve. I got you some asparagus, greens, peas, radishes, rhubarb, and scallions. Got a bit of radicchio left, and oh, the pumpkins! How could I forget the pumpkins!"

Logan chuckles lowly under his breath. "Seth hasn't changed one bit."

Seth continues to dance around his stall like it's his own personal stage, as if this is his world and we're just living in it. His eyes catch mine first, and then Logan's, causing them to almost seemingly glow with excitement.

"Logan!" he booms so loud that everyone standing around us looks over at us. "My man. My friend. My brother," he says, beckoning us both over.

"Seth," Logan says, weaving his way through the rest of the crowd and moving to the front. He leans over the stall, clasping his hand in that *bro, no-homo* hug two men have.

"It's been too long," Seth chastises. "Thought you forgot about me."

"Me, forget about you? Never," Logan promises. "Work's just been busy after losing Lacey."

"If you're here to try and convince me to come work with you in Harper's Cove, I've already told you, I'm happy where I am," he warns, arching his brow.

"I know you're never going to leave this stall; you're going to die here before that happens," Logan chuckles. "No, besides, I've got someone to fill that role for me."

The setup isn't the best, but I let it slide. Grinning, I give a half wave. "Hey. Xavier."

"Seth," he says, giving me a once-over. I'm not sure if I should be offended by how he looks me up and down, as if he's judging me, trying to decide if I'm worthy of the job or something. But the smile that breaks out on his face tells me differently.

"Oh, he's a cute one." Seth smirks. "Good pick, L."

"Seth," Logan warns.

"Has he called you a good boy yet?" Seth asks.

"Not yet. Should I be worried?"

"Once he does, you know you have him hook, line, and—"

"Seth," Logan says more firmly this time.

Seth smirks, making a locked-key motion with his mouth. "I'm just saying. You have a tell, Logan."

"I mean," I interrupt. "I do like to think I'm fairly attractive, but I'm also pretty sure I'm out of Logan's league," I tease, adding to the joke. "Now, you, Seth? Maybe we can make something happen."

Seth lets out a throaty laugh. "Sorry, bud. Never swung that way."

I shrug. "My loss is another woman's gain."

"But if I ever, you know, want to experiment . . ."

"I'll be waiting." I wink.

Seth lets out another bellowing laugh that makes his cheeks turn pink and crow's-feet appear on the side of them. Seth looks like how you'd imagine someone who spends the majority of their life working in the food business. His skin is tan, just a bit leathery. He has that fit-but-not-muscular look about him that comes from someone who spends a lot of time doing manual labor, probably working on some farm, I'm guessing. His hair is dirty blond, and just like Logan, he has tattoos on his arms, and his neck, too.

"You two are an absolute mess," Logan says. "I knew I shouldn't have brought you."

"Aw, come on now, *L*," I tease, using Seth's nickname for him. "Don't be like that. You know you love to have me around."

"Yeah, come on, L," Seth teases back. "You hired him for a reason."

"I hired him because he has the potential of being a talented chef, with the right mentorship."

"And don't forget because I—wait, what?"

The words feel like a knife to the heart. That's the only way to describe it, and it's not the right way, I know. I'm a business-person, not a creative writing professor. But there's honesty in

Logan's voice. I can see it on his face, too. He's only speaking truth. About me. And my skill. There's no subtext there, just pure respect.

"I didn't stutter," he mutters, picking up one of the heads of rhubarb Seth has. "How much for these?"

"On top of your current order?" he asks, jutting his finger to the truck parked in reverse behind us. "Free."

"You know I like to pay you, Seth."

"And you do. Many times, over." Seth turns to me. "Plus, I get to watch this blossom in front of me. That's payment enough."

"I swear to God, Seth, I'm going—"

"Did Logan tell you he was the one who got me this gig?" he interrupts.

"He did not."

"That's an exaggeration," he mutters.

"Horseshit," Seth says. "I bought the land my pa had from him to help him pay some bills. Didn't know what to do with the shit he was harvesting and growing. Logan turned me onto this farmers' market. Talked to the owner."

"Michelle talked to the owner," he corrected.

"Yeah, but you sealed the deal. Plus, we don't like Michelle."

Logan's face twists into disapproval. He wants to defend her, I can tell, but he doesn't say anything. It reminds me of when people break up with their boyfriends or girlfriends, and their posse decides that person deserves to burn in a vat of hellfire. Doesn't matter what you think, your ride-or-die crew is going to . . . well, be ride or die for you.

It's clear Seth is Logan's ride-or-die friend. Everyone deserves that. Just like Mya is for me. I wonder how Seth would take it if Logan just decided to up and leave for years. Even if he had a reason—Anne, getting back with Michelle, a new cooking opportunity—would he still accept it? Would he grin and bear it, knowing his friend's well-being was more important than his own feelings?

Sometimes, I wonder if those thoughts flood Mya's mind. Did I leave her behind without any thought about our friendship? Did it hurt her when I told her I wanted to leave this *horseshit* town behind, lumping her in with everyone and everything else I hated without a second thought?

"Semantics aside," Seth continues. "I got a call a week later that a spot had opened up, and, well . . . that was four years ago, and now look at me."

"Living the dream." I grin.

"Living the motherfuckin' dream, my man."

Logan and Seth continue chatting, with Seth bringing us around back to his truck. Logan's eyes dart from one pile of carefully packed food to another, examining them diligently with his fingers, as if he's trying to decide if the gold brought into this pawnshop is real or not.

"This is more food than you usually give, Seth," he says after what feels like an hour.

Seth shrugs. "I had some extra."

Logan frowns, not buying it. "Did you actually have some extra or . . . ?"

Seth shrugs. "We'll never know, will we?"

Logan sighs, pulling out his wallet, fishing out a check and handing it to Seth.

"Give me thirty minutes to finish here," Seth says. "And we can pass off the goods."

"You make it sound like you're selling contraband," I chuckle.

"We are," both Seth and Logan say at the same time.

"Trust me, once you cook with Seth's vegetables, you'll never go back to store-bought," Logan promises.

"That's a pretty high bar," I say, turning to Seth. "Are you worthy of that much praise?"

"Oh, absolutely." Seth grins. "Probably more."

"Is there an Oscar for farmers?"

"No, and don't get me started," Seth says.

"Oh, lord," Logan interjects, rolling his eyes. "Here we go."

"India. The UK. Bangladesh. Australia. Chile. All of these countries have awards for farmers. Did you know farmers provide up to thirty-one percent of the world's crop production?"

"I did not know that."

"Don't encourage him, Xavier."

"No, no, I love shit like this. Go on."

"People like me," Seth says, pointing to his chest, "help keep mouths fed. And how does America repay us?"

"With tax cuts?" I chime in.

Logan nudges me hard with his boot, causing me to bite back a hiss.

"With nothing!" Seth slaps the side of his truck.

"I see I opened up a whole can of worms here I regret opening."

"I could have told you that," Logan mutters. "Alright, Seth. Before you go off on more of a tangent, Xavier and I are going to go shopping. Meet you back here in thirty minutes?"

"Can do," Seth says, waving his hand dismissively. "I have to go back to selling since—"

"The government screwed you over, we know," Logan and I say at the exact same time.

I grin at him. "Jinx, you owe me—"

"I absolutely owe you nothing," he says, turning to walk

down one of the parallel streets. "Come on, I have some shopping I need to do anyway."

I have a comeback planned, because, well, when do I *not* have a comeback planned. But the pistons don't fire. The gears don't turn to make the words come to life. Instead, I just follow along with Logan. Picking up my pace a bit to keep up with his long legs.

And a part of me, a very small part, is happy he didn't just drop me off back home before heading into Portland.

But he can never know that.

FOURTEEN

'VE HEARD OF COOKSHOP Plus before, so when Logan parks in front of the small shop, I'm not surprised. But Logan's face shows that *he's* surprised I know of his supposed secret.

"My dad got my mom something from here before," I explain. "Some All-Clad pans; a whole set."

He whistles, slamming the squealing door of his truck behind him. "Those are costly."

"Anything for my mother," I say. There's sarcasm dripping from my tongue that isn't intentional—at least, I don't think it's intentional. My dad's love for my mother is adorable and something people should strive for. But it's a near-impossible standard. Mom and Dad always say that I should find someone who has the same *energy* as they do.

Don't they know how hard to obtain that is? People don't meet like that anymore. Now we have dating apps, hookup apps, drug dens. Okay, maybe the last one is a bit of an exaggeration, but the point still stands. People don't date for love anymore, people date for convenience. To help cut down on rent. For the tax break. For dozens of other reasons. It's not reasonable to expect to find love as a priority when you don't need to marry someone to be in love with them.

Logan arches his brow. "We're going to have to unpack that later on," he says. "But for now, I have a list of—"

"Oh. My. God. Xavier?"

I'm not the best when it comes to remembering people's faces. It's a skill that I need to get better at, especially if I want to run a Fortune 500 company. How can I be a powerhouse in my field if I don't know people's faces by heart? How can I make connections with people in country clubs that can lead to multimillion-dollar deals if I don't know some of the most intimate details about them, so I can bring them up and make people feel like I actually care about them when I just care about their business?

But voices? I never forget those.

Stacey Lee was a girl in my class at NYU. She was in a concurrent track to me, going down the path of television and film, and getting her BFA thanks to Stern's 4+1 program. Last I heard, she had gone to Hollywood to pursue her dreams of working on big-budget films, and hopefully meet Jake Gyllenhaal and have his babies.

I mean, solid plan, if I do say so myself.

But also, it begs the question: Why the fuck is she here, 2,900-plus miles away?

"Oh my God, it's actually you!" she squeals, practically flinging herself at me. She doesn't hesitate, doesn't pause to wonder if, I dunno, I actually want to touch her, or if I'm even going to catch her. But that's Stacey Lee for you. Not Stacey. Not Lee. Stacey Lee. Both names and you best remember it, if you know what's good for you.

"Jesus, look at you," she coos. "You haven't changed a bit since college."

Not sure if that's a compliment, but okay. "Neither have you."

She beams. "Why thank you. It's the commitment to the gym and my six-step skin routine three times a day. You know what they say, consistency is key."

That wasn't a compliment, even if Stacey Lee wants to take it as one. The moment she is within four feet of me, I'm hit with a wave of perfume—the same vanilla she used to always wear. It's like she bought it in bulk; there never was a day I didn't smell it on her.

Seriously, nothing at all ever changes. History just repeats itself over and over and over.

"But how are you?" she asks, reaching without permission and squeezing my shoulder. "Last I heard you were in Chicago?"

So, the NYU wannabe *Gossip Girl* grapevine isn't perfect, I see. Does that make me Lonely Boy? Could be worse.

"I was. Moved back home a few weeks ago to help my parents."

Not exactly a lie. Okay, not really the truth either. But I don't want to, nor do I have to, explain myself to Stacey Lee. Plus, I'm *keenly* aware that Logan is standing right next to me. And I don't want him prying into any part of my life if I can avoid it.

"Aw, that's so cute," she says, pressing her right hand to her chest. "Bless your heart."

It's important to understand how out of place that is for Stacey Lee. If you closed your eyes and only listened to her words, you might think she was a rip-off of Alexis from *Schitt's Creek*.

But she's the complete opposite. Jet-black curls in a giant braid, strikingly bright blue eyes, and tall—like, taller than most men. The type of height where you are absolutely asked by every person you meet if you play basketball.

And she did, until she injured her leg junior year.

"And who is this handsome fellow?" she asks, almost purring when she turns to Logan. "Why have I never seen you around here before?"

"Probably because I don't live here, I reckon," Logan says, extending his hand. "Logan."

"Nice to meet you, Logan. Wherever you live, I need to move there."

Does Logan have that effect on everyone? It's like he releases something out of his pores that makes people wanna flirt with him. Or maybe people are just that desperate. I read somewhere in a magazine that late twenties feels like the last jumping-off point that you can have a meaningful relationship. Which isn't true at all; when you're older, you learn that. But in your twenties, when you're in the thick of it, unable to see the forest for the trees, and all your friends are having babies, buying houses, and getting married, it can feel like everything is falling apart. Desperation sets in.

That's another lesson that I learned in grad school: never make a decision when you're desperate.

"What are you doing in Portland?" I ask. "I thought you were in LA?"

"LA is a state of mind," she clarifies. "It never leaves you. No matter where you go."

Of course it is.

"What about you, rock star?"

Kill me.

"What are you doing here? And how do you two know each other?" She gestures between us, as if we look like some odd pair.

I open my mouth to spit out the logical and truthful answer, to tell Stacey Lee that we're just coworkers shopping for kitchen equipment. I prepare myself for the backlash of questions that will follow. Why was I, a kid who got into the University of Chicago, whom Stern sent out an e-blast about my successes when I graduated, in Portland, population sixty-six thousand?

The domino effect is going to feel like an avalanche, but I'm ready for that. These are the consequences of my actions coming home to roost. In some epic tale, this is when the hero is at his lowest point before—

"He's my boyfriend."

Wait a damn minute.

It feels like my whole world just shattered in front of me. Like the universe was inside of a glass aquarium filled with water and just the tiniest crack made everything burst, overwhelming me with feelings.

Did he just say *boyfriend*? He couldn't have. He didn't. That doesn't make any sense, right?

To add to the facade, Logan wraps his left arm around me, pulling me closer. The grin on his face is convincing, and it doesn't falter.

"Oh?" Stacey Lee asks. She arches her brow in that way I know means the moment we separate, she is going to tell everyone she can. "You two?"

"Since he moved back home. Lucky me, am I right?"

At first, she doesn't seem convinced. Stacey Lee lets her eyes move slowly from me to Logan. When she looks at Logan, though—like everyone when it comes to Logan—her eyes slowly go up and down like she's scanning him to keep an image of him in her memory.

No reason I should care. Logan isn't actually my boyfriend; it's just something he probably said to keep this interaction at a minimum because he, too, wanted to rip his eyeballs out. If we set up a scenario that doesn't warrant questions, she'll go about her business. It's a smart move.

But seeing her look at him like that? With a glimmer of—what is that, hunger?—in her eyes? It makes me ball my fist by my side, hidden slightly behind my back.

And I can't fully explain why.

Before she can ask any more questions that might expose me to Logan, I do the unthinkable. I lean up and place a kiss on Logan's cheek, my lips brushing against his stubble.

It only takes a moment. There are no words that need to follow. I see the flicker of astonishment on Stacey Lee's face. Did she think I couldn't secure someone like Logan? Was she surprised someone like Logan would be interested in someone like me?

"You didn't tell me why you left LA," I add, leaning against him, causing Logan to instinctively squeeze my side and let me push the weight of my body against him.

Stacey Lee's eyes sparkle as if I just turned on the engine. "You remember how after my accident I wanted to go into film?"

I nod, trying to stay focused on the conversation as best I can. But the way Logan's fingers stroke against my side is distracting to say the least.

"Turns out getting a job in LA is harder than I thought."

"Who would have thought that?" Logan chimes in. "Would you, babe? Their loss, obviously."

Babe. The word feels heavy when Logan says it. It reminds

me of when Bradley used to call me that. It never got old, the feeling of weightlessness that turned to dizziness to quickly follow each time he said the word. Be it against my lips, against my ear, or calling me out in the store; no matter the inflection, the word meant something. I feel that all over again, rushing back to me so quickly, like I'm rising from the bottom of the ocean too fast. It is dizzying.

Knowing he's saying it just to keep this ruse up helps ground me. Logan is my boss. Plain and simple. There's nothing between us because there can be nothing between us. Even if I understand why people find him attractive—and maybe, in another life far, far away from here when I stayed in Harper's Cove, it's possible for me to see how we could've crossed paths and been something romantic. But that life is so distant from mine, it's nearly impossible to even fantasize about it. Which makes keeping up the lie easier.

"Never," I say.

"I know, right?" Stacey Lee adds. "I mean, don't get me wrong, this is nothing like LA. But the TV station I work at? It'll do. I'm running a whole series about what makes small towns great. It's really quaint."

I give her a tight-lipped smile in return and nod. "Sure, we can go with that."

I don't think she actually knows what it means. It's not her fault, really, since most people use that word and don't know what it means. The dictionary definition of *quaint* is "attractively unusual or old-fashioned." Most people use it to mean "small" or "simple." Those are not the same things at all. Yes, Harper's Cove and other East Coast towns are small and simple, and that's what people like about them. They are an echo of the world from as far back as two centuries ago, when that was the norm. Not big, looming metropolises that swallow you whole, devoid of all personality. Not labyrinthine cities where survival is unlikely; where it's more likely the city will spit you out, but we all pretend we're better for it.

We should start calling cities *quaint* and make small towns like Harper's Cove the norm. Then we really all might be better for it.

Logan must have picked up on my frustration. He gives me one last squeeze before pulling his hand back and extending it to Stacey Lee.

"We really have to get going," he says.

"Oh, no, no! Do not apologize."

He didn't.

"It was so nice to meet you," Logan smoothly lies. Or is it a lie? I'm finding it harder and harder to discover with him what is truth and what is fiction when he speaks. I'm also finding it harder and harder to care if I discover the difference.

"Likewise. Xavier, we have to get together soon. You still have my number?"

I pull out my phone and wave it to her. A silent way of saying yes without saying yes.

I have no idea if I have Stacey Lee's number.

"Splendid. You two lovebirds have a great day. Xavier? I'll be awaiting your call."

Like a wind that carries leaves in some cliché Disney movie, Stacey Lee glides away with an air of confidence and individuality that could be bottled and sold for millions on Amazon in a matter of hours. A lot just happened right there, and I find myself just standing on the sidewalk, blinking, looking back at Logan, who is *also* just watching her walk away.

"Those are the type of people you hung out with, huh?" he asks.

"Don't."

Logan gives me a cheeky smile as he holds the door open to Cookshop Plus for me.

"You're not going to drop this, are you?"

"Oh, absolutely not."

C ARRIE THE MUTT, IF you don't get your face out of there, I swear to God."

I take issue with people who give their animals real-people names. Because when you hear something like *Carrie if you don't get your face out of there I swear to God*, you'd think I must be referring to a human. When, in fact, it's Mya's dog that was forced upon her by a roommate who up and left the puppy when she got expelled.

But who is the weak one when Mya's now got the animal that won't follow orders, and the original parent got off scot-free?

I may be a little biased, because Naga is nearly a perfect dog. She listens to orders; she has a mind of her own but doesn't usually speak out of turn. She's expressive and lovable without being smothering, and most importantly, she learns commands very quickly, even the complicated ones. When my parents came to visit me at NYU and brought Naga with them, one of the students on my floor mentioned that she was the best-behaved Samoyed she had ever seen.

I think I had something to do with that.

I sit at the island nursing my first and only drink of the night with Mya before we head out. Carrie the Mutt—her full government name—has her face buried in the trash, so deep that her back legs are up in the air and she's balancing on the front ones. She doesn't even stop when Mya repeats herself.

"Me and this dog are going to have words."

"Sounds like you already had words, and she has very clearly made her reply."

She narrows her eyes, dipping her fingers in the clear liquid and flicking it at me. The burning that pools out from my right eye where some of it lands tells me it's alcohol.

"You're going to take her side over mine?"

"She's a dog! She needs someone to advocate for her!" I reply, throwing my balled-up napkin at her.

"Traitor."

"Dog hater."

I open my mouth to call out her bullshit, but I decide to let her have this moment. She loves dogs more than I do. When I went away to college, I almost thought about giving Naga to her instead of letting her stay with my parents. Not that I didn't think my parents would treat her right, and they obviously did; it was just that Mya and Naga had a connection that was as close to my connection as I could think of.

"I just don't get it," she says, standing up and taking the drink from me, even though I still have half of it left. "Why is she such a bitch? And don't you say it's 'cause she's actually a bitch."

"I wasn't going to say that," I lie. "Maybe it's because you call her Carrie the Mutt? Or because you named her after a woman who burns a school down with her mind?"

"Okay, let's be clear, *Carrie* is an amazing movie," she barks back, as if I brought dishonor to her family. "Carrie the Mutt should be honored she's named after Carrie."

"Maybe if you named her after another famous Carrie, she'd like you more?"

"What famous person is named Carrie? Come on now."

"Carrie Fisher, Carrie Bradshaw, Carrie Underwood."

"All white women. Do you know a Black Carrie?"

"Is Carrie the Mutt Black?"

"Of course she's Black! Dogs take on the race of their owner. You know this."

"So Naga, a Samoyed, a Siberian breed, is Black?"

Mya pauses and huffs. "Well, what do you know? Are you ready to go?" she asks.

I've been ready for ages. I give Carrie the Mutt one last pat on her head before jumping off the stool and heading out to Mya's bright green Jetta, which she swears was the best investment of her life—besides her husband.

"Why are we going to a place here again?" I ask, buckling up. "Portland isn't far, and no one would recognize us."

"I thought you hate Portland?"

I fall silent. It's grown on me, but if I tell Mya why, she's going to want to dig deeper, and I don't have the bandwidth for that. Besides, this was Mya's idea, her incessant idea, that we needed to de-stress and hang out like real twentysomethings. I'd agreed without really thinking about what that meant. I was happy staying at her place, drinking, watching some movies. That's what fun was to me. But Mya had a completely different idea.

"And besides, I know the bartender at the Aqueduct and the drinks will be strong and free," she says in an annoyed tone, like she's told me this a dozen times. It's only been half a dozen. At most.

I open my mouth to make a quiet comment about money. We can afford more expensive drinks; the trade-off isn't enough. But then I remember: Maybe she can't. Mya is a teacher in a small town. How much does she make? I never asked. And all my money is going toward this fellowship fee. I don't have anything to spare.

Mya snaps her fingers in my face, jolting me out of my mental wormhole.

"You good?"

"Decent," I say. "Let's get going."

The Aqueduct is that awkward distance from Mya's house where it's too far to walk, though it is *technically* walkable, and just far enough that a car is reasonable, but with us drinking, it's going to be a hassle to deal with. Uber and Lyft weren't able to take a foothold in Harper's Cove. Too many people with cars and too many places within walking distance—no reason to have someone else drive you.

But it gives me a perfect excuse to not drink much.

"I'll drive us back," I say as she parks us around back. "My gift to you—you can drink as much as you want."

Mya flips the rearview mirror down and examines herself. Her skin, a half a shade lighter than my own dark skin, is honey-kissed. Her locs are pulled back into a makeshift bun with gold clips intricately placed on specific ends. She clicks her plum-colored lipstick methodically, which matches her plum-colored dress, before smacking her lips and looking at me.

"Do you love it, or do you love it?" she asks, gesturing to herself.

"I love it." I grin. "You sure you don't want to invite Derek out?"

She waves her hand dismissively. "He's busy."

For some, *busy* might sound like a bad thing, like she's avoiding some impending storm in her relationship, choosing to bury her head in the sand. But Derek and Mya are probably the calm-est couple I know. Derek's parents are born-and-raised Harper's Cove residents. He spends more time on the water than he does at home. And that works for them. He and Mya love hard—I know because I've been accidentally called during their lovemaking—and they make the most of their time together.

So, when they are apart, when he's doing long stints on the water or when she needs her alone time, it's not a thing that fractures their foundation. It's something that makes them stronger.

They are just that secure.

Honestly, it's hot. For a straight couple, I guess.

I jump out of the car and check myself in the warped, muted reflection of the passenger-side window. Mya told me early on what she was wearing, having FaceTimed me at the Wharf last week when she was at a boutique trying the outfit on.

"I've been calling you all day, where have you been?" she asked.

"Out," I said, keeping it vague.

She arched her brow. "Is Logan there?"

How could I tell her I spent all day in Portland with him, without her reading into it?

"I'm at work, so yes."

"Don't get smart with me. We'll talk about that later."

Without my permission, she bought me a matching V-neck she showed me, and told me what to wear with it. No ifs, ands, or buts.

"Dark jeans, boots, black blazer. Black belt. You'll look hot as fuck," she said.

"See?" she says confidently, walking around the side of the car to meet me. "I was right. You look fuckable."

"You always think you're right."

"That's because I always am. Where have you been? Why haven't you learned this yet?"

"Maybe you just haven't done a good job training me."

Mya gasps, hand on her face. "Xavier! How cheeky! Save that energy for the boys in the bar!"

I roll my eyes and hold the door open for Mya as we go inside the Aqueduct. It's not like any type of bar that I've seen in New York or Chicago, but then again, most bars inside of major cities are their own enigma. This one doesn't really have a dance floor; it's just some tables and a pool table they pushed out toward the center, using some colored duct tape to crudely outline where people can dance and where people can't. Strings of neon lights give the bar a slightly eerie ambience the owner probably thinks is romantic—but it just makes me nauseated. There's a stage off to the right where a live band is starting to tune their instruments, and the bar off to the left seats individuals whose faces I've seen around town—about half of them I could probably name, and another quarter I know personally. Even the two waitresses, the only two people who work in this restaurant besides the two bartenders and the two chefs in the back of the kitchen, are people who went to school with me.

"Welcome back to the Aqueduct," Mya says. "Fourth largest employer in town. Did you know Marcus still owns it?"

"You're joking."

She shakes her head and sits at one of the tables, not waiting for a hostess or anyone to come over and seat us. "Nope. Somehow this place has stayed in his family and kept afloat."

When Mya and I were in high school, this place was owned by Marcus Wolf, a man who liked to give back to the community more than anybody I've ever known. He always came to our high school and middle school to do show-and-tell, we went on his fisherman's boat at least three times a year for field trips, and he was the guy who would step in to support you (or reprimand you) like a surrogate father if something bad happened with your parents. The best way to describe Marcus Wolf is that if my mom is the matriarch of Harper's Cove, then Marcus is the patriarch.

In another life, they might have been a small-town power couple. Like Brad and Angelina.

Just that image makes me wanna barf.

Amelia, a girl in my class who was aboard the astrology train before it became a hot thing in the media, saunters over to our table. She loudly pops her gum, a violet bubble about half the size of her face obscuring my ability to see her for just a moment.

"Hey, Mya," she says, glancing over at me with what I think is slight surprise. "Xavier."

"Amelia," I say. "How goes it?"

She shrugs; no more explanation than that. "You two here for the band?"

"And for your amazing food," Mya grins. *Amazing* isn't the word I'd use, but Mya has always been a world-class politician when it comes to working people. "What do you all have on tap?"

Amelia lists off the drinks as if she is reciting an order back to a customer in a drive-through on the interstate at 2:00 a.m. Mya narrows her eyes, only for a moment.

"I'll have the Wagner," she says, turning to me.

"Rivers and Valleys," I reply. "The hard cider?" There's barely any alcohol in that.

"Coming right up," Amelia mutters before turning on her heels.

Mya rolls her eyes when Amelia's gone and her back is turned. "Can you believe her?"

I arch my brow in response.

Mya waves her hand. "Come on. Her attitude."

"I mean, I'd have the same attitude if I had to work here," I admit.

There's nothing wrong with the Aqueduct. It's a job, and so many people don't have those. But I understand what Amelia's body language is saying, even if her voice says the opposite.

She, too, sees Harper's Cove as a prison.

"Look, I'm sure this isn't, like, some big flashy bar in Chicago or anything, but it's not bad," Mya replies, almost defensively.

"No, I agree. And I'm not saying it should be."

"But you're saying this isn't good enough for you."

Mya doesn't frame it like a question; she frames it like a statement. I've known her long enough that I know exactly where this is going. I'm going to back myself into a verbal corner that I'm not gonna be able to talk my way out of, Mya's going to give me the silent treatment, and the night is going to be ruined. The logical answer would be to avoid this whole conversation, just agree with her, and move on. Because our different views about Harper's Cove aren't worth ruining the night—or our friendship—over.

But isn't friendship about being honest with each other? It doesn't matter if we disagree, as long as we treat each other civilly. And if it's really a friendship, shouldn't I be able to say what I'm thinking?

I hesitate, deciding how I'm going to phrase this carefully.

"I'm just saying I can understand wanting to be somewhere else and ending up here," I say slowly, carefully picking each word. "It doesn't make this place any less valuable to you, or others, just because she wants to be somewhere else."

"She should be happy she has a job," Mya replies. "You know the unemployment rate—"

"In the country is high, I know," I interject.

"Of course you'd know that. You and your statistics."

"They've always been a comfort to me, you know this." You can rely on statistics, not people. Case in point, only 25 percent of first loves are still together.

I should have known Bradley and I wouldn't be an outlier.

"I'm going to ignore that. But Amelia is allowed to have her opinions. She can be happy she has this job and still wish for more. I mean, few people think they are going to be working at a small-town bar when they graduate. I don't think that's what she wanted for herself. She wanted to be a painter, right?"

Mya opens her mouth, and I can tell she's ready to fight. She's always loved Harper's Cove, more than most people I know, and has no desire to leave. Besides going to college in Portland and living at home and commuting, she hasn't seen the rest of the East Coast, let alone the rest of the world or the country, I don't think. Harper's Cove has everything she's ever wanted, so there's no reason for her to leave, and she can't understand, no matter how much I try to explain it, why anyone else would want more.

Amelia returns with our drinks. Mya makes quick work ordering us some french fries. When she's done, Mya takes a long sip of her beverage and finally speaks.

"You know what?" she says. "I don't want to fight tonight."

"Neither do I."

"I have my best friend here, good food, good drinks, and live music to dance to. We can deal with our ideological differences another day."

"And by *another day* you mean . . . ?"

"Never," she says.

Grinning, I raise my glass of cider to her, clinking it with her beer before taking a drink. Mya's like a flash fire; she burns fast and bright and then simmers down. You just have to ride out the wave and hope you don't get burned.

"You were adamant about coming here," I say, noticing more members of the band beginning to flood the stage. "Is the live music that good?"

"Better than good."

"Like, on a scale from Ariana to Taylor Swift?"

"Janelle Monáe meets H.E.R."

My eyebrows raise. "In Harper's Cove? Black population you and me?"

"And don't forget your parents and Derek," she corrects. "But Harper's Cove is growing. We're *anti*-gentrifying, whatever the term for that is."

"*Diversifying* is what you're looking for. But, seriously? Janelle? H.E.R? We were supposed to see Janelle in concert, remember?"

"Do not remind me!" she wails, groaning and putting her forehead against the table. "I almost emancipated myself from my parents that night!"

"You shouldn't have snuck out to see Derek the night before," I remind her, muttering around the rim of my cider.

"The power of love cannot be stopped, Xavier."

"But parents can stop you from seeing your favorite artist."

"Fuck you."

"Fuck you, too." I wink. "But, my point is, that combo is high praise coming from you."

She grins confidently. "I know how to pick good music."

"And good people. I mean, you're friends with me."

Mya opens her mouth to refute that statement, but luckily for both her and me, the drummer of the band clicks his drumsticks together twice. The mix between live music and dance music is something I would expect in New York's Central Park or Prospect Park, so it's refreshing to see it here in Harper's Cove. It almost, almost makes me relax and settle into the moment.

That's until a familiar face takes the stage.

"Hello," the deep baritone says. "I'm Logan O'Hare, but many of you know me as the owner of the Wharf right down the street. But right now, I'm just the lead singer of Stevie Tricks, named after my good friend here Stevie on drums, who came up with the idea of the band. So, let's all have a good time, enjoy the booze, the food, and most importantly, the music."

I quickly snap my gaze to Mya, who's sipping her drink inconspicuously, trying to avoid my eyes.

"Since when did Janelle and H.E.R. combine and morph into a WHITE MAN, Mya?"

"Okay, but if I had told you Logan was playing, would you have come?"

"Of course not!"

"For the record, the music is good," she claims.

Right now, all I want to do is throw those french fries at her and hope to God Logan doesn't—

"Hey, heads up," Mya mutters. "Your boss is looking at us."

—see me.

CHAPTER
SIXTEEN

SOMETIMES I HAVE TO remember that I am a goddamn adult.

And not just an adult, I'm an adult with a master's degree. I survived some of the toughest cities in the world, cities quintessential to the expression "If you can survive here, then you can survive anywhere." Sure, I may be living at home with my parents in a town that doesn't know the definition of struggle, but that doesn't change the things that I've been through. The things I've seen. The things I've overcome.

I, Xavier Reynolds, am a bad bitch.

So why the hell am I sitting here acting like I'm doing something wrong, just because I'm at a bar?

I've been working at the Wharf for about two weeks now, and this is one of the two free nights I have off. The Wharf is open on Monday, as most restaurants are, and the staff gets one day off a week—every single one of us. It's not like I'm playing hooky; it's not like I'm avoiding my work responsibilities. I'm having fun with my best friend. Normal people do that.

So what if Logan is here?

So what if he's singing an amazing cover of "Ocean Avenue" and hitting all the right notes?

So what if the way his raspy voice cracks intentionally makes it sound like he's singing directly in my ear?

And absolutely so what if he keeps looking at me, enough so that Mya has her eyes practically glued to me instead of the stage?

"Stop looking at me," I mutter. Some people, three songs deep, have already moved to the dance floor. If you can call it dancing. It's mostly just white people thrashing about.

"I'm not looking at you, I'm staring at you."

"You know that's the same thing, right?"

"*You know that's not the same thing, right?*" she mocks. "Are you going to play dumb?"

"Yes."

I'm mostly just being stubborn, I know this. But I don't have the patience for Mya right now. She's going to start probing, because that's what she does, and it's what a best friend does for their other friend. It's a reasonable question anyway—why *is* Logan staring at me during the majority of his songs?

Maybe I can just chalk it up to the fact that he finds comfort in looking at me? Kind of like when you're doing a performance in high school and you only look at your parents and ignore the rest of the crowd? Logan never has come off as a person who is nervous. I mean, he went into the business of owning a restaurant, and that's not for someone who doesn't have a little bit of hubris, right?

Regardless of the reason, I can't ignore the fact that in the bar with the lights down low and the bodies moving to the music, sometimes offbeat but in an almost hypnotic way, combined with the lights focused on Logan and his band, I can't help but look back at him. I can't help but get lost in his eyes.

The music comes to an end, and the crowd cheers. Logan takes a bow, introducing the rest of his bandmates, giving them the credit they deserve.

"We'll be back in fifteen minutes, folks, just need a quick water break."

"And by water, we mean booze," says a guy whose name I just learned is Stevie, the drummer.

The crowd laughs at the joke, and a low hum of meaningless conversation, a pleasant and familiar white noise, falls over me.

"Okay," Mya says. "So, you know now you obviously have to go up and talk to him, right?"

"I don't have to do anything like that." And I won't.

"You obviously do! No one looks at someone that way, during a cover of 'A Thousand Miles,' who doesn't want to—"

"He's my boss, Mya."

She rolls her eyes. "Yeah, only for the next few weeks. Only until you get enough cash. Why not try to have a little fun while you're here?"

"Sounds like you're trying to live vicariously through me."

"Me and every other woman in town. And some men," she mutters, already finishing her second drink fifteen minutes in. "Just go over and talk to him. Or I'll talk to him for you."

"That doesn't sound like the worst—"

Mya gives me that look that tells me I don't have a choice in the matter. Sighing, I wave it off.

"Five minutes," I say.

"And get me another drink while you're over there!"

I have half a mind to bark back something at Mya, but instead, I force my legs to keep walking. Politics is something you learn when you're in business school. You never know who's gonna be your boss, or who might run a company you wanna work for, or who might have a connection that you need in the future. Some people . . . white men . . . like to assume they're always gonna be top of the food chain. For people like me, and women who are minorities, I understand that you have to play the game more carefully if you want to succeed. There's less space at the top for people like us.

I'm using the same logic right now. Logan is my boss, so it would be awkward if we both went to work tomorrow and I was like, *I didn't see you there at the bar*, when it's so obvious we saw each other multiple times. Besides, Logan's been pretty nice to me at work, ever since Portland and the momentary fake-dating situation. One Saturday night shift, Logan brought us all coffee and snuck a latte for me into the mix. And not just any latte. A caramel one. My favorite flavor.

A flavor I offhandedly mentioned to him when hungover.

When I tried to say something, he just made a *shush* motion and winked at me. And of course, Kyle and Angelica. They didn't say anything, but the grin on Kyle's face that made his eyes crinkle, and the way Angelica wouldn't stop staring at me? I knew they knew.

Another way to know my relationship with Logan has changed? I don't think, when I started, I would have asked him for help or admitted I didn't know something; that rule went out the window last week.

"Can you show me that technique you did before? With the onions and the soup?"

"The lozenge cut?" he asked, pulling his glasses off and looking up from the papers he quickly pushed into the drawer.

I didn't think much of it, especially when Logan looks so good with the stubble and the dark glasses on, accenting his face.

"Yeah, that."

"I'd be happy to," he said without hesitation. Standing up, he walked into the kitchen, grabbing an apron and slipping it on.

"You mind?" he asked, gesturing to the strands around his waist.

"I'd be happy to," I replied teasingly, tying him.

Once done, I stood next to him. Logan grabbed one of the knives and twirled it in his hand. "Okay, do you know how to do a baton or bâtonnet chop?"

I shook my head.

"Do you know how to julienne?"

I nodded.

"Show me."

Grabbing one of the knives, I pulled a stack of carrots from his side of the chopping board over to mine. I cut them into roughly three-inch pieces, trimmed the rounded sides of each piece to create a rectangle shape, and then intended to cut each rectangle lengthwise into one-eighth-inch slices, but Logan grabbed my hand.

"Instead of cutting them into eighths, we're going to cut them into quarter-inch pieces," he said.

"Easy enough," I said, following through with the instruction.

"Now . . . do you mind?" he asked, gesturing toward me. When I shook my head, he moved behind me, his chest flush with my back. I could feel the pulsing of his heart, the strength of his body against me, the fullness of his crotch . . .

"We're going to take the knife and cut at a forty-five-degree angle," he muttered against my ear. He guided my hand, slice after slice, until about half of the stack was done. "Got it?"

The point is, Logan and I have changed ever since Portland.

It happened slowly, and went without notice until now. And I'm not really sure I mind it.

So maybe, just maybe, Mya is right. Maybe I should lean into this feeling . . . whatever this warm feeling is. Maybe it's the one cider I had. Maybe it's something else. Maybe it doesn't really matter and I shouldn't read into it, I should just act.

I push my way through the crowd, until I find myself at the front. This is one of maybe two bars in Harper's Cove that has decent drinks, or so Mya told me when she was selling me on our night out. But the crowd feels more like the type of crowd I'd find in a New York bar.

"What can I get for you—oh, hey!" the bartender says when he notices me. "Xavier, right?"

I hate this feeling. It's partially what I hate so much about coming home. For anyone who didn't leave Harper's Cove, you just memorize everyone in your life because you see them almost every day. I am an anomaly. I left and came back, which makes me somehow interesting because Harper's Cove isn't known for its transient population.

Which leads to situations like this. Me standing here trying to figure out who this person is who swears they know me. I can just be honest; tell them I don't remember them. Not everyone takes that well. It's like when a celebrity meets someone at a meet and greet, and that fan says, *I was at your last concert.*

Like there's any way in hell for a celebrity to know every person at their concert.

No, I'm not saying I'm a celebrity. I'm not saying I'm some famous person to discuss, whom they should be honored to know. But I kind of feel the same way. The pressure to try to remember who the person is and not let down their expectations swallows me whole.

"Oliver, remember?" he says. "We were in AP—"

"AP Bio together, yes," I finish for him. Lucky guess. I only had two AP classes, and I remember everyone from my APUSH class. I remember them because I assumed all of us would go on to do things with our lives, and it was important to commit everything to memory. I think maybe, just maybe, three out of fourteen of us actually left Harper's Cove—and both of them, besides me, returned.

I guess I'm following a pattern. Some sort of Harper's Cove high-achiever curse.

"Right!" he says, adjusting his backward baseball cap. It's worn and looks like it's seen better days, along with the rest of his clothes. Oliver just seems like the type of guy who values everything. Frugal, doesn't live off much because he doesn't need much. Probably the type of guy who takes extra shifts here because he likes talking to people.

He fits perfectly in Harper's Cove.

"How have you been?" I ask.

"Great, seriously. Married Shelby a few years back."

"Congrats!" *Who?*

"Thanks, man. She's expecting a little one. Twins, actually."

"Boys or girls?"

"We're keeping it a secret, you know? Want to be surprised when they come."

"Isn't having twins surprise enough?"

Oliver lets a handsome smile spread over his features. "Right you are. But enough about me. What about you? What—"

Nope. We're not going down that rabbit hole.

In Oliver's favor, he isn't Stacey Lee. Not there's anything wrong with her, I honestly do appreciate how honest and unabashedly herself she is. In a sense, he and Stacey Lee are the same, in that what you see is what you get. There's no doubt in my mind that he wouldn't judge me if I tell him the real reason why I'm here. In fact, he'd probably be in support of it. Very few people have as much calming energy as this guy has, and he doesn't even have the quintessential blond hair that most humble guys who fit that trope do. He's just an average-sized guy, with a round face, round eyes, and a bright smile. He's not threatening. He's a good person.

He's Harper's Cove to a tee. And I don't want that. I don't want the sympathy. I don't want to be looked at like someone who needs that to be the glue that'll help me piece myself back together. You know what will help me move on? Going to Berlin and completing the Carey Foundation Fellowship. That's what I have to keep my eyes on—the goal.

There's no easy way to weasel my way out of his conversation, so I just take the most direct route. Turn myself into a battering ram and charge straight through.

"Sorry, I don't mean to cut this short, but someone's waiting on me. Do you think you can get me a Wagner and a Rivers and Valleys?"

He blinks once and pauses. A flicker of hurt passes over his face. "Yeah, man, of course."

Oliver turns without another word, going to get the drinks. A twinge of regret passes through me, but I push it down. I shouldn't feel bad for asserting myself. I didn't want to have this conversation, and he did. I don't owe him anything. I did the right thing. I—

"Well, that was mean of you."

Of course, *he* has an opinion.

I turn my head to the side, seeing Logan move into the open space next to me. He's nursing a beer in his right hand, and half of what looks like some sort of turkey sub in his right.

"I—"

"If you're about to say you were asserting yourself, or that Oliver is supposed to serve you not talk to you, I'm going to say point-blank you sound like an ass. So, do you want to try again?"

"I wasn't going to say any of that. I was going to say Mya is waiting for me, and I don't want to keep her waiting. Do you think that lowly of me?"

Logan doesn't speak at first, just stares at me before a slow grin spreads over his face. "Fair." He takes a chomp of his sub, consuming about a third of it in one bite. "I'm sorry."

In the moment that neither of us are speaking, while waiting for Oliver to return with my drinks so I can leave, I take a moment to look, *really* look, at Logan. I don't think I've seen Logan like this.

His shoulders are relaxed, his posture less rigid. He has a constant light smile on his face and a glow in his cheeks. His eyes aren't darting back and forth, looking for something to focus on, like they are at the Wharf. They move lazily, as if he's enjoying every moment and doesn't need to focus on any specific thing. His black-and-gray hair is pushed back, hidden under a red beanie, but strands extend under it, like wisps of smoke seeping out from under a closed door.

"Forgiven and forgotten. And if it matters . . . never mind."

"What?"

"It doesn't matter."

"Of course it matters," he scoffs. "Look, I don't know what number your ex Brady—"

"Bradley."

"Doesn't matter. I don't know what number Bradley pulled on you, but what you say and think? It matters, I want you to know that. Especially if it's an honest, from-the-heart statement, not some sarcastic quip. I know there's more to you than that, Xavier. I saw that when we were in Portland. That side? That's the real you. *That's* what matters."

Warmth pools in my stomach as Logan rambles. I wiggle my toes in my boots just to remind myself this isn't a dream. I can feel my cheeks turning warm, but my dark skin makes that impossible to see; thank God.

"You're drunk, aren't you?" I brush off.

"Oh, absolutely," he smirks. "But that doesn't make what I said any less true. Now, what were you going to say?"

"And if I don't want to say it anymore?"

Logan shrugs, moving a step closer, pushing me against the counter and causing my back to press into it. He closes in, the smell of his cologne mixing with the scent of beer and sweat, creating something almost musky but intoxicating at the same time.

"Well," he whispers as he leans in, breath skimming my lips. "I'm pretty sure I can think of some ways to get it out of you."

"Oh yeah?"

"Oh, definitely."

"You sure are confident," I whisper back, leaning forward so our lips are barely a half inch apart. "Or is it arrogant? I'm not sure."

"Fine line between them, I'd say. Should I prove you wrong?"

Before I can say anything, he pushes forward, slotting his leg between mine, pushing his hips against my own. I let out a gasp that's swallowed by the live-wire hum of the bar as he slowly and intensely grinds our crotches together, the whole time, eyes locked with me.

"Now," he almost purrs. "Are you going to tell me what you were going to say, or do I have to do more?"

Part of me, a fairly fucking large part of me, if I'm being honest, wants him to do more, wants him to keep going, keep grinding. Another part wants us to go into the nearest seedy bathroom, for him to push my pants down around my ankles, use his spit as lube, and bury his cock inside of me.

But telling him what I was going to say is probably better. And smarter.

"I like this version of you," I suddenly say. "This . . . relaxed version."

He keeps his eyes locked on me, like he's searching for some ounce of a lie he can pick apart until the truth comes to light.

"I'm always relaxed." Another beat. "More so when I'm around you, I've noticed."

My turn to snort. "You don't seriously expect me to believe that, do you? I've seen how you act in the kitchen."

Logan pauses, still well within my personal space. He reaches for one of the Wagners and another Rivers & Valleys that have appeared, and takes a long swig of it, holding the rim of the glass with his two fingers.

"I'm not going to apologize for running a tight ship in the kitchen," he says honestly. "And I meant what I said in Portland. You have the talent to be a great chef. I can see it in the way you study food. How you go through the motions in the kitchen. You might think having an MBA and being some big-shot Fortune 500 CEO is your path, but people can have more than one path, Xavier."

"And you think mine is in the kitchen?"

"I think you should give yourself the chance to find out."

I'm not buying Logan's idealism. Being a restaurant owner, or even working in a restaurant, is his dream, not mine.

"We have very different ideas of what a dream career is."

"How do you know if you haven't tried?"

"You can know you don't want something without having tried it before," I scoff. "I know I don't like fisting, and I haven't tried that."

"Does the reverse apply?" he asks. "Know you'll like something even if you haven't tried it?"

"Of course, it—"

"So it's reasonable for me to assume you might like kissing me? Even though we haven't done that before?"

Before I can answer, Stevie clears his throat in the mic, tapping it with his finger, making the room echo with feedback. Logan glances over his shoulder; the rest of Stevie Tricks is onstage, waiting for him.

And most of the bar is looking at us. And how close Logan and I both are.

Logan clears his throat and pulls back, winking at me as he walks away, a silent way of saying, *Think about it.*

Joke's on him; it's the only thing I'm thinking about.

CHAPTER
SEVENTEEN

WHEN LOGAN RETURNS TO his band to play, I find my way back to Mya, who is looking at me with large eyes, making an O around the rim of the bottle.

"I just have one question."

"Don't," I warn.

"What was *that*?"

"Please don't make a thing out of this," I groan. "It was just some . . ."

"Erotic flirting?" she asks. "People were staring at you for at least a minute and neither of you noticed."

"Harmless flirting," I correct.

"Bullshit. That was intense flirting. WMD-level flirting. With your boss, I might add," she says. She doesn't say it in the sort of way that comes off as a judgment, more of a verbal nudging with her proverbial elbow. There's a twinkle in her eyes, too, that makes the room light up. She's never going to let me live this down.

"First of all, is that something you all say now? WMD this,

WMD that? Second time I've heard it since being here. Second of all, I just prep the vegetables. And it's a short-term thing."

"But he's in charge of you."

"I don't like where this is going."

She shrugs. "Listen, I'm not going to tell you that you shouldn't do this. That's not my job as a friend. All I'm going to say is go with God, good luck, get you some, and if you need me, I'm going to be over here nursing this drink."

Mya is no help. I think, deep in my mind, I was hoping she would tell me not to do this. That this is a bad idea. That I'm making a huge mistake. But in fact, she does the complete opposite. She wants to live vicariously through me.

"Is married life so boring that you—"

"Oh my God, it's the worst," she corrects. "I love Derek deeply. But our life is predictable and boring. He goes to work, he comes home, we have dinner, we talk a bit, maybe you know . . ." She shimmies her hips at the standing table.

"You love it," I mutter back.

"I'm going to plead the Fifth on that one."

She can pretend all she wants that this life she's created for herself is boring, but I remember when we were in high school, when her and Derek broke up for three weeks, how . . . gray she was. As if a mood could have a color.

"You're not a lawyer," I say.

"But I could be. I'd make a great defense attorney."

"That you would." I raise my glass to her in appreciation. No one, and I mean no one, is smarter than my friend Mya.

"Flattery is absolutely the way into my heart, so thank you, but right now we're focused on you," she says, nodding behind me toward Logan. I follow her sight, seeing another waitress bringing the Stevie Tricks drinks. One of them takes the drinks, and the folded piece of paper in her hand. His eyes scan it, and he leans over, tapping Logan's shoulder. Logan turns his attention to the man, reads the note, and smiles a wolfish grin.

"Well, well, well," he says into the microphone. "Seems we have a request. From an unknown admirer: 'Do you and Stevie Tricks know any sea chanteys?'"

Logan looks around at the band. "Well, do we, boys?"

"Damn straight we do!" Stevie says, playing a string of rapid notes on his drums, sweat dripping off his face and bouncing on the instruments. He starts a steady beat that goes for eight counts, before the guitarist jumps in, adding to it. The shortest of the men, who plays a tambourine, adds, making a melody of three instruments, while all three men start tapping their feet in an almost Nordic battle cry that echoes off the walls.

Logan runs his right hand through his sweaty hair, slicking it back. He leans in close to the microphone, almost making out with it. His voice cuts through the air, clear and deep, commanding attention.

There once was a ship that put to sea
And the name of that ship was the Billy o' Tea
The winds blew hard, her bow dipped down
Blow, me bully boys, blow!

The rest of the band jumps in on the chorus.

Soon may the Wellerman come
To bring us sugar and tea and rum
One day, when the tonguin' is done
We'll take our leave and go.

"I hate it here," I mutter.

Hate is a strong word. I hate the warm fuzzy feeling that's starting to boil and bubble in my chest as the song ripples through the Aqueduct. I hate how much my body wants to join in as the rest of the town, even Mya, starts tapping their feet and singing along.

"Did I miss the memo when we learned this?" I ask her.

"It's catchy!"

"It's cringey," I correct.

"That's not the word I'd go with but sure, yeah, it is. But this is also home. It's your home. And it has Logan O'Hare," she says, grabbing my shoulders, forcing me to turn and look at him. "I mean, look at him."

Logan is the loudest member of the group. Not in voice, but in energy. He's singing his heart out, leaving it out on the stage. One arm is over his guitarist's shoulder as he sings joyously along with him. If what I saw before at the bar was Logan at a Relaxation Level 5, this is at a Relaxation Level 10.

"How can you not find that adorable?" she asks.

I'm not going to answer her. Because honestly? It's fucking hot. It's really, really fucking hot. But I don't need to give her another bit of ammunition. Mya would be the first person, after my parents, who would go into a full-court press campaign to get me to stay if I told her I was considering it.

And let me be clear, I'm absolutely not considering staying. But there's a small—a very small—part of me that could see why it might be a good idea.

Maybe.

Possibly.

In some future life.

"Oh, fuck," I mutter.

"Hm?" Mya asks, looking over at me. "You okay?"

I don't answer her at first. I'm not sure I can. Mya's curiosity turns into concern.

"Did you drink too much alcohol?"

I shake my head.

"Do you need me to take you home?"

I shake my head again.

"I think I'm falling for Logan."

Mya's concern morphs into a smile that lights up her beautiful, dark-skinned face.

"Oh, Xavier," she says, and wraps her arms around me. She doesn't say anything else, simply holding me.

Like with most sea chanteys, the song doesn't end when the lyrics are over. Logan moves from the microphone, and the guitarist takes off, riffing and adding his own lyrics, while keeping the beat. With the added percussion of everyone in the bar tapping their feet, even some of the women and men vocalizing, it's like a whole concert, with people dancing, too.

Logan moves from the stage, coming down with his drink. One of the women grins and dances around him. He grabs her hand, twirling her, but only once, before weaving through the crowd.

Heading directly toward me.

Once he's standing there, he extends his hand with a smile. "Dance with me?"

"I—"

Mya nudges me firmly this time.

"Do it," she urges, smiling and turning to Logan. "He'd love to."

"I would?"

"He would," she says, wiggling her way between me and Logan, standing with her back to him, looking me directly in the eyes. "Have a little fun. Compromising your morals one time isn't going to rain down judgment from the heavens above and ruin your chances of being a successful hotshot in the business world. I promise."

"That's not what I was thinking at all."

Maybe it was a little bit. Maybe God actually is some wrathful god, like my parents' Baptist church likes to remind us; God is going to rain hellfire—or, more accurately, small-town eternity—on me for dancing with my boss.

Or maybe I'll actually like it, and the idea of going to Berlin and fulfilling my true purpose in life, the only thing I've ever wanted to do, will become a back-burner thought. And I can't afford that.

I stare at Logan's hand. I see the calluses from working in the restaurant, the faded burns, and the nicks he's gotten from mishandling a knife. His hand is rough, but I know the roughness will feel like a comfort in my own, softer hand.

But for some reason I can't help but think about the movie *The Princess and the Frog*. As if I'm making a deal with the Shadow Man.

"Come on." He grins. "One dance. That's it. You can even pick the song they play."

Something the Shadow Man would say.

"Any song?" I ask.

"Any song."

"Even if I said, 'Freak Nasty' by Megan Thee Stallion?"

Logan opens his mouth but quickly shuts it.

"Didn't think so." I grin. Though it's funny to imagine this alt-rock cover band trying to play and sing along with Megan Thee Stallion.

Actually, the more I think about it . . . that's a horrible idea. But one song comes to mind.

"Do you all know 'Mr. Brightside'?"

Logan's eyes brighten up like a child who just got a Captain Planet T-shirt for Christmas—that child was me, by the way.

"Oh, what self-respecting kid of the early 2000s doesn't know that song?"

"Sorry, early 2000s?" I ask. "If you're thirty-nine, and it's . . ."

"Nope," Logan says, putting his hand over my mouth. "We're not rehashing that conversation. David! Stevie!"

The men stop playing the chantey that has gone on for nearly a dozen stanzas now.

"You all know 'Mr. Brightside'?" he asks

"Do we know 'Mr. Brightside'?" Stevie laughs. "What self-respecting musician doesn't?"

"Well, then you have your orders!" he says, twirling his hand. "Get to playing!"

"I'll take lead vocals," David says. "Want us to just riff afterward? Or are you busy . . . ?"

While Logan is bantering with his band, he moves to stand next to me, wrapping his arm around my waist and holding me close. Not possessively, almost protectively. And I don't mind it, not one fucking bit.

"I think we'll see what happens," he says. "I trust you all. Don't ruin our brand."

"We'd never do that, boss," Clyde, a man with a handlebar mustache, promises, giving a two-finger salute. "Scout's honor."

"That's what scares me," Logan mutters. The group downs the beers offered to them before chatting among them about who is going to take what part.

And through it all, Logan still has his arm around my waist, like we're posing for some photo that'll immortalize our relationship. As if knowing what I was wondering, he leans down, whispering close to my ear, his hot breath practically kissing my ear shell.

"Are you going to be a good boy if I take my hand back?"

The words send a shiver down my spine, no matter how much I try to not give him that pleasure. The way his voice sounds like grinding gravel, rough but smooth at the same time . . . I can't help it. Any person who has a sex drive would feel the same pulsing across their body that I do. I'm not above admitting that Logan absolutely has that effect on people—and I am a person, so . . .

That's the type of mathematical proof we should review in eleventh-grade math class.

"Well," Logan whispers, quieter, huskier. "What's the answer, Xavier?"

I nod; slowly, he pulls his hand away and slides it down my arm to give my right hand a squeeze.

"Then let's go, Xavier, into the unknown." He smiles, tugging me onto the dance floor with him. And for once, maybe for the first time in a really long time, I don't question if this is right or wrong, and I just . . . you know . . . do it.

CHAPTER
EIGHTEEN

'M NOT GOING TO sit here and say that Logan is the best dancer in the world, because I learned at an early age that lying to make someone else feel better about themselves does nothing for anyone.

Logan is the epitome of a man who dances on the one and the three, as if the two and the four are some foreign countries his passport doesn't give him permission to enter. I'll admit, dancing to "Mr. Brightside" isn't the easiest thing on the planet. Generally, just a lot of thrashing around. Which, I mean, I don't blame him. Most people are dancing like that. That's how most people dance to "Mr. Brightside."

But when Logan does it? Oof. But, like, cute oof.

"Mr. Brightside" morphs into "The Great Escape" by Boys Like Girls. "The Great Escape" shifts into "Smells like Teen Spirit," which evolves into "I Write Sins Not Tragedies." We're just going through the decades, it seems. Even Mya finds a group of girls to dance with a little way away from me, doing a visual check-in that friends do with one another. No words needed, just secret visual cues and silent conversations to make sure we're both okay.

Or at least, we both thought they were secret.

"If you wanna go with her, you can," Logan says, five songs in. The Aqueduct isn't the most . . . ventilated place, and a layer of sweat makes his face shimmer, strands of black hair sticking to his forehead. "I won't be mad."

I down a sip of the drink I brought with me to the dance floor. "You saw that, huh?"

"I have a daughter, Xavier. I taught her those cues."

A wave of embarrassment pulses through me, only for a moment. It's not like I'm not enjoying myself, and I don't want him to think that. In fact, it's probably the opposite. It's nice to not have to think, to be able to shut my brain off and move to the music. Bonus points because I'm doing it with a hot-as-fuck guy.

"You didn't answer me," he reminds me. "Do you need to go? Or more importantly, do you want to go?"

This could be my out. All I have to say is yes, turn around, and head over to Mya. She won't question me—she's married after all—and she's always looking for an out to keep her from being tempted and crossing any lines. I can bid farewell and that's that. *Until tomorrow, handsome boss with salt-and-pepper hair and an award-winning smile!*

"No," I say, glancing over at Mya to convey to her I'm good. "I'm going to stay a bit."

Mya nods to me, giving me a discreet—or a not so discreet—thumbs-up. I turn back to Logan just in time to see a grin on his face that lights up his eyes.

"Good," he says.

"Good?"

"I mean"—he shrugs, wiping his hair out of his face—"good that you feel comfortable around me."

"Not good that I'm staying and spending time with you?"

He shakes his head.

"Ah." A beat. "So, you don't care if I stay or go?"

"That's not what I said."

"Pretty sure it's not *not* what you said either."

"Oh my God," he groans. "You're really going to nitpick every word I say, aren't you?"

I shrug. "It's a gift."

"It's annoying."

"Like good annoying or bad annoying?"

"Is there such a thing?"

"Of course," I say. "Good annoying is, like, a best friend who ribs you just enough to get your blood pumping. Bad annoying is like a splinter in your finger you can't get out."

"You're more like a rod protruding through my chest than a splinter," he clarifies.

I put my hand over my chest. "Me? That annoying? My word, dear sir," I say with my best fake British accent. "You offend my common sensibilities. How will you ever win back my honor?"

He laughs, a deep barreling laugh that I never noticed taking over his full face. "Is that what we're doing now? British accents?"

"Just roll with it."

Rolling with it isn't exactly something Logan does. He's too uptight and always focused on being a perfectionist. I think we have that in common, and I can relate to him about that. Everything has its place, and everything has its purpose. And when those things work in concert, success happens. Logan O'Hare doesn't just roll with anything, because people like us don't succeed by just rolling with things.

I open my mouth to make some quippy—and frankly excellent—comment, when he pauses me, pulling his phone out.

"Give me a second; it's Anne," he says. Without hesitating, or even waiting for me to say, *Sure, no problem*, he turns and walks out.

I watch his backside retreat, weaving through the crowd before disappearing out of the Aqueduct. I check my phone for the first time since the night began; we've been here for almost two and a half hours already. It's pushing 10:00 p.m. A knot in my stomach turns and tightens. Nothing good comes from a text from anyone this late at night.

"Hey," Mya says, tapping my shoulder. "You scare him off already?"

I don't answer her at first; instead, I focus on how much I can see of Logan through the window. He seems to be talking rapidly, gesturing with his other hand into his phone. He's pacing up and down the length of a window that spans about half of one side of the wall. I chew on my bottom lip before turning to Mya.

"I'll be right back."

She narrows her eyes, and I can tell she doesn't believe me. "You're going home with him, aren't you? Again?"

"Mya!"

"Look," she says, throwing her hands up. "I'm not judging you. Just want the record to show—"

"I'm not going home with him."

"But if you do," she says, "you have a condom? You know my phone number? Do you know how to get a taxi? Can you walk home from—"

"Goodbye, Mya," I say. "I'll be right back. I'm just going to make sure he's okay."

In my mind, a happy boss means a happy job. If there's something going on with him, it's going to trickle into work tomorrow. Might as well do what I can to be on his good side now, and if someone cares enough to check up on him, it will probably mean that subconsciously, tomorrow, he's going to be nicer to them. This is purely self-preservation and nothing more.

At least, as I wave to the crowd and follow him, that's what I tell myself.

Because no, I'm not going home with him; that's not in the cards for me or him tonight. I don't even know if that's where this is going, but I would be remiss to not at least try to make sure he's okay. Something tells me deep inside my chest that if I don't, if I just let him go, I won't be able to live with myself.

I push the doors open, just in time to hear the tail end of his conversation.

"No problem. Nope, not at all. I'll be right there. I'm heading out now."

Logan hangs up the phone, and I don't think he sees me standing there. Without hesitation, he turns on the heel of his left foot and kicks the wall with his right. The steel-toed tip of his boot collides with the wood, splintering it and causing pieces to flake off, leaving a large gash in the side of the Aqueduct's wall.

"Shit!" he hisses. "Shit, shit, shit."

"Okay," I interject. "Let's calm down, yeah?" I ask, putting my hand on his shoulder. "I don't think you want to use all the money you got this week dealing with a legal battle because Marcus wants to sue you for breaking his bar, do you?"

Logan sighs but doesn't force me to move, doesn't stop me

from squeezing his muscular, strong, well-defined shoulders.
I've found that part of the body to be overlooked by a lot of people. A person with good, strong shoulders is usually a good person. I know that doesn't make any sense, but it makes sense to
me and my wealth of experience with guys.

Trust me.

"Marcus won't sue me," he says. "I cut his fries for him and
give him a discount. He and I are friends."

"Of course you are."

Logan doesn't even bite at the joke I practically laid out for
him to dunk on me. His eyes are focused on his phone, typing
rapidly, already turning his back to me.

"Do me a favor—can you let Marcus know I'll come by to fix
this tomorrow?" he asks, gesturing in the general direction. "I
have to go."

I don't even ask him where or why he needs to go. "Anne?"

"She punched someone at the sleepover. The mother is furi-
ous and demanding I come pick her up. If Anne punched
someone . . ."

"She had to have a good reason," I finish for him.

"Exactly." Logan fishes his keys out of his back pocket, running his hand over his face, slapping his cheeks twice. "Shit, shit,
shit. Fuck."

I can already see the wheels burning behind his head. You
don't need to be a genius to see all the reasons I'm worried. I
don't need his daughter to get into a fight with someone—we've
got no idea how badly she punched the other kid in the face. And
add to that, Logan is drunk. Which means he has to drive drunk
if he wants to go and pick her up. Which also means he's going
to appear drunk when he arrives at this woman's house, which
isn't a good look at all.

And all of that is just compounded because he's divorced. And nothing about being divorced is easy.

I do some quick mental math in my head. I only had two drinks in three hours. I danced enough to have my shirt drenched in sweat, which means I probably burned through most of that alcohol. Plus, two drinks isn't enough to get me drunk.

"I'll drive."

No hesitation, no pause, no trying to figure out how I can twist this to my advantage. It's the right thing to do. Simple.

Logan's features shift from frustration to relaxed surprise; his blue eyes widen. "You don't have to do that. I can get a taxi or something."

"You and I both know taxis take hours around here."

"I'll ask Stevie or someone to drive me."

"Stevie, who has been drinking as much as you?" I ask. "No, I got it." I extend my hand, waiting for him to put the keys in them. "We can't have you driving drunk, especially if your daughter is in the car. I've only had two hard ciders, I'll be fine, better than you."

I put emphasis on the second sentence to really hit home for Logan. There's no part of me that thinks he's a bad father—in fact, I think he's the type of father who would sell his restaurant in a heartbeat if it meant he could make his daughter happy. In this moment, his vision and his thoughts are clouded. All he's thinking about is what's going to happen in the future and how this moment will affect that. He's not seeing the forest for the trees—he's seeing the forest for the whole goddamn national park.

Recollection and understanding ripples across Logan's face. He sighs, grumbling incoherent words under this breath before tossing the keys to me.

"I'll direct you," he says, heading toward his truck in the far corner of the gravel parking lot. At first, Logan opens the door to the driver's side of his truck, before I clear my throat.

"Oh." A beat passes. "You're right. Sorry. Habit," he says, while walking around to the other side, hoisting himself in. He shifts in his seat for a moment, sinking into the worn leather. "Feels weird," he mutters.

"Was that an actual statement, or one of those *I'm drunk and muttering to myself so ignore me* moments?" I ask. Before shifting the car into drive, I send a quick text to Mya to let her know I'm helping Logan with Anne. Once pocketing my phone, I focus all my attention back on driving. I haven't driven a stick in ages.

This is going to be fun.

Would have been nice to think about that before I offered to drive, but too late now.

The truck rumbles to life and jolts for a moment, hard enough for Logan's face to slam forward. And with no seat belt on, his face—like his full-on face—slams right into the dashboard with a sickening loud thump, and a loud string of curse words that follow . . . and droplets of blood dripping down his face from his now-broken nose.

This is not at all how I thought my night would go.

CHAPTER
NINETEEN

Y OU DON'T LOOK BAD with a little red on your face."

Besides Logan giving me curt directions for where to turn, we drive mostly in silence toward the house where Anne is having her sleepover. He sits there, trying to clean up his face with the spare napkins he finds in the glove compartment, stuffing pieces of them into his nose and attempting to stem the bloodshed.

"And honestly, this is your fault," I say, babbling—which is what I do best when I'm uncomfortable.

"How in any fucking world is this"—he gestures to his face—"my fault?"

"Gays can't drive," I say without hesitation. "You should know that. It's your fault for putting me behind the wheel."

"And me not knowing that—"

"Makes all of this your fault, yes."

I don't turn to look at him, instead focusing on the road, because I know he's trying to drill a hole in the side of my head with his piercing blue eyes. Logan mutters under his breath in disapproval, flipping down the visor, light illuminating his handsome face. I see him turn left, then right, then left again, checking his face.

"It's not that bad." I try to provide some sense of solace.

"I look like I got into a bar fight, Xavier."

"Things could be worse, right? I mean, some people like that rugged look on a person."

"*Some people* being you?"

The words evaporate out of my mouth before I can even think about what else to say. It's like he stole them from me, crumpled them up, and tossed them into an incinerator. There doesn't seem to be a right way to reply to that. If I say no, I'm lying. If I say yes, I'm giving him exactly what he wants.

Luckily for both of us, he gives me an out.

"Sorry," he says, shaking his head. He takes the time to guzzle down the half-empty water in the cupholder next to him. "Still buzzed."

"You don't need to apologize," I say, also taking a moment and adding, "people under the influence seem to say things they don't mean."

That, in itself, is a lie. Drunk people speak the truth. I still feel Logan's eyes on me as I round the corner, slowing down when I see the sign for 1813.

"You don't actually think that, do you?" he asks. "After everything we just did in the bar? That wasn't some *Twilight Zone* episode I was starring in, right? You felt that chemistry, too?"

I pull the truck to a rolling stop, half within the driveway and half extended into the street. The lights in the house are on, and before the car can turn quiet, the front door is ripped open. Anne comes storming out, backpack half-unzipped, all the contents threatening to spill all over the lawn with one wrong movement. The woman whose house she's staying in stands in the doorway, arms crossed, face twisted into a look of disgust. Three other girls—I'm guessing who are also at the party—stand at the window, like they're going to watch some show.

Logan is out of the car before she can reach him. "What happened?"

"I don't want to talk about it," she says, brushing past him and slipping into the back seat of the car.

"Anne. Anne!"

No reply. Instead, Anne slams the door shut and sinks into the seat.

"Fuck," Logan sighs, running his hands over his face.

"She's still looking at us," I say, nodding my head toward the woman. She shifts her weight and purses her lips, expecting us to come up to her and talk.

I don't want to say she seems like a Karen but . . . yeah. Karen.

"Of course she does," he mutters. "Can you deal with Anne for me? Just . . . make sure she doesn't run off?"

"Of course. She's the cooler one between the two of you anyway."

"You're not going to hear any disagreements from me. How do I look?" he asks, turning to me. I open my mouth to say the truth—fucking amazing. The blood does look good on him, in a cliché romance movie sort of way. But with his stubble and sparks of gray in his hair, his well-formed, strong jaw? It all works, coming together like a perfect sculpture.

But that's not what I say.

"You look fine."

He stares at me for a moment longer, as if waiting for me to remedy my statement.

"I'll be right back."

I watch Logan's back retreat to the steps, and hear him mutter a greeting to the owner, who does not return his energy. In fact, instead, she starts yelling at him.

"You need to get your daughter under control, Logan," she barks. "I'm serious."

"Okay, hold on, Patricia," he says. "You're going to have to tell me—"

"She punched Kat, Logan. Punched her in the face."

There's no point in me staying here. Instead, I slip into the driver's side of the car.

"My dad's drunk, isn't he?"

Anne doesn't have any judgment in her voice. She sounds defeated, if anything, like a wounded animal who just got kicked.

"He had a few drinks." *Careful words, Xavier.* Careful words.

"So that means yes." Her buckle unclips, and she shifts over in her seat to press her face against the passenger's side back window. "He doesn't look drunk."

"He didn't drink that much."

"Was it a few drinks or was it that much?" she asks, though there's a level of mirth in her voice. "He and his band love to drink. Not in a bad way."

"I didn't think you meant like that," I say.

"He isn't one of those dads who has a drinking problem."

"Anne, I don't think he does."

I look in the rearview mirror, seeing her stare at me, just like her father, as if she's trying to see into my soul.

"I'm not lying to you," I promise. "I don't think your dad is an alcoholic or anything. I actually think your dad is pretty cool."

Another pause. "You promise?"

"I promise."

Like a lock that slips into place, Anne's eyes soften.

"No one he's ever dated has said he's cool."

"Well, I'm not just anyone."

She parts her lips, letting out a breath she had been holding, and settles into the back of her seat, quiet. We both watch, windows rolled up, as Logan argues with Patricia, his hands moving wildly and quickly.

"You want to tell me why you punched Kat?"

"Because Kat's a cunt," she says without hesitation.

"Anne." Even I'm surprised by how sternly I say her name. I'm not her father. I'm nobody to her, just a coworker of her father's. I don't have any right.

But Anne responds decently well. She sighs, shrugging. "Sorry. But she is annoying."

"That's not enough of a reason to punch someone. You're going to have to give me more than *she's annoying*."

"She thinks she's . . ." Anne waves her hands—again, exactly like her father. "She's just . . . she always has something to say."

"Did she say something about you?"

"No."

"About your mother?"

"No."

"About your father?"

Silence.

There it is. "Something about him being divorced?"

"No."

"Something about his job?"

"No."

"Something—"

"She said he's going to hell because he's bisexual."

It's my turn to look astonished. I even turn around and look at her with sheer surprise on my face.

"That's exactly what I said!" she explains, matching my expression. "So, I punched her."

"Okay, lesson one about dealing with bullies—you don't punch them." Especially if you're going to get caught. "And lesson two . . ."

How do I explain to her that Kat's views might not be her own? That she, as a kid, is a by-product of her parents' viewpoints and hasn't yet started to establish her own thoughts? That Kat is probably just a regurgitation of everything her parents say at the dinner table and around the house? How do I explain to her that there's a high likelihood that when she gets older, those views will change? How do I explain to her that there's also a chance that Kat is just a hateful, horrible person and Anne did the right thing?

"Look," I say finally, "I'm not going to tell you what you did was right. But I am going to say standing up for your family is important, and you did that. You stood up for someone you care for."

"That's what I'm trying—"

"But," I interrupt, "that also means you have to be prepared for the consequences. Whatever they may be. And judging by how angry Patricia is, and how angry your father is going to be . . ."

"He's going to kill me."

I shake my head. "I don't think your father is that type of person. But I do think you should be prepared for him to be very, very upset at you."

Before Anne can say anything in her defense, or add context to the situation moments ago inside the home, the door to Patricia's house slams opens a second later, loudly. Both Anne and I snap our heads to see Logan come storming out, Patricia chasing after him.

"Neither you nor your daughter are *ever* welcome back here again!"

"Good!" Logan booms, loud enough for us to hear through the car. "News flash, Patricia, you're not that great a person either!"

I know, in moments like this, what my job is. I turn the car on, ready to peel away as soon as Logan slides into the car. Patricia isn't letting up, though, walking up to the side of the car, banging her fist against the passenger side, where Anne can be seen through the tinted windows.

"If you don't watch your attitude, little girl, you—"

"Hey!" Logan yells. He keeps his distance from her, but that doesn't make him any less of a threat.

"Don't. You. EVER talk to my daughter without my permission, you understand me? You have a problem with her, that's cool. But you do not talk to her without talking to me first. She's my daughter, Patricia. Maybe you should handle yours."

"Maybe," Patricia seethes, "you should set a better example for your daughter."

"Excuse me?"

"You heard me. A daughter like her needs a positive influence. She needs a mother. And you went and divorced Michelle and now are . . . what? Wandering around town with Janice Reynolds's kid? Amber's sister's best friend's daughter saw you both in Portland. And I can smell the alcohol on your breath. What were you and—"

"Enough," I say, rolling down the window of the car. "We're not doing this. Logan, we need to take Anne home."

"So now he speaks for you, too, huh?" Patricia asks. "I didn't know you two were *that* close."

"Oh, shut the hell up, Patricia," I spit.

"You'll call me Ms. Court, young man."

"I'm not going to call you shit. I happen to think Anne is a pretty good judge of character, so if she had a reason to punch your daughter, then I'm going to bet she was in the right, especially based on what I've seen from you as a mother."

"Logan?" I repeat. "Get in."

Logan glances at me, a smirk on his lips. It's not a typical smirk. Not the one you see on someone who is trying to push your buttons, or knows they have the upper hand. It's one of someone who is proud.

Logan slides into the side of the car, and I pull out before either of us can say or do anything to get us into deeper trouble. We're about halfway down the street before one of us speaks.

"That was fucking awesome," Anne whispers.

"You," Logan says, turning to face her, "are grounded. For two weeks. One for punching Kat, and one for cursing."

"So cursing is equal in this hierarchy of punishment to punching?" Anne tries to reason. "That doesn't seem—"

"You're right. Three weeks. One for cursing, two for punching."

"Oh, come on, Logan, that seems—"

Logan gives me that arch of his brow that says, *Do you want to get punished, too?* without any words.

I open my mouth to say *maybe*, but there's a child in the car. Instead, I fall silent, listening to Anne try to barter a lesser sentence, while I drive to the only place I can think is the right place to drive: Logan's home.

Home. Logan's home. That has a nice ring to it.

CHAPTER
TWENTY

S LEEP. NOW."

Logan spares no words as soon as we get to his home. The moment we step inside, he's already blocking the way to the kitchen or living room, leaving only one path for Anne to take: upstairs.

"You were serious about that?" she asks, with mock surprise.

"As serious as a heart attack."

Her face scrunches into a frown. "That's . . . You shouldn't make jokes about myocardial infarctions, Dad. Did you know that more than eight hundred thousand people a year die from heart attacks? Mom's mom died from one."

"Yes, I was there, Anne. You're not going to outsmart your way out of this one. Go. Up. Stairs."

Anne sighs, loudly and obnoxiously, glancing over at me, as if asking for support.

I only shrug. "I'm not going down with this ship."

"Smart move," Logan says.

"Bad move," she says directly to me. "You know if you want

to win over someone's parents, you have to win over the kids first, right?"

"Anne Natalia O'Hare, are you—"

"Blackmailing him? Yes, I am," she says, giving me her full attention. "So, what is it? Are you going to side with me or . . . ?"

Am I seriously going to be shaken down by a fourteen-year-old? I look at her with surprise, but she doesn't let up. Honestly, imagine thinking if I side with her, my support will actually change Logan's mind.

"This is a family affair; I'm not going to get involved."

Anne rolls her eyes and groans, storming up the stairs. "MEN!" she says, throwing her hands in the air. "Worthless."

Logan and I both stand there, listening to her stomps turn softer and softer before she slams the door behind her, muffled sounds of what I think is Olivia Rodrigo playing through the speaker system in her room.

"I thought raising her was going to be easy," Logan mutters, rubbing his temples and shuffling into the kitchen.

"Sorry, you thought raising a girl by yourself was going to be easy?" My eyebrows raise. "In what universe did that thought cross your mind?"

"Please." He puts his hands up. "Not tonight, Xavier. Though I do appreciate your unending sass, I'm getting a hangover, my nose is broken—"

"Not my fault."

"It is your fault. And I'm going to have to tell Michelle tomorrow about this. If Patricia hasn't already."

Logan slumps in his chair with a heavy sigh. He groans, leaning his head back until he's looking directly at the ceiling, as if the answers to his problems are somehow up there.

Before I can stop myself, I mutter, "It must be hard."

"Hm?" he asks, not moving his head to look at me.

I turn to the double-sided fridge, open it, and pull out frozen peas—while normal people might have bought them, Logan seriously has them frozen in a ziplock bag, which means they are probably peas he got from his friend in Portland—and some cold water from the Brita. I push them over to him across the granite island that stands in the center of the kitchen. Logan lets out a grunt of thanks for both, hissing as he gently presses the bag of peas against his face.

"All you're juggling. Being a parent. Running a business. Trying to raise your daughter. Dealing with people in this town. Whatever else comes your way."

"Working to fulfill my dream of being a world-famous rock star," he mutters, mirth dancing in his voice.

"Yeah, sure, let's go with that," I tease back. "But it's a lot. Any person would self-destruct. And you're—"

"Self-destructing every day." Logan sits up, peas pressed to his nose, sipping the water slowly. "I always worry . . . Am I doing right by my staff, doing right by Anne? Am I screwing her up? Should she move in with her mother?" He sighs. "I'm always second-guessing myself."

"I wouldn't know that," I say honestly. "And I bet your staff wouldn't either."

"Then I'm doing my job right," he adds, taking another sip.

The music from upstairs has been turned down. It's almost midnight, judging by the clock on the stove and its flashing colors. I pour myself a glass of water, letting the crisp chill send a jolt through my body that keeps me awake. The high of the bar and the run-in with Patricia is starting to wear off.

"Do you mind if I ask you a question?"

Logan takes a moment to answer, caught in mid-sip. "I mean, you did help me get Anne out of that mess of a situation—nice job by the way—so sure. You've earned it."

"Oh, thank you, great benevolent one," I say, rolling my eyes. "Why did you and your ex-wife divorce? The full story, unfiltered, if you trust me enough to tell me."

Logan pauses, pulling the peas halfway off his head, exposing one of his eyes to me. "Not the question I thought you'd ask."

I flourish my hands in a fake bow. "I like to keep people on their toes." I half want to ask him what question he *did* think I was going to ask, but something tells me it's an answer I don't want to hear. Or maybe I do want to hear? I don't know. Strange things happen around midnight.

"But seriously, why? If you want to, tell me. If not, you don't have to."

"I'm not ashamed about the people I love, or the love that didn't work out for me," he says, voice dripping with confidence. "I'm not trying to hide my and Michelle's relationship."

A moment passes. Logan takes another sip before setting the empty glass down, as if he just guzzled three gulps of courage.

"There's nothing really exceptional about what happened," he says. "She's a musician, you know that. She got the chance to tour for her first album eight years ago. A North American tour. We made it work, having recently moved to Harper's Cove. But then the tour resulted in an LA record label wanting to sign her. Anne was doing well here. I was doing well here—I had just opened the Wharf. I didn't want to move. Anne didn't want to move. But she wanted this. Badly.

"Michelle always wanted to be a famous musician. We met in college; I told you that. But I didn't tell you we met because we were paired for an improv class. I took it as an elective, started singing to fill some prompt, and then . . . we kinda made a band together. It was seamless, and our love for music was strong."

"They say music is a language everyone can understand," I add.

"Right. That's what it was like for Michelle and me. A language we both spoke on a level that no one else could. Until we started speaking a different language and couldn't understand each other any longer."

Logan gets up from the table, walks over to the other side, his hip brushing up against me as he opens the refrigerator—looking for something else to drink, I imagine.

"Sorry," he mutters under his breath. "Need to move this island. It's in the damn way whenever you—"

"There's nothing to apologize for," I whisper back . . . and lean into the touch.

Logan doesn't move. Not at first. The cool air of the fridge chills the warmth on my cheeks, which only grows warmer the more Logan looks at me. Because it's not like he's looking at me; it's like he's looking past me. Through me.

He turns his back to me, showing off his strong back muscles and very, very nice ass. He pulls out two bottles of brightly colored liquid—one red and the other orange.

"Strawberry soda or orange soda?" He holds each one up by the neck.

"Strawberry."

"Good choice; that one's better." He pops the tops on the corner of the counter, passing the drink to me. But he doesn't move, still standing in the cramped space between the fridge and the island. And with me sitting on the stool, there's even less space. So little space I naturally part my legs . . . and he naturally stands between them.

Logan's hip once again presses against my own as he slots himself between my legs. One hand still wrapped around the neck of his bottle, the other resting on the cool countertop. He keeps his eyes locked on mine, almost like a hunter watching his prey, sipping the drink in that masculine way you only see on TV shows where some bad-boy biker drinks a cold beer.

"Can I ask you another question?" I whisper.

"You can ask me anything you want."

"About what Patricia's kid said."

"About me being bisexual?"

I nod. That's easier than talking.

"What about it? You know what bisexuality is, don't you?"

"Don't be glib."

He grins wolfishly. "Sorry, couldn't help it. What's your question?"

What is my question? My heart is pumping at a rate that makes my head feel dizzy. I should say something about his nose. Ask if he's ever been punched before for being bi. If he had any problems growing up being bi. If that's why he and Michelle really broke up. Say anything instead of being silent.

Instead, Logan speaks for me.

"I'll go first then. Three questions. One . . ." he says, leaning his lips close to my ear, whispering, "can I take you out on a date sometime?

"Two, can I kiss you?

"And three," he says, lips skimming against my neck, barely touching as his hot breath burns a brand on my skin. "Can I fuck your brains out afterward?"

The words make my brain short out and reboot all in the span of a few seconds. My mouth turns dry, no words wanting to form. I can hear my heart pumping in my ears, gushing so much blood it sounds like white-water—or rather, red-water—rapids are swirling around me. How do you respond to something like that?

I guess, honestly?

"How about we try for a date first?" I whisper.

Logan pulls back, taking another sip of his drink, now half-gone. I haven't even touched mine. A glint of playfulness dances in his eyes. "We can do that, sure. If that's what you want."

What I want is to push him down, pull his pants down, and sit on his cock, I think. But what I want and what I'm actually going to do are two different things. Thank God for Anne punching Kat, because if he had kept drinking, that's probably exactly what would have happened.

My phone vibrates in my pocket, once, twice, three times. Logan grins but doesn't move to give me enough space to pull it out.

"You going to get that?"

"Are you going to move so that I can?"

"I dunno." A third vibration. "Maybe we should send it to voicemail. Do you want to send it to voicemail?"

Yes. Absolutely yes. When the call stops, a part of me relaxes. But when it starts up again, I know exactly who it is.

Mya.

"I need to get this," I finally say, pulling myself out of the stupor I'm in. Logan nods, stepping back to give me room. I appreciate that—him respecting when I say what I need to do, not pushing any further. There's something hot about consent, even if porn and media don't want to show that side of a relationship.

Jumping off the counter, I catch the phone on its third ring during its second rotation, walking into the living room across the hall.

"It's been two hours since you told me you're leaving, and radio silence. Are you dead?" Mya says.

"If I was dead, would I be able to pick up the phone?" I reply, holding the phone between the right side of my face and my shoulder as I slide the wooden barnyard doors shut. I've always loved barnyard doors and wanted them in the home I idly design in my head when I need a break.

"Fair." I hear barking in the background, loud, constant barking. "Bitch, if you don't shut up," Mya hisses.

"Carrie the Mutt?"

"She saw a rabbit and is very upset I'm not going to let her chase it and get lost. Where are you? Do you need me to pick you up?"

"I'm fine."

"That's not nearly enough information. Did they not teach listening comprehension skills at your MBA program? If they made you spend all that money, I would at least—"

"I'm with Logan."

I whisper that part. Not like I'm ashamed. More like I don't want him to hear that I'm talking about him to my best friend.

"Oh," a pause. "*Oh*. Please, don't let me stop you from getting dicked down."

"Mya."

"No, seriously, you need to tell me how good he is once you do. This will answer all the age-old questions."

"MYA."

"Is he cut? Uncut? Never mind. You go have fun."

"I'm not—"

Mya hangs up before I can get a chance to explain to her that I'm not with Logan in that sense. But of course, I don't get to say that. I just get to put up with Mya *assuming* I'm having sex. Shaking my head, I reenter the room, coming face-to-face with Logan's smirk.

"Don't," I warn, trying not to smile.

"Don't what? Am I not allowed to smile in my own house?"

"Not like that you aren't."

"Like what?" he asks, pushing off the wall, walking toward me. "Like a debonair stud?"

I take a step back. He takes another step forward. "Like the hottest bachelor in Harper's Cove?"

Another step. "So you know people call you that."

"Of course," he purrs, moving with longer strides until he's standing right in front of me. "It's hard not to hear. People aren't that sly. But you don't say that."

"No," I say. "I don't."

"And that's what I like about you."

"Not my good looks or amazing cooking skills?"

He chuckles quietly. "Maybe that."

Slowly, Logan leans down, his face almost an inch from mine. I can smell the cologne on him, evergreen and something citrus based. I can feel the beat of his strong heart thumping through his shirt. A shirt I just want to rip off to reveal a chest I . . .

"Make sure you get home safely, Xavier," he says, pulling back. "And text me when you get home, yeah? I'm thinking our date can be next weekend?"

I stand there, being brought back to my body like I just had an out-of-body experience that treated my soul like a fucking yo-yo. I'm not saying Mya is right about me fucking Logan, but if it did happen, right there, against the wall? I wouldn't have been against it.

"Ass," I mutter, though I obviously don't mean it.

"I do have a great ass." He winks, pouring himself a tea from the pitcher in the fridge. "Hopefully you'll be able to see it one day soon. It looks great facedown and ass up."

Before my brain short-circuits, I walk out as quickly as possible with the goal of getting home and maybe dealing with my quickly growing raging hard-on in a nice cold shower. Halfway down the sidewalk, I pause.

I drove Logan's car. Which means I don't have a car to get home with.

"Shit," I hiss, calling Mya. The phone rings twice.

"You realize you don't have a car to go home in, right?" she asks. "I'm on my way."

TWENTY-ONE

M Y GOD, YOUR CLOSET is a mess."

Leave it to your best friend to be absolutely ruthless when trying to help you decide what to wear on your first date since your brutal breakup. Mya dropped everything she was doing when I finally told her Logan and I had a date.

"Like a date-date?" she asked, calling me during my break at the Wharf. Her call came through exactly thirty seconds after I stepped out the back for my twenty minutes.

"Is there a difference?"

"There's a *date*, where it's really just a prequel to fucking, and then there is a *date*-date that's all Sam Smith playing in the background like a chorus of angels."

"Did you pick Sam Smith because I'm gay?"

"Absolutely—was I wrong?"

"'Like I Can' is a bop."

"Exactly. So, which one is it?"

"Date-date."

That was all she needed to know. That Friday, after we both got off, she was at my home, waiting.

"I brought hair gel, twist ties, and some outfits just in case what you have isn't up to par."

I scrunched my nose in disapproval. "What I have is going to be completely fine."

Turns out it wasn't.

"See, where would you be without me?" she asks now, shouting loud enough so I can hear her from the bathroom. "How is that mess of a hair coming?"

I wipe the mirror free of condensation. Mya has taken over this whole Operation Make Sure Xavier Doesn't Make a Fool of Himself. She gave me strict instructions—twelve steps—written down about how to make sure my hair represents our people and doesn't conform to Anglo-Saxon beauty standards but also—her words—ensures I look fuckable.

I'm only on step five.

"Fine?"

"Fine?" she says, forcing her way into the bathroom. "That doesn't sound confident . . . Let me help."

"Mya!" I bark, barely having enough time to put my towel on. She doesn't care, forcing her way into the bathroom and closing the door behind her. "Stop acting like I haven't seen it before. Sit. I'm going to speed this up."

I know better than to fight when Mya has that look on her face. I sit down obediently, letting her fingers dance around my scalp. Applying coconut oil here, twisting there, blow-drying here.

"Did he tell you where he's taking you?" she asks. "Just, FYI, if he takes you to the Wharf, that's an automatic no."

"I don't think he's going to do that. Give him some credit."

"Look, I think you and him are going to have a great time."

"And," I remind her, "you're the one who was very pro-us doing . . . this." I flourish my hands.

"I was, but I'm also very pro-Xavier. So now this has become something, gears shift, and I'm completely on your side. You deserve the best. Better than Bradley. You haven't talked to him, have you?"

"Nothing meaningful." That's the truth. "He texted me a few days ago to see how I was doing. It was awkward considering, you know—"

"He's the asshole who kicked you out?"

"In so many words, yes."

Mya falls silent, tugging on my hair a little too hard. I know better than to show any sign of pain when a Black woman is dealing with your hair. Instead, I sit as still as I possibly can, letting her tend to my twists.

Almost as if he had a camera in my bathroom, my phone vibrates with a text from Logan.

LOGAN: I'm not sure what a city slicker like you is used to for dates, but I prefer them to be personal.

I read the message, Mya looking at it over my shoulder.

"I swear to God, if he says—"

"He's texting," I interrupt, watching the bubble. A quarter of a minute goes by before another text comes through.

LOGAN: My place? I'll make dinner.

Mya studies the phone for several seconds before walking out of the room.

"I mean, I guess," she says, returning with two different shirts: one floral and one with stripes. "Which one do you prefer?"

"You guess? The floral."

"Works with your skin tone better. Good choice." She hands it to me before walking back into the bedroom, looking for the right pants to pair with the top. "I only say *I guess* because . . . a date at home? With him cooking for you. Doesn't that seem a little . . ."

"Boring?" I ask.

"Yes, boring."

She's not wrong. But there's nothing to say I don't like boring. Maybe I need boring. How many times have I gone on dates that were extravagant expressions of class and wealth? Maybe it's time to try something else. To try something new. Something different.

"Besides," I say, walking into the bedroom with a towel still on. "I don't think Logan is the type to go all out for a date."

"And don't forget his daughter," she reminds me.

"Hey. Anne is badass. You'd love her."

"She's a menace," she argues. "Teachers hate her."

"Maybe you all just don't know what to do with her?"

Mya tosses a pair of boxer briefs at me, a matching shade as the shirt.

"I didn't even know I had these."

"You didn't; I bought them. And also, I don't tell you how to do your job, so how about you don't tell me how to do my job, hmm?"

I put my hands up in a defensive *you're right* style. I have no desire to be a teacher. She's better at that than me. Walking into the bathroom and locking the door this time, I slip on the shirt, pants, and shirt, checking myself in the mirror. Mya's silent while I finish getting ready. Brushing my teeth, putting on deodorant, and of course, lotion—because what Black person can or should go anywhere without lotion on? I check myself in the mirror before stepping out, twirling for her.

"Well?"

Mya stands a bit away to give herself the best vantage point. She spins me around slowly, clockwise and then counterclockwise. "One more thing."

Reaching into her bag, she pulls out a stainless steel necklace, with what looks like a lightning bolt as the pendant. She puts it on for me, with little protest from me—at least, what I consider little protest.

"Just to add a little flair to you," she says. "You're going out on a date with a rock star."

"He plays in an alt-rock cover band."

"Which is one step from a rock star. I'm just making sure you look the part."

At her heart, this is Mya being a good friend, I know this. Controlling? Sure. Always in my business? Sure. But she's still being a good person, and I can't fault her for that.

"So, you really support this?" I ask, narrowing my eyes. "You didn't answer me before."

Mya shrugs, shoving some of the bags from the clothes she brought in the trash. "I support anything that makes you happy. I just have one question."

"I'd expect nothing less from a teacher."

"What are you going to do when you go to Berlin?" she asks. "You've never dated someone like Logan before."

"An older man?"

"A father," she corrects. "Logan is here, Xavier. He has a business, friends, a daughter. He isn't going to uproot his life and go with you to Berlin."

"I think you're thinking too much into this."

"Am I?" she asks. "Look, I don't know what type of boys you dated when you were in Chicago, but Logan is an adult. He isn't looking for someone to flirt with and just have a good time with. He's looking for someone to settle down with. And that means he can't be having some casual sex with—"

"I'm going to stop you right there," I interrupt. "Because you're really assuming a lot about me and my—"

"I'm just going off everything you've ever told me, Xavier. I'm your best friend. I know you better than you know yourself. You've never wanted to stay here. Coming back home? That wasn't part of your plan. Whether I agree or not with your views of this place, I know you want out. You can't want out and stay with Logan. So, I'm asking you, what's your plan? Are you going to stay, or no?" Mya asks in that point-blank manner that makes it impossible to avoid the question even if I wanted to.

Mom has been asking me the same question. Just . . . not as directly. She's never been the most direct person when it comes to talking about things close to her heart. And what's more personal than family?

"Because if you're going to stay, then I say go with God."

"And if I'm not?"

Mya pauses. I can see her thinking what exact words she wants to use to express her feelings. "All I'm going to say is that you should think about what type of impression you're leaving."

"Impression?"

Mya nods. "Logan hasn't dated anyone in town for as long as I've known him. Be it because he's focused on Anne, the Wharf, or whatever; everyone has their thoughts. You're the first. There's a responsibility here when you have someone's heart in your hands."

"Again, you're assuming a lot. Maybe we're just going to fuck."

"And again, I know you better than you know yourself. That's not what's happening here."

"You were the one who told me to go through with this just a few weeks ago!"

"I'm not saying you shouldn't. I . . ."

And then it clicks.

"You were hoping he would get me to stay."

I don't say it with anger, or resentment. Mya is important to me, and we've both been ride or die for each other for years. When I say she's my other half and I'm hers, that's not a lie. I logically can understand wanting her best friend here. I get wanting to push things in motion, or hoping that something would nudge me in the direction of her thinking.

Emotionally, though, the antithesis of logically, I'm not happy about it.

"Look, it's not . . ."

"I need to get going," I say, cutting her off before she can finish.

"Xavier."

"I'm not mad, promise, Mya. Really. I just . . . I'm going to be late; we can talk about this later."

We both know we won't talk about it later.

"Stay as long as you want. Mom loves you."

"Hey," Mya says. I don't turn to look at her. I don't pause slipping on my dress shoes either. "I love you; you know that right?"

"I do," I say honestly, grabbing a sweater and slipping it on. "And I love you, too. I'll let you know how it goes. Want to make sure I leave the right impression, you know?"

I leave the house before Mya can say anything, taking the steps two at a time toward the front door before Mom or Dad can stop me. I don't need to hear any more from either of them, from any of them, about my life choices or what I'm doing: right or wrong. For once, in a very long time, I feel like I'm not doing things just to chase an angle. I'm doing them for me and for myself alone.

There's power in that.

I peel out of the driveway and head over to Logan's place. It takes less than fifteen minutes to get there, but I drive slower than I need to. My heart pulses with the fluttering of a thousand butterflies. Since my last serious relationship was with Bradley, and before then I was so focused on school and succeeding, I haven't been on a date in nearly seven years. Even if I wanted to, I'm not sure I know what to do.

"Just breathe," I tell myself, cruising into his gravel parking lot. "You're fine, and you deserve this. It's like riding a bike. Or swimming."

I don't think anyone really understands what it's like to be me. I don't mean that like I'm some great god who has weight on their shoulders, or that there's just so much pressure to be Black and gay and trying to succeed. But my parents sacrificed a lot. And it feels like, even though I have this degree, without having someone in my life, without having the fellowship, without having a job related to my degree, in some ways, I failed them. And as an extension, I failed myself. I didn't take the gift they gave me and make the most out of it. I didn't live up to my expectations. It may be, in some small way, I feel like I'm not setting the pace for other Black teens who need role models.

When I was at NYU, I was part of the Black Student Union, and Black Business Leaders. We did lessons with individuals across the state, and across the Northeast, teaching teens business strategies and mentoring them about ways to set them up for the future. Not everybody was invited to this. It was the shining achievement on my résumé. When I interviewed at the University of Chicago, I talked about how the Black Business Leader's Association helped me figure out what I wanna do with my life.

"I want to run a Fortune 500 company, but I also want to be someone teens like me can look up to," I said during my first NYU mixer.

And what am I now, just another Black guy who doesn't have a job and instead has hundreds of thousands of student loan debt? Am I just another statistic? Where was that confidence and bravado I had at NYU?

No, I'm not stupid enough to think that having a boyfriend like Logan, or even just dating Logan, will help me get back on my feet. But I need to do something. And maybe, just maybe, doing something for me that doesn't have any specific end goal in mind, something that doesn't help to build my résumé, will help me figure out where along the way I lost track of who Xavier Reynolds is.

Or maybe I'm just talking out of my ass.

CHAPTER
TWENTY-TWO

'M SORRY IT'S A mess. I'm usually more organized than this."

I'm not really sure Logan understands the word *mess*. The kitchen is immaculate, as it always has been. Different areas are set up with different parts of the meal that go from left to right and a natural path that people understand goes from appetizers to dessert. Everything is set up as a kind of make-your-own-taco bar, except make your own is replaced with different cuisines of your choice.

"I wasn't sure what type of food you liked, so . . ." He gestures widely.

Appetizers are custom-made bruschetta from Italy. Main course is gazpacho, with small servings of paella valenciana. Second main course is kabobs from the Mediterranean, and dessert looks like fixings for sundaes, with handwritten labels with different flavors in the freezer.

"Sundaes from . . . ?"

"What?"

"You have different foods from different parts of the world here. Where are sundaes from?"

"Pan-continental?"

"Are you telling me or asking me?"

"I have a feeling you know the answer to your own question, which is why you asked me."

"Me? Give you a test of your food knowledge?"

"You would absolutely do that, don't shit me."

I grin and shrug. "Pan-continental is fine. I don't think anyone can really own ice cream sundaes."

Logan is dressed more casually than me, and for a moment, a pulse of anxiety washes over me. This is a house date—homemade dinner and simple desserts. He isn't trying to impress me with his food knowledge, he's just trying to have fun, get to know me, and enjoy himself. So why did I let Mya make such a fuss about my clothing?

He's wearing a pair of jeans and black socks, very casual and comfortable in his own home, and a T-shirt instead of a button-down; the T-shirt shows me a tattoo on his collarbone. I remember seeing him when he first came over, during our ill-fated first meeting, how his wet shirt clung to his skin, and in Portland, too.

There was no tattoo then.

"That's new." I point.

Logan doesn't even ask me what I'm looking at. "Got it last week." He tugs a bit on the shirt, exposing his bare skin. It's an owl with its wings outstretched and spans from one shoulder to the other.

"Do you like it?" he asks, voice an octave lower.

"Does it matter if I like it?"

"It might. Might help me decide if I get more."

I swallow thickly, my throat suddenly dry. Logan has a way of saying small things that in normal conversation wouldn't mean anything and making them sound like they are the most important thing in the world. Like my words have power to find a way between his cool and collected armor and stab his most vulnerable parts. It's subtle, and if you blink, you'll miss it, but it's there.

My phone vibrates in my pocket. I pull it out, glancing at the screen; a message from the Carey Foundation. I tap the screen quickly, scanning it, a reminder about my payment plan, how much I owe, and a passive-aggressive statement about how much they want me, but if I can't make the payments, they'll have to offer the position to someone else.

I read the email quickly, pocketing my phone when I see Logan's eyes drift down toward it, scanning the message upside down. Two taps and the phone turns dark, slipping it into my pocket.

"Something you need to handle?"

I shake my head. "You have my full attention."

"Me and my tattoos?"

"You and your tattoos." I grin, nodding to him. "To answer your question, I like it. And the ones on your arms, too."

That seems to be what he wanted to hear, and pulls his focus away from even thinking about what he might have seen on my phone. I watch his shoulders relax, the faint tightness in them release. "Good."

"Where's Anne?" I ask while making my plate. "She's grounded, isn't she?"

He points upstairs to the room almost directly above him while pulling out what looks like lemonade from the fridge in a chilled pitcher and pouring us both a large glass. "I imagine she's reading or listening to music or talking with her mom right now. I gave her back her phone so she could do that. Michelle always updates her on new places she's performing, what songs she performed. They work on the music together, you know."

"That's adorable," I say, while plating my own food. Silence falls over us for a moment.

"You want to ask me something, don't you?" he asks. "Go ahead, I'm an open book."

"Why didn't you go into music? Like as a full-time job."

"I love cooking more." There's no hesitation in his voice, no pause. He answers that question like I asked if he had to sacrifice himself or his daughter, which one he'd pick, and he, like any good parent, said themselves.

"Plus, there's more of a job market for chefs than for musicians."

"Michelle seems to be doing well?"

"Let me rephrase. Two parents as musicians isn't good for a kid. Where would Anne live? Where would she call home? I like the fact she has stability in Harper's Cove. I get to see her grow up," he says as he scoops some gazpacho into a small wooden bowl.

"And, I get the best of both worlds: I get to run a kitchen and play music. Wouldn't have it any other way."

Logan makes his way around the counter, sitting on the large stool opposite me. I sit down across from him and put two of the six bruschettas on my plate. I bring the smaller of the two to my mouth, letting the crunch of the bread and the saltiness in the savory mixture flood my senses. The cheese is fresh; I can tell the cubes of tomatoes are seasoned perfectly as they dance around like there's a concert going on in my mouth.

"Okay," I say, mid-crunch. "This is fucking amazing."

"Right? It's the—"

"Coriander," I say before he can finish. "And also, something else . . . thyme?"

He grins, nodding slowly. "Exactly. Can you guess the last ingredient?"

I take another slow, measured bite, letting the food turn into a paste in my mouth. "I want to say . . . nutmeg?"

"Just a dash of it." He smiles.

"That's weird."

"But tastes good, yeah?"

He's right. It does.

If I'm being completely and totally honest, being with Logan feels good. In that I assume from hearing from others.

"So," he says, sucking on his fingers to get some of the juices off them. "You have to explain to me what made you come back home. Truly. Really. Because from my perspective, you aren't a Cover."

I scrunch my nose and focus on the food in front of me instead. This idea that people belong to the land is such a white-centric idea, but I don't know if Logan has woken up enough to have that conversation. Plus, it always makes my skin prickle as though I washed myself with some cheap soap I got from 7-Eleven. It makes me feel like you could only belong to one place and that our bodies are rooted in a location instead of being transient and fluid.

That might sound a little hippie-dippie to anyone else, but it makes sense to me.

"Do you consider yourself a Cover?" I ask.

I catch him mid-chew. Adorably, he tries to cover his mouth with his hand and shakes his head. "Not at all, and I never will be," he says. "Do you?"

"No."

"You didn't even hesitate to answer that."

"It's complicated and not really a first date conversation."

"Hey," he gently nudges. "I'm well past the whole *what's your favorite color?* part of dating. That's some 101-level shit. Dating is about getting to know someone and building trust, that's it. Point-blank. That's the whole point of having someone in your corner. And this seems like an important thing to get to know about you if we're going to date.

"So," he says, pausing for a gulp. "If you feel comfortable telling me, I wish you would. I promise, I'm not going to think less of you or negatively of you. And, if I'm being honest, even if you're not shooting down my question with some sassy remark? That's growth compared to three weeks ago."

A wave of emotion rolls over me that feels like whiplash. At one point, I feel like Logan can be kind and charming and a gentleman. But a part of me is concerned about that. I don't trust people who have such sweet and gentle personalities. And that's probably because I cut my teeth in New York and Chicago. But on the other hand, Logan makes my skin tickle, and that push and pull, that dynamic? I'm comfortable in that space. I'm comfortable being on high alert.

"So, do you trust me?"

More or less, I think, swallowing the remainder of my drink before speaking. I didn't even talk about this with Bradley; he never wanted to hear.

"For a Black queer guy in business school, it's eat or be eaten," I say, wiping my mouth. "You see the movie *Whiplash*?"

"With that guy . . . Mack Teller?"

"Miles, but yes. It's like that. Not the whole running and dragging and throwing things at people. But if you want to succeed, if you want to be somebody, you have to make sure you excel and stand out."

"And is that what you're worried about? Falling behind?"

"I'm worried about being seen."

The words come out faster than I would've liked them to. If I had thought about them, I would've called them back and molded them into something a little bit more palatable for people. When you tell people the truth, when you show them your honest-to-God self, they tend to be afraid. They tend to not like the real you. People are accustomed to seeing a version of people that aligns with their prescribed idea of what a person is.

And that, for me, isn't someone who has fears of never succeeding. But that cat is out of the bag.

I steel myself, waiting for some quippy response from Logan, but nothing comes. In fact, he slips his hand over and threads his fingers with mine, squeezing them. My hand isn't as rough as his; I've only been working in the kitchen for a few weeks, but I'm starting to get pads and burns in the same locations as his.

"I think that's admirable," he whispers. "I think that's brave, and I think more people should be like that."

"Vulnerable?"

"Honest."

The word rolls off his tongue as easily as good wine slips down one's throat. When he speaks, I can tell there's no malice in his voice. No teasing, no judgment, just pure, unadulterated honesty. His fingers don't move, his thumb still running against the back of my knuckles, slow circular motions in a soothing, calming manner.

"Do you feel like you stood out? Or like you fell behind in the pack?" he asks, voice barely above a whisper.

"I mean . . ." I gesture with my free hand to myself. "Yes? And yes?"

Logan doesn't speak.

"That's not enough of an answer for you, is it?"

"You're learning."

I let out a sigh through my nostrils. "I was a Black kid in NYU. I was a Black kid at the University of Chicago, and in both of those environments, I knew if I wanted to be respected, I had to be the best. There was no room for anything less than. A lot of Black people experience this. Like, if we mess up, it not only is a reflection on ourselves but everyone who comes after us."

"Sounds like a lot of pressure."

"It is. No one ever gets that. And look at me now. I'm—"

I catch myself before I say it. Logan doesn't need to know that side of me yet. This is just a first date; nothing more. He furrows his brow, picking up on the fact that I'm holding something back, but he doesn't say anything. At least, not at first.

"I just want you to know you can trust me," he says, pulling his hand back and getting off the table to go and make tacos. "I know it might not feel like you can, since this is only our first date, but I want you to know I'm not the villain here. I'm not the enemy. I'm . . ."

He takes a deep breath, pauses, and closes his eyes. I can see him counting to ten. "I'm just a guy who likes another guy and thinks that maybe there could be something there. I'm just a dude who isn't looking to play games and is hoping to find someone who might be open to making something magical happen. And I'm hoping, just maybe, you might be that guy.

"I'm not perfect either, Xavier. A restaurant is a negative business for a long time. To make sure I can pay Angelica, Kyle, and make rent, sometimes I don't take a paycheck and Michelle's child support is what floats Anne and I. I'm not some hotshot Chicago businessman. I'm just a guy trying to keep his head above water. I hope that's enough."

It's rare that I'm at a loss for words. I always have something to say and always know what to say. Maybe I should have aspired to be a famous author, touring the country. But right now, all I can think about is how no words will justify a response to what Logan just said. Without worrying how I might react. Without worrying how I might react to him showing his underbelly to me in the most honest way possible. Fuck a big dick, fuck a nice ass, fuck money. Someone who is honest like this is probably the hottest thing I've ever seen before my life.

"It's enough. It's more than enough."

And before I know what I'm doing, before I can think about the ramifications of my actions, I'm leaning over the island and pressing my lips hard against Logan's, cupping both sides of his face as if kissing him is the last thing I'll ever do.

CHAPTER
TWENTY-THREE

XAVIER, CAN YOU COME into my office for a moment, please?"

It's been about three month since Logan and I had our first date and first kiss, and we've already spent almost every other night together. It feels weird, almost foreign, to be dating again. Is that we can call this? *Dating.*

That word feels too heavy for what we're doing. Sure, dinner together has been nice. Even getting coffee one morning together was great, especially considering he went out of his way to try to predict my order based on the other beverages he'd seen me drinking, but I don't know if I can consider that dating.

God, I sound like I'm in high school all over again.

Without another job, I am intentionally trying to find a way to keep our dating—or whatever this is—professional. Well, as professional as I think it can be. We don't drive in together; if we do spend the morning together, I'll make sure to leave before he does. He doesn't treat me any differently at the restaurant; we make sure not to leave at the same time. It's not like I'm ashamed of the fact that I'm dating him (or, once again, whatever this is), but I don't want to be judged for it. Many of the people at the Wharf have been working here for several years, ever since he opened the restaurant five years ago. They're like family, and I am the interloper who came in and suddenly took root inside their home. Like a mold.

"You called?"

"Close the door behind you." Logan is already standing when I enter. Arching my brow, I slowly close the door behind me. Logan's desk looks like that of a college student who is studying for an exam. Dozens of half-scribbled papers adorn the top. A quick glance at them, and I can tell most of them are half-finished recipes, with comments and notes in the margins.

"I'm all for risky make-out sessions or sex as much as anyone, but I smell like grease, the rest of the staff is out there, and—"

"I need to ask you a favor."

Logan is barely present when he speaks. He's moving around the room like a butterfly that can't find a place to land. While playing the lead role of a hurricane, he picks up a dress shirt draped over the back of his chair, practically ripping off his shirt and throwing it on.

"Do you need help tying your tie?" I ask, nodding to the twisted pile of fabric on the table.

"Can you?"

I nod, grabbing it and standing in front of him. Logan tilts his head upward without hesitation, exposing his neck to me.

"You know, in some cultures, exposing your neck to someone means you trust them explicitly," I mutter. "Considering doing so meant someone could slit your throat."

"You're not going to slit my throat, are you?"

"Not this time." I smile warmly, patting his shoulder once done thirty seconds later.

Logan grabs his phone, clicks it on, and uses the camera to check himself in the mirror.

"Do we have an important guest coming today?" I ask.

"No, I wish," he sighs. "That would be easier. Michelle is here with her new boyfriend. Surprise visit. Or I missed the voicemail."

"Must be serious. Think she wants you and Anne to move out to Seattle with them?"

I curse myself mentally, the words coming out before I can stop them. Clingy isn't a good trait for anyone. Letting the words slip out like that? Makes me sound desperate and childish. Huge turn-off. Even if she does want that, that's a good thing, right? It would mean Anne gets her father and mother closer together.

And, besides, I'm not staying in Harper's Cove anyway, right? Right.

But Logan just pulls back and grabs my shoulder with one hand. His other hand moves under my chin, gently tipping it up, and he leans forward, pressing a soft kiss against my lips, holding it there for what feels like an hour—a good hour—but is only a matter of seconds.

"That's not going to happen," he mutters quietly. "I promise. No, she and her boyfriend are coming. She wants me to meet him. I think they might be getting ready to, you know."

At first, I expect the follow-up to that to be *and I want you to join me for dinner*, but I know better. A month is absolutely not long enough to go to that step. I don't even know if I would call us boyfriends yet, and I'm not sure Logan wants to call us that yet. Has he even told Anne? She has to know; she's smart enough to know.

Not the time or the place, Xavier.

"Get married?" I ask, clarifying.

"Exactly."

"And how do you feel about that?"

"Fine." He shrugs. "I mean, it makes sense, right? People move on, I'm moving on. And I want what's best for her. I know some people who are divorced don't, but I do. Michelle and I are still close friends; always will be, even if we didn't have Anne.

"But I don't want Anne to get the news by herself. I want to be there with her. Michelle is her mother, too, absolutely, but I have custody of her; her mental well-being is my responsibility."

"And this could wreck her, I get it. What do you need from me?"

Logan sprays one spritz of cologne on his body.

"I need you to cover for me. Can you do that?"

"You mean completely run the kitchen?"

"Exactly."

"I mean, I can, technically speaking, but . . ." Run a kitchen? The Wharf kitchen? All by myself?

"I wouldn't ask you if I didn't have any other choice," he says, grabbing his jean jacket. "I don't want Anne to be there by herself when she hears her mother is getting remarried or meets her new stepfather for the first time. But if you don't think you can handle it—"

"I can handle it."

I say that a bit too quickly. I should have thought and processed the request instead of just spitting out an answer and possibly biting off more than I can chew.

But the way Logan's face lights up, and his shoulders relax just an inch? I can tell what answer he was hoping I'd say. How could I backtrack when he has that look in his eyes like I'm the most important person in the world? Bradley never looked at me like that. I didn't think anyone would ever look at me like that.

"Thank you, Xavier," he whispers, leaning down and kissing my lips softly. He lets them linger for a moment. He pulls back a fraction of an inch, resting his forehead against mine. "I promise, I'll make it up to you."

"No need."

"I'm going to want to," he says, pulling back, zipping up his jacket.

"Any special dishes we're making tonight I don't know about?"

Logan shakes his head. "Just don't burn down my restaurant and you'll be great. Angelica will help you, too. She can answer any questions and knows all my recipes by heart. Even the ones I haven't finished yet."

"And Kyle?"

"I don't trust him to handle anything but the meats," he says honestly, but there's a playful smile on his lips. Kyle would probably agree with him. But there is something bugging me.

"If you trust Angelica so much, why not have her run it?"

He checks himself in the mirror one more time, but doesn't hesitate. "You've shared my bed with me—"

"And your car."

"And my car. My daughter seems to like you. If you can take care of my kitchen, there's no reason you can't take care of my heart, too."

Speaking of hearts, my own heart flutters when he says those words so casually. Like blood is pooling inside of it and it's threatening to burst. Logan has a way with words that could rival a poet. No wonder he's a musician.

"So, this is a test again?" I say, doing my best to hide what I'm sure is astonishment on my face. "Another one."

"No. I already trust you. This is just another favor. And after all, this is what people do for each other, right? Favors?"

I trust you. I'm sure Logan meant that as a good thing, to calm my nerves and make me feel like I have control over my own destiny or whatever, but it makes me feel the complete opposite. Like I'm absolutely going to fuck this up, and because the weight is completely on my shoulders, this will totally be my fault.

"Hey," he says, squeezing my arm. "You got this, yeah? Plus, if something comes up, I'm only a phone call away. You have my number."

He's asking, in so many words, if he needs to stay, I think. If he can count on me. What am I supposed to say to that?

"Totally."

* * * * * * * *

THUMP THUMP THUMP.

I can do this.

I can do this.

I can do this.

I don't know how many times I've chanted those words in my head. How many times I've stared at my reflection in this disgusting mirror that hasn't been cleaned all day in the staff bathroom. Whose turn is it to clean the bathroom? I should check the chore chart. I think.

"Focus."

I hiss the words at myself like I'm some petulant child. I'm trying to distract myself. To avoid what's out there behind the door. A kitchen that's in a mess.

That's wrong and not fair to myself. The kitchen isn't a mess. I've got this. I can do this. I'm a boss. I'm THE boss.

How many people can say that?

Thump thump thump.

"Just a minute!"

"We need you out here."

The voice is Angelica's, thick with stress. She's doing her best to hide it, to keep whatever is driving her insane at bay.

I sigh, splashing shockingly cold water on my face. "You got this."

Taking a deep breath, I push the door open and meet her face-to-face. Her face looks like she's fighting back a look of disgust and frustration. There's something dried and red on her cheek. Food—probably the tomato sauce she was working on.

"Did the sauce fight back?" I ask with a teasing grin. "You know, we seem to have a problem with—"

"A critic is here."

She says the words quickly, cutting my joke off at the legs. There is a directness in her voice that leaves no room for interpretation. *This isn't time for jokes, Xavier,* her voice scolds. *You have to be serious.*

She's right. I need to be serious. Because this isn't just my job on the line, and it isn't my place. This is Logan's. Logan's restaurant. Logan's pride and joy. Logan's heart.

Because what is more romantic than a chef giving me his restaurant for the day? That's literally like giving me his soul, the keys to his kingdom. Or, like he said, his heart.

Great, talk about feeling even *more* responsibility than I did before.

"I'm sorry, what?"

"A food critic," she says. "Here. At Harper's Cove."

"Today?"

"Right now, actually."

"You sure?"

"Table four. He was going to come this month but . . ."

"Of course he turned up today. How do you know?"

"I pick up on these things. Like I knew the moment I saw you and Logan together you'd be fucking within a month."

I open my mouth, but she puts her finger to it. "We'll talk about that later. We should call Logan."

I already have my phone out, tapping on my messages, then Logan's name, and then the call button without hesitation. The phone rings once.

Voicemail.

"Shit."

I try it again. Voicemail again.

"Shit, shit, shit."

Where are you? I send a rapid text. The little delivered symbol doesn't appear.

"Can you call him?" I ask Angelica. She nods, pulling her phone out of her apron. A moment later, she pulls it back from her face.

"Voicemail."

"Fuck!"

Walking out with her, pushing my way into the kitchen, waves of smells and sensations hit me. Thyme. Coriander. Seared meats. Each of them is one pulse after another slamming into my face. Along with the heat. Can't forget the heat.

I wipe my brow with the back of my hand, glancing at Angelica. "Logan didn't tell you where he was going, did he?"

She shakes her head. "I'd assume out of anyone he'd tell you."

"And of course, he didn't." There are only so many places in Harper's Cove he could have gone to dinner. Assuming he's even in the Cove. Maybe he headed to Portland. If he did, he's already on his way, almost halfway there if not more. He couldn't turn around in time and get back here with enough time to cook a meal and impress the critic.

We're on our own.

My chest feels like it's about to explode. The blood pumping into my ears is so loud, it sounds like a river is splashing all around me. Manning a kitchen is one thing. Manning a restaurant when a critic is here is another.

And I'm expected to do both? What if I fail? What if I fuck up? What if he hates the meal? What if . . .

A warm hand on my shoulder pulls me out of my downward spiral. At first, for a moment, I think it's Logan here to save the day, but it's just Angelica, with a gentle smile that almost—almost—hides her own fear.

"Hey, Logan trusted you with his restaurant. He believes in you more than he believes in most people. You got this. We can do this."

"What's going on?" Kyle asks, poking his head from around the corner.

"Xavier is having a panic attack."

"I am not having a panic attack!"

"Sounds about right. He knows there's a critic here, right? That we don't have time for breakdowns?"

"He knows."

"I know!"

Angelica glares at Kyle, turning back to me. "You just tell us what you want us to do, and we'll help you, got it? We're going to succeed together."

"Or fail," Kyle says in a singsong voice.

"KYLE!" Angelica and I both yell. Angelica grins at me, nudging me with her shoulder. "See? You're already a part of our crew."

That doesn't make me feel as good as she thinks it does, but her smile does make everything a bit brighter. I take a deep breath, flexing my fingers, wiggling them, and listening to their cracks.

I can do this.

I can do this.

I can fucking do this.

"Logan said you know all his recipes?"

"Pan—"

"Porcini-dusted grouper with sweet corn puree and cayenne," Kyle interjects, speaking loud enough for us to hear from the other side of the restaurant.

"You're joking," I say.

"You know it?" Kyle asks, bridging the gap and standing next to us.

"No, but I know it's complicated to make. It has almost nine words in its title."

"It's fancy," she says. "He wants to impress. It's a critic, remember?"

"I know." I remember clearly what Logan said. And I know how important this is to him. I know how crucial it is for him to succeed at his dream.

"But?" Kyle says, drawing out the word.

"But nothing."

"There's nothing," Angelica pushes. "I know that look."

"I just . . ." A beat passes. "It's not Harper's Cove. It's . . . seafood you might find in New York, or Paris, or London."

"This critic is from London," she says. "Used to be a chef under Gordon Ramsay."

"Right, I get that, but he's coming here to experience the Wharf. Food that represents Harper's Cove. Food that shows off the warmth and friendliness of our town. Not wannabe European dishes for those with their noses in the sky."

"You're going to suggest something that's going to make me want to quit on the spot, aren't you?" Angelica asks.

"Hear me out," I say, pulling out my phone. I tap three times, bringing up the menu, and zoom in. "The salmon burgers."

"You have got to be kidding me."

"No, no, listen! They are fucking awesome. Seriously. They represent everything about our town: welcoming, inviting, simple, delicious. They are easy to make, and if done right, they show what the Wharf is. A place you come for comfort and a good meal with family and friends. What is more Harper's Cove?"

"It's also completely different than what Logan wanted," she reminds me.

"Different isn't bad."

"Yes, but if we fail?"

"But what if we don't?" Kyle asks.

Angelica glares at him. Kyle puts his hands up in a defensive, surrender position.

"I'm not saying he's right," he says quickly. "But, what I am saying is that I get where he's coming from."

Angelica frowns, showing off the dimples in her cheeks. "It's a risk."

"Running a restaurant is a risk," Kyle says, and then adds,

while waggling his brows, "falling in love is a risk. And you fell in love with me."

"Never said I was in love with you."

"That's not what you said last night when I put my tongue . . ."

"Fine!" she interrupts, putting her hand on his mouth. "Fine. But if we fuck up and ruin this for Logan? I'm blaming you two. I'm not losing my job."

"That's my girl." Kyle beams like a loving boyfriend, pulling her hand away.

"Not your girl," she reminds him.

"Yeah, but maybe you should be." I grin. "Everyone sees how you two—"

"Really?" she barks, arching a brow. "You want to talk about the way someone looks at someone?"

I mimic Kyle's surrender motion. "Fair, fair," I concede.

"As you should. Now, what do you need from me and Kyle?"

"You mean I get to boss you both around?"

"Absolutely," Kyle says. "What's that expression? Rising tides . . ."

"Lift all ships," I finish for him. "We succeed together, we fail together."

"And we also get fired together if we ruin this for Logan," he reminds us.

"That too. But what's the fun in doing something if there isn't any risk involved, you know?"

"You're a masochist, you know that?" Angelica asks me.

I shrug. "I've never tried it before, but I wouldn't be against experimenting with a little pain play."

Kyle lets out a hearty laugh, clasping his large, almost Viking-like hands on our shoulders. "That's what I like to hear! So, we doing this?"

I look at Angelica. "We doing this?"

"We're doing this."

The salmon burgers are a staple on the menu. We've made them at least one hundred times. It only takes us about thirty minutes to slice the fresh salmon, toast the bun, make the hollandaise mayo, cook the salmon perfectly with the right seasoning, and garnish it.

"We should add a salad, right?" Kyle interjects as Angelica carefully places the salmon on the bun, like she's removing a nuclear reactor. "Some vegetable? To complement the meal?"

"We have the bitter green salad?" I say. "We have the goat cheese, the fruits, the greens already ready to go?"

"Dressing?" Angelica asks.

"Pineapple vinaigrette," we all say together, without hesitation.

"Jinx," Angelica adds. "You owe me a drink after this."

"I was going to pay for a round anyway. The Aqueduct?"

"Yes, please."

I open one of the two large fridges and bring over a bowl with a freshly made batch of the salad. Using one of the large sets of tongs, I scoop a helping into the bowl, shaping it into a perfect mound. Kyle follows up, quickly whisking together the vinaigrette, drizzling it over, while sprinkling the blueberries, walnuts, and cheese.

"Done?" I ask.

Angelica lets out a grunt of a response. Kyle gives me a thumbs-up.

"Can I say it actually looks pretty beautiful?" he asks, sniffling almost as if he just saw the big bang for the first time, looking at it through the open window of the Doctor's TARDIS. "We can call a meal beautiful, right?"

"You are such an idiot." Angelica rolls her eyes.

"Yeah, but I'm your idiot." He grins.

"Jury is still out on that."

"But there's still hope."

"Oh my God." She rolls her eyes, looking over at me. "Look, we have a server who can do this but . . ."

"You think I should take it out," I say without letting her finish.

"You are the owner, for all intents and purposes right now, and it's important he sees your face."

"I agree with Angelica," Kyle chimes in. "You're the big dog right now. And if anyone should take the credit . . ."

"Or the blame?"

He shrugs. "I like to think positive. It's my ethos. Keeps me young looking."

"I can see why she can barely put up with you," I tease back. But they're both right. It should be me who takes the plate. Making a decision that could make or break the restaurant shouldn't be the responsibility of some twenty-year-old.

I sigh and roll my shoulders. Quickly, I take off my stained white apron, looking myself up and down. I wasn't dressed for this. I'm a sous chef. It's my job to make sure things run smoothly. I work in the kitchen. And I look like it. Just a nondescript dark-colored shirt and some pants that I can get dirty. I wasn't prepared to be seen. To be perceived.

That's not the point. Someone has to do it. And that someone is me.

I sigh again, making a quick pass over my body with a towel to wipe off any evident flecks of food. Once done, I take the plate, carrying it on the palm of my right hand.

"No, no," Kyle says, gently taking the plate. "Don't try and be someone you aren't. Critics can smell that a mile away. Hold it like you normally would."

I frown. "That's not professional. First impressions are—"

"Bullshit," he interrupts. "Most people fail them. Let the food speak for itself. It's like lovemaking or like relationships. It's not about who you are when you first make eyes, or make love, it's about how you are in the long haul. What you stand for. What your heart says when it's quiet, and no one but you and your lover can hear it. When everyone falls away, who are you, and what do you want to be known for? What is your truth? Fuck pleasantries. Let you and the food speak for itself."

Both Angelica and I stand there quietly. Kyle looks at both of us, eyes darting back and forth.

"What?"

"Nothing." Angelica grins. "That was just . . ."

"Deep. Deeper than I thought you were capable of."

"Excuse me?" Kyle roars.

Before he can say anything else, I do exactly what he says, grabbing the plate with both hands on either side, cupping it carefully. I cradle it in my hands, feeling the warmth and the weight, not fighting it or fearing it, but embracing it. This is now or never.

I got this.

I can do this.

I'm a fucking boss.

And no critic, no matter how big their reach is, is going to get the best of Logan.

TWENTY-FOUR

"CAN YOU PLEASE STOP refreshing your phone?"

Ever since the critic stopped by, Logan has been glued to his phone and computer, spending more time around them than Anne or me. We've both noticed it, and today is no different.

I finally got him to relax. Finally got him to not spend the evening sitting at the counter on his computer, refreshing his email or the *Portland Gazette*, and instead, he's found a loophole around it, sitting on his phone. I even got him to leave his house—albeit outside and in his backyard—with Anne, and still, he's just refreshing the screen over and over again.

"And he says I spend too much time on my phone." Anne rolls her eyes, blowing on her hands. Her Bluetooth speaker is playing some new pop music, and we're sitting by the creek that lines the back of his house. The sun has just set, no more than thirty or so minutes ago. It's cooler than a normal September in Harper's Cove. A recent rain storm brought down the temperature, and Anne has been debating with Logan if she can start a fire or not.

So far, she's lost the argument. Plus, she made grilled cheese—and who can say no to grilled cheese?

"Your father isn't going to stop refreshing that phone until he either gets a review or his fingers fall off," I say, sitting in the chair next to him. "Which I'm starting to think is more likely than not to happen."

"Har har har," Logan says. "You know I can hear you both, right?"

"Your ears still work?" I gasp. "And here I thought your body had optimized itself to make sure the only things that worked were your eyes and fingers. You know, directing blood to the most important body parts, considering you haven't stopped looking at your phone for the past five days."

"I just wish you had gone with the pan-crusted . . ."

"Listen to me," I say, shifting on the couch. "It's going to be okay. I promise. We blew it out of the park. He loved the burger."

Logan glances over at me, still not convinced.

"You trust me, don't you?"

"I think."

"Going to ignore that apprehension for a second. I know people. Even you said I know food, and Angelica and Kyle wouldn't let me go down that road if they didn't agree with me. It's going to be okay. Also it's just one review, right?"

For some reason, Logan doesn't answer me there. He just shifts his weight and sinks into the couch, staring at the TV.

"Logan?" I ask. "Right?"

"I think this is a perfect time for me to ask for whatever I want," Anne suggests.

I stare at him for a moment longer, waiting for an answer. Something about how he's acting . . . it's odd and makes my hackles rise. But maybe it's just his nerves. Some people become closed off when they are nervous. Logan could be one of those people.

Instead, I turn back to Anne. No reason for both Logan and me to be nervous wrecks.

"Go for it. I mean, he's in such a state he'd probably just say yes."

"A pony?"

"A dog?"

"A house?"

"A car?"

"The continent Europe?"

"You two are insufferable," Logan mutters, finally admitting defeat and pocketing his phone. "You do understand this review could make or break us, right? You both understand that?"

I have to appreciate Logan's teaching style as a parent. He doesn't shy away from saying the big and scary things around his daughter. She gets to experience it all. The good, the bad, the big, the small, the ugly, and the beautiful. She'll grow up knowing that men are just men, the importance of fighting for what you believe in, and of putting real elbow grease and blood into accomplishing your goals. What more can a parent do for their daughter?

"It's going to do fine," I say, discreetly squeezing his hand. He may be open with his daughter, but I'm still not trying to be that person. *That person* being the person who just flaunts in the kid's face that I'm dating their parent. That's weird. I would have hated that.

"I need to do better than fine." He sighs. Logan squeezes my hand back, but leans forward, pressing his palms against his eyes.

There's no more to it than that. Each time he's talked about the restaurant since this critic came, it's been short sentences like that. I should push him more, each time he hesitates and catches his tongue. I should force him to tell me because I can tell there's something more there, buried just underneath the surface.

But forcing someone to tell the truth never ends in actually getting the full truth; it just ends in you getting flaky fragments, enough to satisfy the urge but never quell the demons. And that's not what I want. That's not what either of us need.

"You stress too much, Dad," Anne says in a bored tone, standing up and arching her back until her bones pop. Logan makes a face. I think she does that just to get a rise out of him.

Logan lets out a throaty chuckle. "Oh, I stress too much?"

"Mhm," Anne says, turning to face us both. She puts her hands on her hips, looking like we need to absolutely listen to whatever smartness she is going to spill to us. "The world is going to melt away anyway in the next twenty years."

"It is?" he says, looking at me. "What am I missing?"

"Global warming," we both say at the same time, though Anne's voice has more annoyance than mine.

"The polar ice caps. Pollution. Rising temperatures. Tides," Anne lists off on each finger.

"And this means . . . ?" Logan asks.

"Nothing matters in the grand scheme of things."

I know what Anne is saying. Trust me, I get it. I remember being a teenager and being nihilistic about everything. But I also see how Logan's face flickers with hurt for a moment. Just a moment. I don't even know if Anne notices. But I do know that Logan doesn't say anything, not at first. But more importantly, I can see that Logan and Anne might need a moment to discuss some things. Father-and-daughter things.

"I'm going to go get the Popsicles we made," I say, thinking that's a smooth way to exit the impending conversation that's going to happen. "Anyone want one?"

"They aren't done yet," she says with more attitude, as if I should know that. "You're the chef, aren't you?"

"Anne," Logan says like a warning.

"Of course they aren't, but between you and me, the first Popsicle is the best one after all, so I'm just being—"

Anne frowns. "How old do you think I am?"

"Anne," Logan says firmly again.

"What? He's acting like I'm—"

"Anne Natalia O'Hare. Inside. Now."

Anne pushes her lips into a thin line and grabs her boom box. "Screw you."

"Excuse me?" Logan says, half standing. But by the time he gets up, she's already trotting up the stone steps and into the house, closing the door loudly behind her.

Logan sits back down. No, *sits* isn't the right word; he collapses back down into the chair. We both sit in silence, letting the soft sounds of the creek and the muted sounds of the boom box from Anne's rear-facing room fill the melody of the summertime in Harper's Cove.

"I don't know what I'm going to do with her. She's just . . . at that age where she's finding herself. You remember being that old. I remember being that old. Everything and everyone is against her. She needs to learn that people aren't always out to get her, or out to prove she's wrong, or to treat her like a child." He sighs, pinching his nose.

I can see the tension in Logan's shoulders. They are tight and hunched, so tight that I think the muscles and tendons will snap. It's not healthy. It can't be comfortable.

Carefully, I reach over and dig my knuckles into his left shoulder. Logan tenses up even more at first, but slowly starts to relax. His right hand drops from his face, and he lets out a small sigh, almost like a balloon deflating.

I stand slowly, moving behind him and digging both of my hands into his shoulders, starting to rub and knead at whatever tight muscles I can find. Logan's body slowly gives way and unspools in my hands like yarn. He lets his shoulders drop, his head leaning backward, and he lets out another sigh, almost a groan.

I continue to silently knead at the muscles. I'm not a masseuse, but Bradley used to get this same tension in his shoulders after studying too hard. I used to do this for him.

"Simple acts of simple kindness," I mutter.

"Sorry?" Logan says, his voice groggy as if his mind and body are separate.

"Nothing."

That's what Bradley used to call them. It feels stupid now. Not the act—he was right about that—but how close I thought we were. How important I thought the world in his small apartment was. How everything seemed to be of the biggest consequence. Like the smallest things would have the biggest consequences in the whole entire world.

The world is so much bigger than Bradley and I thought it was. Not in the sense of actual size, because if you use that metric, it's gotten smaller, but with so many different people with so many different intersecting and conflicting lives. Every person has their own struggles and their own battles, and no person's life is any more or less important than any others.

I'm sure if I told my mother that I just came to that discovery, she would just be happy that I finally got here.

Which is something, I guess.

"Hey," Logan whispers. I feel his rough fingers rubbing against my forearm, the pads of his fingers, covered with cuts and small burns, scratching against my skin. "Where did you go?"

Good question.

I look down at him and his handsome, upside-down face. Slowly, I lean forward, about to press a kiss against his lips. But I pause, glancing upward at Anne's window.

"She's not looking," he mutters, his eyes closed, not even opening his eyes to see why I paused. He just knows. "You can kiss me."

"Do you want me to?"

"I always want you to kiss me," he whispers.

I grin and slowly lean forward, pressing another soft kiss against his lips. Even though it's been over a month since our first kiss, each one feels as electric as the first time, like his lips are the pure source of magic and power and electricity all combined into one.

"Come here," Logan asks quietly. In a fairly graceful move, he pulls me around the side and into his lap, forcing me to straddle him in the process, his hands gripping my hips.

"That's better." He smirks as he leans up, nipping at my bottom lip. Naturally, my arms move to wrap around his shoulders. It just happens. I don't think about it. I'm not sure if you would or could say it's natural submission, because I don't think I would call it that. But our bodies fit well together. My arms around his neck. My hips pressing down against his hot lap. My lips against his lips.

Or his cheek.

Or his neck.

It just feels . . . almost right.

Logan grins up at me, peppering my lips with hot kisses, like his lips can spell out some sort of Morse code. He hums with each one and growls with a few others, fingers digging and rubbing against my flesh. His fingers slip under my shirt and press against my bare skin.

Each touch is just as electric as his kiss. Each one, even in the hot summertime, sends shivers down my spine. My mind feels like it's running at a million miles an hour, but at the same time, it feels like it's moving at half a mile an hour. So fast I can't think. So slow I can only focus on one thought at a time.

Finally, as his fingers start to crawl up my skin, walking up my chest, I speak.

"Your daughter might see us."

There's nothing sexual or sexy about saying someone's daughter might see you're about to have sex—assuming that's where we're going. But it's right, and it's fair to stop now before we get so far in that stopping is impossible.

"Do you want me to stop?" he mutters, his lips pressed against my neck, speaking into my skin in a lower octave. "Is that what you want, Xavier?"

I don't know if that's what I want. I don't know if I can trust what I want right now.

"Because if you want me to stop," he whispers, "just let me know. But if you want me to keep going. If you want me to keep touching you . . . keep . . ." His hands slip into the back of my pants, cupping my ass, squeezing both cheeks. "Then you just say the word."

I've never fully understood what people mean when they say their mind is misfiring. But that's exactly what's happening right now. Every nerve in my body is going on red alert. A good type of red alert. A happy type of red alert. But still, fire and passion burn inside of me, threatening to push logic and reason out the window.

"I don't want you to stop," I breathe out. Probably one of the few honest and true statements I can say right now. It's easiest to be that. To be honest. To be real. To be truthful. I can lean into that. Trust in that, the most primal and utterly honest of feelings.

"Then how about you let me do what I'm doing and—"

"Your car," I blurt out, doing exactly what I said I would do, trusting my feelings.

Logan pauses all actions, pulling back and looking up at me. "I'm sorry, what?"

I pull back again, looking down at him. The horny fog in my brain slowly starts to lift, even if only for a moment. "We should do this in your car."

Logan just stares. "You know I'm an adult, right?"

"I do. You'd be an old-looking teenager if you weren't."

"With a house that I built myself."

"Yep, and that's hot."

"And I own a business? Can chop wood? Gut a fish? Fix a car?"

"All traditionally masculine things, but yes."

"And you want me to have sex in my truck?"

"Why not?"

Logan looks up at me. He isn't convinced, I can tell. Does this show my age? Does this make me seem like a kid? He's never really questioned our age difference before. It's roughly thirteen years. That's a significant age difference, isn't it? Most people would shy away from that. It's more than my parents'. I'm closer to his daughter's age than—

Logan presses his lips quickly against my lips. A hot, passionate kiss that's the type of kiss you do in a club on a dance floor, when you know you'll never see that person again.

"Fuck, that sounds hot," he growls—actually growls—against my lips. "Is this some fantasy of yours you've always had? Sex in a car?"

"Absolutely not," I lie. "Just the practical, logical, easy solution for a problem that has no real easy solution right now."

"Ah, I see," Logan says, smirking. "How about you just admit you've always wanted to get fucked in a Jeep."

"Maybe I've always wanted to do the fucking in a Jeep?"

"Good, because I've always wanted to do both, too. Glad we're on the same page. Now we don't have to have that awkward conversation."

Logan stands up, barely giving me time to stand along with him. I stumble backward when he rises, my legs not acting correctly and twisting together. I brace myself for the fall. It's not far, and I'm sure Logan will laugh at me and my pain, which I'll chastise him for, and he'll kiss it better. I've fallen from higher places before.

But, even as my body braces for the impact, it never comes. My body doesn't fall more than a couple of inches. Logan, holding on to me with both hands, one hand on my hip and the other on my shoulder as he keeps me close, and pulls me up as he stands, our lips barely an inch apart.

"You don't think I'd ever let something bad happen to you, do you?" he whispers to me against my lips. "You should know me better by now, Xavier."

There it is again. That shiver that doesn't belong here. I grin slowly at him, our eyes locked, his beautiful blue ones and my dark brown-black ones. My fingers rest against his hips.

"Foolish me," I tease quietly.

"Yeah." He nips at my lips. "Foolish you. Stick around with me, and I'll teach you a thing or two."

Logan pulls back slowly. He releases the hand on my shoulder, the other hand on my hip moving down to thread between my fingers as he leads me around the side to his garage, where his car resides.

CHAPTER
TWENTY-FIVE

LOGAN UNLOCKS HIS TRUCK with a click but not before pushing me back gently against the passenger side door. He doesn't let the handle dig into my back, wrapping his right hand around my lower back to protect me.

Slowly, he leans forward, pressing his lips against my full ones. He nips slowly at my lips, pushing his tongue forward, quietly begging, yearning for entrance. My own hands move almost automatically, wrapping around Logan's strong waist. My fingers dig into his muscles, feeling them, memorizing them.

I pull Logan's shirt up, and he helps me take it off quickly, tossing it to the floor. Reaching around me, he unlocks the back doors of the truck, walking me backward until my back is against the seat and he's hovering above me. He grins down at me, strands of his dark black hair shuttering in front of his eyes.

"Hi," he teases. "Fancy seeing you here."

"Yeah, I think I made a wrong turn somewhere," I tease back. "Think you can help me?"

"Really? The lost traveler role play?" he asks, slowly undoing my shirt before pulling it off. "That's such a cliché."

"It's a cliché because it's still hot. Tell me you haven't watched a porno with that and jerked off to it."

But you know what is jerk-off worthy? Logan. Tattoos adorn his arms and chest, telling a story that I can't translate. I've grown fond of the bird and mammal tattoos on his arms, but his chest? There he has music notes, an outline of Nevada, I'm guessing where he's from. But there are also lyrics, book quotes, random cartoons, and so much more. It's like his body is literally a canvas that he—

"Oh fuck."

Logan's lips are like a hot iron against my skin. He presses kisses down my neck, moving toward my right nipple, where he swirls his tongue around at least three times, before moving with hot fire kisses down my stomach. Four hot kisses later, he's right against my navel, and stops.

Lukewarm air breathes raggedly against my skin, forcing my eyes to look down at him. Of course my pants are tighter now, of course I'm sporting a hard-on . . . and of fucking course he's doing nothing about it.

"Do I have your permission, Xavier?" Logan asks quietly, his voice laced with horniness.

"You think I'd let you get this far if you didn't?"

"I need to hear you say it," he says. "I can't teach—"

"Do not say your daughter's name when we are about to have sex, please," I interrupt quickly. "You are going to absolutely kill the mood."

Logan blinks and lets out a laugh, pressing another kiss on my skin. "You're right."

There is something very . . . hot about Logan asking for permission. When I broke up with Bradley and wandered back into the dating pool—aka the Grindr pool—most guys were just *down to fuck* or sent dick shots without warning. There's something almost romantic about consent.

Even if we're fucking in his car.

"You have my permission," I whisper.

Logan smirks, pulling my belt off with an easy tug and flick of his hand. He throws the belt on the floor, unbuttons my pants, and with one harsh pull, yanks them down to my ankles, leaving me mostly in just my black briefs. I let out a mix of a yelp and a laugh as Logan sits up, grinning proudly.

"You liked that didn't you?" he teases. "How masculine and manly that was? Just say the word, babe, and I'll manhandle the fuck out of you," he playfully grunts.

"Oh my God please stop," I laugh, shielding my face with my fingers while kicking off my pants tangled around my ankles. "You are leaning too much into nineties porn star territory."

"Hey, those porn stars helped make me," he scolds, slapping my exposed thigh. "Those helped make me the man I am today."

I wanted to say something. Make some comment about how his defense of nineties porn makes me question his ability in the bedroom. But his words cut off any sarcastic thoughts I have going through my head.

"You look so fucking beautiful, you know that?"

I stare up at him, my mouth slightly open. I want to say so many things: brush it off like he's making a joke, thank him, say it back to him. But none of those words come out. Like my mouth has suddenly turned dry and words are impossible.

Until what *does* come out is the last thing I thought I'd ever say: the truth.

"No one has ever said that to me before."

Logan's face twists into a look of confusion. "You had a boyfriend, didn't you? Brandon?"

"Bradley. And no, he never said it."

"You're kidding."

I shake my head.

Logan scoffs. "Again, you have bad taste in men."

"I picked you, didn't I?"

"Like I said, bad taste in men," he says, leaning down once again and pressing his lips against mine. This time, I move one arm around his neck, holding him close, while with the other, I undo his pants; not as gracefully as he did mine, but it gets the job done.

Logan shimmies out of his pants, wearing a pair of baby-blue boxer briefs that hug his thick thighs perfectly. My hand slips into his boxer briefs, wrapping around his cock gently. Even the soft touch causes Logan to let out a deep groan that I feel vibrating in his chest.

"Fuck," he hisses, lips moving from mine to my neck. "Stroke it," he whispers, almost begging. "Please."

He doesn't need to tell me twice. Twisting my hand slowly, I pump his cock up and down, using the tip of my thumb to rub against his crown. Each touch causes him to groan, each stroke and gentle squeeze causes him to pant right in my ear.

"Jesus, Xavier," Logan says breathlessly, letting out a strangled laugh mixed with a gasp. "You're going to make me come before I even fuck you."

"Someone needs to build up some tolerance," I tease.

"If you even think about edging me I'll—"

"You'll what?" I playfully add.

"Fuck you even harder," he says without hesitation.

"I don't see how that is bad for me. Maybe I should . . ." I pull my hand away slowly, pulling it out of his pants. Logan pulls back enough to look back at me, glaring.

"You better not," he warns.

Spontaneously, I take my hand that was wrapped around his cock and now has a small sheen of precome on it, and lick the precome off my fingers while looking at him.

"Oh fuck," Logan groans out. Then, he pins both of my arms above my head with one hand. His lips crash against mine, hard enough that our teeth almost touch, and he pushes his tongue into my mouth. It's unceremonious, it's rough, it's hungry . . . and it's so fucking hot.

Logan's other hand pulls my briefs off. Pressing our hips together, almost desperately, he begins to grind against me. It's not long before our bodies start to roll together in harmony, as if the friction could somehow make electricity spark between us and that electricity could be turned into power.

But I don't mind any of it. I don't mind the hormonal sex in the car. I don't mind his tongue down my throat, strangling a groan of pleasure and a whimper of desire from me. I don't care how fucking badly I want him to fuck me, how I'm chanting it in my head as if he can mentally hear me.

Right now, the only thing I care about is Logan.

In that moment, it's almost as if he can hear my thoughts. He pulls back for just a moment, grinning almost wolfishly at me.

"I'm going to fuck you now," he says.

"You don't need to announce it, you know that, right?"

He chuckles, taking his free hand and grabbing the base of his cock. "I know. You can tell me to stop at any time, you know that, right? Just say the word and I'll listen. No hesitation, no hard feelings, no . . ."

"Logan, it's pretty obvious at least two things are hard, and I want one of those hard things inside of me, so if you don't shut the hell up and fuck me, I'm never going to talk to you again. That direct enough for you?"

He stares at me for a moment, a surprised look like he's caught off guard plastered on his face, before he grins.

"Sir, yes, sir," he says, quickly pressing his lips against mine. He reaches down into his pants, pulling out his wallet and fishing out a red condom, ripping the package open with his teeth.

"You just have that in your wallet?" I ask. "How very HBO drama."

"I've had it in my wallet ever since our trip to Portland," he says directly. "I wanted to be prepared if this happened."

"Oh? You thought you'd get lucky since then?"

"No," he says, shaking his head, slipping the rubber onto his hard cock. "I was hoping I'd be able to make love to you since. I've wanted to fuck you since you assaulted me in your home."

"You mean when you broke into my house to steal my family cupcakes."

"Tomato tomato." He grins.

Without a moment more of hesitation, Logan slowly pushes his thick cock inside of me. There's a moment of burning, a sharp feeling of pain that pools from my hips and expands outward. Besides fingering myself and a dildo I bought and used a few times, I haven't been fucked since Bradley, and my body has tightened.

Logan doesn't ignore that either. He's slow and careful, pulling back and gathering spit in his mouth, using it as lube as he tries again. This time as he pushes in, he moves more slowly, working himself until his cock is nestled inside of me, his chest flush with mine.

"You okay?" he pants quietly in my face.

"Perfect," I say without hesitation. The burn is a welcome one, especially since it comes from Logan.

His grin is mixed with pride and joy. Burying his face back in my neck, he begins to rock his hips in and out of me. My legs shift, one wrapping around his waist, the other pressing against the doorjamb. Logan's movements get faster and faster, his pants and grunts following suit, matching mine.

A moment later, we both have the same thought. Silencing each other, we kiss each other desperately, our groans of pleasure getting swallowed into each other's mouths. My hips move in time with his, rocking up faster, harder, more desperate than his. Almost as if I can't get enough of his touch.

After all, just being this close to someone is an addicting feeling. It never felt like this with Bradley. Sure, it felt good; it felt great sometimes, but this is different, this is a new high. This is . . .

"Oh fuck, Xavier," Logan whispers. "I'm going to come."

I nod frantically. The concept of words feels like an ideal my human brain can't even comprehend right now. I reach down, wrapping my hand around my own cock, beginning to pump it, but Logan moves my hand away.

"Let me," he says, stroking me in time with his thrust. Electric white-fire feelings rocket through my body, almost blinding me with pleasure. My toes curl, my body tightening around him. His hips thrust in, almost sporadically, desperately, as we kiss hard one more time before that feeling of intensity overwhelms every fucking nerve in my body.

And my body can't stop shaking.

Logan collapses on top of me, panting so hard I think he's going to have a heart attack. Part of me wants to make a joke, but in the moment, just being there, our bodies slick in the back of his car? It's perfect.

We stay there for what feels like an hour, just letting our heartbeats sync and calm down, reaching a normal pace. Finally, he pulls back, grinning with lazy, lidded eyes at me.

"Think it's cool if I call you my boyfriend now? For real?"

I grin back without hesitation, kissing him gently.

"As long as I can call you my DILFriend."

"I'm going to fucking kill you."

"Why not just fuck me again?"

"Now that"—he grins—"I can do. Different position?"

"Surprise me."

CHAPTER
TWENTY-SIX

'M NOT SURE IF this is part of being a good, loyal, and frankly badass boyfriend, but I'm going to chalk it up to all those things.

"I forgot I promised Anne if she got an A on her math test, I'd take her out of school for a girl's day. She's been struggling with math, so this was an incentive. Don't tell her I didn't actually expect her to get a one hundred percent," he says over the phone when he calls at 5:00 a.m. the following week. "I know it's last minute but . . ."

"I'll do it," I say, without hesitation.

"You sure?"

I'm sure he's asking that because I sound like I just came out of a Sleeping Beauty–level stupor. Which would be correct. The only thing that woke me is that Logan's name is under "priority contacts," so his call broke through my sleep.

"I'm already up."

A lie, but he doesn't need to know that. To make the lie more believable, I roll out of my bed and saunter over to the closet. I loudly yank some clothes off the hangers so he can hear.

"See?" I ask. "I'm getting dressed."

"Wear something cute," he teases. I can hear the sounds of the coffee maker in the background.

"For your friend?"

A beat passes. "I didn't think that through."

"I mean, he is hot."

"Xavier," he growls lowly.

"I'm serious. He has that rugged look about him."

"I'm going to—"

"Spank me?"

A throaty laugh. "If that's what you want. I was going to say make it up to you, not punish you."

"Who said those two things are exclusive?"

I stare at the bathroom, wondering if I have time for a quick shower. Opting for yes, I turn on the faucet, listening to the hot hiss.

"Anything special you're picking up?"

"Nope. Just a normal run. I'd ask him to just come to town, pay for his gas and beer or something, but—"

"Why do that when you have a hot boyfriend?"

"Eh," he grunts out.

"Eh? Eh to what? The hot or to the boyfriend?"

"I plead the Fifth on that one—I need to go. Anne isn't up yet, and she hasn't finished her project yet."

"Oh no! You can't just ignore me like that!"

"Goodbye, Xavier, and thank you for this."

He makes the sound of a kiss through the phone before hanging up.

"Asshole," I growl. But there isn't a moment that I think about not helping him. Not for one second. Logan needs me to do something for him, I'll do it. No questions asked.

I take a quick shower, just fast enough to wash off the sweat from sleep. By the time I'm out, fifteen minutes later and dressed, my phone has a text from him.

You're both hot and my boyfriend, in case you were wondering.

I can't help but smile, glancing at the heart and kiss emoji that follow the text.

You don't text in emojis, I send back. Is this Anne?

Asshole, he sends back a moment later

But your asshole. Plus, you like how tight my asshole is.

I'm blocking you.

I make the commute to Portland in less than forty-five minutes, closer to thirty-five. I wasn't speeding, but the gods are on my side. Clear skies, nice sixty-six-degree weather, no one on the roads. All perfection. I blast Tinashe, H.E.R., Doja Cat, the new Lizzo track, and a few Aretha and Beyoncé classics.

This is the Black run.

I park in the same parking garage as we did before. It almost feels familiar. Like muscle memory, if that's a thing. Can you have muscle memory from something you've only done once?

No, it's not that. That's not the right word. It's familiar. It's comforting, that's what it is. My body has already started to settle into a routine.

It feels odd. To assume that this could be my life. That it's possible for me to be this calm. I've never felt this relaxed and at ease in New York or Chicago. Sure, part of that comes from the fact life is slower here. But I work at a restaurant. It's not that much slower. It's not like I'm running a cake-decorating supply shop, I prep, I worry, just like Logan, about the future of the Wharf.

I worry about it like it's my own.

And maybe there is a future where it can be my own. I don't want to jump ahead of anything—which I have a tendency to do—but the more I'm with Logan, the more that future seems likely.

What a weird feeling.

Logan's produce dealer smiles brightly when he sees me. His laugh and smoke lines blend together to narrow his eyes, and he waves at me like a happy child. My cheeks burn as I wave back. I think, weeks ago, the smile I gave him would have been fake, but now? It's honest, and I can actually admit I'm excited to see him. Seth's energy is an infectious and welcome ray of sunshine. I can see why Logan comes here, for more reasons than just his friendship or the produce.

"Ladies and gentlemen, you might not know it, but this man here?" He points to me. "Prep chef at one of the best restaurants in the New England area. You haven't eaten until you've eaten food made by him. And trust me, I know food!"

The crowd looks over at me, as if half expecting me to have some sign on my shirt that says ADDRESS: HERE, PHONE NUMBER: HERE.

But all they get is me in a worn Beyoncé ON THE RUN T-shirt that has seen better days and a pair of joggers and high-tops.

"It's in Harper's Cove," I chime in. "Go down to the end of Main Street, you can't miss it."

"Oh, that's a quaint town," a woman says.

Quaint. That word has a different meaning to me now. Before, when I first arrived, I thought quaint was such a bad thing. Claustrophobic, even. But now? It feels more like a warm embrace. Like hands and arms wrapped tightly around my shoulders.

Not just any hands or arms. Logan's arms.

When I close my eyes and think, that's what comes to mind. The scent of his cologne. The smell of sweat prickled on his skin. It's him. No one else.

"Fuck," I mutter.

The woman next to me, a woman with a fashionable silver-haired bob cut, who looks more like she belongs in NYC than here, quirks her brow at me. I wave it off with an apology.

I'm really head over heels for this guy.

The crowd thins, especially the judgmental woman with the fashionable bob, and goes their way. Too many quaint little shops and not enough time. Once everyone is gone, I make my way over to Seth.

"Well, well, well. Logan sick of me already? Send you to tell me he isn't doing business with me anymore?"

"Hardly," I scoff. "He's busy with Anne. Thought I'd help out. While I'm at it, you need some help?"

Seth hoists the remainder of his crates into the back of the truck. They're fuller than before, not as much produce sold. I don't know an average rate of return for someone who spends their life selling produce at an open food market, but I have known, as a business major, more freelancers than I like to count.

We spent the next twenty minutes sifting through contents, dividing up produce, putting them into piles. It's a different sort of working with my hands than working in the restaurant, and

I like it. I like feeling that I'm physically doing something. Like I'm contributing and actually adding to the world. I guess that's why people take up gardening.

Seth rubs his hands on a dirty towel, tossing it to me to clean mine off. Small flecks of wood from the crates, dirt from the vegetables, and some other sticky debris I can't name covers my palms.

"So, are you going to tell me why you're giving off some weird vibe?"

I glance over at Seth, who has that slight arched-brow look that tells me he knows something is up, even if he doesn't know what EXACTLY is up. I chew a bit on my bottom lip, enough to draw the copper taste of blood.

"That obvious?"

"Very." A beat. "The produce run is Logan's thing. Says it helps calm him and gives him time away from Anne."

I don't judge him for that. Even parents get sick of their kids, no matter how much they love them. Raising a child is a responsibility, as much as it is a gift.

"So, for him to give it up?" Seth says. "Means he either trusts you more than most people, or you were adamant about coming out here because you wanted to tell me something without him being around."

"Can't it be both?"

Seth shrugs. "Probably. Possibly. But I'm more interested in the former than the latter."

A twinge of annoyance, not directed at Seth, floods through me like hot oil. I used to be better at this. Better at keeping my cards closer to my chest. But this lifestyle . . . it dulls your senses. When you live easy, you forget how to be hard. You forget how you have to be sharp and prickly to survive. And as such, you forget all your coping skills you had, because you don't need them anymore.

Old Xavier wouldn't have given so much away. Showing that much of himself to Seth would be giving away too much free knowledge. But new Xavier? The one who does favors without asking anything in return? Who *dates* his boss? Who is actually considering staying here, living this reality? He doesn't care that Seth might get the best of him.

He might even trust Seth.

But this Xavier isn't concerned with those ideals. This Xavier is going out of his way to help someone, to do something for someone that doesn't help him at all. We call that growth.

"I need a favor from you."

Seth arches his brow. "Now I'm curious."

"Logan had a food critic come by a week and a half ago."

Seth's face turns darker. "Oh."

"Oh? He didn't tell you?"

Seth sighs, shaking his head. "But I'm not surprised. What would you say if I told you that Logan internalizes everything? And I mean everything?"

"I would say that tracks. Most successful people take things too seriously. If everything is a stab at your core, then you'll do everything you can to ensure everything you do is exceptional."

"That's Logan for you. He doesn't take critique well."

"Who does?"

Seth shrugs.

"Every time I ask him about it, he brushes me off."

"Again, that's Logan for you," Seth says.

"And I'm Logan's . . ."

Seth seems to agree. "Boyfriend, I know. He's called me about you."

"Good things I hope?"

"Very good things."

"Even more of a reason for you to help me," I explain. "I want to help him, Seth. He checks his phone constantly. It's all he thinks about."

"It's not that simple."

"What do you mean? I get being hung up about a review, I would be, too, but . . ."

"It's not that simple, Xavier."

Seth pauses, like something is on the tip of his tongue that he's hesitating to say.

"If you know something that can help me help him, you should tell me. You're Logan's best friend."

Seth picks up the cooler that he had under the table and opens it, pulling out two cans of Coke submerged in what used to be ice and is now just ice water. I take the one he offers, open it, and wait for him to take a sip.

"Can I ask you something before I tell you?"

I nod.

"You're not going to break his heart, are you?"

Seth's proclamation catches me mid-sip. The bubbles ride into my nostrils and burn my face. I force a warm swallow down, shaking my head, eyes red.

"Logan doesn't fall for people easily, not since the divorce. He's been focusing on building a life for Anne. But when he was with you last time? That was a side of Logan I hadn't seen in a while."

"I feel like Logan's bossy all the time," I mutter, but there isn't any animosity in my voice. His bossiness is understandable now, and I've kinda grown to like it about him.

Seth chuckles around the rim of his drink. "Relaxed. Honest.

Playful. For the first time in a long time, when I saw him with you, I saw a guy who hadn't given up on having a life for himself. A guy who hadn't resigned himself to simply be a chef or a father but someone who can live for more than that."

Seth takes a longer sip from his Coke. "The Wharf is about to be foreclosed on."

The words feel like a sledgehammer that slams right into the center of my chest. As if Thor's hammer slammed right into the center of my body without mercy in the climax of some overly produced Marvel film that relies more on rippling muscles than on plot and subtext. Honestly, in the moment, I'm impressed and pretty proud of myself that I don't spit all over Seth. That deserves a pat on the back. Spit takes are rarely actually funny in real life.

"Sorry, come again?"

Seth studies me. Really studies me. "He didn't tell you?"

I shake my head.

"I'm not surprised," he sighs, combing his fingers through his hair. It's the first time I notice his receding hairline.

"I shouldn't be telling you this. Logan would kill me. He doesn't like people in his business. But you're not just people, are you? Since you're staying around, right?"

The call from the foundation replays in my head. I'm so close to being able to pay that off. Just a few more shifts, and I'll be good. What I've always wanted so close to within my grasp. I just need to hold on.

But now? Now all I want to do is help Logan out.

"I'm sticking around," I say. I'm not sure if that's true, but there are worse things that can happen than this little white lie.

Plus, sticking around in Harper's Cove doesn't seem as bad an option as it did six weeks ago.

The words seem to convince Seth enough. He gives a small

nod, pulls out a cigarette, and goes through the automatic motions of lighting it.

I bite my tongue; he doesn't need to know almost half a million people in the US die a year from smoking.

"The Wharf hasn't been doing well recently," Seth says bluntly. "A seafood restaurant in a fisherman's town? Everyone there knows how to make their own seafood. Why go to a restaurant for it when you can make it at home? Plus, Logan's not a Cover, he's an outsider. No matter how much he wants to pretend that doesn't matter, it matters."

Seth loads a final container into his truck.

"Also, most restaurants fail," I add. "Seventy percent in their first five years?"

"Eighty," he corrects. "It's one of the reasons he and Michelle broke up."

"I thought that was because of her music?"

"Everything is two sided, Xavier," he says. "Michelle's music was part of it, but Logan wouldn't see reason. Now, to his credit, Logan had a dream, and he followed through with it. He's always wanted to own a restaurant, and when he saw a way to make it happen, he went for it. Most people aren't brave enough to follow their dreams. It's why him and Michelle worked so well. In some ways, they are two sides of the same coin.

"Michelle saw the restaurant as a bad investment. There were dozens of other things she suggested he put his money into, instead of a bleeding pit of cash, but he wasn't having it. Call it stubbornness or drive or both, but he just kept pouring more and more money into that place, into that dream. Took out more and more loans just to prove that the Wharf isn't a mistake."

Seth takes a drag, sitting in the back of his truck. It hisses and whines as the metal bends under his weight.

"You know Logan, he's a charming guy and a good chef, if not a great one. He's gotten by for the past few years on that. Goodwill with the bank, favors, eking by every month, each time rent is due, barely making a profit. But even that has its limits. Banks only have so much grace. There's only so many months you can live so close to the edge, and he's hit that limit. This review? It's the spark he needs to keep the bank at bay. A good review from a nationally respected critic will show the restaurant has promise, bring in a wave of customers, and is the collateral he needs to keep the bank at bay a little while longer."

"He knows that's all a gamble, right?" I ask. "Like, yes, banks, especially in Harper's Cove, will make decisions based on if they like people or not. It's the benefit of a small town over, let's say, Portland, but basing everything off a good review?"

Seth shrugs. "Logan is an idealist at heart. He's a romantic who believes in the good of people and happy endings. This is just another representation of that. He thinks a glowing review and his good heart, the work and investment he's put into The Wharf, will be enough to get another month, or six weeks, or eight from the bank. And that's all he needs."

"And a bad review will tank all of that."

"It's not just that, though," he says, not looking at me while organizing his remaining produce. "He's afraid losing the restaurant will mean he won't be able to provide for Anne, that he'll let his daughter down. And besides the Wharf, and maybe you, there isn't much he cares more about."

Seth's statement doesn't go without notice, and I feel my cheeks burning hot. I push through the discomfort; this isn't about me.

"Why doesn't he just ask for help? There are so many services to help get people out of debt. Michelle doesn't seem like the type, from what I've heard, to hold this against him."

"She isn't."

"So why doesn't—"

"Pride, Xavier," Seth interrupts. "It cometh before the fall."

I chew on my bottom lip, letting Seth smoke his cancer stick in silence. My analytical brain is already starting to work, trying to find a solution to Logan's problem. My body buzzes with a live-wire-type vibration that is akin to getting high. This is literally my field of expertise. This is what I wanted to do with my life. And what's the point of living if we can't help the people we care about?

Seth nudges me with his foot. "You gonna pick that up?"

I blink back into consciousness, Logan's calling. I stare at the phone, chewing on my bottom lip until I draw blood. Clicking the side twice, I send it to voicemail and quickly type out: Driving hit you up soon.

Seth doesn't say anything about me declining Logan's call, and I'm thankful for that. Jumping off the back of the truck, I finish my soda in three burning gulps.

"I should get this food back. Thanks for telling me, Seth."

He gives me a two-finger salute as I walk with Seth to get my Prius in the parking garage. Before I can put my seat belt on, Seth taps his knuckles against the window.

"Logan's a good guy, Xavier."

"Never said he isn't."

"No, you didn't. But I know that look in someone's eyes. It's the look of someone who is trying to fix things."

I open my mouth to dispute his ridiculous statement, but nothing comes out, just silence. Seth smirks. "I feel like you being silent is a rare thing, so I'm going to chalk that up to a win."

"I see where Logan gets his humor from."

Seth shrugs. "But seriously. You can't fix everything. And if you actually care for Logan, you won't try and fix him or change him, you'll take him as he is. Because if he does lose the Wharf, he's going to need someone on his side."

"I'm not going to do anything, Seth."

I avoid looking at him, focusing on fiddling with the gear, the radio, even shifting the car into drive.

That doesn't stop him from staring at me with that *bullshit, Xavier* expression.

"I promise," I say. "Scout's honor."

"Are you even a Boy Scout?"

I shrug, revving the engine, which isn't much of a growl since a Prius doesn't exactly roar to life, but it's enough to make him step back. I give him a nod before pulling off and heading back to Harper's Cove.

On the way, my phone vibrates. Another text from Logan. This time it's a photo of the TV with *The Devil Wears Prada* on it, purchased. The caption reads:

Alright let's see what's so good about this movie. You free tomorrow after work?

I don't hesitate to text back **yes**.

And almost completely miss my exit along the way.

TWENTY-SEVEN

THOUGHT PEOPLE HATED ANNE Hathaway."

That is the thing Logan takes away from us finishing *The Devil Wears Prada*. Not the iconic lines. Not the outfits. Not how it changed a generation. But asking me if people hated Anne Hathaway.

"Seriously?"

I have to give him some credit, though. The pita chips he made, drizzled with olive oil and lightly dusted with Parmesan? They are the perfect movie snack. Coupled with the apples drizzled with honey? Exceptional.

This guy might have the cooking thing down. But his slander of Queen Anne? I can't let that slide.

"Ow!" he hisses as I hit him with a pillow. "What was THAT for?"

"If you're going to critique someone in the movie, the first thing you have to say is if you enjoyed it or not."

"That's NOT how that—OW! STOP, Xavier!"

Logan isn't worried about being too loud, even though it's

approaching 11:00 p.m. Anne is with a friend for the evening and will be back in the morning, so we have the house to ourselves. Seems like we should be taking advantage of that. Spending our time doing . . . something more than just watching a movie nearly twenty years old.

"You still haven't told me if you liked the movie!"

"I liked it, okay? Jesus!"

He grabs the pillow before I can hit him for a fourth time and tosses it on the floor. With easy and quick movements, Logan is once again on top of me, like he was before. His body straddles mine, crotch pressing firmly against my own, adding just the right amount of needed and wanted pressure.

"But I like you better," he whispers, leaning down and pressing a hot, burning kiss against my lips.

Any obstinance I was thinking of throwing his way goes out the window when he kisses me like that. Sure, sex is great, but being kissed? Like that? Ten times better. It's dizzying almost, like the world is collapsing around me in the best way possible.

His kisses are soft, they aren't hurried. There's no one in the room but us and the faint light of the TV's credits rolling barely illuminates Logan's midsection. My arms slip around Logan's firm body, squeezing his sides. He lets out a shiver.

I love that shiver.

Deftly, my fingers slide down his sides and move to fumble with the drawstring of the gray sweats he's wearing. Honestly, boys in gray sweats? God's gift to humanity.

"Don't hurt me," he whispers almost huskily, with lust dripping in his voice right in my ear. There's a level of teasing playfulness in his words. But the statement pulls me out of the moment more than I'm sure he intended.

All I can see, all I can hear, is Seth asking me if I was going to leave Logan, if I was going to hurt him. It reminds me, bringing the memory right to the forefront of my mind, the truth Logan has been hiding about the Wharf.

"Hey, can we stop?"

Logan doesn't need more than that. He pulls back without another thought. He sits up, black shirt riding up slightly to show the happy trail on his abs. "Of course." He looks down at me with a concerned furrow of his brow. "Everything okay?"

How do I tell him what's on my mind? How do I confess that I know something so personal about him, only because his best friend thought he could confide in me?

I nod, shifting to sit up. He gives me the space I need, moving away as I rise, like a magnet of the same polarity, unable to touch.

"That's not an answer," he gently reminds me.

Logan stands, frowning as I buy myself a moment by finishing the ginger beer he made and was oh so proud of. The sting sends prickles down my throat, but it's a nice and almost familiar feeling. Mom loves to cook spicy food, like she's some mad scientist who is trying to test Dad's and my limits.

"I'm fine." A beat. "Promise."

Which is true. I am fine. I'm just . . . trying to navigate all of this. Trying to decide what person I want to be.

I can see the paths diverging in front of me. I can tell him what Seth told me, confess it all and expect him to actually be able to hold a conversation after he was "betrayed" by his friend and me.

I can ignore everything that I learned. Push it aside and remind myself this isn't my life, it's his. I'm not responsible for him. Logan is an adult. Whatever happens, happens. Trust in the universe or whatever.

Both are valid options. Both have responsible outcomes.

But what do I do? I just turn on my heels and walk into the kitchen, putting distance between Logan and me. For as long as that lasts.

Space will help me think, I reason, turning on the faucet to swallow a glass of cool water. I know, according to most people, I'm probably overthinking this. Logan didn't technically lie to me. I didn't ask him point-blank how the restaurant was doing. He didn't try to hide phone calls from me. This is, after all, like Seth told me, his lifeblood.

But that doesn't mean there isn't a small bit of me, deep inside my chest, that feels like something was kept from me. I worked my whole academic life to be someone who can help put businesses on the path to success. If he needed help, why didn't he come to me? I would have been more use fixing his books than prepping carrots.

Maybe that's what upsets me the most. He could have asked me for help and yet he didn't. Why? One reason only.

He didn't and doesn't trust me.

Logan taps my shoulder twice, pulling me from my mind. It's not the first thing I should have noticed. I should have noticed the burning hot water overflowing the cup and turning my hand red.

"Shit!" I hiss, doing what any normal person would do. The glass shatters in the farm sink. "Sorry."

"It's just a glass, babe," Logan reminds me. "I have plenty of them. But maybe I should dock that from your pay."

He's joking, I know, and I try to let out a snort under my breath to show him that I know he's joking. But the notes fall flat, the joke doesn't hit its mark. I catch Logan arching his brow again, a puzzled expression that shifts into a frown.

He wants to ask what's wrong. He wants to ask why I'm holding back and hiding. Thirty percent of people said, in a study I read, that lying ruined their relationship. I'm doing the exact thing I know can doom us.

"Sit," Logan says, gesturing to the bar stools. Maybe he doesn't want to know what I'm keeping from him. Maybe he already knows.

I listen obediently, watching as Logan practically glides around the room. He pulls a stool in front of me, balancing the first aid kit on his lap.

"Anne always gets into some shit," he explains, cutting a long string of gauze. "I have these all over the house."

"I bet you were a wild child too when you were her age."

"Oh, absolutely." He grins. "But you don't get to know that yet."

"Let me guess, I haven't earned it?"

"You haven't earned it."

He scoots closer to me, focusing on slowly wrapping the palm of my hand with gauze. His touch is gentle, soothing almost like a human version of aloe vera. Logan hums, pressing a kiss to my wrist.

"All better," he mutters, keeping the palm of my hand against his cheek. His eyes, thoughtful and pensive, look up at me through his dark lashes.

It's intoxicating.

It's breathtaking.

It's the most beautiful thing I've ever seen.

"You know you can tell me anything, right?" he whispers. "You don't need to hide anything from me. I'm not going to hurt you."

The funny thing is? I believe him. With every fiber of my

chest, pulse of my blood, and flex of my muscles. Logan isn't going to hurt me. He isn't the enemy here. Whatever he is hiding from me and for whatever reason, he deserves to have his own secrets.

That doesn't make it feel any better or any easier.

"I know," I promise. Leaning forward, I gently grab both sides of his face and pull him into a kiss, my full lips brushing against his own. I try to pull back a moment later, but his right hand moves up, slips up to curl his fingers into my locs, and deepens the kiss.

Our lips stay like that for what feels like eternity—an eternity I'd be happy to spend with Logan. But I'm the one to end it, the one who pulls back and speaks words that feel like molasses on my tongue.

"I should get going," I whisper. "I have to help Mom with something tomorrow morning, I just remembered."

Judging by the way Logan looks at me, he doesn't buy it. But that doesn't stop him from standing up and letting me go. It doesn't stop him from stealing another kiss as I stand in the doorway.

"Text me when you get home?"

"You sound like a parent."

"I am a parent," he reminds me. "Text me?"

"I will."

I don't look at Logan as I walk to my car. I have other things on my mind anyway. It's like that simple lie opened up the floodgates.

I pull out my phone as I get into my car, scrolling through the contacts. Luckily, I did in fact save Stacey Lee's. I tap her name twice while pulling out of the driveway, waving to Logan. It's late, but Stacey was always a night owl in college, so I'm betting that—

"Hell-lo," she says in a singsong voice, less of a question and more of a statement.

"Stacey Lee? It's Xavier."

"I know who you are, silly. But do you know what time it is?"

"Sorry, were you sleeping?"

"God no, I just came from a booty call. Well, your phone call saved me. Tragic man really."

"So would you say you owe me?"

Stacey Lee pauses. "Possibly, what did you have in mind?"

CHAPTER
TWENTY-EIGHT

STACEY LEE DEMANDS, IN the kindest way that Stacey Lee demands anything, that we meet in person. Which means another trip to Portland twice in one week?

I feel a heaviness in my joints as my phone vibrates while I sit in some small French bistro that I didn't even know existed. It's not a text from Stacey, not an update on why she is already twelve minutes late to a meeting she picked at 9:00 a.m., but a text from Logan.

You want me to bring you anything?

I read somewhere that gay people tend to love things like Disney and other childish things at an older age because they didn't get to live their authentic selves as youths. Being in the closet steals that from you. I don't think this is the same, but skipping out of work to meet with Stacey? Lying to my boss about being sick? That feels like how college kids would call in sick from class when they were really just hungover.

I'm fine, I text back, adding, **just caught a bug. I'll be better tomorrow, I think.**

Logan sends back a heart without hesitation.

Let me know if you need anything. Anything at all.

My stomach turns from lying to him. But, if my plan works, it won't matter. He'll appreciate me doing this. I'm helping save his restaurant. There's no way he can—

"My God why is it so early?"

Stacey flops down opposite me with larger-than-life shades on her face. She sighs, pulling off her hat with an exaggerated action that makes her look like some TikToker playing a skit of Alexis's from *Schitt's Creek*, rather than her actually being a person who pulled inspiration from Alexis from *Schitt's Creek*. As always, Stacey Lee looks exceptional. She's complaining about it being morning, and yet, every hair is in place. There isn't a single bag under her eyes. Her skin is vibrant, and her dress is perfectly pressed.

She leans forward expectantly. I only miss my cue for half a moment.

"Oh, shit, right."

Leaning forward to meet her, I kiss both of her cheeks. Emily from *Emily in Paris* has nothing on Stacey Lee.

"Hi there," a cheerful waitress with far too much energy says, bouncing over to us. "Welcome to the Continental, what can—"

"Do you have espresso?" Stacey Lee interrupts. "And not just coffee you call espresso, but real espresso."

"I believe we do; I can check in—"

"Do you know the difference?"

The woman blinks. "Between . . . ?"

Oh, dear God.

"Espresso and coffee," Stacey Lee asks, checking herself in the reflection of her iPhone. She doesn't give the woman a chance to answer. "All coffee can be espresso but not all espresso can be coffee, did you know that? In general, espresso requires a dark roast, fine grind, and high pressure to create an ounce or two—aka a 'shot'—of concentrated coffee."

"I didn't know that."

I give the waitress a sideways glance, slowly mouthing, *Sorry*, to her. She gives me a tight-lipped smile that reads, *I get this all the time*.

It's funny, Stacey Lee hasn't changed at all. I've never loved her, that's for sure, but in college, her directness? This curtness? I loved it. Now, I want to interrupt her and tell her we don't talk to people like that. Assuming this woman doesn't know such a basic difference, when she actually works in a restaurant? It's childish, it's insulting, and it reinforces the idea that anyone who isn't from a big city is a country bumpkin.

It makes my blood want to boil.

"Of course you didn't, it's not your fault. Please make sure it's actually espresso. And I'll have grapefruit. You have that, right?"

"We sure do."

"Light sugar. Splenda. That'll be all."

The woman turns to me.

"Just some iced tea. Whatever kind you have is fine, thank you, Amy."

Amy. I make sure to look at her in her eyes when I say her name, showing her silently that I see her and that I actually read her name tag.

Amy gives a small thankful smile in return before muttering she'll have our orders soon. When she's gone, Stacey Lee sighs.

"I swear, getting good service anywhere outside of New York or LA? Impossible."

That's a load of crap, but sure.

"And I imagine it's even harder in . . . where is it where you live now? Hartford's Cove?"

A twinge of white fire surges through me. Protectiveness over my town, my home, almost rears its ugly head, but I pull it back.

"Harper's Cove."

"Right," she snaps. "Cute name."

"It is a cute place."

I say that honestly, without any mendacity. Harper's Cove is a great place to grow up. Stacey Lee is the complete opposite of me, and though she's only one person—one extreme case—growing up in the big city could have meant I'd end up like her.

But she isn't alone in those thoughts. I can't solely blame her. So many kids in college and grad school, when I told them where I was from, would scrunch their noses. Like I was lesser than them or didn't belong because of where I came from. Saying, *I'm from Portland,* just became easier. At least they knew that place.

How could I have let myself get so close to that toxic flame? How could I let myself be sucked into this vortex of self-deprecation, like shunning the place that made me who I am today was some sort of bad thing? I'm not going to beat myself up for it. Being like Stacey Lee and being accepted? That's a hell of a drug. I don't think wanting that is bad.

I think putting down, even for just laughs and jokes and social clout in a bar at 2:00 a.m., the people and place that raised me, though? That's something I'll always have to live with.

Amy returns with our drinks and food. Stacey Lee studies the brown drink with the perfectly coiffed froth toupee in front of her. Like a puppy inspecting its food for the first time, she gives it a careful sniff, and then a sip.

"This'll do."

It takes all the energy I have to not roll my eyes. Okay, sure, Jan. Couldn't say, *This is good*, could you? That would have just absolutely have killed you, huh?

"I'm glad our food here at the Continental suits your highly specific desires. We want nothing more than to serve you here and to make sure your most specific wants are met."

The rib was perfectly timed, honestly. Before Stacey Lee can finish her sip, Amy is already gone and talking to another table. I tip my head downward, sipping my tea, so Stacey Lee doesn't see me smirking.

Stacey Lee, one. Amy, one. Who will win?

"Honestly, the service here in this place? Horrible," she mutters. "I don't understand how you came out of here, Xavier. You're so cosmopolitan compared to everyone else."

"I'm really not."

The words leave my mouth before I can stop them. Thankfully, Stacey Lee doesn't actually push. I can ignore her eyebrow raise and chalk it up, mentally, to her being curious and nothing more.

"Anyway," I say, a complete ninety-degree shift. "Thanks for making it out here so early, I really appreciate it, Stacey Lee."

She waves her hand dismissively. "Anything for you, Xavier. We were so close in college . . ."

We weren't.

"I'm just hoping we can get back to that."

Stacey Lee has, obviously, very selective memory. We weren't close. We floated in the same circles. I, maybe, was pulled into her magnetic orbit because, well . . . Stacey Lee is Stacey Lee. But actual friends? Close? Yeah, I wouldn't go that far.

"Sure, sure, of course." The lie feels like someone squeezing a sour lemon on open wounds. But I'm not here for me. Eating some shit feels like a decent enough penance considering the person I was when I first got here.

"Which is why, when I was thinking of who could help me, who else rather than my old friend Stacey Lee?"

Stacey Lee smirks, flipping her long dark hair over her right shoulder. "I do have a way of helping people reach their full potential. You know, friends in high school called me their fairy godmother."

"Really?"

Gag. Logan better be worth this.

He's absolutely worth this.

I gulp down half of my unsweetened tea, letting the flavors and chill coat my throat, almost as if it numbs my vocal cords, preventing my body from seizing up to stop me from asking what I need from her.

"This weekend, there's a festival in Harper's Cove. I know you said you're covering a small-town series for your network?"

Stacey Lee nods, big blue pools staring almost baby doll–like at me.

"I was wondering if you might want to come to Harper's Cove and cover it? I think it's perfect for your segment. Harper's Cove is, like, the quintessential East Coast small town. Generations still living there. We still have a drive-in movie theater. People don't lock their doors."

"That's cute."

"Sure." I flex my fingers under the table, scratching at my thigh through my jeans to steel myself. "Plus, the Wharf, Logan's—"

"Your boyfriend?"

"My boyfriend's restaurant is going to be there. He's manning a booth that's all about bringing old Harper's Cove recipes, since the 1800s, and modernizing them for—"

"Are you going to stay here, Xavier?" Stacey Lee interrupts. The question feels like she hit me in the side of the head with a baseball bat, right in my gut. Which is why she only gets a blank expression in return.

"Here, in Harper's Cove or Portland or whatever."

"I know what the word *here* means, Stacey Lee."

"Are you going to stay?" she repeats. "Because, let me be clear, I'm happy to help you and your small-town boyfriend, but I'm just wondering if this . . . the town, him . . . are just some sort of rebound thing?"

Stacey Lee leans forward. "You didn't hear this from me, but I heard Bradley misses you. He's just not man enough to reach out."

"I'm good. How do you know about that, anyway?"

Stacey Lee shrugs. "I pride myself in keeping up with my classmates."

"You should reach out. I mean, you know how much money his parents have. He might even run for mayor of Chicago in the next few years. Think of how hot it would be to be the mayor of Chicago's significant other? That's—"

"Stacey," I say firmly, not even her full name. "I'm good."

There's nothing I want less than to be on Bradley's arm again. There's nothing I want less than to be in Chicago. Honestly, there's nothing I want less than to be around Stacey Lee or any reminder of the person I was before Harper's Cove. Before the breakup.

Before Logan.

Stacey Lee studies me. Like, really studies me, as if she'll find some secret switch hidden under my skin that'll make me come to my senses. I wonder what she sees when she looks into my eyes. Does she see someone who needs saving or someone who finally found their way back home and is comfortable in their own skin, for once? Someone who doesn't feel like they're playing catch-up and trying to be someone they aren't just to appeal to others.

I hope she sees the latter.

Stacey Lee's phone vibrates. She pulls it out, scans the message, and then downs the espresso as if it wasn't boiling hot.

"I need to get going," she says, standing. "Emergency at the station. You know how picky and particular talent can be."

Stacey Lee fishes out twenty bucks, throwing it on the table. "That should cover my half."

She had an espresso. Mentally, I like to think she's just a really good tipper and not that she has no idea how much an espresso cost.

"When is this festival thing? This weekend?"

I nod. "Sunday, is that too soon?"

My phone vibrates, a notification from my bank.

DIRECT DEPOSIT—$600, it reads.

I do a quick swipe up, logging in with my face. I'm still eight hundred dollars short; an obtainable amount, but not my goal.

"I'll bring a crew," she says, perfectly positioning her beret on top of her beachy blond hair. "We'll get a few shots, an interview of your man. It'll be great. I'll do a whole profile on him. I'll make him look . . . less rugged."

"People like his rugged look," I remind her.

"People, or you?"

"Is there a difference?"

Stacey Lee shrugs. "You must really like him, huh? To give up a possible First Gentleman mayoral position for . . . well . . . this."

I ignore the way she says *this*, instead focusing on the first part of her sentence. "I do. You'll love him, too."

"It only matters if the camera loves him," she says in a sing-song voice, blowing me a kiss. "Ciao, bello, Xavier."

I give her a wave, chuckling to myself while I take a moment to finish the tea.

Stacey Lee has never been to Italy in her entire life. I know this, because she's terrified of planes.

TWENTY-NINE

THE HARPER'S COVE FAIR is our version of the Chicago world's fair. Except, you know, without people getting locked into murder houses across the street or the first display of electricity as a modern marvel.

And not in Chicago.

It's all hands on deck at the Wharf, and the night before, people just seem to accept that. No one is against coming in early the next day to finish cooking a stew or the gourmet pigs in a blanket or whatever it is we were assigned. And like any good prep chef, I prepare the team for battle with the most important thing, coffee.

"Shit, shit, shit," I whisper, trying to balance the trays of six coffees without spilling them. The sudden, last-minute rain last night left the park soaked. The boots make a sopping sound that reminds me of a Vine that anyone with any sort of class would slap the shit out of me for referencing.

But right now, I'm more concerned about spilling the coffee everywhere and being late. Because if you can count on one thing, it's that Xavier will always run on CP time, no matter how early he leaves.

"Here, lemme help," Logan says. He doesn't give me a chance to protest, taking one of the trays in his rough hands. Our fingers touch for a moment, and even still, it's like electricity runs through my body.

"My knight in shining armor," I tease.

Carefully, somehow with the coffee in hand, he flexes his toned right bicep. "I don't think silver's my color, but for you, I'll make an exception."

We walk across the lawn, following the sounds of Kyle and Angelica arguing over which direction to turn the table. Their bickering, at first, was childish and annoying, but it isn't the Wharf if these two aren't arguing about something.

"Thanks for this," Logan says. "You know how Angelica is without her coffee."

"It's the least I could do. You know, rally the troops."

"You didn't have to, though," he argues while we walk, our steps easily falling into stride. "Your only job is to make sure the food gets done."

"And to be your boyfriend."

Logan shrugs almost bashfully. "If you still want to, sure."

I arch my brow, setting the coffee down on the table. If I still want to? What does that mean? Is there something I don't know that he's avoiding telling me?

No, I think while lining up the cups. It's not that, I know better. By the way Logan looks at me—like really looks at me—I can tell he senses it, too. I've been distracted the past few days. Stuck in my own head trying to deal with how I feel about everything going on with Logan and the Wharf. It's like I've been here but not fully present.

That's why he came over. That's what that look that lingers a bit longer than it should means. It's a silent question.

I squeeze his shoulder a moment and lean over, kissing his cheek.

"There's an answer to your question."

"Nope." Logan shakes his head. "Not the answer I was looking for."

Before I can ask what exactly that answer could be, Logan shows me. He grabs both sides of my face, gently forcing me to look at him and get lost in those bright blue eyes of his. The weather is cool from yesterday's rain, making the seventy-degree 6 a.m. weather tolerable. It makes the fact our bodies are so close, even in the summertime, not unbearable. The gray T-shirt Logan's wearing hasn't become dark with sweat yet either. His toned muscles are evident, sure, because what fit man doesn't look just fucking perfect in a gray T-shirt, dark jeans, and boots?

Exactly.

But I can't focus on how handsome he is, even in a simple outfit he probably paid twenty bucks for, because suddenly his lips are pressed chastely against my own. It's a soft kiss, the type that reminds me of spinning the bottle in high school and not knowing what I was doing.

But he knows exactly what he's doing. And I want him to keep doing it and never stop. No matter if our staff is looking.

"We have company," I mutter.

"Let them look," Logan whispers. "Being with you like this is my happy place, and I'm not going to let anyone take that from me. Even—"

"Finally," Kyle's deep voice booms. "I mean, come on, how long were we going to keep up with this whole 'will they won't they'?"

"You seriously thought they were hiding anything?" Angelica asks. "Straight men are as dense emotionally as a brick."

Kyle's face twists into mock hurt. "Oh, come on, you can't pretend that—"

"About six weeks, right?" Angelica asks. "That's how long you've been dating?"

Logan opens his mouth and then closes it, narrowing his eyes at Angelica.

"What, don't look at me like that," she scolds. "Listen, I'm happy for you. You're nicer when you're in love."

"Dick will do that to somebody," Kyle mutters under his breath. All three of us glance over at him. Judging by how Kyle has a folded-up croissant twisted into a bite-sized ball about to get lobbed into his mouth, he wasn't expecting that.

"You heard that, didn't you? You weren't supposed to hear that," he says.

"Everyone did," I say.

"Probably the whole park," Logan adds.

"People across the sound heard it, too, I'm sure," Angelica finishes.

Kyle puts his hands up in defense. "All I'm saying is that you've been nicer since you two started hooking up."

"Hooking up?" I ask, arching my brow and looking at Logan. "So now we're just hooking up, huh?"

Logan shrugs. "I mean, I guess that's what the kids call it nowadays. Hooking up."

"Oh, for fuck's sakes. I'm just going to shut up now," Kyle says.

"Probably for the best," Angelica adds, turning to us. "Look, I'm happy if you two are happy. Are you happy?"

It's relaxing in the moment to see Logan banter playfully

with his two employees. Right then, I kind of forget that we work in the restaurant. It kind of just feels like friends ripping into each other at a picnic during summertime. Logan, even though he has so much weight bearing down on him regarding the Wharf and this impending review from the critic, has relaxed shoulders and his laugh lines are showing. I think, maybe just for a moment, he forgot that with one review, everything can come tumbling down.

"Well, whatever you want to call it," Kyle finally chimes in. "It's nice to see you happy, boss. Really."

Logan slips his arm around my waist, pulling me close before I can protest. He presses a warm and wet kiss against my cheek, the type that makes a loud popping noise, before pulling back, a boyish grin painted over his features.

"Yeah, I'm happy."

This is the point in the script where I would say, *Me too*. The point when I would tell him, without hesitation, with Kyle and Angelica as our witnesses, he brings to the forefront the happiest version of myself that I've ever experienced. This will be the part where we, metaphorically, sail off into the sunset and live happily ever after. The camera would pan up, showing the whole park, with credits rolling on the screen while some pop song plays in the background as people leave the theater.

This would be the beginning of the happily ever after that, when I was younger, I didn't think was possible because people like me—Black queer boys growing up in small towns—don't get happily ever afters. But instead, I say probably the worst thing anyone in my situation could say.

"Can I talk to you privately?"

Tone in the park drastically shifts. Kyle and Angelica glance at each other in that knowing way that people who know shit's about to go down look at another person. It's how I probably imagined people on the *Titanic* looked at one another when they heard the sound of the ship hitting the iceberg.

For someone who doesn't know what's about to happen, Logan keeps his composure. The smile on his lips is soft, almost like a goofy golden retriever with his head in the clouds. He squeezes my hand gently.

"Course," he says. He turns to Kyle and Angelica. They don't even give him a moment to speak.

"We'll handle things here," Angelica says.

"People are going to start coming soon, though," Kyle warns.

And he's right. It may be morning, but the cars are already starting to pull in. The Harper's Cove festival is going to be a daylong thing. It will start at nine o'clock and go until the wee hours of the morning. Once things get going, there won't be time to pull Logan aside and talk to him. There won't be a moment to tell him what I did or to confess what I know. It has to be now.

"We'll be back in a second," I promise.

I pull Logan off to the side, with more force than I would probably need to make him move. Under one of the large oak trees, which have been here since as long as I can remember, I find the courage inside of me to say what I wanna say. To confess what I need to confess.

"Before you say anything," Logan interrupts. "I want to say something first."

Shit.

What am I supposed to say to that? *No, you can't, because I need you to understand that maybe, just maybe, I might have over-stepped a boundary?*

My face must have completely given me away, because Logan

makes his eyes wide, almost like saucers, lacing his fingers together and resting his chin on top of his knuckles. He looks cute, almost innocent, replicating that childish pleading look that is a quintessential example of someone using their cuteness to get what they want.

"You know you're not that cute to be able to pull that off," I scold, trying to hold back a smile.

"Oh, I'm plenty fucking cute, Xavier. That's why you like me."

"Nah, I think I love you."

Record scratch.

Record. Mother. Fucking. Scratch.

Logan's eyes shift from being wide as a cute tactic, to being wide in surprise. My eyes, I know, do the exact same thing. If I could pull them out of their sockets and turn them to look at my lips, I'm sure I'd get all the confirmation I need.

"Shit."

"Did you just say . . . ?"

"Fuck."

"Wait, hold on."

"Shit fuck shit."

"Did you just say you love me?"

Obviously, I just said I love you, I hiss mentally. Even if that wasn't the intention, here we are, stuck between a confessional and a love-drunk confession.

Maybe it's for the best. Maybe Logan will tell me I'm moving too fast. Maybe he'll say he doesn't love me because he can't love anyone else because he's still getting over his wife. Maybe . . . Maybe . . . Maybe . . .

"I love you, too."

The words come out of Logan's mouth so casually. That doesn't lessen the weight of them, in fact it feels like a ton of bricks was dropped from a passing airplane and landed directly on my head. There's a lot of responsibility when someone says *I love you* and they mean it. It's not that I don't love him back. I don't think if I had the power to turn back time, I would take back what I said.

It's just scary to know that someone might have my heart in their hand, and theirs in mine.

"And before you say we haven't been dating long enough to say that, because I know that logical annoying brain of yours is thinking it or trying to back yourself out of what you think is a cage you've walked into," Logan scolds, "it doesn't have to be that deep. It doesn't have to be a life-changing thing. We're both adults, Xavier, and we know our hearts and our minds. I know what I'm feeling, and I don't need society to tell me when it's okay to admit that I care about someone deeply, fully, and completely. And I know that I care about you in that way right now. And I'm not afraid to admit that."

The words sound perfect. Almost too perfect. Like when you're in a dream and everything is going so right that you just know that nothing is real. I guess I could say that I deserve happiness. I mean, who in the world doesn't deserve to have a little bit of peace and love?

But it's not that simple. It's never that simple.

"Look," I say quietly. "I don't want you to think my hesitation means I didn't mean what I said."

"Did you? Mean what you said?"

"Yes. I did."

That was easier to say than I thought. Maybe when you're with the right person, the words just naturally come out. Maybe things aren't supposed to be so hard when you're with the right person?

What's that song? *There's no music, no confetti. / Crowds don't cheer, and bells don't ring.*

Maybe, just maybe, Logan is that right person.

"I just think you need to hear me out before—"

"Logan?"

Sugary-sweet words flit through the air. Logan and I turn in the direction of the question, almost at the exact same time, but only one of us shows any sort of recognition for the woman with a dirty blond high ponytail, standing in capri jeans, a leather jacket, and what looks like a distressed-jeans-patterned T-shirt.

"Michelle? Hey! I mean, what are you doing here?"

Of course. *Of course* Logan's *ex-wife* would show up exactly at this moment.

And of course, she's turned to me, looking directly at me, and says as innocently as possible. "Xavier, right? I got your invitation. Where do I set up?"

CHAPTER
THIRTY

LOGAN HAS A RIGHT to be angry at me. He has every right to volley any sort of profanity, accusation, or anything he wants directly at me with little concern for my own emotional well-being. If the situation were reversed and my current boyfriend had been in contact with Bradley when I was dating them, I would be pissed, too.

But he's not angry. Not in the typical sense. Sure, his jaw is tight, and his lips are thin, but he's quiet, giving me a chance to explain myself. As if that would fix anything.

"That's not exactly true," I finally say.

Michelle cocks her head to the side. "You didn't invite me?"

"No."

"To perform?"

"No."

"Are you sure?" Logan asks.

"I'm pretty sure I would remember if I invited your ex-wife, Logan."

The words come out sharper than I wanted them to. But the

way my heart beats so loudly in my ears makes it so the tips of my fingers and toes feel like ice. I'm on the defensive, caught, metaphorically, with my pants down around my ankles, trying to figure out what in the hell is going on and why this woman, probably the second-most important person in Logan's life, after Anne, is suddenly here looking at me. Acting like she knows me.

Michelle pushes her lips into a thin line. Objectively, Michelle is a beautiful woman. With her dirty-blond hair and her heart-shaped face, she looks like Brooke Shields, just younger. Tall, with perfect skin, and an air of casual confidence that isn't oppressive or that makes you think she thinks she's better than you, even though she was absolutely the popular kid in high school and probably college.

"You reached out to Stacey Lee, right?" she asks. "The reporter for WCBA?"

And there it is. There's the other fucking shoe I knew was going to drop.

Recognition passes over Logan's face. I see his eyes process the information, kind of like an AI system in some multimillion-dollar-budget science fiction movie processing data. I don't need to be inside his head to know what he's thinking, seeing the image of our time in Portland a few months ago passing through his mind's eye, remembering who Stacey Lee is.

And that means he's starting to see how I overstepped.

"I didn't know she was going to contact you," I say. I'm not sure if I'm speaking to Logan or to Michelle. "I'm not sure why she contacted you, if I'm being honest."

"The Harper's Cove Fair?" Michelle asks, glancing at Logan. "You have a booth for the Wharf?"

"I do," Logan says in that curt way that shows he's trying to hold back what he's really feeling. Part of me hopes he wants to direct that curtness toward Stacey Lee, but I know who is going to receive the brunt of it when Michelle leaves.

"Reporter reached out and said she's doing a piece on you and the restaurant," Michelle explains to both of us, her brow twisted in a puzzled manner as she speaks slowly. "Said she was a big fan of my music, asked if I would be there to help support you . . . of course, I had to say yes. It would have been nice to know you needed the support."

"That's because I don't," Logan snaps. Almost instantly he sighs, rubbing his face with both his hands. "Sorry. Didn't mean it come out like that. What I meant to say was I'm fine. I appreciate you coming but everything is good."

Michelle opens her mouth to say something but pauses. I can see why she and Logan dated, and married. The same signs of recognition passing over Logan's face just moments before mimics hers.

"You didn't know about this?"

He shakes his head.

"You . . . didn't reach out to the reporter? Didn't mention me?"

"Nope."

"So you don't know she's going to be here in fifteen minutes or less?"

"Trust me, Michelle, I would have given you a heads-up before asking you to fly across the country, when you were just here. Honestly, and I mean this as nicely as possible, but I don't really know why they reached out to you. But I bet someone does."

Both Michelle's and Logan's eyes settle on me, and for the first time in a long time, I feel something I haven't felt before. Small. Like I've stepped into a room where everyone is in on a joke about me, except me.

Michelle clears her throat, speaking first. "I can go if you want."

"No, no." A beat. "It's great to see you again; seriously. I mean it. And I'm sure Anne will be happy you're here. You know she can't ever get enough time with her mom. She'll be here in a bit; she spent the night at a friend's house and then is heading over. This will be a nice surprise."

Michelle nods. "I'm not against helping you, Logan," she says softly. "You know that. You could have asked—"

"I know," he interrupts. The moment lingers heavily in the air, as if Logan isn't sure what he wants to say. All signs point to Michelle and Logan having a great relationship. I never thought otherwise. If there was a pairing that could be a poster child for a solid co-parenting situation, it would be these two.

But something *is* off. It's like when someone sneaks into a room and rearranges everything just an inch to the left. You can't see it, or place it, but you know something's wrong. That's me right now.

"Can you give me a second?" he asks Michelle.

"Of course." Her bright eyes glance over at me, studying me, for only a moment, but that moment carries so much weight in it. It makes me feel like a child again. Like she's judging me or chastising me, or both.

"I'm going to go ahead and get set up," she says. "Anywhere work?"

"Anywhere," Logan replies. "You going to play your greatest hits?"

She smirks. "Of course, Lo. What else would I play?"

A part of me—a large part of me—doesn't want Michelle to leave, because once she does, I'm going to have to have the conversation with Logan I don't want to have. I'm going to have to confess how and why I meddled. I'm on the defensive right now, ready to defend myself and my reasons. And when you get defensive, you get snappy; you say things you regret. This isn't a place I want to be. Ever.

Especially not with Logan.

I watch Michelle's backside retreat, blending in with the growing crowd of attendees at the festival. My eyes lock onto Angelica's for a moment, and she quirks her brow, questioning silently why Logan and I aren't over there, helping her and Kyle.

"Come with me," Logan growls under his breath. "Now."

He doesn't give me a chance to respond, turning on the heels of his boots and walking quickly toward the parking lot. His stride is long, almost as if he's trying to keep the distance between us from shortening.

"Wait up," I hiss. "Logan, slow down!"

He doesn't listen; of course he doesn't listen. Would I listen if I were in his situation? If someone had gone behind my back and contacted Bradley, what would I have done?

I wouldn't talk to them anymore, I think. I know that. I know how stubborn I am. How this would be considered, to me, a violation of our trust.

I'm going to be sick.

Logan finally stops when we reach the edge of the park, where the green bleeds into gray and the nearly full concrete takes over. He flashes a smile that doesn't reach his eyes at the few of the passersby; customers at the Wharf we both know very well, the regulars. It's a fake grin, though. Not his usual bright and cheerful golden retriever–like grin I've grown to adore, no matter how much it annoys me to see.

Logan crosses his arms over his chest, looking almost like a peacock puffing his chest to make himself look more threatening. The sad part? It works. It feels like he's a few inches taller, like he dwarfs me more so than usual.

"Spill."

Direct and to the point.

"Okay," I say. "You have to promise you won't get mad."

"Oh, we're already past that," he warns. "I'm not promising you anything. You're going to tell me why my ex-wife is here, why she knows you by name, and what the *hell* she's talking about."

Logan's voice grows louder and louder with each word, approaching a yell. I open my mouth to tell him to calm down, but—

"You're seriously not about to tell me to calm down, are you?" he asks.

"I just don't think we should be yelling. It's going to draw attention."

"How about we focus more on what I asked. Again, why is my ex-wife here?"

I could probably talk my way out of this. I could find a way to work around his anger and find a viable solution. I'm good at that. Cost-benefit analysis, falling on your own sword for the greater good? I'm an expert at shit like that. It's how I survive. It's how any smart businessperson survives.

But I don't want to be a business wonk right now. I don't want to be obsessed with the probability and numbers. I don't want to try to lessen the blow. I want—and this feels weird even thinking—to be honest. I want to be real. I want to be . . . authentic.

Because that's what love is, right? If Logan really loves me, if he meant it, then it shouldn't matter how badly I fucked up. I mean, yeah, it *does*, and it *will*, but we should be able to get through it. Because love will pull us through. Love will conquer all.

I have to believe that. I *want* to believe that.

So, I take a deep breath and tell him everything. I take that leap of faith.

"A few days ago, when I left, I went to Portland and met with Stacey Lee. You remember her."

"The girl from your college," he says, no emotion, just shortness in his voice.

"Yeah, her. She works at the station. They're doing a series on—"

"I remember, Xavier," he interrupts. "So, she's coming here?"

I nod.

"To do a profile on the Wharf?"

I nod again.

"And how does my ex-wife play into this?"

That, I don't know. But saying that isn't a worthwhile solution. That's not being honest.

"I'm guessing, like Michelle says, she wants to get the whole picture. It's a profile piece on you and the restaurant. You told me she was partially the inspiration for the Wharf."

"For me getting into cooking," he corrects.

"Right. I'm sure the reporter did her research. Helps shape you as a romantic. I'm sure she had your best interest at heart."

"I'm sure she did."

The snideness of those words feels like silver being directly injected into my vein, but I ignore it as best I can. Again, he has every right to be mad.

"My question is, why did you reach out to her without asking me?" Logan questions, scratching at his beard, his eyes narrowed.

And there it is. The quiet part said out loud. The part I was hoping he wasn't going to ask.

"Does it matter?" I ask, as if that doesn't make me suspicious.

"It absolutely matters," he says. "Because there had to be a reason you felt like you couldn't tell me directly. Or ask my permission."

There was. Of course there was.

There's no point in avoiding it. I can't hide from the truth and the mess I've made by sticking my nose in a place where it doesn't belong. All I can do is trust Logan. Trust what he said about loving me, and hope that wasn't a lie.

"You have to understand, before I tell you, that I was just trying to help," I say. My voice only comes out a whisper, though. And I can't even focus on his face—his handsome face. All I can look at are his boots.

"What did you do, Xavier?" he asks slowly.

"Promise me you'll—"

"What. Did. You. Do?"

I tap my finger against my jeans, an offbeat rhythm that didn't come from any lingering song in my head, just random notes. Something else to focus on besides what's about to happen.

Leap of faith, I say in my head. *Just take a leap of faith.*

"I went to do the produce run, like you asked me to. Seth and I got to talking. I was . . . I just mentioned to him about how worried you were about the review and—"

"And he told you," Logan finishes for me. "He fucking opened his mouth and told you."

There it is. The truth. Out there in the open for everyone to see. There was no point in hiding anymore, no point in lying.

"He always had such a big fucking mouth," Logan growls.

"He was just trying to help you," I say slowly. "I was just trying to help you."

"So, you told a reporter, what exactly? That my restaurant was failing? That I needed some cheap publicity to what? Keep the Wharf afloat? Make it seem viable?"

"I told her you'd be a good subject for her series because I believe that."

Logan lets out a condescending chortle that bubbles from the back of his throat. "Yeah, sure you do."

"What does *that* mean?"

"Oh, come on, Xavier. You're not stupid. And neither am I. This was all just a project for you. A 'rebound job' before you went off to live your life in Chicago or wherever. A pit stop."

"That's not—"

"You're not going to sit here and tell me that's not true."

"I am, because it's fucking not!"

"Sure, keep telling yourself that if it makes you feel better," he says, turning on his heels.

"No, absolutely not," I mutter, moving around him, blocking his path. "Logan. Listen. I was just trying to help! That's all! Maybe I shouldn't have reached out to Stacey Lee, but . . . the intention was good."

"Intention means shit, even Anne knows that, and she's fourteen. What you did? This publicity stunt? It's cheap, a stupid idea, and one that I didn't ask for. And you may think it shows me you care, or you're looking out for me, but you know what it shows me? That you don't trust me, and you didn't think I could succeed on my own. That you're just like everyone else who thought I was going to fail."

Logan's words aren't just loud; they're booming. It's not like he's yelling at me, but he's speaking from so deep in his chest, from his heart, that every word finds its way into any microscopic crack in my armor and expands it.

"That's not true," I whisper, flexing my fists by my side, like I'm a lightning rod grounding my frustration and hurt into my fists.

"Yeah? Then answer something for me, honestly this time. What's the Carey Foundation?"

That last sentence comes at me like a sniper's bullet piercing directly through my heart. Accurate, efficient, and merciless. Just like a sniper, it takes me a moment to realize what he actually said.

"What?"

"You heard me. What. Is. The. Carey. Foundation?"

"How do you know about that?"

"Answer my question first."

I hesitate, trying to parse through my thoughts and decide what I'm going to say, before breathing out heavily through my nose. "It's something I applied for before moving here. Months before. A fellowship in Berlin I missed out on."

"And?"

"And they reached out offering me a spot."

He crosses his arms over his chest. "When?"

"That isn't—"

"When, Xavier."

"A few days before I came to you for a job," I mutter.

"Right. Exactly. You just came to work for me so you could get out of here as quickly as possible. Like I said," Logan seethes. "I saw the alert on your phone during dinner. During our first date."

"That was a while ago?"

"Exactly. You seemed intently focused on your phone. I saw your body tense up when you saw the message, so I did some research. Found the fellowship. Even found your application on their website for it. Great essay by the way. You look fucking hot in that suit."

A million thoughts are going a hundred million miles an hour in my head. "Then why didn't you say anything? Why didn't you ask me about it before now?"

"And you still don't get it," he says. "I didn't tell you anything because I didn't care. I liked you for you. I liked what we had. And maybe, foolishly, there was a part of me that thought we would still make this, whatever this is, work even with you in Berlin for a year. There are phones and FaceTime and every form of communication under the sun. Maybe the Wharf would get to a place I could come see you, maybe show Anne the world.

"But even if none of that happened, I was okay with it because, for now, I had you. You were mine and I was yours and that was enough. To be with someone who liked me for me. Foolish fucking me."

"There's no reason you can't still have me."

"That is where we disagree."

I shake my head. "No, absolutely not," I say quickly, almost desperately. "I do like you for you. I wouldn't have done all this if I didn't. I wouldn't be considering not going to Berlin if I didn't. Seth told me you needed help, and the first thing that came to mind was HOW I could help you. I thought, if we could get enough good publicity, then the review wouldn't matter. The bank couldn't take your restaurant because the popularity would lead to more customers."

"That's exactly what I was doing, Xavier. That's *why* the review was so important."

"If it was so important, then why did you leave me, considering there was a chance the critic might show up? I know Michelle was here, but—"

He doesn't miss a beat. "Yes, it was important. But what's more important to me? Living a life I'm proud of. Being someone who can wake up every day and know I did right by Anne and by those by my side. I want Anne to grow up knowing her dad fought like hell for everything he has. But I also want her to know he's someone who doesn't shy away from love, from happiness, and who teaches her waking up with someone you care for, who cares for you, and someone who you trust by your side is more important than any review. I thought I had that in you. I was wrong."

Another shot, except this time, with a shotgun pressed right against my chest. Dozens of words, like sharp shrapnel, impale me.

"You don't mean that."

"Yeah, I do," he says. "You went behind my back."

"To *help you!*"

"What would have helped me was being HONEST!" he booms, so loudly his body shakes. It's not anger that floods through him, it's a well of hurt, be it misdirected at me or accurately zeroed in. "That's all! I didn't ask you to be my fixer, or my business consultant! I just asked you to be yourself, to be with me, and to be happy with me! To care about me for me!"

"Look," I say, after taking a deep breath. "I'm sorry, okay? I thought I was doing the right thing. I thought I was helping you. I thought—"

"I'm sorry, too, Xavier," he says, almost in a whisper. "Really, really sorry. I'm sorry we never got to actually see what this between us could become. But I have a restaurant, and Anne, and Kyle and Angelica to worry about. I don't have the bandwidth to deal with a dramatic relationship. I just want something simple and easy and quiet."

Time stops. The world stands still, and the only thing I can focus on is the sadness in his eyes.

"And honestly? I don't think you know what you want yet or where you want to be. That's okay, you're young, you don't have to know yet. I didn't know when I was your age. But I can't afford that. I just can't."

I don't want to open my mouth. I don't want to ask him for clarification because, if I do, what I think he's saying will come true. Words have power, and once we put them out into the universe, we can't stop what happens next.

But I have to know. I have to be clear with him. Because if I am, then I can do damage control. Then I can do what I do best. I can save this. I can show him what I was trying to accomplish— and failed at doing. I can save us.

"What do you mean, Logan?"

"We're done, Xavier. As boyfriends and as coworkers," he says without hesitation. "You can gather your last check on Monday. Actually, I'll just mail it to you. I'm guessing you need, what? 1K? 2K more? Consider it your severance. I hope you do great work in Berlin. I'm sure you'll do great."

And before I can say anything else, Logan walks right past me, walking quickly with his long legs back toward the Wharf table, with me standing there with my broken, shattered heart in my hand from that leap of faith that ended with me completely broken on the ground.

THIRTY-ONE

GET BY WITH A little help from my friends.

I never thought much about that song. Probably because I'm not a Beatles fan. But it's true. Fuck relationships. Fuck men. The only thing that matters in the world is your friendships, and Mya comes through clutch as she always does.

She hasn't left for the fair yet when I arrive at her house. If I had been five minutes later, gone around the block a few more times, trying to gather my emotions so I *don't* look like a complete and total wreck, then sure, I would have missed her. Then I would have been standing on her porch, looking like an idiot, with my broken heart in my hand.

"If you're here to sell me something, I promise, I don't need it, and I can get it faster on—"

I don't know what I look like. I don't know if I even want to know what I look like. The tears in my eyes make my vision so blurry, it's impossible to see anything but large, blocky shapes of Mya in front of me.

But she doesn't hesitate. She doesn't even ask me what happened. Instead, she pulls me close, wraps her arms around me, and lets me fall into her arms and mango-smelling perfume.

"It's okay," she whispers, rubbing my back. "It's okay, I got you, Xavier. I've got you."

Mya didn't even go to the fair. She, as she said, had enough leave she could take off for the rest of the year and no one could tell her shit.

"After all, what's the point of weekends if I don't use it to help bring my best friend from the brink of romantic despair?"

I don't go home for four days. Sure, I update my parents that I'm not going to *be* home. They don't ask why; I'm with Mya, and that, to them, is enough security to make sure I'm not going to do something stupid.

Enter my "Rachel Chu lying in bed at the end of act 3 of *Crazy Rich Asians*" montage. Lying in bed, ignoring all my phone calls, Mya bringing me breakfast, lunch, and dinner, while I . . . do what any person on the brink of romantic depression does. I disassociate.

I know this sounds dramatic. I know it sounds like *Xavier, it's just a breakup. You've had a breakup before. You had a breakup a few months ago that didn't wreck you like this.*

But that's the point. This isn't that. Logan isn't Bradley. I might have known him for a shorter amount of time, but I could, despite everything, see a life with Logan. I could see a life here, in Harper's Cove. It was blurry, covered in fog and not fully formed, but it was there: a goal and future I could walk toward and guide myself to. It made more sense than going to Germany for the Carey Foundation.

How stupid of me. How foolish of me. How dumb of me to forget what I've fought for, for my whole life. How idiotic of me to think that I could be happy here.

I played myself. I set myself up for this. I let my guard down. I deserve this feeling. I deserve this pain.

The buzzing in the bed from my phone is muffled by the dozens of pillows and blankets I have buried around myself. I let it ring three times before sighing, heavy bones and muscles reaching out and patting around trying to find it. On the fifth ring I grab it, press answer without looking, and put the phone to my ear.

"Hello?"

"Xavier? It's me, Ms. Cunningham, from the Carey Foundation. How are you doing?"

I sit up and pull the phone away from my face, swallowing thickly. Closing my eyes, I count to three before putting the phone back to my face and making sure there's just the right amount of pep in my voice.

"I'm great, thanks for calling."

"That's great to hear. I wanted to call you about your spot. Are you still interested? We at the Carey Foundation hope you are and think you would be a great addition to the program."

Of course they do. How many Black Americans do they have? I mean, I know that was a selling point. I laid that point on heavy during my interview process a year ago. You need more people of color in you program, and people of color need to be in higher leadership positions. And that's why you need me as part of your incoming class of Carey Fellows. To help rectify the diversity problem in C-suite positions across the country and across the world.

That version of myself who believed in things like that feels so far away. Feels like that was a completely different version of me who cared about one thing and one thing only—being successful and getting as far away from my past as possible. When all I want to do now is stay as close to home as I possibly can. To make this my home. Right now, the Carey Foundation and its fellowship and that future feels like the most distant version of myself possible.

"Are you still interested, Xavier?" she repeats.

She asks like I missed the question the first time, repeating herself to make sure she can get an answer so she can either ramp up her recruiting efforts or put me down as a loss.

"Why?"

"Excuse me?"

"I mean, why do you want me now?"

"Well, as I said before—"

"No, I know, another fellow got married. But you didn't want me before that, and now, all of the sudden, because you have a free slot, I'm worth acceptance?"

Ms. Cunningham goes silent. No rustling of papers, no heavy breathing, just stillness as she tries to think of an answer.

"The review panel goes through an extensive process to select the proper candidates for each fellowship class. The composition of the class is important to us, and a lot of the choices depend on synergy—"

"No, I know. I get that. But the thing that puzzles me is that suddenly, with this guy gone, I'm now the right type of person for the cohort when, for whatever reason, I wasn't before."

Ms. Cunningham lets out an under-the-breath scoff. "Are you assuming that the Carey Foundation makes a decision on its fellowship class based on race or sexuality?"

"I'm not. I don't know anything about this man who dropped out. Maybe he was a person of color, maybe he was queer, who knows. But I do know that having a Black openly queer American boy does fit a few boxes that would be nice for the foundation."

Silence, but this time I can hear the papers rustling. "Xavier, I take offense to that accusation. Our fellowship panel makes every decision based on creating the best class dynamic possible."

"By ensuring every person who attends is the best fit, right?"

"Exactly. And, once again, I think you'd be a great fit. Even you asking these questions shows me you're the perfect type of person to usher in the new generation of business leaders."

Of course. *Fit* is that thing white people in leadership say and don't understand how loaded it is. How can a person of color be the right presumed fit when every person you hire or include is a white person who comes from the exact same background? How can anyone who comes from a different experience and has a different point of view fit into your idea of correctness when that idea has been the same for years?

And the biggest problem? She doesn't know how wrong what she just said is.

There's a knock on my door. A heavy one. Probably just Mya wanting to check up on me, especially since she can hear me talking on the phone.

"So, regarding your deposit . . ."

I sit up in the bed, licking my lips and rubbing my hand over my exposed thigh, considering I've been in only boxer briefs for the past two days—I changed them out, of course; I'm not a complete monster.

"Xavier? Are you there?"

My palms are sweaty, and my knees are weak, with the quietest voice in my head growing louder. I know what I need to say to her. I know what I should say. But I've already done one self-destructive thing this week; two is the beginning of a pattern.

"Xavier? Hello?"

There's a part of me, such a large part of me, that wants to tell her, *Screw it*. To tell her that I'm not going to be some Black queer American token for her and the foundation. But there's nothing for me here. Logan and I are broken up. I don't have a job. At least in the world of business, I can be someone. I can excel and bury myself in my work, in the 8:00 a.m. to 7:00 p.m. hustle. I can get lost in the glitz and the glam of the big city and the expensive life.

There's a lot of maybes there, but what I do know is the Carey Foundation is my ticket to getting to a place I've always wanted to be. If they want me because I'm actually a great applicant, or just because I'm Black, doesn't matter. They want me, and I can use that to my advantage. I can use that to start a better life. A different life.

"I have the money for you; I'll log into the portal and pay it today."

Another knock. This time I get up, holding my phone between my shoulder and my ear while quickly slipping on sweats and a T-shirt to at least be presentable.

"That's great news! We're so excited to have you and welcome you into the next class of Carey fellows."

I swallow thickly. It doesn't feel as good as I thought it would. Getting what I've always wanted. In fact, it feels almost hollow.

"Xavier?" Mya says on the other side of the door. "I need you to open up."

"Ms. Cunningham, I have to go, but like I said, I'll get the money in today."

"Of course, of course, please let me know if you have any questions."

I hang up before I can rethink my life-changing choice, opening the door at the same time. Sure enough, Mya stands there, dressed in the clothes she wore to work today.

"Hey," she says, glancing at my phone. "Everything okay?"

"I'm fine." I think. "I'm better than fine. I wasn't—"

"Talking with Logan, I know," she says hurriedly, extending the phone to me. "He wants to talk to you."

I frown, giving her my full attention. "What? Mya, I don't . . ."

"Just . . ." She takes a deep breath. "Can you please talk with him? For me, Xavier?"

Well, that's ominous. I study her for a moment, but notice the telltale tightness in her face. Mya isn't usually scared, but right now, she looks damn near terrified and is trying to hide it.

I take the phone from her and take a deep breath, making my voice as light as possible, like it was when Ms. Cunningham called. He can't know I've been in a state of near depression for the past few days. He can't know the hold he had on my heart or how I so badly want to apologize. He can't—

"Anne's not with you, is she?" he asks before I can even say anything.

"What? No. I haven't seen her since the fair." A fraction of a moment passes before the fear sets in.

"Logan . . ."

"I can't find her. I can't find my daughter, Xavier."

THIRTY-TWO

LOGAN GIVES ME THE rundown of Anne's disappearance over the phone.

Ever since Michelle has been in town, Logan and her have been spending more time together. Logan and Michelle had a fight—as divorced parents do—Anne misunderstood the source of the argument, thought it was about her, and ran away. Pretty simple and direct. A tale as old as time.

"How long has she been missing?" I ask, putting the phone on the bed on speaker while I throw on a long-sleeve shirt and jeans.

"Since this morning. I thought, when I woke up, she had already gone to school without me. Then Michelle called. She was supposed to pick up Anne, and she wasn't at school."

Logan's voice is heavy, as if he feels like he's somehow to blame. There's weight in his voice, depth, and unspoken guilt that I feel like I can—or, rather, I should help resolve.

"Kids run away," I say gently. "Hell, I ran away a lot when I was her age. I'm sure you did."

"But did your parents not know you were missing for almost seven hours?"

That I can't agree to. My parents knew I was missing instantly. But my parents shouldn't be the barometer for being a good or bad parent.

"We'll find her."

That's more of a promise to myself than to Logan. I mean, she couldn't have gone far. Harper's Cove isn't the biggest place in the world. She doesn't have a car. Anne, from what I can tell, isn't some popular kid who has a bunch of friends she can run to. She's probably just . . . hiding out somewhere.

At least, that's what I hope.

"You don't have to help, I just wanted to know if . . ."

"I'm not letting you look for your daughter alone." A beat. "You're not alone, what am I talking about. Michelle's here, right?"

"Doing her own search with her new fiancé. Seriously, Xavier. I appreciate it, but you don't need to help me. I don't deserve that."

"Anne is missing, Logan. She's a child. A good kid. I'm going to help you, no matter what happened between us. Just because we're broken up—" Oof, that hurts to say. "Doesn't mean I'm not going to help you find your daughter, Logan."

After all, I like Anne. A lot. I see myself in her. I can see her wanting to leave Harper's Cove when she's seventeen, just like I did. It'll infect her, be the only thought she can think about. Every choice she'll make will be based on the thesis that this town is too small for her. She'll look for reasons to want to leave. Thinking there's more out there for her than here.

"Xavier, I think—"

"I'm going to look around. I'm a Cover after all, there's some place neither you nor Michelle would even think to look. I'll call you if I find anything."

I hang up the phone before Logan can say anything else. Hearing Logan's voice on the phone like a weighted blanket is pressing down against my chest and suffocating me, but it's a wanted feeling of pressure. I yearn for it. I crave that feeling again.

A feeling I'll never be able to have.

When I come downstairs, Mya is already grabbing her keys.

"I'm joining you," she says. "Two additional sets of eyes are better than one."

"I'll take the east?"

"And I'll take the west."

Mya and I give each other a fist bump as we walk out to our cars. Before I can get into mine, Mya calls my name.

"You good?" she asks. "I mean, are you really good?"

"No." I don't even hesitate. "But I'll be better once we find Anne. Call me if you find anything?"

Mya agrees, giving me one last look before getting into her car. We both back out, going opposite directions.

There are so many places in Harper's Cove Anne could be. The town isn't large, but there are alleyways, parks, fields, forests that meld and blend with other nearby towns, where the borders are nebulous and county lines are blurry. Harper's Cove is a great place to grow a family, not simply because it's a small town but also because of the proximity to nature. I mean, we even have access to the ocean.

Which means she could be anywhere.

"Think," I mutter. "Where would you go when you were fourteen?"

Logan and Michelle probably already checked the places Anne would most likely be found. Mya, being a teacher, will check the next most logical locations. I need to look outside the box, be the person who finds the nooks and crannies no one would expect.

I spend the next hour doing just that. The underpass that no one uses and, when I was a kid, I used to try to catch tadpoles in? Check. The old hardware shop that is supposedly haunted thanks to the man who died when a shelf fell on him? Explored. The county lines that kids love to step over, so you can essentially be in two places at once? Not there.

All places I would have gone if I needed to be alone. All places that meant something to me.

Funny how easily those places come to mind. It's almost as if I'm on autopilot, driving around town, exploring old haunts that I haven't thought about in years but are so ingrained into my mind that pulling those memories from the bank is the easiest withdrawal I've ever done. If you had asked me three years ago to name those places, I would have laughed it off. No one cares in NYC or Chicago about the small-town life that made me.

So, I pushed that aside. I buried it deep and erased it. If it didn't help me make the perfect persona of myself, the version of me that got me Bradley, got me into NYU or UChicago, or the Carey Foundation, then it wasn't useful, and I didn't need it. I eroded everything that made me who I was, every rough, imperfect, unique edge, to be someone . . . acceptable to everyone.

I lost myself along the way and found it in this small town that means so much more to me than I could have ever imagined.

I might have fucked it up with Logan here, but the one thing I learned is that I can do anything. I can meet any challenge and overcome it. Learning a kitchen? Check. Rekindling a friendship with my best friend that if I stayed in Chicago might have withered away? Check. Find love again even if only for a minute? Check. And most importantly, find out who I really am and not lose myself along the way like before? Triple check.

How many people can say that? Not many. And I should be proud of that. No matter how it happened, no matter how rocky the journey was, I made it here, I know who I am, and for the first time in a long time, I'm proud of who I am.

That's worth whatever suffering I had to experience along the way to get here. And it'll make me better for whoever comes into my life next.

For the first time in a really long time, I feel like I can do anything. And maybe, just maybe, that freedom is actually what I need. Not a plan laid out that takes into consideration my next ten years, not logic. I know I'm going to Berlin for the Carey Foundation, and that's it. I don't know what I'll specialize in. I don't know if I'll stay in Europe or come back to the States. I dunno what I'm going to do a year from now. And that's okay. I don't NEED to know that. I just need to be someone I can proudly smile at when I see myself in the mirror. I just need to keep moving forward, no matter how hard it is, and know I'll come out the other side better than I was going in.

It's like the Calhoun River, one of the largest rivers that run through the woods in Harper's Cove. The river is one of the oldest in New England. It burrows through stone and earth, and anything in its way. It disrupts and has always, to me, represented what it might mean to find my own path when the world was just too much to handle. It reminded me I can get through anything. I can get through this. I—

"Fuck."

I pull out my phone, texting Logan while making a U-turn that causes another car to honk and narrowly miss me.

I think I might know where Anne is.

· · · · · · · ·

THE RIVER THAT LEADS to Harper's Sound is a hidden gem of Harper's Cove and Maine as a whole. Most people have no idea how to reach it. Deep within the forests that are safe havens for hipsters and those who need to be even more removed from the hustle and bustle of Portland, it's one of those boxes you check on your list of things to do if you make it into the forests and want to feel like you accomplished something.

Supposedly, over the years, it's gotten smaller and smaller. Pollution, erosion, and prioritizing commercial buildings over nature have made the golden nugget of the forests within Harper's Cove no longer a spectacle to go searching for. But little things that teens and young adults consider valuable have a way of passing down from generation to generation. And even Mya told me one time, kids in her classes still talk about searching for the river.

I told Logan to meet me here. He instantly texted back saying he was on the other side of town; it would take him twenty-five minutes to get here. That was ten minutes ago.

Closing the door of my car, I look around, searching for the path I used to take. It's overgrown with tangles of vines and unruly roots, but I can still see the opening, like it's burned inside my memory. I spent many days here, looking at my reflection in the river, trying to imagine what type of life I'd live or person I'd be when I left this town.

"Might as well give it a shot," I mutter.

Pushing through the brambles, I lean backward while walking down the hill toward where the river used to be. Each step brings back flashes of memories. I practiced my debate team talking points here. I wrote the first draft of my valedictorian speech here. I would say, out of any part of Harper's Cove, this place has my heart more than any other location.

My heart swells, and I swallow thickly, pushing through the emotion. I'm such an idiot. I wouldn't be who I am without Harper's Cove, and for so long, I thought Harper's Cove did nothing to make me who I was. I thought it held me back, when so much—the opportunities, the good and the bad—came together to make me, well, me.

Once I reach the bottom of the hill, the river—or what's left of it—comes into view. The river is maybe a tenth the size it was before, mostly just a trickle. You can walk through it now, and only two inches of your shoes would be drenched. When I was in high school, it was so deep it would come up to your mid-calf.

"Time changes everything," I mutter to myself, shoving my hands into my pockets, sighing. I close my eyes, taking a deep breath. The sharp stench of pollution fills the air, but I can still smell the flowers, the ones that have survived, that before were here by the thousands. This was my spot. This was my happy place. This . . .

"Xavier?"

Anne's voice breaks through my moment. Opening my eyes, I glance over to my right. About twenty feet or so, she's sitting on rock, a small pile of pebbles next to her.

"Hey, you." I smile, walking over to her. I keep my voice light and easy. I don't want to scare her, and it's not my place to chastise her or yell at her. All that matters is she's safe. Logan's on his way. He'll see my car and will come down here and find us both.

"You know, a lot of people are looking for you," I say once I stand next to her.

Anne simply shrugs, looking off at the water.

"Mind if I sit next to you?"

A moment passes before she moves over, giving me space. I sit on the corner of the large boulder, nodding to the water.

"I used to come here all the time, you know. When I was a little older than you. How did you find this place? I didn't think anyone knew about it."

"I know a lot of things people don't know," she says. "People think I don't pay attention or that I'm too glued to my phone."

"When in fact you're more perceptive than people give you credit for."

She nods, pulling her knees up to her chest. "I haven't seen you and my dad together for a few days."

I don't know how to answer that. Did Logan not tell her? Again, it's not my place to say anything about that if Logan hasn't.

"Are you going to come over again sometime?" she asks, looking over at me. "My dad's always happier when you're around."

I swallow thickly, pushing the burning tears away by turning my head to cough and clear my throat. Right now, I'd love nothing more than to go back to Logan's place, watch one of the dozens of movies he hasn't seen, and make popcorn with Anne. But Logan's right. I overstepped. I broke his trust, and that's not something that can be fixed. I don't have to go, but I want to get out of Harper's Cove, start my new life, and if that means leaving early, so be it. Gives my heart wound more time to heal before I have to start the fellowship.

That's not enough time to fix anything.

"You know what would make your dad happiest? Knowing

you're safe." I smile, nudging her gently. "How about we get you back to him and then we can talk about—"

"Anne?"

Logan's voice, filled with desperation, breaks through the silence. He, Michelle, Michelle's fiancé, Mya, and a police officer come running down the hill, almost stumbling and falling face-first into the mud and rocky bed of the river. Logan and Michelle make a beeline for Anne, me moving out of the way just in time for Anne to stand and her family to collide in an embrace.

"We thought we lost you," Michelle whispers, barely above the sound of the water.

Logan pulls his face back, quickly studying her, scanning for wounds most likely.

"Why did you run away?"

Anne doesn't answer at first. Her eyes dart from her father, to me, to the river, back to Logan. The reason why Anne ran away doesn't concern me. In fact, it feels like a personal moment that I shouldn't be privy to. I did my part. I helped Logan find his daughter and reunited a girl with her father. I feel like, for the first time in a long time, I've done something; accomplished something. Like I've closed a chapter in a book. I did something right and have done what I've always wanted to do, since going to college. I helped someone. I did something only I could have done.

It feels like I can finally be on my way. That feels surprisingly good to say.

I walk over to Mya, who's standing the furthest away from the group. She smiles softly at me.

"You okay?" she asks.

"Yeah." There's no hesitation in my voice. "Let's go home, I have a trip to pack for."

Mya arches one brow at first. "So, you're doing it? Berlin?"

I nod. "I'm not going to be a stranger this time, though. I promise."

"Oh, I don't care," she says, turning with me to walk up the hill. "Now I have a reason to visit Berlin. So, this benefits me more than you."

I let out a laugh, grabbing a tree branch to hoist myself up. I turn back, offering my hand to Mya to help her up, too. As we reach the top of the hill, Logan's voice calls my name, sounding almost like a distant ghost calling for its lost love.

Mya turns back, then looks at me. "You want to go back down?"

I shake my head, digging my heels into the earth to make sure I don't fall. I know if I go back down there, I'm not going to ever effectively leave this town.

Going to Berlin is the right thing to do and is a choice I'm making for myself. Not for my résumé, not to prove anything to anyone, but what I want to do for me.

THIRTY-THREE

"YOU SURE YOU DON'T want me to drive you to the airport?"

The first reasonable flight to Berlin was a week after the whole Anne debacle and leaves in eight hours. And of course, Mya says I have to get there six hours before the flight takes off, meaning we need to leave in thirty minutes, and I'm still not packed.

"It's fine, Mom, really, I promise." I smile, kissing her cheek while walking into the bathroom to get my toiletries. "Mya offered and she's already going that direction. Plus, you have that community center meeting this afternoon."

"I could have pushed that to take my son to the airport," she scoffs, sitting on the edge of the bed, folding my T-shirts and tucking them into the bag.

"It's better than him taking a taxi," Mya says, leaning against the wall and glancing at me. "That was his first choice. You really think I was going to let you do that? You're not that dumb, though you are pretty dumb."

"Ouch." I grin, putting my hand on my chest. "My heart."

"You'll live." Mya offers me half of her Snickers bar from her purse. "For the road."

"How long has this been in there?"

"Don't ask that question. It's still good."

I can't help but snort, say my thanks, and shove the bar into my backpack. Once the last of the items are placed in, I do a quick check, counting on my fingers to make sure I have everything I need.

"I think we're good."

"You're missing one thing," Mom says, standing up and reaching into her purse.

"Mom. No, you're not giving me money. I'm going to be fine. The foundation is giving us a stipend." A big one, too. Three thousand euros a month. Considering our room and board is paid for, that's huge. "I don't need any money."

"I'm not giving you that," she says, pulling a rolled-up newspaper from her purse.

Frowning, I take the *Portland Gazette* from her, unfurling it. "Check the circled article," she says. "Page five."

I lick my fingers, flipping through the pages until I settle on page five. Circled in red in the food section is . . .

"No."

"Read it out loud, will you?"

I snap my eyes up to her, closing the paper. "Mom, I don't . . ."

"Oh, just read it, Xavier," Mya scoffs.

I throw a glare at her. "I thought you were my friend?"

"I am, and sometimes you do stupid things and I have to be the voice of reason, which is what I'm doing right now. Read it."

"I hate you."

"You love me," she says. "Now stop stalling."

Reopening the paper to page five, I take a deep breath. "Review: The Wharf, written by Alistair Westbrook.

"Harper's Cove is a location you could easily miss. A short drive from Portland, Maine, the small, quaint town is like a gentle embrace from a grandmother or a friend you haven't seen in ages. Tangential to Harper's Sound, which leads right into the Atlantic Ocean, the town is known for its fishing community. Naturally, I was skeptical of a seafood restaurant in a town that isn't for tourists and where everyone can make their own seafood, probably better than most restaurants across the country. Harper's Cove isn't a tourist town. No one is stopping here for their vacation. It's a town for residents and those who want a quiet life. Which also made me wonder why Logan O'Hare would even try to open a restaurant here instead of, let's say, Portland.

"But, to my surprise, what is the Wharf's weakness, is also the Wharf's strength. The restaurant personifies everything that is Harper's Cove. It's friendly. It's comforting. No one feels out of place here. The meals—fish and chips, salads, steamed seafood, and chowders—may seem simple to the outside viewer, but if you look closely, Chef O'Hare has done something so few restaurants can accomplish: created simple, welcoming, and delicious food, without alienating the core base of restaurant-goers, people whose memories of food are centered on family, the home, and most importantly, love.

"If you want a pretentious restaurant that will open up your palate to different types of foods, then the Wharf isn't the place for you. But if you want someplace where you'll feel like you have been in a hundred times, somewhere you can release the stress from your shoulders, and forget about the world for a while? The

Wharf is the place for you. And make sure you get the salmon burger. Trust me, you won't regret it. Well worth the drive. Rating: Five out of five."

I read the review three more times, just standing in the middle of my bedroom before finally looking up at Mya and Mom.

"When did this come out?"

"Today," Mom says. "It's on the website, too."

"Has Logan seen this?"

"I imagine so," Mya says. "He's called my phone three times asking about you."

"And you told him?"

"Nothing. Not my place. Do you want to call him before you go?"

"No," I say without hesitation.

"You sure?"

I nod, folding the paper back up and giving it to Mom. "I'm sure. We should get going anyway, right?"

Mom glances at Mya, who looks back, both exchanging a whole paragraph of words without saying a single thing.

"I know what that look means and I want nothing of it," I say, grabbing my bag. "I'm going to be downstairs, in your car, Mya, when you're ready to take me to the airport."

"Okay, but—"

"Nope, not having it."

"No, seriously, Xavier, you—"

"If you're not in the car in five minutes, I'm going to drive it myself!" I say, kissing my sleeping dad's forehead and ruffling Naga's fur when I come downstairs. This isn't goodbye like before. I'll be back after Berlin and for the holidays.

Mya follows me to the steps, shuffling quickly behind me.

"Xavier, just listen for a second."

"Oh, good, you're here. So I think while we're in the car, we should plan your trip to Berlin," I say, throwing my bag over my shoulder and opening the door. "I'm thinking you come in the winter. Maybe go all over Europe, make a trip—"

As I turn to walk out, my face slams right into something firm and hard. I hiss, a string of curses coming out of my mouth, my bag dropping from my shoulder.

"Shit, sorry," Logan says, picking up the bag from the floor. "You okay?"

No. I'm not okay. At least my nose isn't bleeding; that's a core memory right there.

But the last thing I wanted to do was see Logan right before leaving. I intentionally avoided him. Not only to give him time with Anne and Michelle, but because that chapter of my life is over. And that's okay! Not everything is supposed to last forever.

"I'm fine, what are you doing here?"

"That's what I was trying to tell you," Mya hisses, smiling at Logan.

"Oh, so you knew about this?"

"If you had let me *talk*, you would have known."

"Speaking of talking," Logan says. "Do you mind?"

"I actually—"

"No, we have a few minutes," Mya interrupts. "I need to warm my car up anyway."

"It's not that cold outside, Mya."

"You don't know how cars work, you're gay, hush," she says, wiggling by Logan and me. "You have five minutes."

I'm not sure if she's talking to me or Logan.

Sighing, I look up at him. He looks handsome as usual. This time, he's wearing a blue-and-black-checkered shirt with a black undershirt that shows a new tattoo in the shape of a sailboat on his chest, peeking out from above the collar. His jeans have a few specks of paint on them, probably from an arts-and-crafts project with Anne. A matching blue beanie tucks most of his strands of hair under it.

"So, Berlin, huh?" he finally says. "Leaving one small town for another."

"I wouldn't call Berlin a small town. Especially if you call Harper's Cove one. The population is like, three hundred and sixty times bigger. It's also one of the top five biggest cities in Europe."

"Okay, but why?"

"Excuse me?"

"Why Berlin?"

I look at him, puzzled. "You know I had the offer from the foundation. You gave me the money to go."

"I know," he says quietly. "But . . . shit."

Logan sighs, taking off his beanie and rubbing his fingers through his hair. "Look, I know I only have five minutes and maybe I'm being dumb, but I want to be honest with you. I was wrong. I wasn't just wrong, I was absolutely horrible to you."

"Logan, you don't need to apologize," I say honestly. "I overstepped. I fucked up."

"Sure, but I shouldn't have reacted the way I did. What you did might have been an overstep, but the way I yelled at you? It was wrong. It was horrible."

"It's in the past," I say. "I appreciate you apologizing, and I'm sorry for overstepping, but—"

"I signed up for therapy," he interrupts. "Starting next week. Going once a week in Portland. Going to do it before the produce run. Think it might help with some of the insecurities I have."

"Wait, seriously?" I ask. "No, that's great, Logan. There's no shame in that."

"No, I know. I just think, how I reacted to you, how obsessed I was with the review . . . I need to talk to someone. I can't carry it all on my shoulders and expect to not crack."

"Nor should you. That's really brave and awesome." I smile. I want to reach out and squeeze his bicep, but if I touch him, I'm pretty sure I'll never want to leave.

"Did you see the review by the way?" he asks. "He loved the burger. He loved the Wharf."

"Mya showed me."

"That was because of you. You did that. You helped me."

"That's my job." I smile again, flashing a grin at him that doesn't make him smile back at me.

"I'm being serious, Xavier. I wasn't lying before when I said you have the chops to be a great chef. Your business mind is great. Your cooking skills are good. You understand people and this town better than almost anyone, even if you don't want to admit it. I'm not saying you couldn't do great things in Berlin, but you could most definitely succeed here."

"I can't stay here." The words leave my mouth before I think them through. "I mean . . . I'm going to Berlin, Logan."

I'm repeating myself now, like it's the only talking point I have.

"Why? Can you honestly tell me the Carey Foundation is going to give you everything you need to achieve whatever goal it is you want out of life?"

"No, I can't." And I don't want to. I *like* the fact that I don't know what I'm going to do after the fellowship. I don't need to look that far ahead.

"If you don't know, then why don't you try and find that out here?"

It is so casual, like he's just asking me to pass him a salt-and-pepper shaker, or asking me what I want for breakfast. It's admirable. How he just wants to move past everything that happened. Or is it naive? I suppose it's possible to be both.

"You know I can't do that."

"Can't or won't?"

"Shouldn't," I correct. "I shouldn't. We shouldn't."

"Why?" he asks, taking a step forward. I don't attempt to move or stop him from grabbing my hands, holding them between his large ones. "Why can't we try? Why can't we try again?"

Maybe there is a universe or a timeline where Logan and I can start again. Or maybe there's a timeline where none of this is happening, and our lives didn't blow up because I had to stick my nose in someplace where it didn't belong. I believe in the multiverse theory that some physicists latch on to. I like to think that there are other realities where there's a version of me that made the right choice or found a way to recover from stumbling down the wrong path.

"I only decided to work for you so I could make money for a fellowship," I remind him. "From the get-go, I only wanted to leave Harper's Cove."

"I don't care." Logan shakes his head. "Xavier, listen to me. I don't fucking care."

Logan has always been a few inches taller than me, and to compensate for that, he pulls me to the side, gently forcing us both to sit on one of the benches so we're eye level.

"I don't care why you came back to Harper's Cove. I don't care why we ran into each other or fell into each other's lives. All I care about is that we did, and we're here and together. Life is messy, people are messy, and they make mistakes. I'm not asking for perfect, or flawless, I'm just looking for someone who will accept me for my flaws, of which I have many, and will let me accept them for theirs."

Each word that Logan says is like a hammer hitting against marble. Each word helps to crack and break through the thick facade of protection that I have layered myself with. I don't know exactly when it started, or why it started, but over the years, even before I met Bradley, love was always something that was an afterthought. Romance and companionship were an expectation, a check box in the game of Life to get the highest score.

But, standing here, listening to Logan and what his idea of love is? What companionship is? It sounds nice. It sounds *right*. It sounds like something that maybe, just maybe, is worth having instead of the Fortune 500 C-suite office, or the safe and predictable life that comes from being single and always buried in my work.

"I'm just asking you to stay, just for a bit. To take that leap of faith with me and give this a try. I'm not saying it'll end up perfect, or we'll get that happily ever after people dream about, but what I am saying is right now, we are the most honest version of ourselves. All the cards in both of our decks are laid out in front. There aren't any more secrets or lies holding us back, and I think we deserve to give ourselves a chance at being happy. And I think I can be happy with you, Xavier. Do you think you can be happy with me?"

I glance over my shoulder at Mya. She's gotten out of her car, crossing her arms over her chest, brow arched, silently saying, *If you're going to go, you need to go now.* I look over at Anne, still sitting in the car in the front seat, but leaning forward like she's watching a movie that she can't predict the ending of, and she doesn't want to miss the climax.

And then there's Logan, sitting here, so close to me, with nothing but his heart laid out in front of me. His neck is bared, his soul exposed, and what happens next to him, to us, is completely my decision.

"Look, I know you're scared. I know you're nervous because Berlin at least gives you a year of guidance and guardrails you can stay between. Staying here doesn't provide any of that. And I can't promise you it'll be some love story where we end up living happily ever after. But I think we owe it to ourselves to try.

"But, if you really don't think we should. If you really think we can't make it work, then at least let me give you this."

Logan reaches into his back pocket, pulling out an envelope with my name written on it in chicken scratch. He hands it to me, nodding.

"Read it. Make sure it's good."

Curiously, I open the letter.

To whom it may concern,

Xavier Reynolds worked in my restaurant, the Wharf, for six weeks as a prep chef. As a prep chef he was responsible for assisting the head chef in preparing food by chopping and washing vegetables and meats and arranging salads, breads, sauces, and dressings.

Though Xavier had no experience working in a restaurant, he learned quickly and became an integral part of my staff. Xavier's business skills transferred easily into the kitchen, and I'm confident whatever job he takes, he'll be an asset to your company, just like he was with me.

But, by far his strongest skill is Xavier's ability to touch and change people in ways they can't imagine, even himself. Xavier is a headstrong, confident, talented individual who changes the lives of everyone he meets. You can't put a price on that skill. But if I could, I would pay or do whatever I could to get him to stay with me.

Although, since you're reading this reference, it's clear Xavier has made his choice. It is with my full heart, mind, and soul I recommend Xavier Reynolds for this job, without an ounce of hesitation. My only regret is that I couldn't get him to stay with me.

Yours truly,
Logan O'Hare
Owner of the Wharf

"You think that will work?" he asks, his voice quiet. "Think it'll help you? I can change it if I need to. Or you can type up a reference and email it to me and I'll sign it, scan it, and send it back. If I can't be part of your life, if I can't wake up next to you and see you every day, at least I can know I helped you achieve your dreams. Just promise you'll remember me when you make your first million. I like to think I'm responsible, in part, for helping you be awesome."

I stare at the words on the page until the ink begins to blur. I'm not sure if it's because of tears or because I'm looking at it so long my vision crosses. I hear Mya call my name, though her voice seems miles away.

"Hey," Logan says gently. "You need to get going if you're going to make your flight."

"I'm scared," I say honestly, looking up at him. "I'm scared I'm going to mess up. I'm scared I'm going to hurt us more, hurt *you* and Anne more. I'm just . . . I don't know how to do this."

Logan stares back, saying nothing for a moment until he squeezes both of my shoulders. "Neither do I. I'm scared, too, but that doesn't mean we don't try. How about we take some time and find out together, huh? I've heard it's easier to handle difficult tasks when you have someone by your side."

He's saying all the right words. There's no reason for me to think he's lying. Logan doesn't lie. He's kind, he's caring, he does everything fully with his heart, and that might not always be the best thing, but he doesn't lie. So why would he start now?

"Just a leap of faith," I whisper.

Logan smiles. "Just a leap of faith," he repeats. "Put your faith in me, I promise, Xavier, I won't let you down."

I'm not sure if that's a promise he can actually keep. Or if we'll find out that maybe we're expecting too much of each other, but I know the idea of discovering that answer seems far more appealing than running away to Berlin and regretting ever trying.

"Berlin will always be there," I say, smiling at Logan. "I might as well stay a little bit longer."

A smile so bright I think it might burn through the ozone layer erupts on Logan's face as, without any hesitation, he grabs both sides of my face and kisses me deeply. No tongue, no lust, just a pure exchange of electric, unbridled emotion that cannot be contained passing through us.

"You just made me the happiest person on the Eastern Seaboard, Xavier," Logan whispers.

"Not in the United States? Wow. Maybe I should get in the car."

"Oh, for fuck's sakes," he laughs, kissing my lips quickly this time.

"Give me a month, I'm pretty sure I'll get there."

"I have no doubt in my mind that whatever you put your mind to, you can do, and if making me happy is what has your attention, then I'm the luckiest man in the world."

How do I tell him I think that title goes to me?

EPILOGUE

Eleven months later

"ANNE! XAVIER? YOU HERE?"

Nearly a year later and spending most of my evenings at Logan's house is a commonplace occurrence. I have my own apartment now, two blocks away from the Wharf, but Logan's place is bigger and feels more like home. Plus, I get to spend more time with Anne, which we all enjoy.

Especially Anne; she doesn't have to work as the dishwasher anymore.

"In the living room!" I yell, going over Anne's lines with her, scratching out and putting notes on the script for her. "I think you should put some emotion here, go out with a bang."

"You don't think it'll be too over the top?" she asks.

"Absolutely not. And even if it is, don't you want to make a good impression?"

"What's going on in here?" Logan asks. "Are you both plotting a mutiny?"

"Yes," we both say at the same time.

Logan rolls his eyes, kissing the top of Anne's head. I stand, embracing him and kissing him on the cheek.

"Hey, you." He smiles, kissing my lips quickly.

"Hey yourself, how's the Wharf?"

After I decided to stay, I decided to work at the Wharf for a few months while getting myself on my feet. Like every other twentysomething, I've embraced the idea of freelance work, and there are more than enough businesses in Harper's Cove that need some business advice. My "clients," if you can call them that, and the electives I teach are more than enough income to afford an apartment here.

"Good, Angelica's doing great as head chef," Logan says, pulling out foam containers of food from the restaurant for dinner. "You were right, she was the right choice to promote."

"She was always the right choice," I tease, helping him with the containers. Anne springs up, dashing into the kitchen to get some of the sparkling lemonade we made today for dinner. "And the bank? I know you had a meeting with them today, too, but I was busy helping Maria Beth Clements expand her dog-washing business."

"We got another six-month extension based on the new influx of customers and reviews, so that's great. And I decided on a dishwasher. Still looking for a prep chef, though. It's hard to replace you. Sure you don't want to come back?"

"I'm sure. And I know," I tease, playfully throwing my fake hair over my shoulder. "I'm just that exceptional."

"And you're so modest," he teases back. Crab legs, clam chowder, lobster bisque, and of course, a salmon burger adorn the distressed oak coffee table.

Carefully, Anne brings back three glasses of the lemonade,

placing them on the table without spilling a drop. She pulls out of her pocket the utensils she brought, too, putting a full set in front of each of us.

"She made it herself," I tell Logan.

"You did? I thought you hated working in the kitchen."

"I do," she corrects. "But making drinks doesn't count."

"Oh, obviously," Logan says seriously. "How could I be so foolish."

He sits down to eat, pulling off his black beanie and tossing it on the unused chair, and grabbing one of the forks to serve himself. At the same time, Anne and I exchange a look that doesn't escape Logan.

"What is that look for?"

"Before you eat," I say slowly, "Anne wants to show you something."

"Okay . . ." He hesitates, leaning back. "Should I be worried?"

"Absolutely not," I say, grabbing the papers we had, handing one to Anne. "You know how she's applying for the drama club this year?"

"Mhm. We've been working on her audition monologue. She's going for Lady Macbeth."

"Yeah . . . about that," Anne says, moving in front of the coffee table.

"What about it?"

"Anne and I had . . . a different idea."

"Oh God."

"You're going to love it!"

"If you have to preface it with that, I'm not going to."

"Trust me," I say. "It's going to wow the drama teacher. Anne has a real future in acting."

"I know she does, which is why . . ."

I put my finger to Logan's lips. "Shush and just trust us."

His eyes cross, looking at the finger. A flicker of playful darkness flashes over his eyes before I move my finger away, grinning back at him.

"Alright," he sighs, gesturing widely to both of us. "Show me what you got."

"Perfect." I turn to Anne and give her a thumbs-up. "Need me to set you up?"

"Would you mind?"

"Never," I say, taking off my belt and handing it to her. Logan arches his brow.

"I have no idea where this is going."

"Shush!" Anne and I both say. I turn to her, wink, and nod. "Ready?"

"Ready."

I clear my throat and straighten my back, glancing down at my paper.

"Something funny?" Anne asks me, not even looking at her paper.

"No. No, no, nothing's . . . you know, it's just that . . . both those belts look exactly the same to me. Y'know, I'm still learning about this stuff, and uh . . ."

"This . . . 'stuff'?" she asks, ice dripping from her voice. "Oh, okay. I see, you think this has nothing to do with you. You . . . go to your closet, and you select . . . I don't know, that lumpy blue sweater for instance, because you're trying to tell the world that you take yourself too seriously to care about what you put on your back, but what you don't know is that that sweater is not just blue, it's not turquoise, it's not lapis, it's actually cerulean."

"Is this the monologue from—"

"SHUSH!" Anne snaps, never breaking character as she turns back to me.

"You're also blithely unaware of the fact that, in 2002, Oscar de la Renta did a collection of cerulean gowns, and then I think it was Yves Saint Laurent, wasn't it? . . . Who showed cerulean military jackets. I think we need a jacket here."

While speaking, Anne practically glides around the room, head held high, completely embodying Miranda Priestly. When she circles the couch, she stands in front of me, pushing me back until I fall onto the couch, and she is now effectively taller than me.

"And then cerulean quickly showed up in the collections of eight different designers. Then it filtered down through the department stores, and then trickled on down into some tragic Casual Corner where you, no doubt, fished it out of some clearance bin.

"However, that blue represents millions of dollars and countless jobs, and it's sort of comical how you think that you've made a choice that exempts you from the fashion industry, when in fact, you're wearing a sweater that was selected for you by the people in this room . . . from a pile of 'stuff.'"

Silence hangs in the room for a moment before I stand up, exploding into a round of applause. Anne grins brightly, instantly breaking character.

"You did so freaking good!" I exclaim. "Shoving me? That was such a good touch!"

"Really?" she asks. "I thought it was too much."

"Oh my God, no, that was PERFECT! I loved it! You're absolutely going to get the part!"

For a moment, Anne and I forgot Logan existed. Slowly, we both turn to him and his stunned face.

"Well?" I ask. "How was it?"

Logan still doesn't speak, just . . . stares at both of us. Finally, his soul returns to his body.

"You are never, ever, helping my daughter with her homework again," he says, though there's no real malice in his voice. "That being said, you fucking killed it, Anne."

"Language!" we both say at the same time.

ACKNOWLEDGMENTS

A Dash of Salt and Pepper was the hardest book I've ever written.

To my agent, Jim McCarthy, for always being in my corner. To my editor, Kristine Swartz, for always helping elevate my ideas and books . . . even if they change halfway through. To Stephanie Felty, Jessica Mangicaro, and Mary Baker, for being the greatest team a writer could ever ask for.

To my copyeditor and everyone at Berkley I haven't met who helped make this book a reality—thank you. And of course, to my parents, my friends, my boyfriend, and to anyone who picked up *I'm So (Not) Over You*; thanks for continuing to support me and my dream of being an author.

Keep reading for an excerpt from
Kosoko Jackson's debut rom-com . . .

I'M SO (NOT) OVER YOU

Available in paperback from Berkley!

THE FIRST RULE, AND only rule, of getting over your ex is not to answer your ex's messages. This can be done in many different ways, depending on the person.

One, change his contact to read: **DO NOT ANSWER**.

Two, block his number.

Three, glue a horrible weave to your scalp, so you look and act like a completely different person.

Four, restart your life as the owner of a mom-and-pop shop in rural Indiana and call it a day. That's one I'm particularly partial to.

All of those are good and valid options. Do what you need to do—no judgment.

And yet, somehow I found a way to break this simple rule. Not just break it, burst it wide open. Shatter it, if you will.

Because it's one thing to open a text and answer it, but it's another to decide to follow through with your ex's request.

Look up *Bad Idea* on Google, and our helpful search engine

will bring up, *Did you mean: Kian Andrews's choices whenever they involve Hudson Rivers?*

My phone in my pocket vibrates once. My heart skips a beat. Maybe Hudson will cancel. Or maybe he'll realize the past three months apart have been a mistake and he's going to confess he's still madly in love with me? Maybe . . .

Nope, just Divya.

DIVYA EVANS: Let the record show this is a horrible idea.

"Of course you'd say that," I mutter, forgetting she can't, you know, hear me. And she may be right, but that's not the point.

When I got the text from Hudson a week ago, asking me to meet him at the Watering Hole, Divya was not amused. She scrunched her nose, like she tasted something rancid in the air, which wasn't entirely off.

Because to her, that's exactly what my relationship with Hudson was: rancid. Which, sure, everyone says that about their ex because it makes them feel better.

KIAN ANDREWS: You've said that—multiple times.

DIVYA EVANS: And yet, you still refuse to listen. Remind me, who is getting their law degree from Harvard?

KIAN ANDREWS: Wow . . . we went . . . 12 hours without you bringing up your Harvard degree. That's a new record!

DIVYA EVANS: But seriously, K. This is a bad idea. Closure is not as good as you think it is.

As a lawyer-in-training, she should understand why I need to meet with Hudson: to process what happened, to close that chapter of my life, and to seal it shut with a glue made of truth. The memory of us breaking up is an open wound that never healed. It was a volatile separation, ending with me blocking him on every social media account possible and drinking myself into a stupor that made the two weeks after the breakup a blur.

Maybe that's why Divya's a prosecutor and not a defense attorney.

Another vibration, another text.

DIVYA EVANS: I'm only a few blocks away if you need me.

KIAN ANDREWS: What are the chances of that happening? 🖤

Pretty high, if I'm being honest. Divya has always been my rock, no matter what. Whether keeping me from embarrassing myself when I started crying in the club two weeks after my breakup, making sure I got my worthless self out of bed so I didn't lose my partial scholarship, or even finding some men with absolute dump-truck asses to help me get over my head-over-heels obsession with Hudson, Divya has been that ride-or-die friend for me.

So it's reasonable to assume that when I'm about to go through another major, traumatizing Hudson experience, Divya Evans is the big guns I have on speed dial. What's that expression? Behind every great gay guy, there's a badass woman?

Again, my phone pings. I pull it out of my pocket without looking, expecting another (well-deserved) quippy barb from Divya. But instead, an e-mail stares back at me.

I stare at the screen for so long, the colorful background of one of the many lighthouses on the North Carolina coast. I want to savor this moment. Hold on to it, keep it in its box, and put it on the top shelf somewhere out of the way. When I'm a famous journalist, with sources sliding into my DMs, begging me to write Pulitzer-winning stories, and I'm giving a guest lecture at Northeastern, they'll ask me, *How did you get started in this competitive, cutthroat business?*

And I'll say, *I got my first job at Spotlight.* Will Spotlight be around twelve years from now? Probably not. News websites cannibalize themselves like bacteria. But it's the hottest place to work in journalism right now. Getting an Investigative Journalism Fellowship there would change my life. It's like . . . do not pass Go; instead, get Park Place on your second turn.

I tap the screen, bringing it back to life. Still, the e-mail alert taunts me. Maybe it's an interview request? Maybe my pitch on the lack of education programs in Appalachia and how it's setting students back several grade levels that I spent all last week making really did impress them, and they are going to offer me a position sight unseen. That's not unreasonable. It happens to white guys all the time. And I have good—no, fucking *great* credentials.

Like Divya says, they would be *lucky* to have me.

But at the same time, as my journalism professor said, *Journalists are a dime a dozen. Why should they pick you over anyone else?*

Which takes us back to Divya Evans, and her exact words: *You're a goddamn star, Kian Andrews.*

I wish I had the same level of confidence as her. I do a good job faking it when I'm around her, at least I think I do. But now? Alone in this café? Doing something stupid like waiting for the boy who broke my heart—who is now seven minutes late—*and* staring at the e-mail that could change my career? That confident facade is pushed far back into the closet; a place I haven't been since middle school.

And I promised I'd never go back there again.

Without overthinking it, I tap on the screen one more time, and then enter my passcode before I can change my mind. One more tap, and the e-mail fills the screen.

Dear Mr. Andrews,

Thank you for your application for the Investigative Journalism Fellowship at Spotlight's Boston branch. At this time, we've decided—

"Shit."

There's no need to read any more. I could do a CTRL-F in my inbox, search for "we've decided," and bring up more than a dozen results. This is no different, despite how badly I want it to be different.

I'm halfway through a text to Divya, informing her about the rejection from Spotlight, which will undoubtedly result in her replying with drinks on me tonight, when a baritone clearing of a throat behind me causes my fingers to stop. The deep voice cuts through the low sensual tones of the Esperanza Spalding cover artist serenading us in the Watering Hole, even if it is as out of place as a Black guy in Boston—aka Me.

But the voice is unmistakable. Even after three months of

avoiding everything related to Hudson, the way he speaks effortlessly from the depths of his diaphragm still sends shivers down my spine. And the way his boyish grin plays off his chiseled jaw makes me want to melt.

"Kian?"

I do my best to turn slowly. Eagerness isn't a good look on anyone, especially around your ex when you're trying to act like you've moved on and are living your best single twentysomething life.

But my *God* does he look nice.

No, not nice.

Hot.

"Hey," he says while smirking. "Thanks for coming."

There it is. That smile. The same lopsided grin that he gave me when we were paired together in freshman English to come up with a presentation of *The Bell Jar.* That smile he gave before our first kiss, after almost two years of mutual pining and "will they/won't they"s.

That Southern drawl. The same one that he would make more prominent when we lay in bed on Sunday morning because he knew what it did to me.

Put them together with a dash of traditionally accepted masculine features, a heaping of generational wealth, and you've got Hudson Rivers.

I can already feel the weightlessness taking over. That sickening feeling that's akin to carbon monoxide poisoning. That's what Hudson is: a toxin that makes my best judgment and practical senses go haywire. He's dangerous. He's a mistake. He's going to hurt me.

But he's so damn beautiful. And I miss him. I miss him so fucking much.

"Sure, no problem." *Act relaxed. Act like you don't care.* "I wasn't doing anything anyway. I mean I was in town. I mean I was in the area. I mean I was in the area because I live around here and I wasn't doing anything." *Besides neurotically refreshing my e-mail for a response from Spotlight and obviously looking like an idiot who can't put together a decent sentence to save my life.*

Divya and I went over this, like a witness being prepped for a dangerous cross-examination, multiple times. I have to hold my ground. I have to stay aloof. I have to stay in control. Thirty seconds in, and I'm doing the exact opposite of that.

Hudson just keeps that soft, charming grin on his face. It's like he knows my brain is short-circuiting, because he does. He's seen me spiral like this before; multiple times in college when I had too many assignments due and I didn't know where to start. And all those times he let me just talk myself out of the hole I created, smiling at me, maybe rubbing his thumbs over my knuckles in a soft, circular, soothing motion.

There's none of those touches this time, though, and that smile, once cute and teasing, now seems like it's twisted into one of mockery. Even if I know that's not true, it's what my head, and my heart, thinks. Funny how when you break up with someone, everything you loved about them turns into everything you hate.

"I don't have much time, though," I add to recover some dignity and take some power back. "So, whatever you want, let's get this over with, yeah?"

"Course, darlin'."

I twitch, like this word is the trigger of a shock collar. He sits, frozen, as though he whispered some command that put a spotlight on him, and shakes his head.

"Sorry. Habit."

"You call a lot of boys that now?" That was uncalled for.

"That's not what I meant, and you know it, K."

"Kian," I remind him. "K is reserved for boyfriends, and you, Hudson, are no longer my boyfriend."

There. I did it. Advantage: Kian. The ball's back in my court. I've taken control of the narrative. Hudson, the smooth-talking Georgian, is not the one who has the power anymore. I . . .

"That's exactly why I called you, actually." Hudson avoids my gaze, fiddling with the sugar packet I ripped open and threw on the counter. He folds it into a nondescript shape, unfolds it, and refolds it again, like some poor man's origami experiment.

I know that tick. He fiddles with things when he's nervous—truly, actually worried. It's just so rare that I see it. It's . . . about as common as finding a bad picture of Beyoncé.

Is it possible the great Hudson Rivers is more nervous than me?

"Screw it." He tosses the crumpled paper on the counter. "Nothing good comes from beatin' around the bush."

"I'm pretty sure I'm the one who t—"

"I called you here because I want you to be my boyfriend."

And at that moment, I've never been so happy to be Black. Not only because Black don't crack, but because the way the blood rushes to my cheeks would make me look like an overly ripe tomato.

And there is nothing sexy about tomatoes.

Photo by Louisa Wells

KOSOKO JACKSON is a digital media specialist who lives in the New York Metro Area and spends too much time listening to Halsey and Taylor Swift. *I'm So (Not) Over You* was his debut rom-com, published by Berkley.

Ready to find
your next great read?

Let us help.

Visit prh.com/nextread

Penguin
Random
House